Also by Jerome R. Corsi, Ph.D.

America for Sale: Fighting the New World Order, Surviving a Global Depression, and Preserving USA Sovereignty

Why Israel Can't Wait: The Coming War Between Israel and Iran

The Obama Nation: Leftist Politics and the Cult of Personality

The Late Great USA: The Coming Merger with Mexico and Canada

Atomic Iran: How the Terrorist Regime Bought the Bomb and American Politicians

Black Gold Stranglehold: The Politics of Oil and the Myth of Scarcity

Unfit for Command: Swift Boat Veterans Speak Out Against John Kerry

Minutemen: The Battle to Secure America's Borders

JEROME R. CORSI, Ph.D.

THE
SHROUD
CODEX

THRESHOLD EDITIONS

New York   London   Toronto   Sydney

Threshold Editions
A Division of Simon & Schuster, Inc.
1230 Avenue of the Americas
New York, NY 10020

First Threshold Editions hardcover edition April 2010

THRESHOLD EDITIONS and colophon are
trademarks of Simon & Schuster, Inc.

For information about special discounts for bulk purchases,
please contact Simon & Schuster Special Sales at
1-866-506-1949 or business@simonandschuster.com.

The Simon & Schuster Speakers Bureau can bring authors
to your live event. For more information or to book an event
contact the Simon & Schuster Speakers Bureau at 1-866-248-3049
or visit our website at www.simonspeakers.com.

Designed by Joy O'Meara

Manufactured in the United States of America

1   3   5   7   9   10   8   6   4   2

ISBN 978-1-4391-9041-8
ISBN 978-1-4391-9045-6 (ebook)

For
Melania M. Menzani,
who made it possible for me to view the Shroud
in Turin, Italy, in 1998;
with loving memory
and continuing appreciation

And he [Joseph of Arimathea] bought fine linen, and took him [Jesus] down, and wrapped him in the linen, and laid him in a sepulchre which was hewn out of a rock, and rolled a stone unto the door of the sepulchre.

MARK 15:46

THE
SHROUD
CODEX

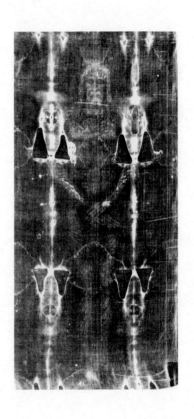

CHAPTER ONE

Liberated, he felt himself moving free, as a spirit. Easily, he moved upward, leaving behind the police and ambulance sirens below, as rescue workers rushed to the scene.

Ahead of him, he could see the purest of white light streaming from a tunnel that loomed in the sky above him.

In the depths of his soul he felt a peace he had never felt before, a peace he had always longed to feel. He was happy to be free of his broken body and he felt no sorrow at leaving his life behind.

As he entered the tunnel, the luminescence surrounded him. He held his hands in front of his face and turned them so he could see his palms. He was intact. He felt his legs and they too were fine. He was uninjured.

He wondered, Why am I surprised?

Then the car crash flashed back to him in horrific detail.

He had been at the wheel of his car, applying the brakes as hard as he could. He had just come around a sharp curve to find ahead of him two semi-trucks jackknifed together in a multiple-vehicle wreck that blocked both lanes of the interstate.

As if watching a movie, he saw himself behind the wheel of his car, screaming and bracing for the impact. At sixty-five miles per hour, the hood of his car crushed back upon him like an accordion. The impact was a more powerful jolt than he had ever imagined possible.

An unexpected summer thunderstorm had sent a driving rain down on the highway and he should have known to slow down, but he was preoccupied, lost in thought, totally unaware of the oil on the highway that had turned slick in the rain, causing the trucks ahead of him to collide and jackknife, setting off a chain reaction of a dozen more vehicles.

Yes, that afternoon, Father Paul Bartholomew, a Catholic priest, died.

The police report would read that he was killed in a motor vehicle accident at 3:35 P.M. ET on August 15.

He died on the operating room table after the horrific car crash he suffered while driving that Sunday afternoon to the cabin in the Finger Lakes region of New York State, where he had spent summers as a boy.

But now all that seemed like a dream. The luminescence in the tunnel surrounded him like a fog and he felt drawn to move forward.

As he approached the end of the tunnel, he could see people milling about. Strangely, they all seemed to be floating with the light and the fog enveloping them. Vaguely he thought he could detect friends and relatives who had been dead now for many years.

Suddenly, he was thrilled to see his mother coming forward to embrace him. His mother had died ten years earlier of Lou Gehrig's disease, a progressive nerve disease in which the brain loses the ability to move the body's muscles. The disease took five years to kill her and in the last two months of her life her paralysis increased to near total.

Paul at that time was on the faculty of the Institute for Advanced Study at Princeton. He was the youngest physicist ever to be asked to join the esteemed institute. Before his mother's illness, Dr. Bartholomew was considered one of the most promising young physicists in the world.

When his mother was diagnosed with amyotrophic lateral sclerosis, or ALS, his life was shattered. Six months before she died, he moved his mother out of the hospital and brought her back home, where he hired nurses around the clock to care for her. As his mother's paralysis became complete in her final days of life, the institute gave Bartholomew a leave of absence. He never left his mother's side until she died; he moved a small cot into her room so he could take care of her in the middle of the night. He prayed that God would take him and spare his mother.

Then, as she went into a coma, he spent hours at her bedside, holding her hand, trying to communicate with her one last time. In the middle of the night, as she took her final labored breaths, Bartholomew wiped her brow with a cold cloth, trying to ease her pain. When she died, he felt desolate and abandoned, his tears unable to bring her back or express his pain. At her funeral, Bartholomew wished there was a way he could join her in death, and he would have, except he felt it was against God's law for him to commit suicide.

The death of his mother marked a turning point in Bartholomew's life. What kept him going was a determination to understand what his life was about. Why was he here on earth in this here and now? He had no ready answer.

In the depths of his crisis, he railed against God for taking from him the only person in his life who truly understood him. As he grieved his loss, he realized he had gone into physics in an attempt to find God, and now, with the despair he felt with his mother gone, he was ending up with nothing. Regardless of how brilliant he had been in science, having received his Ph.D. from

Princeton when he was only twenty-five years-old, the death of his mother made him realize that God could not be found in a particle accelerator or a quantum equation. The head of the physics department was shocked when Bartholomew came into his office and announced he had decided to resign from the prestigious Institute for Advanced Study.

"What do you mean you want to resign?" asked Dr. Horton Silver, himself a renowned physicist and Bartholomew's most trusted advisor at the university. "Your appointment at the Institute is an appointment for life. Your particle physics work has broken new ground internationally. You can't resign."

Dr. Silver was right. Bartholomew was on the verge of a major theoretical breakthrough dealing with one of the most important unanswered mysteries that had eluded the most brilliant minds in physics since Einstein had been at the very same institute. Bartholomew had spent the last three years developing a series of equations that Silver felt were the most promising approach he had yet seen to explain the Heisenberg uncertainty principle, a quantum physics problem: if the position of a particle were known, its momentum could not be determined with precision. Dr. Silver believed Bartholomew would solve the problem and that if he abandoned physics now, it might be decades before another physicist emerged who was brilliant enough to tackle the problem and advance beyond the progress Bartholomew had made.

Silver refused to accept Bartholomew's decision. Instead he insisted that Bartholomew take some time off to get himself back together emotionally. They had known each other since Bartholomew was an undergraduate in one of Silver's advanced physics courses at Princeton. He encouraged Bartholomew to pursue graduate studies in physics and when Bartholomew was accepted as a graduate student in physics, Silver became his advisor.

"Your leaving physics will be a great loss both to physics and to the institute," Silver insisted. "Travel. Go to Europe for a few months. You need some time to grieve. When you get back, you'll be ready to resume your work."

"I've made my decision and it's final," Bartholomew explained to Dr. Silver. "I have come to the conclusion that I have made all the contributions to physics that I want to make."

"What do you mean? You're already famous and you're not yet at the height of your career."

"That may be, but my decision is final."

Dr. Silver finally had to accept the fact that he could not change Bartholomew's mind.

"What are you going to do with the rest of your life?" he asked. "You're a young man, not yet forty years old. You can't mourn your mother for the rest of your life."

"I've decided to go into the priesthood," Bartholomew said without hesitation. "I have come to the conclusion that I have to find God and that physics isn't going to get me there."

Silver was flabbergasted. "So, you're dropping out altogether then?"

"No," Bartholomew protested. "I'm not dropping out. It's just the opposite. I think for the first time in my life I know what I'm doing. My mother always told me that I had a vocation for the priesthood and I had never believed her. If she communicated anything to me in the last days of her life, even if it was just with her eyes before she went into a coma, she was telling me I had to find God. She always said I was born to do something in my life more important than physics. Now I believe her."

THE DAY OF the car accident was a Sunday. After saying Mass that morning at his parish, St. Joseph's on New York City's Upper East Side, he drove over to his mother's grave site in Morristown, New Jersey. He brought fresh flowers to place on her grave, as he always did. Kneeling at his mother's grave that morning, he prayed for her soul and asked God once more that he might join her soon.

Little did Bartholomew realize, as he left the cemetery in Morristown to head up to his cabin, that this was to be the last day of his life.

Now, surrounded by the luminescence in what he imagined must be Heaven, Bartholomew and his mother embraced for what seemed the longest time, thrilled to be reunited.

"Come with me, Paul," his mother said. "There's someone else who has been waiting here for you, along with me."

She took his hand and together they approached a man seated at a table.

Bartholomew felt this man was the oldest and wisest man he had ever seen. His hair and beard were flowing with silver and his eyes were the softest and most understanding blue eyes Bartholomew had ever seen.

Entering the Ancient One's presence and returning his gaze, Bartholomew felt pouring toward him an unqualified love and acceptance he had never imagined possible. For the first time, he felt at home.

"We have a special place prepared here for you," the Ancient One said lovingly.

Bartholomew looked around him and he was aware of legions of other souls who were on every side of them, listening and watching intently.

"You are free to stay here forever," the silver-haired Ancient One continued. "This is your home and you never have to leave."

Bartholomew himself was now listening intently, sensing there was more.

"If you choose to stay here with us, you will always feel as happy and fulfilled as you do right now."

Bartholomew understood.

"But you have a choice," the wise man said seriously. "If you choose to return to earth and resume your life there, I will give you an important mission that I believe only you can accomplish. The mission is more important than I can explain to you. The future of human beings on earth hinges on whether you can manage to convey the message I will entrust to you to convey."

"What message is that?" Bartholomew asked.

"It's a message my son Jesus embedded in this burial cloth after his crucifixion," the Ancient One explained. "The cloth is known as the Shroud of Turin. Even though the gospels of the New Testament tell the story of Jesus' life and death, Jesus never wrote a book. The Shroud of Turin is his book, a codex in which a message for humanity was buried in the cloth, along with the body of my son. Deciphering that message for the world will be your mission if you choose to return to life."

"I'm not sure I understand fully what you mean," Bartholomew said with honest humility.

"I don't expect you to understand now," the Ancient One acknowledged. "But if you accept this mission, what you experience will bring forward to the world a new understanding of themselves and of the divine."

Bartholomew felt torn. He had just been reunited with his mother and it pained him terribly to think he would be separated from her once again. He looked at his mother for advice. "I don't want to leave you ever again," he said from his heart.

"The choice is yours, son," she said lovingly. "Either way, if you return to earth or choose to stay here, we will always be together."

"If you do choose to return," the Ancient One explained, "I will bring forth people to work with you, each selected for a particular reason. You will be given certain gifts that will bring to you the attention of the world. Your mother will return to be with you to help you accomplish your mission. Trust that I will enlighten those I send to you. To understand what is happening to you, it will be necessary to unravel the Shroud codex, the message I have imprinted into the burial cloth of my Son, waiting for the world to decipher."

Bartholomew listened intently, not at all sure he comprehended what he was being told.

"If you choose to return to your life, you will be fulfilling the destiny for which you were created," the Ancient one continued. "But you will not experience adulation or earthly riches. Instead, you will suffer much pain. You will be disbelieved, rejected, and scorned by Church authorities as well as millions of people who no longer believe in anything or anyone higher than themselves. But if you do return to earth, as I am asking you to do, what you do there will be written here with me in eternity."

Bartholomew looked at his mother and their eyes met.

"What should I do, Mother?" he asked.

Right then, his mother took both his hands in hers and a brilliant flash of light surrounded them.

Bartholomew felt a surge of energy, as if he and his mother were being rushed through a warp in time to a distant dimension. Swirling around them was what seemed a blur of stars. He felt as if they were passing through distant galaxies on the way to what felt like another dimension.

Transported in space and time, Bartholomew looked around to find he was standing on a hill outside a city with his mother at his side. They were dressed in robes and wearing sandals. It felt like ancient times. He had no idea what had just happened.

"Where are we?" he asked his mother.

Looking around, he saw little that was familiar, but he thought the overall landscape looked like a place he had been in before.

Then he recognized the cream-colored limestone that he knew to be distinct to Jerusalem.

He had visited the Holy Land twice and both times he had stayed at a hotel with a view of the walls of Jerusalem. He had loved watching the daylight from dawn to sunset as it delicately changed the limestone walls of the old city from a soft pale yellow at dawn to a rich red rose at sundown.

Just then he was startled to realize that he and his mother were standing outside the walls of Jerusalem at Golgotha on the very day Christ was crucified. If this was Jerusalem two thousand years ago, how did they get there?

In front of him, everything was happening as if they were there, at the hour of Jesus Christ's death. In front of Paul and his mother was Jesus nailed to the cross, with a criminal crucified on either side of him.

The agony that Christ was suffering overwhelmed Bartholomew as he observed the details of the crucifixion—the nails that fixed his wrists and feet to the cross, the beating Jesus had taken, the crown of thorns.

Christ struggled to raise his head from his chest. He looked up toward Bartholomew and his mother. Their eyes met.

"Bartholomew." Jesus spoke in recognition.

"My Lord," Bartholomew replied, feeling a sorrow deeper than he had ever before imagined possible. "I am here."

"I knew you would never abandon me," Jesus said with infinite love.

As Jesus spoke these words, his mother held Paul's hand even more tightly.

She turned to him, wanting to know his decision. "Understand only that I have always been with you in spirit," she explained, "even in death. You were born with a mind gifted to grapple brilliantly with complex issues of time and space. By the time of my death, you had reached the height of your work as a physicist. My death was destined by God to force you to accept the vocation to the priesthood I always knew you had. The last and greatest part of your destiny remains before you, if you choose to return to earth as God has asked you to do."

Paul listened, not sure he understood.

"When you return to earth, you must see yourself as a messenger from God, across time and space," she said with all her heart.

"What exactly is the Ancient One asking me to do?" Bartholomew asked his mother. "I've studied the Shroud of Turin for much of my life, but there are many scientists who have worked on the Shroud for decades. I'm not one of them. How can I possibly explain to the world the message of the Shroud of Turin when I'm not one of the top experts in the field?"

"As the Ancient One said, if you return to earth, the right people will come forth so your life can unlock for the world the Shroud codex. You won't need to be a top scientific expert on the Shroud. Your life and what you experience back on earth will force the world to decipher the message Jesus left in that burial cloth. Also, as the Ancient One promised, I will return to earth as well, to assist you."

"How is that possible?" Paul asked. "You have died."

"And so have you," she pointed out. "Yet God has given you the grace to return to life. If you accept this mission, God will grant the same grace to me as well."

At that instant, Bartholomew made his decision. "I don't know if I understand any of this," he said truthfully, "but I will do as you and God ask me to do."

She embraced him warmly.

"May your destiny be fulfilled," she prayed.

Silently, Paul prayed the same.

"I must warn you that once you are back on earth, you must be patient," she explained. "Now that you have agreed, the Ancient One gave me permission to explain to you that you will experience three years of rehabilitation before your mission begins. This is the time you will need to rebuild your body after the car accident that caused your death."

Bartholomew listened intently.

"From the moment your body begins manifesting the passion and death of Jesus that you see here before you today, your mission will be accomplished in thirty days. I will join you on earth and you will recognize that I have returned, though others will not be permitted to know precisely who I am or why I have returned. On the thirtieth day, we will be reunited again, here in the loving presence of God, this time to stay forever."

"As you say, Mother," Paul said, accepting his fate as she explained it to him.

The next thing Bartholomew knew, he was moving back through time and space. Suddenly he saw, from above, his body lying on an operating table in the hospital. He still felt outside his body, as if he were hovering above, an unencumbered spirit looking down at a scene below that really didn't concern him.

The doctors and nurses were working frantically to save his life, but all the monitors had flatlined.

One of the doctors moved forward and prepared to give Bartholomew a cardiac shock with a defibrillator.

On the second try, Bartholomew felt himself jolted back in his body.

He was alive once more, gasping for breath.

Back in his body, the pain was overwhelming.

Quietly he slipped from consciousness as the doctors and nurses frantically resumed their efforts to save his life.

CHAPTER TWO

Three Years Later
St. Joseph's Church, New York City
Thursday, Day 1

Father Bartholomew was back at St. Joseph's Church on the Upper East Side of Manhattan, where he had returned to serve as pastor after three hard years of hospitalization and rehabilitation. He spent one year bedridden, followed by another year in a wheelchair. The final year he learned to walk with leg braces and crutches before he gained enough strength to walk again on his own power. Steel pins and rods that had been inserted in more operations than he could recall held together the multiple broken bones throughout his body. Truly his body would never be the same, but he felt God's grace had been abundant. The doctors advised him that the pain from the car accident would never entirely leave him. Still, he thanked God that he had lived and he was overwhelmed with joy that he had recovered enough to return to his duties as a parish priest.

This Thursday, Father Bartholomew was saying Mass at the central altar under the dome of the venerable church. He enjoyed wearing the vestments, the long formal robes the priest wore when celebrating Mass—the alb, the thin tunic worn by priests since antiquity; the chasuble, the stiff outer mantle with its Latin cross embroidered on front and back, and special colors for each part of the church liturgy. The vestments might seem medieval to the iPod generation, but to Father Bartholomew the formal priestly garments worn to celebrate Mass were essential to conveying the solemnity he felt the Mass was intended to create: a community of worshippers brought together to celebrate Christ's life, death, and perpetual resurrection.

Always, Father Bartholomew felt moved as he approached the consecration of the bread and wine, the most holy part of the Mass. Ever since being ordained, Bartholomew never got over the awe of the mystical power he had been given to transform the bread and wine into the body and blood of Jesus Christ. The memory of having seen with his own eyes Christ's passion and death continued to haunt him. How great was God's love for us to have allowed his only Son to die on the cross for our sins? The sight of the nails driven through Christ's flesh had become the constant theme of his quiet prayer and meditation.

In this era of the Internet and big-screen TVs, the number of true believers in Christianity had diminished, but Bartholomew's faith had never wavered. Having been given the grace to return among the living after the dreadful accident that had nearly cost him his life, Bartholomew counted every day as a blessing God had personally bestowed upon him.

Slowly, he genuflected and raised the host above his head. "Behold the body of Christ," he told the assembled congregation.

This he had done hundreds of time, so many he could not count. But today it was different. As he held the host between the thumb and forefingers of each hand and raised the host upward with both his arms elevated, he felt a sudden violent shock pound at his right wrist. The pain was immediate. Looking up, he saw what he perceived to be blood trickling down his arm.

His mind suddenly tripped, ripping him from the here and now of the central altar of St. Joseph's Church in New York City to a distant time and place. Here, in a distant place separated from New York City by countless miles and what felt like thousands of years, he found himself stripped naked, lying flat on the ground, atop what seemed to be a long board. Though it made no sense at all, a Roman centurion was holding down his right arm with his knee, preparing to pound a nail large enough to be a railroad spike into his wrist. Carefully the centurion placed the nail on his wrist and lifted a mallet high above his head. Almost uncomprehending, Bartholomew realized the centurion was intent on driving the nail through his wrist. With the first crushing blow, the pain was unbearable. Though his mind struggled to grasp whether this was really happening, Bartholomew realized he was being nailed to the cross.

It took a second blow to drive the spike completely through his wrist. The third and fourth blows succeeded in pounding the spike into the wooden crossbeam on which his outstretched right arm was being nailed. The centurion worked methodically, without emotion. The muscles bulged in his arms as the sweat streaked his face. With the fifth and final blow, Bartholomew's right wrist was pinned so firmly to the wooden crossbeam that he could not imagine prying himself loose. The fingers of his right hand writhed in agony.

Back at the altar, Bartholomew fell to the ground. The host tumbled out of his hands and crashed on the floor. His right wrist had been pierced clear through in a horrible gaping wound and blood from the wound was pouring down his vestments.

Then, in another sudden jolt, he felt his left arm wrenched violently out to his side. Almost immediately he felt a violent blow pounding in that wrist as well.

Again his mind tripped and a second centurion had pinned Bartholomew's left arm with his knees as he prepared to nail his outstretched left arm to the crossbeam. He could smell the centurion's stale breath and he felt panic surge through him in the realization there was no escape.

With the same precision and lack of emotion, the second centurion drove a second spike into his left wrist, following in succession one hammer blow, followed by another—five in total. Again the pain with each blow was excruciating. In desperation, Bartholomew whipped his head from side to side, realizing his outstretched arms were completely pinned to the cross and he was helpless to move or free himself. A cold shiver spread through his whole body. He screamed repeatedly as his mind grasped that he was at Golgotha outside the walls of ancient Jerusalem two thousand years ago and his outstretched arms were now nailed to the cross exactly as the arms of Jesus Christ had been.

He knew that next the cross would be lifted to an upright position and he would be hung to die. His feet would be nailed to the body beam of the cross and he would be completely immobilized. Even now, lying with his back against the wooden crossbeam on the hard, cold ground, every slight movement of his outstretched arms sent a new spasm of agony though his body as the nails driven through his wrists rubbed hard against his bones. He couldn't begin to contemplate the agony he would be in when the soldiers lifted the crossbeam to set it into the slot that waited on top of the vertical pole of the cross permanently fixed here, in this desperate place of execution. The final agony would come when his feet were placed one on top of the other so they too could be nailed to the cross, fixing him to this tree like a butterfly pinned to a display.

• • •

AT THE ALTAR, Bartholomew saw that the second wound had pierced through his left wrist. Blood poured forth from both wrists, soaking his vestments red.

His screams of agony filled the interior of the church as the parishioners at Mass stood in fear, trying to comprehend what was going on. Blood was pouring from wounds that had developed on Father Bartholomew's wrists seemingly from nowhere. Several in the church began gasping in shock and screaming in horror. Thinking quickly, several took their cell phones and dialed 911 as fast as they could. Others took their cell phones and filmed the event, thinking to email what they were seeing to friends or to post the videos on the Internet.

Holding his wounded wrists in front of his face so he could inspect the wounds more precisely, Bartholomew's mind spun out of control. He lost consciousness and collapsed on the church floor in front of the altar.

CHAPTER THREE

What does the Vatican want with me? Dr. Stephen Castle had wondered when Archbishop Carl Duncan, an old friend, had called him from his office at St. Patrick's Cathedral, asking for some of his time.

"His Holiness Pope John-Paul Peter I is sending a special envoy to New York and I'm recommending you are the man to see him," Duncan had explained over the telephone on Friday. "This is an important case involving a priest in the archdiocese and we need to deal with it immediately."

"What's so important that the pope is sending an envoy from Rome, and why me, of all people?" Castle protested. "Surely you've got plenty of psychiatrists in Rome. Why not send the priest to Rome and have him analyzed out of the country, where the publicity about the case could be more easily controlled?"

Duncan sensed Castle's hesitation. "We've worked together before and I need your help again," he said, getting straight to why he called Castle this morning. "The pope trusts you and so do I."

Castle appreciated what Duncan was saying. Castle liked Duncan personally, even though much of Castle's international reputation was built on his atheism and his criticism of religion as a dangerous mass delusion that caused human beings to wage war and kill each other as infidels, just because their beliefs in God happened to be different. When Castle walked past St. Patrick's Cathedral on Fifth Avenue in New York City he frequently thought of the Crusades and wondered how anyone could ever kill another human being in the name of God. As Castle had argued in books and in interviews, religious wars were all the proof he needed that man had invented God, rather than the other way around.

Castle's professional reputation went global after he wrote *The God Illusion* five years ago. In *The God Illusion*, Castle had taken Freud's argument that religion was nothing more than a popular delusion that societies through time have created. But he asked why. Was it because societies need to give human beings an explanation for what has always been fundamentally unknowable about the human condition? Was it to answer the questions of where we human beings come from and where we are headed after death?

As Freud had done in *Civilization and Its Discontents*, Castle saw religion as nothing more than a mass neurosis imposed on people by society to control their otherwise disorderly sexual impulses. The problem to Freud was that religion imposes moral constraints of "right and wrong" in order to restrain artificially human impulses that are considered embarrassing or unattractive, such as sex. But Castle went one step further: in his book, he argued that religion not only produces sexual neuroses, it also divides people and causes wars, thereby producing additional neuroses and mass hatred. What is the point, he asked, of holy wars fought over the true God when the whole idea of God itself may be nothing more than a fiction people made up in the first place?

The psychiatrist had first worked with Duncan ten years earlier, when Duncan had been newly appointed archbishop. Castle and Duncan had met socially, at an Upper East Side cocktail party held by a wealthy Catholic donor to the church who was also one of Castle's patients at the time. When the archdiocese was sued over alleged sexual abuses committed several decades ago by a few renegade priests, Duncan called Castle.

"Yes, I understand some of your priests have a fondness for boys," Castle had told Duncan in their first private conference ten years ago. "What do you expect? The Catholic Church does not allow the clergy to marry. Yet the Church gives priests privileged access to advise boys and young men. Boys come to the priest's attention every day when they serve as altar boys. You've got to understand that for a pedophile attracted to young boys, meeting a prepubescent altar boy for the first time is a lot like a heterosexual man being introduced to Megan Fox. Pedophiles get the point that the Catholic Church is advertising 'pedophiles, apply here.'"

Duncan listened quietly, not disagreeing. "I understand what you're saying, but the case I am asking you to take is complicated. It involves a priest I believe was abused sexually when he was a child."

Castle's psychoanalysis revealed the priest's history of abuse had led to a neurosis that was more complicated than simply his own wrongdoing. As a result, the archdiocese was able to settle the case in a way that was financially acceptable to those who had been offended, as well as fair to the priest. Moreover, Castle was able to recommend to Archbishop Duncan the type of psychological assistance the church might offer to the victims involved and to the priests currently under his direction.

When the final lawsuit was settled, Cardinal Marco Vicente called Dr. Castle from Rome.

"The Catholic Church is deeply appreciative of what you have done for us," Cardinal Vicente had said over the telephone.

"I did my job," Castle said modestly.

"You did more than your job. You provided Archbishop Duncan with sound advice. Here in the Vatican, I did not initially appreciate your judgment about the psychological implications of a celibate priesthood, but I have come to see that you offered your views to be constructive."

"You have to know that I'm an atheist and that I don't support the Catholic Church, or any other church, for that matter."

"I understand," Vicente answered quietly. "But it seems to me that you are our atheist. It's ironic that sometimes the Catholic Church's greatest critics end up being our greatest allies. God works in wondrous ways."

"You paid my bills and I did my job," Castle said in agreement.

Castle appreciated the phone call from the Vatican at the time and was especially amused after Cardinal Vicente was subsequently elected pope. "Not a bad connection for a devout atheist," he said to friends.

So, when the crisis with Father Bartholomew developed, Castle was the first person whom Cardinal Vicente, now Pope John-Paul Peter I, wanted Archbishop Duncan to call for help.

Duncan did so.

"I've got another crisis on my hands that I have to deal with immediately," Archbishop Duncan explained to Castle on the phone.

"What's the problem this time?"

"It involves a parish priest at St. Joseph's Church, a few blocks away from you," Duncan explained. "A few years ago, Father Bartholomew had a car accident. Technically he died after his heart stopped on the operating table. But then he revived."

"Happens all the time," Castle responded.

"But there is an urgency here," the archbishop continued. "This case could be as threatening to the Church as the priest crisis had been. Otherwise we never would have come to you."

Castle knew St. Joseph's well. It was an old parish, tracing its origins back to the 1870s.

"So, what are the medical aspects of this case?"

"It's more than just the case of a priest who may have psychological problems, which is what I'm sure you are going to suspect. Father Bartholomew had an after-life experience in which he thought he had died and he saw God. He says God gave him the choice of staying in Heaven or returning to earth. Obviously, he chose coming back to earth. But what Father Bartholomew says is that God told him he would have a mission if he came back to earth, that he would have certain gifts but that his life back on earth would not be easy."

"What gifts?" Castle wondered.

"His parishioners are beginning to say he is not just absolving their sins but that he is also healing their physical illnesses in the confessional," Archbishop Duncan explained. "Then yesterday at Mass, Father Bartholomew began to, shall we say, manifest Christ's wounds of crucifixion."

"What wounds?"

"The nail wounds in his wrists."

Castle's mind raced ahead. He had studied Christianity intensely, even if his curiosity derived from the perspective of a disbeliever. He also loved traveling, especially in Italy. As a result he had a decent command of Italian and could easily order meals in Italian in restaurants and navigate in taxis and trains around Italy without having to rely on English. On his many trips to Italy, Castle took an interest in the story of Padre Pio, a simple parish priest in a small town in southern Italy who gained fame worldwide in the 1950s after he suffered the bleeding wounds in his wrists that the faithful believed were manifestations of Christ's wounds on the cross.

Castle had always wanted to study Padre Pio, suspecting his wounds were self-inflicted—not that Padre Pio had driven nails through his wrists to produce the wounds of Christ on the cross, but that Pio's religious fervor had reached the point of becoming equivalent to a mental illness. As a psychiatrist, Castle suspected that Padre Pio's disturbed subconscious had become sufficiently strong to cause Christ's nail wounds in his wrists to manifest themselves as the bleeding wounds from which Padre Pio suffered.

Castle understood that Padre Pio himself had always maintained the wounds were mystical, caused by the direct action of God and inflicted upon him as a confirmation of his complete devotion to the crucified Jesus. Truthfully, Castle doubted Padre Pio, or anyone else for that matter, could say exactly what the wrist wounds of the historical Jesus Christ crucified had looked like two thousand years ago. As soon as Archbishop Duncan mentioned that Father Bartholomew had "manifested" the nail wounds of Christ's crucifixion on his wrists, Castle was excited to realize he was being handed an opportunity right here in New York to study the phenomenon in person.

"Stigmata?" Castle asked the archbishop, using the Church's name for the wounds of Christ on the cross that a few Catholic mystics have manifested over the centuries. "You're telling me that this Father Bartholomew has begun to display the stigmata?"

"Not just the stigmata, but also the blood Christ shed on the cross," Duncan said seriously. "Trust my judgment on this. This case is already drawing attention in the city right now. The pope is worried that Father Bartholomew could become an international sensation if we don't get on top of this right away."

"Why wouldn't that appeal to the Catholic Church? It might get you more believers."

"I'm in agreement with that sentiment," Archbishop Duncan admitted. "I'd like more believers, especially if they would come to church on Sunday in my archdiocese. But the pope is worried that Father Bartholomew could be a fraud, or even worse."

"What could be worse?"

"That's why we are calling you," Archbishop Duncan admitted honestly. "If Father Bartholomew turns out to have a psychological disorder, this is not the way the Church wants to get believers, and I don't want them either, especially not in the Archdiocese of New York."

"So, you're confirming to me that Pope John-Paul Peter I is involved in this case already?"

"Yes," Duncan acknowledged. "He is sending Father Morelli to the United States to work on the case. Morelli is a Jesuit and he's one of the pope's most trusted advisors. You've spoken with the pope yourself and I suspect you can judge for yourself how serious a man Marco Vicente is. He is the same man as pope that he was as a cardinal."

Castle listened intently, but he was not yet convinced this was the case for him. "But why doesn't the Vatican choose a Catholic psychiatrist? I can recommend several right here in New York City who are top-notch."

"The pope asked for you to take this case," Duncan said firmly. "The pope was very specific. The pope knows you and he trusts you, and he knows you have the skills we need. You're a psychiatrist, and you're also a very accomplished medical doctor."

Castle appreciated what Duncan was saying. Before he had

decided to switch careers and become a psychiatrist, Castle had been a well-known surgeon.

"If you had stayed with surgery, you would today be one of the best in the world," Duncan insisted. "This case is going to demand more than psychiatry to understand the problem. Stigmata are a complicated medical issue and the Vatican feels we need a surgeon to handle the case. You cover both skills we need—you were a surgeon and you are now a psychiatrist. The Vatican doesn't know any medical doctor anywhere in the world more qualified to handle this case than you—certainly no one whom Rome trusts as much as the pope trusts you."

Castle appreciated what Duncan was telling him, and he saw an opportunity in taking the case. He began to sense that analyzing Bartholomew would only end up confirming his suspicion that human beings typically created religious experience to control sexuality and compensate for a lack of meaning in their lives. Besides, his publisher was pushing him for another book and the thought crossed his mind that Father Bartholomew might provide just the inspiration he needed to get started writing. Nothing would be more interesting to his readers than debunking a psychologically disturbed priest who had begun to think of himself as Jesus Christ.

Then too, Archbishop Duncan was an important figure in New York and Castle himself was now at a top level of New York society. So it was better to have the archbishop as his friend than antagonize him by neglecting to help when asked directly by the pope to do so.

"You have to understand I'm close to Bartholomew," Archbishop Duncan continued. "We go back many years. When Bartholomew was in grade school, he and his mother were parishioners at St. Margaret's over in Morristown, the first church where I was a parish priest after the seminary. When his mother died, I counseled Bartholomew on his vocation and I've been his spiritual advisor ever since. Over the years, Bartholomew has become a personal friend, as well as a priest I supervise in the archdiocese."

Castle listened carefully. Reading between the lines, he understood that Archbishop Duncan was telling him he was going to be protective of Father Bartholomew. Any attempt Castle might make to discredit the priest on psychological grounds would have to be well substantiated; otherwise Duncan would end up trying to discredit the psychiatrist in order to protect the Church and his friend Father Bartholomew.

"Truly, Bartholomew is a lot like you," Duncan continued.

"How's that?" Castle asked, surprised at the comment.

"Bartholomew also changed careers. He was a brilliant physicist at Princeton. You have to know he was brilliant, simply because he was one of the youngest Ph.D.'s ever to be accepted to the faculty of the Institute for Advanced Studies. He went through a personal crisis when his mother died. His mother was the only person he ever was really close to. When she died, he left physics and entered the seminary. I counseled him through the crisis. Now I'm calling you because I need your help on this one, just like I did when we first met."

Castle figured he might as well stop protesting. "Okay, then tell me exactly what you want me to do."

"Meet with Father Morelli and hear out the details of the case. Morelli will explain to you why the Vatican is so concerned."

"Can't you tell me why the Vatican is so involved in this case, after only one day of hearing about it?"

"Let Morelli explain it. He is the pope's top advisor on miracles, anything paranormal that affects the Church—appearances of the Virgin Mary, miracles—all that type of thing. He has played the role of devil's advocate in prosecuting the case against those being considered by the pope to be canonized as saints. Father Bartholomew manifested the stigmata yesterday when saying Mass. There were people in the church who filmed the event with their cell phones. The videos are already starting to show up on the Internet."

"I see," Castle commented, making a mental note to look up some of the videos and watch them for himself.

"All I'm asking you to do right now is to meet with Father Morelli. Then, if you decide to take the case, you can meet with Father Bartholomew. The Church would like you to take on Father Bartholomew as one of your psychiatric patients."

"Okay, so you say Father Morelli is prepared to travel from Rome to meet me here in New York?"

"Yes."

"How soon?"

"Today is Friday," Duncan calculated. "If you agree to see Father Morelli, I will call the Vatican immediately. Morelli can take a flight from Rome to New York and be here tomorrow, especially if you can see him on Monday."

The Vatican doesn't want to waste any time, Castle realized. "That fast?"

"Yes, first thing on Monday, if possible," Duncan said firmly. "We need to move on this right now. I sent the details of the case to the Vatican on Thursday night, complete with photos of Father Bartholomew and his wounds. The pope himself was on the phone to me, waking me up this morning at five-thirty A.M. I know I'm pushing it to call you on a Friday morning and ask you to make time in your schedule on Monday."

"How much time will Morelli need?"

"How much time can you give him?"

Castle quickly reviewed mentally the patients he had scheduled for Monday. "If Morelli can be at my office at eight A.M. on Monday, I think I can push my first appointment back an hour. I know that's early, but that's the best I can do."

"Thank you," the archbishop said, very pleased Castle had agreed. "Morelli will be at your office at eight A.M. Monday."

CHAPTER FOUR

Castle rose at 6:30 A.M., looking forward to starting off the week by seeing the pope's mysterious emissary from Rome.

Scrutinizing his face in the bathroom mirror, Dr. Stephen Castle carefully combed into place his ample head of soft black hair, which was now distinguished by traces of gray, as was his closely cropped beard. He was pleased at what he saw, confident he was at the height of his professional prowess.

Standing before the full-length hall mirror on his way out of the apartment, he took a minute to arrange precisely the four-pointed handkerchief in the pocket of his expensively tailored black cashmere sport coat. Taking one last look into his steely blue-gray eyes reflected back from the mirror, Castle was reassured that his exercise routine was working to maintain his muscle tone and control his waistline. At fifty-four years old, Castle found his psychiatric practice to be thriving beyond his wildest expectations. Castle had every intention of staying healthy and productive for maybe twenty more years of active medical practice.

Truthfully, Castle was pleased with what he saw reflected back in his mirrors. His gray-lined pinstripe shirt with a button-down collar open at the neck nicely complemented his sport jacket and his carefully pressed gray slacks. He liked the elegance of his neatly trimmed beard and, while he had to exercise more now to maintain his trim and fit appearance, it was easy with the gym he had built into a section of his living quarters, which had a particularly stunning view over Central Park.

Psychoanalyzing difficult patients was like playing a game of chess in which Castle could lose, despite his advantage of understanding how the human psyche worked. Some of his better patients were also brilliant, more than capable of playing the game of psychoanalysis like chess masters themselves.

He knew Archbishop Duncan was right. If he had never gone into psychiatry, he believed he would have become one of the top heart surgeons in the world; he would have made his millions either way. Returning to medical residency to get his psychiatric training after his wife died cost him a couple of valuable years. Still, he judged it had been worth it. He was a young man in his thirties when he was first board-certified in psychiatry.

Castle got his B.A. degree from New York University, in his native city. He had always wanted to go to Harvard, and when Harvard Medical School admitted him, his decision was already made. He did his medical residency at Mass. General in Boston. When he decided to change careers after his wife died, he did his psychiatric residency at Beth Israel Hospital in New York City, where he was already on staff as a surgeon. Castle enjoyed his time in Boston, but he had always planned to return to practice medicine in New York, the city he loved more than any other in the world.

Though he had never remarried, he considered himself a

young fifty-four-year-old and he felt he had plenty of years left to enjoy his money. At this point in his career, he was doing what he wanted to do professionally, especially since he could afford to take only those cases he wanted to psychoanalyze. The thought crossed his mind that he might never retire. He traveled the world as he pleased, always first-class; he managed to spend a month or two a year in Italy—what more did he need? He was happy with his life and he felt fulfilled professionally. At fifty-four, and with his social prominence in New York, he had all the divorcées he wanted for dinner or theater guests. He enjoyed their company, but he had no intentions of remarrying. The complications of maintaining a long-term relationship with a second wife did not interest him at all.

Castle had never lost his enthusiasm for starting his days early and he knew from experience that if he could manage to keep his mind open, each day had the prospect of opening up to him a new and exciting level of knowledge. Confident that Father Bartholomew's story would form the core of his new book, Castle looked forward to meeting the priest from the Vatican.

Wondering what Father Morelli would tell him about Father Bartholomew that Archbishop Duncan had intentionally left out, Castle walked confidently through his comfortable and elegantly appointed apartment to take the stairway down to his office on the floor below.

Decades ago, when he was dependent on his wife working as a legal secretary to help pay for his residency at Mass. General, Castle had never imagined he would one day have the resources to buy these two top floors of this exclusive Fifth Avenue address, in a prewar apartment building located right on Central Park across from the Metropolitan Museum of Art. But his practice had grown until his patient list included some of the most prominent business leaders in New York and most powerful politicians in Washington. Castle could easily afford his pricey address. By picking a residential apartment building for his medical practice and getting the co-op board to allow him to locate his office in his home, Castle had managed to combine upscale New York living with a discreet location for his office.

Senators traveled from the nation's capital to see him here, as did top investment bankers and CEOs from Wall Street. When coming for medical advice, the rich and the prominent could just as easily be visiting friends. Limousines were nothing out of the ordinary in this neighborhood. Yet, with its address and entrance on the cross street, this building was particularly appropriate for his psychiatric practice. Since visitors did not have to enter the building on Fifth Avenue, Castle's patients could more easily stay out of view from the public and the press, even when their limousines dropped them off at Castle's front door.

Castle loved his perch on the top two floors, complete with a penthouse roof garden that made a lovely setting for a catered late evening dinner in the summer. It was hard to beat the backdrop of Central Park with its changing beauty through every different season of the year—the lush green of the summer, the array of colors as the trees changed in the fall, the stark beauty of the bare trees in the winter, the promise of spring with the first light green as the trees budded anew. In the judgment of many New York social scene reporters, there was no better apartment in New York to hold a cocktail party for the rich and famous.

When he descended from his living quarters to his sumptuous office space on the floor below, Castle entered his massive, mahogany-lined library. His thousand volumes encompassed one of the world's most impressive collections of psychiatric literature in private hands, including signed first editions by nearly every giant in the field. He was most pleased with his collection of Sigmund Freud first editions originally published in German and inscribed by the psychiatrist himself. The library opened onto his treatment room, which filled most of the floor.

Every detail of Castle's treatment room had been carefully calculated for effect. His chair was centrally positioned in the room, with windows onto Central Park to his back. The buildings lining Central Park South and Central Park West provided a bigger-than-life backdrop, which the psychiatrist felt underscored his important role.

The patient's chair, a little less sumptuous and a lot less comfortable, was positioned directly opposite him, across from a small coffee table. From the patient's perspective, Castle was backlit, making it difficult to see all the details of the psychiatrist's face. In contrast, the light from the spacious windows pouring onto the patient gave Castle the advantage of being able to scrutinize every reaction of his patient in nicely lighted detail. Keeping the light to his back was an unfair advantage in the psychiatric setting and Castle liked unfair advantages when they played to his favor.

Around the perimeter of the room behind Castle were comfortable, overstuffed connecting couches, generously punctuated with pillows and positioned for the occasional group meetings Castle hosted in his office.

Entering the treatment room, Castle stopped to allow himself to soak in fully the dazzling beauty as the morning sun danced across the rich yellow and red leaves of Central Park's changing fall trees.

Castle worked alone, without a secretary or appointments clerk. That too was a step he took to protect the privacy of his patients. Regardless of how trusted an assistant might be, a second person in the practice necessarily risked a breach of confidentiality, especially when the clients were well-known. When he was expecting patients, Castle simply left the outside door to his waiting room open.

This Monday morning at 8:00 A.M., as expected, Dr. Castle found Father Morelli comfortably seated in his waiting room, ready for the appointment Archbishop Duncan had scheduled over the phone on Friday.

Seeing the priest for the first time, Castle judged him to be in his early forties. Observing Morelli's wire-frame glasses and frail build, Castle concluded he was most likely the scholarly type who had never excelled in athletics. Still, Duncan said Morelli was a Jesuit, so Castle knew not only that he was smart, but also that he was political—both of which made sense to Castle, especially since Duncan had told him that Morelli was one of the pope's most trusted advisors.

Castle also noted that Morelli dressed modestly, in his black priest's suit and Roman collar. Yet there were signs Father Morelli had money and enjoyed fine things. Without being ostentatious, Morelli wore handmade Italian leather shoes and he carried under his arm an elegant soft leather briefcase that Castle guessed had been handmade in Florence. Today, the briefcase looked like it was bulging with papers that Castle guessed were meant for him.

"Archbishop Duncan said you have come from Rome to discuss with me Father Bartholomew," Castle began, as he settled into his chair opposite Morelli in the treatment room. "What's the problem?"

"*Va bene*," Morelli began instinctively in Italian, reminding himself instantly to switch into English. Proceeding with a heavy Italian accent, Morelli explained in grammatically perfect and fluent English that Father Paul Bartholomew's problems began when he was in a massive car accident that should have killed him.

"Archbishop Duncan mentioned to me the car accident," Castle commented, "but he did not give me any details other than to suggest that Father Bartholomew revived from a near-death experience."

"Technically, Father Bartholomew did die," Morelli stressed, making sure the psychiatrist was prepared to understand that as far as the Church was concerned, the experience was more than just near death. "Father Bartholomew's heart actually stopped on the operating table. The doctors worked on him frantically and it was a miracle, but his heart started beating again and he came back to life."

"How long was he considered dead?" Castle asked.

From his briefcase, Morelli handed Castle a thick medical file.

"Maybe as long as ten minutes," Morelli answered. "You can read all the medical details here. I'm not a medical doctor, but from what I've read in that file, Father Bartholomew's heart had stopped long enough for the doctors and nurses in the operating room to be startled when the monitors jumped back to life and started registering a pulse."

Castle took in the information, but from what he was reading in the medical file, the case was not remarkable. Father Bartholomew had been revived after the doctors in the operating room applied cardiac electric shock procedures. *A lot of people die for a while on the operating table and revive back to life*, Castle thought. *So what?* That Morelli thought otherwise was all Castle needed to hear to understand not only that Morelli had no professional medical training, but also that Morelli had very little understanding of medicine.

"You might not realize it, Father Morelli, but it's not all that unusual for a patient's heart to come back like that," Castle said as he calmly perused the medical file. "For many patients, the cardiac electric shock works. That's why the doctors in the operating room applied the procedure."

"I understand," Morelli said, undeterred. "But there's more. Father Bartholomew reported to his religious superiors in the archdiocese that he experienced an out-of-body experience on the operating table. When he was aware his heart had stopped, he felt himself lifting out of his body and hovering above the scene of the doctors below working frantically to revive him. Next, he says, a brilliant light surrounded him and he went through a tunnel he saw suspended high in the air above him. At the end of the tunnel, he recognized many friends and relatives who had died years before. Finally, he was reunited with his mother, who had died only a few years earlier, after a long illness."

Again Bartholomew was not sure there was anything remarkable about this. In the medical profession, these were considered "near-death" experiences, not "after-life" experiences, despite how much Father Morelli or the Catholic Church might protest the difference. As far as Dr. Castle was concerned, in his professional medical judgment, people who are truly dead do not return to life. People who are near death may have experiences that they interpret as if they had died and returned to life. But to Castle, this important distinction needed to be made. Just because some people reported this experience did not mean the experience of dying and returning to life happened as they thought. As far as the psychiatrist was concerned, no truly dead person had ever returned to life to report on what happens after we die.

"People who go through near-death experiences commonly report seeing brilliant lights or going through tunnels at the end of which are waiting long-deceased friends and relatives," Castle explained. "All this is explainable from natural causes, from the physiology of how the brain dies. It doesn't mean a person going through a near-death experience is really floating as a disconnected spirit that hovers above their body lying dead below, or that they actually enter a tunnel where they meet long-lost acquaintances. Near-death experiences do not prove the continued existence of the soul after death, nor do they confirm the existence of Heaven. Medically speaking, near-death experiences do not prove the person has actually died, even if the person thinks that is the case. More precisely, near-death experiences tell us how the brain shuts down right before the brain dies."

Morelli seemed to get the point, so Castle continued.

"That seems to be what happened to Father Bartholomew. In the cases where people appear to come back to life, maybe the heart has stopped, but the brain doesn't die. I will admit that medical science does not understand the phenomenon completely. But a patient who revives from a near-death experience did not actually die. That must be accepted. Again, we don't always understand why, but some patients can be technically dead for several minutes, even longer, yet for some reason or other, when their vital functions come back to life, there is no permanent damage. Sometimes, as seems to be the case with Father Bartholomew, the patient has a memory of what happened in their minds when their hearts stopped."

But Morelli was not convinced Castle was right. "What if," he asked Castle, "your medical theory is just a convenient explanation to avoid having to deal with messy religious concepts, like the soul or the afterlife? How do we know that these near-death experiences aren't just the first part of what everybody who dies actually experiences?"

"Truthfully, we don't," Castle admitted. "Until we cross over, none of us may know what death is. But what we do know is that people reporting near-death experiences tend to revive relatively quickly. We don't have anybody who has been dead for years coming back to life to tell us what the other side looked like."

"Ah," Morelli exclaimed, "but in this case, despite what may be the reality of what happened, Father Bartholomew insists he experienced everything I just described, including dying and going to Heaven. He reports having had a meeting with an ancient wise man he took to be God. You have to admit that, for Father Bartholomew, this description of an after-life experience is his actual current psychological reality."

Castle had to agree. "That's why you called me. I'm a psychiatrist and I spend much of my life dealing with people's psychological interpretation of reality, whether or not their personal interpretations of what is happening have anything to do with what is really happening, outside that personal psychological reality."

"Let me continue," Morelli said, wanting to make sure Castle heard the whole story. "Bartholomew says he was reunited with his mother and he felt an inner peace and an acceptance from this wise figure that he took to be God. He felt completely at home there and he says God gave him a choice to stay there in Heaven with his mother, or return back to earth. If he decided to return to earth, Father Bartholomew says, God said he could not promise him an easy life, but he would give Father Bartholomew a gift he would need to accomplish his mission."

None of this altered Castle's preliminary diagnostic hypothesis, namely, that Bartholomew was experiencing some disturbed psychological reaction in which he was hallucinating. *How severe was the brain damage Bartholomew suffered in his near-death experience?* Castle wrote in the margin of the medical file.

"What gifts does Father Bartholomew claim to have brought with him back to earth?" Castle asked.

"One gift Bartholomew came back with appears to be the ability to heal people."

Castle was still skeptical. "I appreciate immediately how a priest claiming healing powers could potentially create a lot of publicity in the news media. If Father Bartholomew is successful in generating a group hysteria, in which masses of people came to believe he has supernatural healing powers that came from an after-life encounter with God, the Church could be inundated with millions of people demanding to see the priest in order to be healed."

"Yes, that is a problem," Morelli agreed. "This priest is only one person, but if his healing abilities become widely believed, Father Bartholomew, like Padre Pio before him, could well be on the way to becoming an international celebrity."

"Can you tell me more about these healing abilities?" Castle asked, framing once again an open-ended question designed to encourage Morelli to tell him what he knew, regardless of where Morelli might begin or end up in the explanation.

"It started in the confessional," Morelli answered. "Father Bartholomew hears confessions twice a week at St. Joseph's. Before the accident, Father Bartholomew's time at St. Joseph's was pretty much normal. He did his work just as Archbishop Duncan and the archdiocese expected. He celebrated Mass without incident. He heard confessions and gave people absolution, just like any priest would. Generally, he was a very good priest who did his job quietly and competently. Father Bartholomew was successful as a parish priest. He had a growing congregation and was well liked by his parishioners. But now that he is back at St. Joseph's, everything is changed."

"How so?"

"In the first weeks after Father Bartholomew was back at St. Joseph's after the accident, we began getting reports from parishioners that he had begun telling some of those in the confessional that they had a particular illness that Father Bartholomew had no way of knowing they had. Then, Father Bartholomew went further. He began recommending to these people in the confessional what they should do to get healed. Others he told not to have an operation or to wait a few days before they did anything. Many of the people didn't know they were sick."

"Is Father Bartholomew medically trained?"

"Not that I know. In the past few weeks, the archdiocese began to get reports that Father Bartholomew was performing miracles. Parishioners who went to confession with Father Bartholomew began calling Archbishop Duncan's office to tell him they could hear Bartholomew talking with Jesus in the confessional."

"How did people know it was Jesus that Bartholomew was speaking to?"

"Truly, they didn't. What people could hear was a second voice in the confessional and they knew the second voice was not Bartholomew's. They began to assume Bartholomew was talking to Jesus, because when Bartholomew discussed their illnesses, he told them things about their lives that Bartholomew had no way of knowing. Then, when Bartholomew told them what to do about their illnesses, they were healed, if they followed his instructions. So the word spread that Father Bartholomew was consulting with Jesus in the confessional."

"And what does Bartholomew say about all this? Does Bartholomew say Jesus is there with him in the confessional?"

"Yes. He says Jesus sits in the box next to him in the confessional, where the person who is waiting to go to confession next usually kneels and waits their turn. Bartholomew has begun locking off that side of the confessional, allowing people to enter the confessional only from one side. He says that once people say, 'Bless me, Father; it has been three weeks, or whatever, since my last confession,' Jesus begins talking to him about the person making the confession."

Castle took notes. "And what does this Jesus say?"

"According to Father Bartholomew, Jesus tells him intimate secrets that no one else knows about the lives of the people who come to confess their sins. Father Bartholomew seems to know if the confessors have been faithful to their spouses, or if they have committed crimes or other offenses they have kept successfully hidden for years. Father Bartholomew then tells them that Jesus wants those Father Bartholomew has absolved of their sins in the confessional to know they are forgiven. People are impressed because the sins and trespasses that Father Bartholomew seems to know without being told often involve offenses those in the confessional may have kept hidden as secrets or lies, sometimes for as long as decades."

Hearing this, Castle refined his diagnostic hypothesis to include the observation that Father Bartholomew's neurosis evidently permitted him to manifest a second voice, as if he were communicating with another secret person sitting unseen in the confession box next to him. Castle made another marginal note: *Does Father Bartholomew have multiple personality disorder?*

"Sometimes Father Bartholomew gives very personal advice," Morelli continued, "like telling a person they must stop an extramarital affair, or that they must admit to their spouses or children various lies or secrets they have held for years. The problem for the Vatican is that confession is not supposed to be about medical healing. Confession is about absolution of sins. The Vatican has a problem when one person going to confession with Father Bartholomew claims to be cured of cancer, and then another claims to be cured of heart disease. The word is spreading fast. Now Father Bartholomew has people lined up around the block to go to confession."

"How about in the hospital? Is Bartholomew beginning to cure people there, too?"

"Yes," Morelli admitted. "It's beginning to happen even in the hospital. Father Bartholomew has had to be restrained from walking on the hospital floor and offering to hear the confessions of the other patients on the floor. The doctors and nurses are concerned Father Bartholomew appears to be giving out medical advice, where he isn't qualified."

"I can appreciate the problem," Castle acknowledged. He also realized how little Archbishop Duncan would like seeing the New York media turn Father Bartholomew into a freak sideshow that would draw a circus crowd. Besides, it wouldn't be long before some smart lawyer caught on and convinced a patient to file a suit against the archdiocese for allowing a priest to give medical advice without possessing a license to practice medicine.

"But there's more," Morelli continued. "Father Bartholomew has begun to experience flashbacks."

"What type of flashbacks?"

"Bartholomew reports that part of his after-life experience, or near-death experience, as you put it, was an instant where he felt he was actually standing at Golgotha with his mother, on the day Christ died."

Listening, Castle showed no emotion. He calmly made additional notes in Bartholomew's medical file.

"Archbishop Duncan told me Father Bartholomew has begun to manifest the stigmata," Castle pressed forward. "What can you tell me about this?"

"The stigmata first appeared last Thursday, when Father Bartholomew was saying Mass," Morelli explained. "I brought with me a few photographs that were taken at the hospital. The photos show the wounds Bartholomew suffered while saying Mass. The wounds bled quite heavily and Father Bartholomew collapsed unconscious at the altar."

Castle sorted through the photographs of Bartholomew at the hospital. The wounds on his wrist were severe. Both wrists appeared to have been complete punctures, all the way through.

"The Catholic Church has had centuries of experience with

people experiencing the stigmata," Morelli explained. "The first was St. Francis of Assisi in La Verna, Italy, in 1224. Since then, we have documented maybe a thousand authentic cases. The most common wounds of Christ's passion and death that manifest in Christian mystics are the nail wounds in the wrists from the crucifixion."

Right," Castle mused. "As I recall, Christ suffered five wounds on the cross—nail wounds on both wrists, both feet, and a spear wound in the side."

"Yes," Morelli affirmed. "In addition, there were the wounds from the scourging at the pillar and the crowning with thorns. These wounds rarely appear as stigmata."

"Where does the word *stigmata* come from?"

"It dates back to St. Paul's Letter to the Galatians in the Acts of the Apostles," Morelli answered. "St. Paul wrote, 'I bear on my body the stigmata of Jesus.' *Stigmata* is the plural of the Greek word *stigma,* which is translated as 'mark' or 'brand,' like one you might place on an animal, like cowboys brand cows."

"Isn't Father Bartholomew's first name Paul?" Castle asked, sure he was right.

"Yes, it is," Morelli noted. "St. Paul was a Jew who was also a Roman citizen. As a young man, he despised Christianity. He worked for the Romans and was known for brutally persecuting Christians prior to his conversion. His conversion came when he was blinded on the road to Damascus by a burst of light and a vision of the resurrected Jesus. As I'm sure you know, St. Paul is considered perhaps the most important early Christian mission-ary, credited with bringing Christianity to the Gentiles, even to Rome. According to tradition, he was beheaded by the emperor Nero after being imprisoned in Rome."

"How about Bartholomew? Wasn't Bartholomew one of the disciples of Jesus?"

"Yes, he was. He is counted among the twelve apostles of Jesus in the gospels of Matthew, Mark, and Luke. He is also credited with having been present at the ascension of Jesus into Heaven following the resurrection. Tradition holds that Bartholomew traveled to India, where he took up a mission of preaching about Jesus."

"How do the stigmata typically appear?" Castle asked.

"The wounds typically appear mystically," Morelli went on. "There's usually no evidence of a cause. As I said, over the centuries, the Church has had experience with many people who experience the wounds of Christ on the cross. Only in the most rare of cases does a religious mystic experience all five of the wounds Christ suffered on the cross. And, as I mentioned, we almost never see stigmata from the scourging at the pillar or the crown of thorns."

"Does the Church consider stigmata to be mystical events? Do you consider them miracles?"

"In some cases, yes," Morelli noted. "Padre Pio had the stigmata on his wrists and he was canonized just a few years ago."

"Does Bartholomew have all five wounds?"

"No, he has just the nail wounds in his wrists."

"So, the story here is that Bartholomew suffered these wounds while saying Mass," Castle said, making sure he had his facts right. "That's what Archbishop Duncan told me, it's what you are saying, and it's what I saw on the YouTube videos on the Internet."

"Right. Father Bartholomew was in the middle of consecrating the bread and wine, the most solemn part of the Mass. When he held the host above the altar, the wounds started appearing. He blanked out and collapsed at the altar."

This evidence caused Castle to suspect his initial diagnostic hunches were correct—that Bartholomew's neurosis involved a multiple personality disorder and had progressed to the point where Bartholomew was hallucinating conversations with Jesus in the confessional. The additional evidence also suggested to Dr. Castle that Father Bartholomew was engaging in psychosomatically induced self-mutilations, even if it appeared to those not psychiatrically trained that Bartholomew played no role in causing the injuries. Castle understood that to most people, including Archbishop Duncan and Father Morelli, possibly even to the pope, it would appear as if the wounds were manifesting themselves from some mystical cause. Bartholomew's stigmata, like those of Padre Pio, Castle judged, were most likely caused by Bartholomew's subconscious being fixated on what he imagined was the physical pain Christ suffered being crucified.

He made notes on Bartholomew's medical file questioning whether a mass hysteria had begun to develop in which parishioners believed they were being cured in the confessional when Father Bartholomew gave them absolution from their sins. If a mass hysteria was beginning to develop over Father Bartholomew's supposed power to communicate with Jesus in the confessional and to heal illnesses, it would be accelerated even more if people believed Bartholomew was mystically manifesting the wounds of Christ on the cross.

"You brought with you the medical files on Bartholomew's wrist injuries?"

"Yes, they're right here," Morelli said, pulling the files from his briefcase and handing them over to Castle.

"As I said, I'm not a medical doctor," Morelli continued. "But from the extensive research I have done in the Vatican on the stigmata, I can tell you that Bartholomew's case is very much like what the Church has come to expect. For most people experiencing the stigmata, the wounds can bleed profusely and are terribly painful. Still, the bleeding is not constant and wounds are not typically fatal. Many who experience the stigmata live for years and go into and out of a religious ecstasy in which they often see visions and sometimes report they see Christ and can speak with him."

"From my conversation with the archbishop, I understand Father Bartholomew returned to St. Joseph's only recently," Castle noted.

"Yes," Morelli acknowledged. "It was only two months ago that Archbishop Duncan allowed Father Bartholomew to return to St. Joseph's. He was in rehabilitation for nearly three years. It was two years after the accident before Bartholomew could walk on his own power again. He still uses a cane and sometimes crutches. Right now, recovering in the hospital from the stigmata, he is confined to bed, able to move around only in a wheelchair. The stigmata took away much of the strength Bartholomew had recovered since the accident."

Castle was beginning to get the picture; still, there was something he didn't understand.

"Father Morelli, excuse me," Castle interrupted, "but Archbishop Duncan said you sometimes worked for the Vatican as a devil's advocate in cases where saints are being considered for canonization. Is that correct?"

"Yes, it is."

"Then what I don't understand is why you appear to be accepting Father Bartholomew's story so uncritically."

Morelli knew that was a good question. "Have you heard about the Shroud of Turin?" he asked in return.

Castle vaguely remembered that the Shroud of Turin was a relic the Catholic Church owned and that many believers claimed it was the burial cloth of the historical Jesus Christ.

Morelli confirmed this was correct. "The Shroud has an image on it of a crucified man that for centuries the Catholic Church has venerated as a relic. While the Church has never proclaimed the Shroud to be from the time of Christ or the actual burial cloth of Christ, millions of believers have concluded just that, over centuries."

"What's the point?" Castle asked.

"The point is that Father Bartholomew has begun to resemble the man in the Shroud of Turin, both in terms of his physical appearance and now in terms of his wrist injuries. This is what has drawn the Vatican's attention."

Morelli pulled two more photographs from his briefcase and handed them to Castle one at a time. "This is what Bartholomew looked like before the accident and this is what he looks like today."

Castle was shocked. What he saw in the first photograph was a smiling young man in his early forties who looked confident of his future. What he saw in the second photograph was a much older man. Bartholomew had grown a long beard and his hair flowed down to his shoulders.

"When were these two photos taken?"

"The first was about four years ago, before his accident," Morelli explained. "The second was taken yesterday, in the hospital."

Castle could not believe the difference. "In four years, the man in the photographs had gone from a clean-shaven young man who appeared alive and full of health, to a bearded, long-haired, much older man who looked very troubled with pain and sorrow."

"Now look at this." Morelli handed Castle yet a third photo. "This is the image of the man in the Shroud of Turin. When you meet Father Bartholomew, it should be obvious how closely today Father Bartholomew has come to look exactly like the man in the Shroud."

The image of the man in the Shroud of Turin looked ghostly, yet it had a clearly photographic quality about it.

At first the face looked blurry to Castle, but the more he studied it, the more distinct the facial features became to him. Studying the face, Castle began to see the man many believe to be Jesus. The man in the Shroud appeared to have his eyes closed, as if in sleep or in death. Somehow the face conveyed a quiet dignity in its strong, square lines and elongated rectangular shape. The nose was prominent, but well proportioned. The mouth was closed in what looked like a thoughtful repose. The man in the Shroud looked almost as if he could be sleeping, not dead. Still, Castle could read sorrow and pain in the face, and he noted what looked like white streaks, possibly of blood, that streamed from the forehead and seemed to saturate the long hair that draped down on each side of the man's face.

"How is this photograph possible if the Shroud is two thousand years old?" Castle asked. "Photography was not invented until the 1820s." Castle was struggling to understand how this image had such photographic qualities when it was made either 1,800 years before photography was discovered, if the Shroud was the actual burial cloth of Christ, or some five hundred to six hundred years before photography was discovered, if the Shroud was a medieval forgery.

"It's complicated," Morelli answered. "But to give you the simple explanation, the Church has discovered over time that the Shroud itself is a sort of negative. Surprisingly, the man in the Shroud is most clearly seen when you look at a photographic negative of the Shroud."

"When did the Church discover the photographic qualities of the Shroud?"

"It wasn't until 1898, when Secondo Pia, an Italian amateur photographer, was allowed to photograph the Shroud. Working with his negatives in the darkroom, Secondo Pia was shocked when he realized his negative had produced a face. He said he felt that in his darkroom he was looking back centuries, the first person since Christ died to be looking into the living face of the Lord. Pia realized that the image of the man on the Shroud became easier to see when the light values are reversed, such that the brownish red lines on the Shroud show up as highlights in the photographic negative. In other words, the image of the crucified man that is somehow imprinted into the linen of the Shroud is most clearly seen when the brownish red lines that your eye sees as the image on the Shroud are reversed to white in the photographic negative."

"So what I am looking at here is the negative that results when a photograph of the Shroud is taken, is that correct?" Castle asked, wanting to make sure he understood what Morelli was attempting to explain.

"That's right," Morelli said. "You're looking at a photographic negative. The brownish red lines visible to the naked eye on the Shroud show up in a photographic negative as white highlights. You can easily imagine that Secondo Pia's contemporaries in the late 1890s accused him of having perpetrated a fraud. They claimed he concocted the image of Jesus Christ that you are look-ing at, using darkroom tricks to produce an image that was not visible to the naked eye looking at the Shroud. Pia's results weren't accepted until 1931, when Giuseppe Enrie, an Italian professional photographer, was permitted to photograph the Shroud a second time and got the same results."

From his briefcase, Morelli handed Castle a second image of the face of the man in the Shroud. "Take a look at this image and compare it with the other. I think comparing the two will give you a better idea how the process works. This is what a photographic print of the Shroud looks like. The actual Shroud looks much the same, except that the lines that mark the face would be brownish red, not the black and white of the photographic print you see here."

Castle looked back and forth between the two images, appreciating how Secondo Pia's photographic process had worked.

"What you are looking at now in the photographic print is how the face of the man appears on the linen of the Shroud to the naked eye," Morelli explained. "Looking at the Shroud with your naked eye, the face of the man in the Shroud looks faint—so faint that at first you might not even see him. But then, after you study the image for a while, the face becomes clearer, as you begin to be able to see and distinguish the brownish red lines that appear on the surface."

"So you're telling me that whoever painted the Shroud painted a negative?" Castle asked.

"Yes," Morelli said, pleased to see Castle was getting the point. "That's exactly what I am saying. In other words, if you assume some medieval painter forged the Shroud, that painter would have had to be brilliant enough to understand how photographic negatives work, even though they hadn't been invented yet. Why wouldn't a medieval forger simply have painted a positive image onto the burial cloth, the way a painter portrays a life scene the way the eye sees it? Nobody in the Middle Ages had ever seen a photographic negative."

"But not all photographs require a negative," Castle observed. "Daguerreotypes are one of the earliest forms of photographs and they don't require a negative as an intermediary step in the photographic process. If I am right, in a daguerreotype, a positive image is formed directly on a plate that is coated with light-sensitive chemicals."

"You are exactly right," Morelli said. "Negatives are only used in photographic processes where the image is imprinted first on an intermediary surface that has been treated with photosensitive chemicals, like silver halide. There is also no negative formed in digital photography. If the painter of the Shroud was medieval, that person had to be brilliant enough to anticipate not only the invention of photographic processes that required negatives as an intermediary step in producing the positive photographic image, but that negatives would be a surviving photographic process. Negatives, it turns out, have been the dominant photographic process from the early Kodak cameras up until the recent advent of digital cameras. But my guess is that photographic negatives will fade away in our current era of digital imaging."

"So you recommend I should study the negative images of the Shroud if I want to see the man more clearly?"

"Yes, that is exactly what I am saying," Morelli said in confirmation once again. "I want you to have the clearest possible idea what the man in the Shroud of Turin looks like, for a very important reason."

"What's that?" Castle asked.

"I believe that when you meet Father Bartholomew you will agree he looks today just like the man in the Shroud of Turin. Father Bartholomew has the same double-pointed beard with a fork at the chin. They both have long hair covering their ears and draping over their shoulders. They both have the same face with square lines. If you permit me to interpret how they look, you will see in both the same quiet dignity, the same suggestion of inner peace despite the obvious pain and suffering. The same wrinkles in the brow."

Castle quickly got the point. "So, what you are telling me is that if the man in the Shroud is Jesus, then Bartholomew today looks just like Jesus did the day he died. Is that right?"

"Yes, that's precisely the point," Morelli said slowly. "The Vatican is concerned that Bartholomew is becoming Jesus. What we don't know is whether this is a psychological process or some other reality we don't understand."

With that, Castle appreciated even more deeply why the pope

had asked for his help. "What you also don't know is whether the Shroud is authentic or a fake. Isn't that also what you are telling me?"

"Yes, it is, but before we get to that point, I want you to look at one more image." Morelli pulled from his briefcase yet another photo of the Shroud of Turin. "This is a close-up photographic negative of the arms of the man in the Shroud. It shows the nail wounds on the wrists and the blood flows on the forearms."

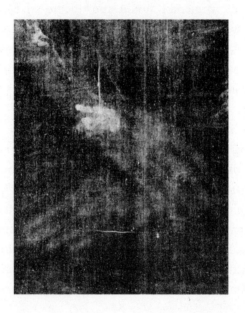

Castle examined the image carefully. Reading the medical file, Castle had observed that Father Bartholomew's wounds were in his wrists, not in the palms of the hands. It was the same with the Shroud. The nail wounds were through the wrists, not the hands, and they looked remarkably like the stigmata wounds Bartholomew had suffered in his wrists. Anatomically, that made sense to Castle. The wounds in the arms could not have gone through the palm of the hand. The nails had to be driven through the wrist. Otherwise, the weight of the body would have ripped the nails loose.

Castle's medical mind envisioned how a nail driven through the junction of bones in the wrist would hold an adult male's weight. "A nail through the palm of the hand above the wrist would tear free over time," he suggested. "The nail would have to be placed just right in the wrist. If the nail hit the major arteries in the hand, the person being crucified might die before they were ever lifted to the cross. Nailing a person to a cross must have been an expert operation that required experienced executioners."

"Right," Morelli confirmed. "The Romans crucified hundreds of thousands of people. They were very good at crucifixion. Crucifixion was designed to be a brutal and humiliating form of death, typically reserved for hardened criminals or traitors foolish enough to foment insurrection against Rome."

"How long was Christ on the cross?" Castle asked.

"Christ hung on the cross for at least three hours," Morelli answered. "He was not dead when the sun was going down. The problem was that Christ was crucified on Friday and he had to be buried before the Jewish Sabbath began, at sundown on Friday. According to Jewish law, Christ's body had to be taken from the cross and buried before the start of the Sabbath, which means the followers of Jesus did not have much time. Before the Roman soldiers allowed his followers to take the body off the cross, they wanted to make sure he was dead. So a Roman centurion took his lance and pierced it through Christ's side, puncturing his heart. Only then did the Roman soldiers give Christ's followers permission to remove his body from the cross."

Looking closely, Castle marveled at how correct anatomically the Shroud image appeared to be. The exit wound on the back of the hand on top—really the left hand in a Shroud image that needed to be reversed right to left like most negatives—looked like an exit wound. It appeared the nail had been driven through where several small carpal bones meet in the wrist, below the metacarpal bones that branch to the fingers, on the thumb side of the hand. The thumbs in both hands appeared to have been pulled back toward the palms of the hands such that they were not visible when the hands were viewed from above. "Driving the nails through the wrists in this area probably damaged the median nerve, with the result that the thumb would have been pulled under the palm in an action not unlike an automatic muscle reflex. So, you're probably also asking me how any artist at the time of Christ—or even during the Middle Ages—would have been sufficiently skilled in medicine as to have captured this anatomically important detail. Is that right?"

"Yes," Morelli answered without hesitation. "How the Shroud of Turin was created is hard to explain. The Shroud provides a remarkably detailed view of the crucifixion of Jesus as described in the Gospels and the practice itself as described in contemporary Roman accounts. Moreover, the Shroud is anatomically correct, even by our current medical standards, in documenting the effects of crucifixion on the human body."

"Where is the Shroud now?" Castle asked.

"The Catholic Church owns the Shroud of Turin," Morelli explained. "It is kept in the Chapel of the Shroud in the Cathedral of St. John the Baptist in Turin, Italy. Typically, the Shroud is kept locked away in a controlled-atmosphere vault that the scientists have designed to maximize preservation of the cloth."

"Does the Catholic Church have an official position on whether the Shroud of Turin is the authentic burial cloth of Christ?" Castle asked.

"The Shroud is one of the Catholic Church's most treasured ancient relics," Morelli answered. "Officially, the Church maintains the Shroud is a venerated object, but there is no Church declaration or judgment that the Shroud is authentic. Officially, the Church's position is that no relic or object is needed to justify faith in Jesus Christ. Still, many Catholics and non-Catholics believe the Shroud of Turin is the actual burial cloth of Jesus Christ."

Before he became an atheist, Castle had been raised an Episcopalian and he was not brought up to put much trust in relics. "I seem to remember reading that there was carbon dating done on the Shroud and that the scientists doing the testing determined that the Shroud came from the medieval period, that it simply did not trace back two thousand years to Jesus."

"Yes," Morelli acknowledged. "That's right, but several more recent studies have challenged the carbon-dating procedures. Whether the Shroud is the burial cloth of Christ is still very much being debated, even within the Church. Archbishop Duncan is arranging for you to meet Father Middagh, one of the Church's most knowledgeable experts on the Shroud in the world. Let's save the question of the carbon dating until we meet with Father Middagh. For now, please just take it that the experts you will meet consider the carbon-testing results showing the Shroud to be a medieval fake are now in question. My job here today is to give you enough information about Father Bartholomew to get you to agree to take the case."

"What is it that the Vatican wants me to conclude?" Castle asked, seriously wanting to get to the point. "Is the Vatican trying to prove that Father Bartholomew is a fake or that he has become Jesus? Is the question whether or not Jesus is somehow taking over the body of Father Bartholomew? You've got to level with me, Father Morelli. What does the Vatican believe has happened as a result of Bartholomew's near-death experience? Does the Vatican believe that Father Bartholomew has become more than a healer, that he has somehow become the crucified Jesus Christ once again reincarnated?"

"Truthfully, the Vatican does not know what is happening with Father Bartholomew," Morelli said honestly. "The pope asked me the same questions you just posed. I have no answers and neither does the pope. That's why I am here."

"Okay, then, let me try to explain to you how I proceed as a psychiatrist," Castle said slowly, wanting to make sure there were no misunderstandings. "You have to understand that the human subconscious is very strong, strong enough to cause many people to modify their physical appearance based on this or that neurosis. My suspicion from looking at these photos and listening to your story is that Bartholomew has a mental condition that looks maybe like a neurosis, or maybe even a more serious psychosis."

"I understand," Morelli said.

"What interests me is that Father Bartholomew's mental illness involves his religious beliefs. Father Bartholomew's case is precisely what I write about in my books. What I suspect is that Bartholomew is undergoing what is commonly known as a multiple personality disorder. His mental illness may cause Bartholomew to imitate Christ—even physically—but I cannot believe this man is somehow mystically becoming Jesus Christ, in real life, today, in New York City. If that's what the Catholic Church wants me to conclude, I'm not your guy."

"The Catholic Church has centuries of experience of dealing with clergy, and in those hundreds of years some of the clergy have had psychological problems, just like any other group of people over hundreds of years of experience," Morelli said. "The Catholic Church also has centuries of dealing with mystics and through those centuries many mystics have demonstrated the stigmata."

"What's your point?" Castle asked directly.

"My point is that sometimes psychology does not explain all of religious experience," Morelli answered equally directly.

"That leads me to conclude that you believe the Shroud is indeed the actual burial cloth of the historical Jesus," Castle said, wanting to make sure he understood Morelli.

"Yes, I do," Morelli admitted. "I struggled with the evidence for years, but finally I concluded I could not explain by any scientific methods how the Shroud of Turin had been created, regardless of how brilliant the forger might have been."

"And you also believe Father Bartholomew died and returned to life, much as Jesus Christ himself did," Castle said, pressing on.

"I'm not as sure of that," Morelli admitted. "I didn't get to be an advisor to the pope, especially not this pope, by giving him easy answers. My training is to question everything. The Vatican and I believe we need your expertise to get to the bottom of what is really going on with Father Bartholomew."

Castle was beginning to feel more comfortable about the assignment, but there was still something he had to be clear about.

"One more thing," he stressed. "I can't promise you I can cure Father Bartholomew of whatever is going on. Father Bartholomew could spend years with me in therapy and I still can't promise you I could cure him. Years from now, he might be much worse than he is today."

"I understand."

"Okay, then," Dr. Castle said, having made up his mind. "I will take the case, but it will cost the Catholic Church a lot of money for me to do so."

"The Vatican is prepared to pay your fees."

"And I reserve the right to publish a book on my findings, with or without the approval of the Catholic Church."

"The pope is prepared to agree to that as well."

"One more thing."

"What's that?"

"I want to speak with the pope myself. I spoke to him when he was Cardinal Vicente and I want to talk with him again before I take on this assignment."

"The pope wants to talk with you, too, but he wants to talk with you after you meet with Father Bartholomew."

"Okay." Castle agreed. "I will do that. But I have one last concern."

"What's that?"

"You are sure the pope doesn't want to have it both ways?" Castle asked cynically.

"What do you mean?"

"If I conclude Bartholomew has a mental illness, the Vatican could always just say, 'Castle is not a Catholic and he doesn't believe in God. What did you expect him to find?'"

"In the final analysis," Morelli said seriously, "you're the doctor and the public will believe you, regardless of what the archbishop, the pope, or me—the used-to-be devil's advocate, as you put it—has to say."

"Okay, then. I will agree to see Father Bartholomew as a patient."

"Thank you," Morelli said in conclusion, reaching out to shake Dr. Castle's hand. "I look forward to working with you."

CHAPTER FIVE

Morelli brought Father Bartholomew to Dr. Castle's office in a wheelchair. The priest was dressed in a full-length hospital robe, not his black priest's suit and black shirt with its Roman collar.

Scrutinizing Bartholomew carefully, Castle realized how deceptive were the wheelchair, the hospital robe, and the heavy bandages on the priest's arms. Far from being weak, Bartholomew had an athletic build.

Judging the priest to be less than six feet tall, Castle could see that Bartholomew, a mature man in his early forties, was still very strong, fully muscled in the upper body and shoulders. Though he was sitting in the wheelchair, the hospital robe appeared to cover well-exercised legs. If Bartholomew had ever played football, Castle was sure he had been a guard or a tackle, not the quarterback. Castle guessed the priest was no stranger to the gymnasium and he wondered if the priest had a history of weight lifting. Castle immediately suspected Bartholomew's physical strength and stamina had been critical to his ability to survive the violent car accident that had nearly killed him, as well as the stigmata that were afflicting him now.

After Morelli excused himself to the waiting room, Castle settled into his chair. "I assume you know why you are here, Father Bartholomew," Castle said.

"Archbishop Duncan asked me to see you," he replied, "and you can call me by my first name, Paul, since I assume we are going to get to know one another pretty well."

"Very well, Paul," Castle began, taking Bartholomew's file from the coffee table and paging through his notes. "You can call me Dr. Castle."

Castle was not interested in his patients becoming his friends. Besides, he knew from decades of experience that the process psychiatrists call "transference" would begin almost immediately. Once transference began, most patients would begin imagining the psychiatrist understood their inner thoughts and feelings, believing the psychiatrist was the only person in the world who could truly understand them and help them.

Both Bartholomew's forearms were heavily bandaged. Long white gloves with the fingers cut out had been drawn over his hands to help mask the sight of the bandages that reached from the fingers of both hands up the forearms to his elbows.

In person, the impression that Bartholomew looked remarkably like images of Jesus Christ was unavoidable. Bartholomew's long brown hair and thick reddish beard framed a long, thin face with prominent cheekbones. The beard ended with a double-pointed fork at the chin, just as Father Morelli pointed out with the man in the Shroud. Bartholomew's mouth was well defined by a neatly trimmed mustache. His hair was twisted in a braid that trailed down his back to beyond his waist. Bartholomew's soft brown eyes looked out from beneath bushy eyebrows that also appeared to need a serious trimming. In the two thousand years since the death of Christ, the image of Jesus had become an icon. Now something resembling that icon was sitting across from Castle as a patient in his treatment room.

Bartholomew may have felt this change in his appearance had come upon him as a result of his mystical experience on the operating table. But Castle knew better.

From decades of clinical practice, Castle knew without doubt that the priest's exterior impression reflected his inner psychological realities. Castle speculated that Bartholomew, now in the grips of his mental illness, was becoming his mental image of what Christ had looked like in life. As an accomplished psychiatrist, Dr. Castle did not believe he was looking at the physical manifestation of the historical Jesus Christ in modern-day New York. He was simply looking at Father Paul Bartholomew's idea of what he imagined Jesus Christ looked like, perhaps heavily influenced by the Shroud. Castle made a note on Bartholomew's file to remind him to find out when Bartholomew had first seen the Shroud and to inquire about what impact the Shroud had had on the priest.

"So do you think you can cure me, Dr. Castle?" Bartholomew asked.

"Do you want to be cured?" Castle asked.

"I'm not sure there's anything wrong with me."

"Look at you, Paul. Do you think there's anything about you that's normal?"

"Let me return the favor," Bartholomew said wryly. "So you don't think that your trimmed beard and nicely tailored clothes make you look like Sigmund Freud? All you need is the cigar."

"Touché," Castle laughed, appreciating the priest's intelligence and his wit. "So that's how you see it? Christ meets Sigmund Freud."

Bartholomew enjoyed the joke as well. "So, tell me, Dr. Freud, are you sure you don't want me to help cure you of this delusion? You must have heard by now that I have exceptional healing powers—maybe not as great as yours, but I'm told they're pretty considerable, just the same. If you let me take you into my own form of analysis, I am sure I could convince you not only that Sigmund Freud died a long time ago but also that there is a God who is very much alive."

Castle appreciated that Bartholomew was highly intelligent, smart enough to be a particle physicist invited to join the faculty of the Institute for Advanced Study in Princeton at a young age. Einstein had ended his career at the institute and Bartholomew in his years as a physicist had aspired to solve the problems of a unified field theory that Einstein himself had failed to solve.

"But I've got to ask you a question," Castle said, wanting to get serious.

"I'm here to answer your questions," Bartholomew acknowledged. "Ask away."

"Why don't you cut your hair and trim the beard? Maybe if you looked a little less like Jesus Christ, you wouldn't be seeing a psychiatrist."

"That's possible," Bartholomew answered honestly, "but even if I could return to having short hair and being clean-shaven, I still have the stigmata."

"Are you telling me there is nothing you can do about your hair?"

"Every time I cut my hair and shave the beard, within a day or two the long hair and beard are back. I've tried cutting my hair and trimming my beard three or four times a day, so they don't get a running start. But even that doesn't seem to work. If you want to prove it for yourself, we can head to the barber shop right now."

"That won't be necessary," Castle said, taking off his reading glasses so he could look Bartholomew directly in the eye. "I'm sure you know I'm an atheist."

"Yes, I do."

"I'm not even certain that Jesus Christ ever really existed. The events happened two thousand years ago. That's a long time ago. You're familiar with the Dead Sea scrolls, I assume."

"Of course."

"Then it's quite possible the whole story of Jesus Christ had been made up, out of a misunderstanding about the Essenes, the splinter religious sect that wrote the Dead Sea scrolls, or—who knows?—maybe by some other splinter Jewish religious sect wandering around in the desert of ancient Israel. Who knows if Christianity was invented simply to meet psychological needs these dissident religious groups faced in coping with their occupying captors from Imperial Rome. Besides, the Romans crucified countless thousands of people all over the ancient world. What was so significant about this one particular Jew? If there was a historical Christ and the ancient Romans did crucify him, I'm quite sure it was just another day's hard work for the centurions in Jerusalem unlucky enough not to be home in Rome. Instead they got the thankless job of nailing yet another unlucky Jew to boards and watching him die."

"There's one problem with your theory, Dr. Castle, as good and as interesting as I have to admit it is."

"What's that?"

"I died after that accident and I saw with my own eyes Jesus crucified. I stood there with my mother at Golgotha and I watched Jesus die."

"And I'm told you see Jesus in the confessional and that he tells you how to heal people. Is that correct, or did I get the wrong information."

"You have the right information," the priest said without showing emotion.

Then a thought occurred to Castle. "Do you see Jesus now?"

"Yes."

"Where is he, then?"

"He's with us right now, sitting right over there on your couch."

"I don't see him. How come you can see Jesus when I can't?"

"I can't answer that question," Bartholomew said. "But there's something I need to say to you."

Castle sat back in his chair. "What's that? Is it a message from Jesus?"

"I will let you decide that for yourself," Bartholomew said. "The only thing I want you to know is that you were not responsible for the death of your wife."

This took Castle by surprise. He rarely talked about his wife. He had loved Elizabeth since they were teenage sweethearts in high school. They married just as he entered medical school and she worked in an office as a legal secretary to support his medical education. He was in the operating room, in the middle of a very complicated heart surgery, when Elizabeth died. He learned after the operation that she had a brain aneurism that nobody realized she had.

Castle never forgave himself. If only he had listened when Elizabeth complained of headaches. He should have insisted Elizabeth get more thorough diagnostic checkups. If he had been more loving and attentive, the aneurism that killed his wife might have been discovered in time and her life could have been saved. He never would have gotten through medical school without her. Castle, for all his brilliance as a heart surgeon and psychiatrist, never got over the guilt that there was nothing he did to save his young wife's life.

Still, Castle was not impressed. "You're good, Paul. I will have to admit that. But it is no secret my wife died early in my career. You're an intelligent man and you could easily have surmised I felt guilty. It may surprise you but a lot of my patients are very intuitive. Sometimes I think the more psychologically disturbed my patients are, the more intuitive they become. You're not the first patient to try to intimidate me or throw me off the track by trying to turn the tables with imagined insights you think you have gleaned from my past."

"You never remarried." Bartholomew persisted, ignoring what Castle had said. "Was that because you still feel guilty? Or, do you worry you would kill another woman by marrying her and neglecting her, too, just as you did with Elizabeth?"

"We're not here to psychoanalyze me," Castle said firmly. "And I'm not impressed with your little guessing game, or with you calling me Dr. Freud. I don't believe for a minute that Jesus is here in this room with you, or that you have any secret friend who squirrels away insights to you about people's lives. A lot of people have imaginary friends as children. It's time, Paul, for you to grow up."

Bartholomew listened silently, not seeing any point in responding. He felt he had nothing to prove to Dr. Castle.

"So far all you are accomplishing is to confirm my suspicion you have a form of multiple personality disorder," Castle continued. "That Jesus you imagine you see sitting on my couches is nothing more than your manifestation of your subconscious."

"That's where there's a big difference between you and me, Dr. Castle."

"What's that?"

"Simple. Jesus showed me your soul and you obviously seem to hate God as much as you seem to hate religion."

"I don't hate anybody," Castle objected. "You're projecting onto me what you want to believe about me. That's all."

"No, it's not all," Bartholomew said very slowly and very seriously. "Believing in God is an experience, not a matter of logical proof. If the existence of God could have been proved by logic or by argumentation, the issue would have been settled by Aristotle or maybe St. Thomas Aquinas at the very latest."

"I concede the point," Castle argued. "But so what? That the existence of God cannot be deduced from logic is hardly a news flash."

"I understand," Bartholomew said, returning Dr. Castle's direct stare. "But if you'll permit me to predict something: before you are done with me, you will end up believing in God."

"I doubt it," Castle answered skeptically. "You are the one here with the Jesus haircut and the stigmata, not me. This is my office you are sitting in and we're on Fifth Avenue in the heart of New York City, not Jerusalem two thousand years ago at the time of Christ's crucifixion and death. I'm not looking for a religious conversion and we are simply getting off track here."

"There's one more thing Jesus wants you to know." Bartholomew pushed on, undeterred.

"What's that," Castle responded cautiously. "I can hardly wait to hear what secret Jesus has revealed about me now."

"Jesus understands that you blamed yourself when your wife died. He also understands that you changed careers because you felt you might have caught her illness if you had been more attentive to her needs, to her mental state."

"That's actually not why I decided to become a psychiatrist," Castle said firmly, rejecting Bartholomew's suggestion that he changed careers out of guilt. "And again, you're veering us off course."

"Maybe so, but you have to forgive yourself."

"What's your point?" Castle shot back.

"My point is that you will remain dead inside until you open your heart to God, and you won't find what you are looking for with your success as a psychiatrist or with the millions of dollars you have earned from medicine."

"Paul, I hope you won't take offense, but that's what other religious people have told me before. You may think your comments are filled with great insight, but frankly I find them sophomoric. A college student taking Psychology 101 would have to do better to get an A. Quite frankly, you don't know what you are talking about."

"Maybe not," Bartholomew said, "but I doubt if anyone has ever told you that you have to take the first step toward your own mental health by forgiving yourself for your wife's death. God decides when each of us lives and when each of us dies. You may think you are more brilliant than anybody else you have ever met, including me, Dr. Castle, but you are not God."

"That may be," Castle responded calmly. "But since I'm the doctor here and you are the patient, you're going to have to let me do the question asking; otherwise I won't be able to work with you as a patient. Right now you are merely wasting time."

"As smart as you are, Dr. Castle, you are not as clever as God," Bartholomew said, folding his hands in his lap and sitting securely back in his wheelchair. "That is all I had to say."

"Good, I'm glad we're finished with that," Castle said, determined to get back control of the interview. "Again, if we are going to make any progress here, you are going to have to let me do the question asking. I am the doctor here and you are the patient. Do you understand that?"

"Yes, I do," Bartholomew said without argument.

"Okay, then," Castle said, ready to start over again. "I'm going to accept for a minute that you died after your car accident, just exactly as you have said. Can you explain to me why exactly you returned back to life?"

"God asked me to return to life," Bartholomew explained. "I was with my mother in Heaven and God said he had a mission for me to accomplish."

"What was that mission?" Castle asked.

"First, let me ask you this." Bartholomew wanted to make sure he had the right information. "Father Morelli said he discussed with you the Shroud of Turin. Is that right?"

"Yes," Castle affirmed.

"All right, then," Bartholomew continued. "What I am going to tell you is the truth, whether you can accept it or not. God asked me to return to earth to interpret to the world the Shroud codex."

"But a codex is a book, an ancient manuscript," Castle objected. "An image of a crucified man on a burial cloth is not a book. When you say the Shroud is a codex, what do you mean?"

"Learning to read the Shroud is like learning to read an ancient manuscript written in a language you can no longer decipher." Bartholomew tried to explain as clearly as he could. "You may think I have stopped being a physicist. But that isn't the case. I've never stopped being a physicist. Deciphering the meaning of the Shroud is like solving the most challenging equation physics has yet to solve. I will decipher the Shroud codex for the world, and when I understand the message of the Shroud and when I communicate that message to the world, the world will understand. When I had the experience of dying, after the car accident, God assured me that I would be able to communicate the message Jesus embedded in the Shroud. When I finally break through, you will be there to experience it firsthand. I'm confident you are the psychiatrist God meant me to see. Otherwise we would not be here together this day."

Castle's first reaction was that everything Bartholomew had just explained was delusional. "Is this why you are manifesting Jesus, with the long hair and the beard, and now with the stigmata?"

"Yes," Bartholomew answered. "I am manifesting Jesus. It started with my physical appearance and now I am beginning to manifest the wounds Jesus experienced in his passion and death."

Castle decided to get to his core question right away. "Are you Jesus Christ? Is that what you want me to believe?"

"No," Bartholomew said emphatically. "I am not Jesus Christ. I am manifesting Jesus Christ."

"Are you manifesting Jesus Christ, or your idea of Jesus Christ?" Castle asked sharply. "This is an important distinction. How do you know what Jesus Christ looked like? He's been dead two thousand years and there's no photographs."

Bartholomew sat back in his chair and took a deep breath. He began slowly. "I know you don't believe me, but when I was dead I traveled to Golgotha and I saw Jesus on the cross dying. I was there with my mother. I know I look like Jesus because I saw Jesus with my own eyes. Whether you believe it or not, the Shroud of Turin is the actual burial cloth of Jesus Christ. God told me that was true and I saw with my own eyes that the physical Jesus who lived and died two thousand years ago is the crucified man you see today in the Shroud of Turin."

Hearing this, Castle no longer had any doubt that Bartholomew believed his delusion was reality. Still, he knew Bartholomew was highly intelligent and he wondered how the priest would react to Castle's hypothesis that his subconscious was manifesting the physical characteristics of the man in the Shroud because Bartholomew wanted to believe that man was Jesus. "When was the first time you saw the Shroud of Turin?" he asked.

"I was in high school. We had a weekend retreat and one of the priests showed us photographs of the Shroud of Turin as one of our meditations."

"What impact did the Shroud of Turin make on you?"

"Profound. I had never heard about the Shroud before and I was overwhelmed to learn how precisely the image of the man in the Shroud matched the passion and death of Jesus."

"Did you study the Shroud after that?"

"Yes, I have never stopped studying the Shroud."

That confirmed for Castle that Bartholomew had internalized the image of the man on the Shroud, such that his subconscious was capable of projecting that image back in the manifestations Castle was currently seeing. "Maybe studying the Shroud has made such an impact on you that your imagination has taken over. Surely you must realize that all of us project onto reality what we want to believe is true."

Bartholomew thought for a minute, formulating his answer. "I know you think I am mentally ill," Bartholomew said. "But you have to accept that I really did experience dying. I'm not trying to make myself look like Jesus. All this is just happening, exactly like God told me it would."

Castle made some additional notes in Bartholomew's file.

"Are your wrist wounds painful?" he asked.

"Not all the time."

"How about now?"

"No, they are not painful now."

"Are they bleeding now?"

"Not that I know."

"You went unconscious at the altar when the wounds on your wrists appeared. Tell me what happened."

"Again, you won't believe me if I tell you."

"Tell me anyway."

"When the stigmata hit me, while I was saying Mass, it felt like I had traveled back in time again. I was right back at Golgotha on the day of Christ's crucifixion, just like I experienced when I died and went to Heaven. Only this time, I was the person being nailed to the cross. Somehow I had taken the place of Christ and I was feeling his pain. The nails were being driven through my wrists. The pain was excruciating. I blacked out because I couldn't bear the pain. When I woke up, I was in the hospital. I have no idea how I got to Golgotha and I have no idea how I got back here."

"You were a successful physicist," Castle said. "Don't you consider time travel far-fetched?"

"No, I don't," Bartholomew said, responding firmly. "You may not know much about modern physics, but I was a particle physicist. I was looking for what Einstein called the unified field theory. Multiple dimensions and time travel were part of what I studied."

"Do you think time travel is possible?" Castle asked skeptically.

"It's a lot more than what Jules Verne imagined," Bartholomew answered. "I doubt if you want me to give you a graduate course in particle physics, but a lot of physicists, including me, think there are multiple dimensions, maybe as many as ten dimensions, that define our universe, not just length, height, width, and time."

"What made you change careers and decide to become a priest?" Castle asked.

"It was my mother's death. My mother raised me and I was devoted to her. She is maybe the only person in my life that I truly loved. After her death, I felt I needed to get closer to God. Suddenly, physics seemed to me to be going nowhere. Searching for a unified field theory only took me away from my mother while she was alive and the knowledge I gained there was no help to me whatsoever in healing her illness. She slipped away from me before I was ready to let her go."

"How did your mother die?"

"She had ALS. I did everything I could to save her, but day by day her condition deteriorated. At the end, she lost all control of her muscles. She couldn't even speak. I was with her, but I never really got to say good-bye to her."

"How did you feel when she died?"

"At first I was angry," he recalled. "Then I felt lost. I was aimless. Nothing seemed to matter."

"Did you blame God when she died?"

"No, I blamed myself. Maybe if I had been a better son, I would have seen her illness coming on earlier, when there might have been something we could have done to prolong her life."

"That's exactly what you said Jesus told you about me and my wife," Castle said. *Interesting,* he thought to himself. "Now tell me why you decided to become a priest."

"I remembered my mother had always told me she believed I had a vocation and that I would have been happier had I become a priest."

"Did you agree?"

"Not when she was alive, but after she died, it all made sense to me. I was searching for God in physics and getting nowhere. I decided to search for God in the priesthood and ever since I made that decision, my life seems to have suddenly gained purpose."

"What about your father?"

"He died three months before I was born. In a work-related accident, I believe. I know almost nothing about my father, not even what he looked like. My mother was always reluctant to speak about him, even when I asked, and there were no photographs of him that I ever saw."

"How about other family? Do you have any brothers or sisters that I should know about?"

"No, I was an only child."

"Your file says you saw your mother with God, in the experience you had after your accident. Is that correct?"

Bartholomew noted carefully how Castle framed the question.

"You are being very careful to avoid asking about my experience of dying after my car accident in any way that would give credence to it. But I did see her in the afterlife," the priest insisted. "The car accident happened a few hours after I visited her grave in Morristown. I'm sure that part of the story is in my file, too. But I doubt you are ready to accept anything I could tell you about what happened to me on the operating table as if it were real."

"Pretty much, you're right," Castle said. "A lot of study has been done on near-death experiences. You describe feeling yourself drawn into a tunnel and experiencing a white light—that's a lot of what we know about how the brain dies. As far as I'm concerned, what you went through might be explained physiologically, without any reference to God whatsoever. Unfortunately, when it comes to proving something about the afterlife, we don't have a lot of people to interview who are still dead."

"How about me having a mental illness?" Bartholomew asked. "Have you come to any conclusions there?"

"That's it for today," he announced, looking at his watch. "The hour is up and it's time for you to return to the hospital."

"That's all?" Bartholomew asked, surprised. "We were only getting started."

"We will take it up again next week," Castle said firmly, closing Bartholomew's file and standing up. "We're done for now."

As Castle got up and ushered Morelli back into the room, he had some instructions.

"Father Bartholomew, I will be sending over papers to your hospital room later today so Father Morelli can have you transferred to Beth Israel Hospital. I am on staff there and I need to become your physician."

"How much longer will I be in the hospital?"

"That depends. First, I want to run a series of tests on you. Then we will decide. I want to examine your wrist wounds with a

CT scan and an MRI. Then I need to see if we can do anything to control your hair growth."

"I want to get back to my parish as soon as possible."

"I understand that," Castle said. "But you are my patient now and your health is my primary concern, both physically and mentally. I won't keep you in the hospital any longer than necessary, but I'm your doctor now and you are going to have to follow my instructions."

"Whether I like them or not?" Bartholomew asked.

"Yes," Castle answered firmly. "Whether you like them or not."

CHAPTER SIX

Same day
Dr. Stephen Castle's office, New York City
1:00 P.M. ET in New York City, 7:00 P.M. in Rome

That afternoon, Castle telephoned Marco Gabrielli in Italy. Gabrielli was a professor of chemistry at the University of Bologna who had developed an international reputation for debunking various paranormal "miracles" that various frauds and con men had perpetrated over decades on a gullible religious public eager and willing to have concrete physical demonstrations that their beliefs in God were justified. Castle managed to meet Gabrielli on his first trip to Italy years ago, at a conference held in Rome by CISAP, an organization whose name roughly translates as the Italian Committee for Scientific Examination of Paranormal Phenomena. Castle was drawn to the CISAP meeting because the group applied the scientific method to a wide range of phenomena presumed to be explainable as paranormal, including ghosts, magic, astrology, psychic and spiritual healing, and UFOs. Gabrielli was one of CISAP's most famous members. In their brief conversation at the meeting, Gabrielli let Castle know that he could help the psychiatrist with patients who claimed or exhibited supposedly paranormal phenomena related to religion.

Castle had worked with Gabrielli several times before. One patient, in particular, believed that the Jesus in the crucifix on his wall was crying blood. Gabrielli proved the patient had concocted an elaborate fake in which the Jesus on the crucifix turned out to be a statue with a hollow space in the head that was filled with a porous powder. The patient had glazed the statue with an impermeable liquid that was transparent to light. He then took a syringe with a long needle and inserted a syrupy red fluid into the statue through a tiny hole in its head. The porous material absorbed the red liquid, but the impermeable coating prevented the liquid from oozing out.

The crying Jesus was created when the patient scratched imperceptibly around the eyes, just enough to allow drops of the red liquid to start leaking out, appearing as if they were tears. The cavity in the head was small, so once the liquid oozed out, there typically weren't any traces left in the statue. When the patient wanted the Jesus statue to start crying once again, all he had to do was to take the syringe and refill the cavity in the head. The patient was making a good living with the fraud, until he got careless. A would-be believer got upset when he noticed drops of the red liquid forming on the top of Christ's head. When he pointed it out, the religious fraud threatened the would-be believer to keep quiet and, when the skeptic refused, the religious fraud beat him unmercifully. The case was referred to Castle when criminal charges were pressed and the lawyer defending the religious fraud decided to pursue an insanity defense. Castle was hired by the court to determine if the religious fraud was psychologicaly disturbed or not. Gabrielli provided the proof that the cleverness of how the blood-crying Jesus had been crafted proved the religious fraud was quite sane and very money-motivated.

Gabrielli was a man in his late forties, with a European build he kept thin from vigorous walking and a modest diet. He sported a Van Dyke beard and mustache. With his disheveled black hair, he looked like either an inspired artist whose mind was always somewhere else, or a mad scientist, which was probably the more apt conclusion. Gabrielli favored turtleneck sweaters and tweed sport jackets; he could have stepped out of a university lecture hall. In his many videos, which peppered Italian websites and were increasingly gravitating, in English translation, to YouTube, Gabrielli could be seen in his laboratory, wearing a white lab coat and working over one of the various apparatuses that he used to reproduce scientifically the "supernatural" phenomenon that had captured the public imagination. But what gained Gabrielli his large following was his sarcastic wit. His wry smile and green eyes darting beneath his bushy eyebrows gave many the impression that Gabrielli was a little boy who had discovered all by himself that there never was any Wizard of Oz behind the curtain.

Over the telephone, Castle described Father Bartholomew's case.

"Did you examine the stigmata?" Gabrielli asked.

"No, his arms were bandaged and I typically don't perform medical examinations in my psychiatric office," Castle explained. "I am a physician on staff at Beth Israel Hospital here in New York City and I'm in the process of transferring Father Bartholomew to my care. I plan to examine his stigmata once I get him admitted as my patient."

"Have you seen his medical charts?"

"Yes. The attending physician noted that the wounds did appear to have pierced through the wrists. Still, until I examine the wounds myself, I won't be able to tell for sure. The attending physician did not have a CT scan or MRI performed. Until I order those tests and examine Father Bartholomew myself, I won't know if the stigmata wounds penetrate his wrists or if the wounds always were just superficial."

"I'm sure you know that in Padre Pio's case there were no wounds at all. His stigmata were completely faked."

"What do you mean?" Castle asked, surprised to hear this.

"Padre Pio died on September 23, 1968, and he was buried four days later at the San Giovani Rotondo shrine in Pietrelcina, the little town where he lived most of his life as a priest," Gabrielli said. "In April 2008, on the fortieth anniversary of his death, his body was exhumed. The Church kept Padre Pio's body on display for well over a year. Thousands of people made the trip, some from the United States, to Pietrelcina to see Padre Pio's body on display."

"Sounds bizarre," Castle said.

"In a way it is. But the faithful believe that because Padre Pio's body had not deteriorated in death, it was a sign from God that his life was holy and he is now a saint. Otherwise they think the body would not have been preserved like this, in an incorrupt state, some forty years after he died."

"Do you believe that?"

"Not for a minute," Gabrielli answered without hesitation. "But that's not the important part of the story. When the body was first exhumed, Bishop Domenico d'Ambrosio examined the body. I know Bishop d'Ambrosio quite well. He told me Padre Pio's body was well preserved; that part is true. From the very beginning of the exhumation, you could clearly see his beard and he was still wearing the mittens that covered the stigmata on his wrists. There were parts of his body that had decayed. You could see the skull and part of the cheekbone was exposed. The public never saw his whole body, just his body in his brown Capuchin habit with an elaborate silk stole embroidered with crystals and gold. His face was covered with a silicone mask that was very lifelike. But the hands were so well preserved that d'Ambrosio said Padre Pio's fingernails were intact. The point is that d'Ambrosio examined Padre Pio's hands and feet and swore there were no signs of the stigmata. Legend has it that Padre Pio's stigmata disappeared at the moment of his death. That was the testimony of his fellow friars and the doctor who attended to him at his death."

"That's convenient, isn't it," Castle said sarcastically. "The moment he dies, the stigmata just disappear."

"But there's more," Gabrielli went on. "A historian digging through the Vatican archives found a letter from a pharmacist who claimed he visited Padre Pio in 1919 and Padre Pio gave him an empty bottle that he asked him to fill with carbolic acid. The pharmacist said Padre Pio claimed he needed the carbolic acid to disinfect syringes for injections. Padre Pio also used other common medications of the time, like Valda tablets, which were a mild, plant-based antiseptic that people used to take for throat or bronchial ailments."

"What's the significance of the carbolic acid?"

"I've got a video right now on the Internet that shows how you can create stigmata with commonly available chemicals. You apply iron chloride on one hand and let it dry and put potassium ferrocyanide on the other hand and let it dry. Then when you rub your two palms together the chemicals combine to produce what looks like stigmata wounds. The chemical action is painless and disappears quickly, once you wash your hands. On the same video I show how you can customize a razor to scrape the palms of your hands to produce bleeding sores that look exactly like stigmata. Carbolic acid is a mild disinfectant that will keep open wounds from getting disinfected. Going back to 1918, visitors to Padre Pio claimed his wounds had a smell of carbolic acid and that he covered up the smell with eau de cologne, claiming his blood had a miraculous fragrance."

"So you are convinced Padre Pio was a fraud?" Castle asked.

"Yes, there is no doubt in my mind whatsoever," the chemist answered.

"Padre Pio would never let any physician examine his wounds to see if they penetrated clear through his wrists. He always claimed the pain was too severe when doctors tried to see whether or not their fingers would meet through the stigmata wounds on his wrists, and no physician ever managed to convince him to go under anesthetic to be examined in a hospital setting. Padre Pio always wore those mittens over his hands, so that the stigmata were largely covered up. Padre Pio was serious about hiding his wounds. All you could ever see were photographs that showed bleeding palms from a distance, or what appeared to be scabs of crusted blood at the edges of the mittens, supposedly resulting from blood flowing from the wounds. But who knew? As far as I am concerned, Padre Pio's stigmata were never subjected to rigorous medical examination when he was alive."

"Why hasn't this come out?"

"It has come out. There are even persistent rumors in Italy that Pope John XXIII was confronted with evidence by a Vatican investigator who examined Padre Pio's secret files in the process of declaring him to be a saint. There is evidently a journal entry John XXIII wrote in his diary lamenting the evidence that Padre Pio committed sexual indiscretions with women who were part of his inner circle. There were even accusations that he had sex with women in the confessional, or that he invited them to visit him privately in his cell, where they stayed the night. Other accusations were that he took money in the confessional, enriching himself. Padre Pio finally admitted that this was true, but he claimed he gave the money to poor penitents."

"Did this come out during his lifetime?"

"Yes. In 1922, the Vatican forbade Padre Pio from hearing the confessions of women, then the next year the Vatican forbade him from teaching teenage boys. He was famous for claiming the devil came to him every night with every sort of sexual fantasy to tempt him to what he called 'uncleanness.' The Holy See eventually became convinced Padre Pio used his fame to sexually pervert boys, that he was a pedophile, just like the priests you had to deal with in the New York archdiocese."

"Why didn't this prevent Padre Pio from being declared a saint?"

"Padre Pio was loved, especially in southern Italy. Even today, more Italian Catholics pray to Padre Pio than to any other saint. He is venerated as a celebrity in Italy and he is constantly covered in the Italian equivalents of *People* magazine, even though he has been dead for over forty years."

"It's remarkable, isn't it?" Castle said.

"Believers say Padre Pio had the gift of bilocation, the ability to be in two places at once, proof to many that he had supernatural powers God would only have granted him if his faith in Christ was genuine and his stigmata real. Others claimed that he could heal the sick. It goes on and on. Padre Pio's Masses were very unpredictable. He seemed to go into trances at the altar and he claimed he had visions with Jesus, or with the Virgin Mary, the mother of Jesus, where he could speak with them and they would advise him or tell him intimate secrets."

"Sounds very much like what Father Bartholomew told me," Castle said. "That he could see and speak with Jesus, even that Jesus was present with him in my treatment room."

"Mass with Padre Pio got so bizarre that parishioners just sat in the church, sometimes for hours, and waited for him to come back to reality so he could finish the Mass. Others say he could prophesize the future, that he told a young Karol Wojtyla, visiting from Poland, that he would be elected pope one day, even though

Padre Pio said he would never live to see that day. It's part of the lore. A lot like Nostradamus. Those who believe Nostradamus predicted the future claim he met a young monk one day, Felice Paretti, when the young man stopped to take a drink from a fountain in the street. Nostradamus evidently saw him in the street for the first time and immediately predicted he would be pope. Paretti did become Pope Sixtus V, but this supposed meeting-in-the-street prediction came to light only decades later, long after Nostradamus was dead and Paretti's papacy was an historical fact."

"So do you think you could explain Father Bartholomew's stigmata by a similar fraud? Do you think his stigmata are not real?"

"I don't know," Gabrielli said honestly. "You're the doctor. I will leave the medical examination up to you. I'm a chemist. All I could do is examine Father Bartholomew's claimed stigmata to see if I could figure out a natural way chemicals could have been used to produce the wounds."

The discussion with Gabrielli was opening Castle's mind. Up to now, the psychiatrist had assumed that Father Bartholomew's wounds might be real, even if they were produced by the action of his subconscious. Gabrielli was suggesting that historically important religious figures—like Padre Pio—who had manifested supernatural phenomena might have been brilliant frauds who had actually concocted their miracle manifestations with sophisticated chemical legerdemain, such that their trickery could not be easily detected. Gabrielli had proved it was possible to create stigmata by clever application of chemicals, then carefully obscure the wounds so no one got too close a look, especially not medical doctors.

Gabrielli was also very careful in how he attacked Padre Pio. What he said was "this is how it could have been done," a discreet way of raising doubt that the only explanation for Padre Pio's stigmata had to be supernatural. While he had not proved Padre Pio was a fraud, Gabrielli had managed to suggest the possibility very convincingly.

Castle next explained to Gabrielli about how Father Bartholomew was manifesting the Shroud of Turin.

"That's another fake," Gabrielli answered instantly. "I've been working on it for years."

"How do you know it is fake?"

"In 1988, the Vatican allowed three laboratories to do carbon dating on the Shroud. All three labs were highly reputable—at Oxford University, the University of Arizona, and the Swiss Federal Institute of Technology in Zurich. The Church gave each of the researchers a sample of the Shroud and their results were all the same. The Shroud dates from 1260 to 1390. It's a medieval fake produced in the thirteenth or fourteenth century when Europe was full of Christians eager to venerate any relic of Christ's crucifixion."

Investigating the carbon-dating tests conducted on the Shroud was on Castle's to-do list, but he still did not know the details.

"Would you like to see some nails from the True Cross? There are golden reliquaries in the Cathedral of Notre Dame in Paris that even today hold what many Christians venerate as the actual nails used to crucify Jesus. If you could have taken all the pieces of wood that were claimed in medieval times to have come from the true cross of Jesus and put them together, you would have had a forest. Then, if you took all the nails claimed in medieval times to be nails from the crucifixion of Jesus, you could have taken true cross boards and built a house. Forgers in medieval times made a fortune producing and selling to believers relics of Christ's crucifixion."

"You have a point," Castle said. Forging relics must have been a big business.

Gabrielli continued: "Besides, there's a medieval letter that says the Shroud is a fake."

"What letter is that?" Castle asked.

"It was written in 1389 by Bishop Pierre d'Arcis to the Avignon pope Clement VII stating that the Shroud was a clever fake. According to the letter, Bishop d'Arcis claimed that his predecessor, Bishop Henri de Poitiers of Troyes, had conducted an inquiry that identified a painter who confessed to having painted the Shroud."

"Who was the painter?"

"Unfortunately, the letter did not identify the painter by name."

"So, if the Shroud is a fake, do you think you could duplicate it, using only medieval materials and processes?" Castle asked, getting to the key point.

"I believe I can," Gabrielli said. "I've already done some preliminary work and I think I can produce a fake Shroud that looks a lot like the original."

Castle was not convinced Gabrielli would succeed, but it was worth a try. Maybe Father Bartholomew was trying to perpetrate a huge hoax, starting with making up the nonsense about seeing God after supposedly dying on the operating table following his car accident. Could Bartholomew have been crazy enough to have actually caused the accident, with the intent to perpetrate this hoax? He would have needed some luck to survive the crash, even if he had planned it. Castle doubted anyone would go so far, but he did not discount the other possibility: that the hoax came to Father Bartholomew's imagination after he woke up in the hospital having survived the car crash. Castle recalled a Brooklyn crime ring that set up fake car accidents in which people were "killed" or "hurt" so they could file bogus insurance claims for hundreds of thousands of dollars.

What was clear to Castle was that if Gabrielli could produce a credible fake Shroud, then he could say to the Church that there was no way Father Bartholomew was mystically manifesting the real crucified Jesus as part of a mission given him by God. Having a credible fake Shroud would certainly support Castle's hypothesis that Father Bartholomew had an overactive subconscious that was working below the surface to manifest what Father Bartholomew unconsciously thought the historical Jesus looked like, based on Father Bartholomew's admitted study of the Shroud.

Castle proposed that he and Gabrielli work together. "I can easily get a book contract for this," Castle explained, "and we could coauthor the work. I will supply the psychiatric analysis and you provide the scientific analysis. Father Bartholomew will be our case study. The book will proceed from the findings of my previous book, *The God Illusion,* in that I want to argue people invent God to satisfy their own inadequacies and make up for their own perceived fears and deficiencies. You will just be advancing your work that there are scientific explanations that explain paranormal religious phenomena, just as you did with stigmata."

"Makes sense to me," Gabrielli said. "I would love to collaborate with you on such a project."

CHAPTER SEVEN

Same day
Dr. Stephen Castle's office, New York City
Midnight in New York City, 6:00 A.M. next day in Rome

The pope called Dr. Castle at midnight, just as Archbishop Duncan had arranged after Castle's first interview with Father Bartholomew.

"Dr. Castle, I want to thank you for taking this case," the pope began.

"You're welcome, your Holiness," Castle answered respectfully. "I just want to make sure we understand one another before I get too deeply into it. I helped you and Archbishop Duncan once before, but that doesn't mean I'm a great friend of the Catholic Church. I'm still an atheist and I still think religion is basically a neurosis."

"I know that's what you believe," the pope answered. "I didn't expect you had changed your views."

"And now I want to make sure you are not hiring me to prove the Shroud of Turin is the burial cloth of the historical Jesus. If that's your goal, I'm the wrong man for the job."

"Why don't you believe the Shroud is the burial cloth of Jesus, then?"

"For starters, the face of the man in the Shroud is all wrong for me. My first impression when I saw the photographs of the Shroud was that the face looks like the face a medieval European artist would have painted for Jesus. The historical Jesus was Semitic. The man in the Shroud looks Italian. It makes sense. If you wanted to sell a forgery, you would probably make Jesus look like the people you were trying to get to buy your handiwork."

"I'm not surprised that's your conclusion."

"You should also know that I spent most of the afternoon today on the telephone with Professor Marco Gabrielli at the University of Bologna."

The pope knew Gabrielli well. "Then you probably heard a lot about why he thinks Padre Pio was a fraud."

"I did," Castle said. "We spent a lot of time talking about how carbolic acid could have been used to cause those wounds to appear on Padre Pio's palms."

"This case is not about Padre Pio," the pope said without hesitation. "Pope John Paul II declared Padre Pio a saint in 2002 and that declaration is now a dogma of faith that is affirmed by the infallibility of the pope. The Church heard all those arguments decades ago and rejected them. I don't for a minute want to consider anything about Padre Pio being a fraud. That's not why I'm interested in Father Bartholomew."

Castle's mind worked rapidly to process what he was being told. If the pope did not want any questions raised about Padre Pio, why did the pope want him to work on Father Bartholomew, especially when both cases involved stigmata? If Father Bartholomew were proven to be a fraud, then new doubt would undoubtedly fall on Padre Pio, a saint the Catholic Church rushed to get canonized. So why was it, exactly, that the pope wanted him to work on this case when everybody knew he was an avowed atheist? He had just told the pope he was planning to work with an Italian chemist who had built an international reputation by debunking miracles. It didn't make any sense.

"Why would you want to prove Father Bartholomew is a hoax?" Castle asked the pope. "It has to be obvious to you that I am setting out to do just that."

"Yes, it is obvious to me what you are doing," the pope admitted. "But there is also something I want to try to explain to you."

"What's that?"

"Have you ever heard of Bishop Malachy?"

"Yes, vaguely," Castle responded. "Wasn't he the first Irish saint?"

"Yes, and he is associated with a prophecy that I am going to be the last pope. A Benedictine historian named Arnold Wion published a book in 1559 titled *Lignum Vitae,* in which a list attributed to the Irish Malachy listed one hundred and twelve popes yet to come, each designated by a Latin phrase that identified the pope. Pope Benedict XVI, my predecessor, was next to last. Malachy designated him as 'Gloria Olivae,' or 'Glory of the Olive.' Joseph Ratzinger, Pope Benedict XVI, was not a Benedictine priest, yet he chose the name of St. Benedict, the founder of the Benedictine order. The symbol of the Benedictine order includes an olive branch. Each of the one hundred and ten before Benedict XVI were identified equally as well by Malachy."

Castle listened, wondering where the pope was headed with this.

"The designation for the last pope was 'Petrus Romanus,' or 'Peter the Roman.' I did not want to take Peter II as my name for several reasons. I thought it presumptuous to name myself second to the disciple of Jesus who founded the Catholic Church. Jesus designated St. Peter to lead his church with the famous blessing, 'Upon this rock I found my church.' I'm sure you know that 'Peter' is the English translation of the Latin and Greek word for 'rock.' I greatly admire Pope John Paul II and taking the name Pope John-Paul Peter I permitted me to put Peter in my name without having to be Peter II. Maybe it was just superstitious, but I was born in Rome, so I fit the 'Petrus Romanus' description Malachy gave to the last pope."

"So you believe in these predictions then?" Castle asked.

"I'm not entirely sure. It's altogether possible the predictions were just attributed to Bishop Malachy, or maybe the believers in the predictions have just interpreted Malachy's descriptors so that they match after the fact, regardless of who was chosen pope in Malachy's number sequence. The descriptors are vague. Malachy's descriptor for Pope John Paul II was 'From a solar eclipse.' The believers have gone pretty far afield to identify Karol Wojtyla with that phrase, even arguing that it was fulfilled because Wojtyla was born on May 18, 1920, a day when there was a solar eclipse over the Indian Ocean. I don't know. But still, I have had a feeling since the College of Cardinals moved to elect me pope that my papacy would have momentous consequences for the Catholic Church. I don't need to list our problems for you. The Catholic faithful in the United States have dropped church attendance dramatically since the priest scandal. I worry for the future of the Church's finances."

"How does this tie into Father Bartholomew?"

"The Shroud of Turin has fascinated me since I first heard about it as a child."

"You believe it is the burial cloth of Jesus Christ?"

"Yes, I do," the pope answered directly. "But that is not the official position of the Vatican, now or ever before. Officially, the

Catholic Church considers the Shroud of Turin to be an important relic worthy of veneration. The Church maintains that belief in the authenticity of the Shroud as the actual burial cloth of Jesus is not important for the faithful to believe in the resurrection of Jesus. This is important because the resurrection of Jesus is the key article of faith the Church considers dogma concerning Christ's passion and death. That Christ rose from the dead is the proof he was the Son of God. The Church does not need the Shroud of Turin to prove Christ rose from the dead."

Castle got the point. "I've challenged Gabrielli to replicate the Shroud with techniques and materials that would have been available to medieval artists. I plan to work closely with Gabrielli, and if he can replicate the Shroud, I intend to invite him to coauthor my next book with me."

"Will that book focus on Father Bartholomew?" the pope asked.

"Most likely it will."

"Then I take it you believe Father Bartholomew is psychologically disturbed."

"Yes, I do."

The pope appreciated Castle's honesty. It was exactly what he expected. "I want to make sure you understand that I picked you because you are a formidable nonbeliever. Beginning in 1977, Anastasio Cardinal Ballestrero, the archbishop of Turin, gave permission to a group of scientists who organized themselves as STURP, the Shroud of Turin Research Project, to conduct tests on the Shroud over a five-day period. Pope Paul VI was not initially in favor of Ballestrero's decision. Pope Paul VI did not think establishing the scientific authenticity of the Shroud as the burial cloth of Christ was a good idea, even if it could be proved the Shroud is authentic. He thought moving the Church in that direction would put us back in the relic business. Since the medieval period, the Church has been moving away from any idea that relics should be used to buttress faith."

"I get the point."

"I always believed Pope Paul VI had a valid point and I disagreed with the decision to open the Shroud to scientific investigation," the pope continued. "But I am intellectually curious, especially since Pope Paul VI ultimately agreed to head down that route. So now I want to know if the Shroud can be proved to be a fake. I doubt anyone will ever prove for an absolute certainty that it is Christ's burial cloth. After all, we don't have any photographs of Christ to compare with the Shroud and we aren't likely to get any."

"So what do you want me to do?" Castle asked.

"I expect you to do your best to prove Bartholomew is deranged and I expect your Italian chemist friend will do his best to show he can make a Shroud as good as the original one. I will even pay you to do so."

"What do you mean?" Castle asked.

"I'm having one million dollars transferred to your account in New York immediately," the pope said without emotion. "I hope that will be enough to cover your time and the services of Dr. Gabrielli?"

"I am sure it is more than generous," Castle answered, quite surprised at how much the pope was willing to spend on this project.

"If you need more than that, I will need a precise accounting on how the one million dollars were spent," the pope clarified. "If one million turns out to be enough, I don't care how you spend the money. Do you understand?"

"Yes," Castle said.

"Do you agree?"

"Yes," Castle said again quickly. "The terms are most generous."

"My only condition is that you work closely with Father Morelli on my staff," the pope continued. "Father Morelli is devoted to the Shroud. Father Morelli came to the conclusion that the Shroud is the burial cloth of Christ, but he came to that conclusion only after studying the Shroud's history and the evidence intensely, both pro and con."

"No problem," Castle affirmed. "I met with Father Morelli earlier today and I will be happy to work with him."

"One more thing," the pope said. "Father Morelli will introduce you to a Father Middagh in New York. Father Middagh has studied the Shroud for more than forty years and he is one of the Catholic Church's leading experts on the Shroud. He too has a Ph.D. in chemistry, much like your friend in Bologna. Your conclusions on Bartholomew and Gabrielli's conclusions on the Shroud will not be meaningful to me until you both survive Father Middagh's examination."

Again, Castle saw the point. The pope was willing to pay, but the job was not going to be easy.

"I'm sure you appreciate that your reputation will depend on your conclusions," the pope said, almost as a veiled threat.

"What do you mean?" Castle wondered.

"The Catholic Church will not tell you what you can or cannot say or publish about Father Bartholomew," the pope clarified, "but if your analysis suffers from any inadequacy, the Church will be quick to defend her own."

"Of course," Castle said, realizing the seriousness of the assignment.

"We understand one another, then?" the pope asked in conclusion.

"We do," Castle agreed.

"One last thing. If you need anything from me, please feel free to call on me. Father Morelli will know how to reach me instantly, on a twenty-four-hour basis, seven days a week. If I am otherwise disposed, I will get back to you as soon as possible, once I hear from Father Morelli that it is imperative we speak again."

CHAPTER EIGHT

Dr. Castle met with Dr. Constance Lin, a petite Chinese medical specialist who ran the CT scan and MRI sections at Beth Israel. At Dr. Castle's request, Dr. Lin had just completed taking an extensive set of CT scans and MRI images on Father Bartholomew's wrists. She had key frames from both exhibited on the lightboards that lined two walls of her office.

"What's the verdict?" Castle asked Dr. Lin. He had always had a soft spot for Dr. Lin. Even though she was more than two decades his junior, Castle was attracted to her petite frame and soft-spoken manner. Still, she was a top professional and he thoroughly trusted her judgment. As far as Castle was concerned, no physician in New York City could read an MRI or CT scan better than Constance Lin.

"I've never seen a case like this before," she said right off. "Both wounds are clearly penetrated by injuries that were caused by an object that could have been a nail." Lin understood she was

studying the possibility of stigmata in examining Father Bartholomew's wrists. "The wounds on the bottom of each wrist clearly
exhibit signs of an entry wound, with a small opening and the
skin protruding down into the wound. The wounds on the top of
the wrist are much more open and severe, with the skin protruding out from the wound."

"Okay," Castle said. "That's consistent with what we would
expect to see if the stigmata were real. I would assume that in a
crucifixion, the victim's arms would be stretched out along the
crossbeam, with the palms upward. The nails fixing the arms to
the crossbeam would have been driven through the wrist by entering the palm and exiting on the back of the hand."

"That's exactly what we see here," Lin confirmed. "The problem is with the penetration through the wrist. It does not look
like the wound penetrates all the way through the wrist. But there
is one more possibility."

"What's that?"

"Well," she began carefully, "it is hard for me to say with certainty. But it is possible the wound is healing very rapidly from
the center outward. The wounds on the top of the palm and the
back of the wrist are still very raw and open, but the bleeding
from the wounds is minimal. When I opened the bandages to do
the tests, the wounds exhibited almost no sign of bleeding. It was
very strange, almost like the wounds had been cauterized from
within. I've never seen anything like it."

Castle could see the possibilities, especially if there was a mystical element to the wounds themselves.

"There's something more I can't explain," Lin began
cautiously.

"What's that?"

"The carpal bones in each hand were severely damaged by the
wound," she observed. "Let's assume the hand was penetrated by a

nail. The bones show signs not only of displacement, but of having been chipped and fractured."

"Isn't that what you would expect?" Castle asked.

"Yes, but when I observed Father Bartholomew take both the CT scans and the MRI exams, he seemed to have pretty good use of his hands. Even in these results, in both hands the radial nerve going to the thumb shows signs of abrasion, yet Father Bartholomew used both his thumbs freely. I would have expected to see much more impairment of function."

"What did the tests show?"

"That's the point," she said. "I could see the damage, but it was as if the carpal bones in both hands were well along in recovering, almost like the radial nerve was regenerating. I never expect to see that with severe hand trauma, especially not so soon after the injury."

Castle saw the point. Father Bartholomew's hand appeared severely injured, but the internal damage was either less than expected or healing remarkably fast.

"Also, if the wounds were from someone driving a nail through each wrist, I would have to say the person who drove the nails did so expertly. In each wrist, there was no damage to the radial artery, even though the nail was driven through each hand on the thumb side. Suicides usually try to cut the radial artery because it's closest to the surface on the back of the wrist. If the radial artery had been severed, Father Bartholomew would only have lived a few minutes."

Castle realized that Father Bartholomew's wrists were recovering almost as miraculously as the injuries that had occurred in the first place.

"The same is true with the muscles and tendons of the wrist," Lin went on. "Again, I can see signs of damage, but somehow either the person driving the nails worked to move aside key muscles, or the muscle and tendon tissue is regenerating."

"Is there any way Father Bartholomew's wounds could have been self-inflicted?" Castle asked.

"No," Dr. Lin replied quickly. "I don't see how it would have been possible. The damage done on the entry wounds in both wrists would have incapacitated the thumbs. One wound might have been self-inflicted, but not both."

Castle had not completely dismissed the possibility that Father Bartholomew had an accomplice. But from the descriptions of how the wounds occurred, it seemed that Father Bartholomew was in full view of the congregation and no one was close enough to him to have caused such deep wounds on both wrists, front and back.

"You are sure there was no obvious cause of the wounds?" Lin asked. "I believe Father Bartholomew's medical records show these wounds on his wrists appeared while he was saying Mass, but there was no attack on him or other cause of something physical penetrating his wrist to cause these wounds?"

"That's correct," Castle affirmed.

"What's your explanation, then?" Lin asked.

"I'm a psychiatrist," Castle reminded her. "I think the wounds were induced by the action of Father Bartholomew's subconscious. Psychosomatic illnesses are common. People give themselves all kinds of disorders, ranging from intestinal problems to heart problems, probably even cancer, simply by the action of their mental state. I would hate to admit to you how many placebos I have prescribed in dealing with mental patients over the years."

"Still," Lin said, "I cannot explain these CT scans and MRIs from what I know of trauma medicine. The raw nature of the wounds on the front and back surface of the wrist would only be consistent with more bleeding. These wounds are healing rapidly, and from the medical charts I see that they developed only a few days ago. Also, I cannot confirm to you that the wounds definitely penetrated the wrist, even though the wound in the palm has the characteristics of an entry wound and the wound on the back of the wrist has the characteristic of an exit wound."

"Do you think the wounds will regenerate completely, such that Father Bartholomew will recover complete use of his hand functions?" Castle asked. "I can't imagine how it would be possible with a wound that appears as severe as these do."

"Neither can I," Lin said. "But this is no usual case. Already I see signs of internal regeneration within the hand that are surprising. Who knows if the regeneration will extend to the surface of the skin? I guess anything is possible, but I know of no medical history that would suggest it is likely."

"Thank you. You've been most thorough," Castle said, grateful for her analysis. "Just one more question."

"What's that?"

"Do you see any reason I should not release Father Bartholomew from the hospital now?"

"You're the attending physician," she said appropriately, "and you know much better than I would what Father Bartholomew's overall physical condition is. But if you're asking me to make a judgment about the condition of these wounds, I would say the major risk now is infection. The wounds have to be irrigated and disinfected, with the bandages changed regularly. Other than that, the wounds look to me like they are healing nicely, more like wounds I would expect to be several weeks old, not just a few days old."

"Thank you again," Castle said. "You have been most helpful."

Back in the hospital room with Bartholomew and Morelli, Castle explained to them the results of the CT scans and MRI.

"How much longer will I be in the hospital?" Bartholomew asked. "I want to get back to my parish as soon as possible."

"How do you feel?" Castle asked. "Your vital signs look good and you appear to be eating and functioning normally."

Castle could keep him here in the hospital under observation for a few more days, but Father Bartholomew was clearly impatient. Castle also had a motive for releasing Bartholomew in that he wanted to observe right now what would happen if he sent Bartholomew back to his parishioners. Would the stigmata continue recovering, or would the wounds worsen? Since Castle believed the wounds were psychologically induced, he expected to see them worsen once Castle had the chance to act out his neurosis in public. By keeping Bartholomew isolated here in the hospital, Castle feared he would only postpone the inevitable second act of Father Bartholomew's self-inflicted psychodrama. Castle shared Father Bartholomew's desire to see him back in the parish as soon as possible.

"I feel a bit weak," Bartholomew said, "but that is probably to be expected. Father Morelli is planning to stay with me at the parish and I don't plan to resume active duties immediately. I may say Mass every day if I can, but I plan to get a lot of rest."

"Father Morelli, can you hold him to that promise?" Castle asked.

"I will do my best." The priest from the Vatican answered as honestly as he could.

"Okay, then," Castle said. "I will prepare the paperwork and you will be released this afternoon. I want to see you in my office two days from now."

CHAPTER NINE

Long lines have been forming outside St. Joseph's Church on Manhattan's Upper East Side since six this morning," Robin Blair, the anchor for Channel 5 television's early evening news report, said in introducing her story. "Our correspondent Fernando Ferrar is on scene. Fernando, what's drawing the crowd?"

"You might not believe it, Robin, but these people are lined up around the block outside St. Joseph's Catholic Church," Ferrar said as he broadcast live from the street outside the church. "And what they're doing is waiting to go to confession."

Ferrar, born in Puerto Rico, was becoming a fixture on the New York local news scene. Already, his uncanny ability to sense a good story and capture a tough-to-get interview had drawn the attention of the network bosses who were always on the search for promising news talent that might break into the big time of network nightly news. He fancied himself to be a younger Geraldo Rivera and he hoped his career would have equally as meteoric a rise. Like Geraldo, Ferrar had an angular, almost sculpted face made even more distinctive by the presence of a neatly trimmed but ample mustache. His sandy brown hair and his chocolate-rich brown eyes made him a heartthrob not only in the Latino community but with the Anglo television audience as well.

"What's going on?" Blair asked. "Do these people know something we don't? Is the end of the world finally at hand?"

"It's the parish priest here at St. Joseph's," Ferrar answered. "Father Paul Bartholomew is inside, hearing confession right now, and these people have lined up to see him."

"I'm Catholic, too," Robin Blair said in astonishment, "and I can't believe it. You mean you've got a line there that runs blocks long just because people want to go to confession?"

"That's right, Robin. People have lined up outside St. Joseph's because they believe Father Bartholomew has the ability to do more than just forgive their sins. They also believe he has the power to heal their illnesses."

In his Fifth Avenue apartment, Castle had just turned on the television with the remote, but he stopped surfing channels when he heard Ferrar mention Father Bartholomew.

Castle had settled into his recliner in his spacious living room overlooking Central Park, ready to watch a Yankees game on his wall-sized flat-screen television. He had decided not to go to the Bronx that evening to see the game in person from his season box behind third base. It had been a long day and he wanted to relax, with the likelihood he would drift off to sleep, especially if the Yankees got a comfortable lead in the early innings. This was one of the final games of the regular season and the Yankees were going into the postseason playoffs with the best record in the major leagues.

Even better, it was a year that had the possibility of turning into a subway Series, with the Mets looking like they could win the National League Championship Series. If that happened, he planned to see every World Series game in person. Castle was one of those New York fans who liked both the Yankees and the Mets, depending on which team was doing best in any particular year. In a subway Series, he would resolve his conflict by pulling for whichever team happened to be the home team that night.

Once he saw the news report come on about Father Bartholomew, he forgot momentarily about the baseball game.

"Tell me, sir, what are you doing standing here in line outside the church?" Fernando Ferrar asked an older gentleman standing in line.

"I'm here to see the priest," the man said.

"Is St. Joseph's your neighborhood parish?"

"No, I'm not even Catholic."

"Then, if you don't mind me asking, why are you here to go to confession?"

"I'm here because they say the priest can heal illnesses and my arthritis is so bad I can barely walk, even with this cane."

"How about you, ma'am. Are you here to see Father Bartholomew?"

"Yes, I am," the woman answered, a little nervous. "Am I on television now?"

"Yes, ma'am, you are."

"Well, I've never been on television before."

"Do you have something you want the priest to cure?"

"Not me, it's my daughter. She just learned she has breast cancer. I want to see if Father Bartholomew can cure my daughter. She's supposed to have an operation next week."

"That's about it, Robin," Ferrar said, speaking directly into the camera. "Hundreds of people lined up around the block just like you see here, to go to confession with Father Bartholomew here at St. Joseph's on the Upper East Side."

"He is the same priest that people say suffered the stigmata, the nail wounds of Christ on his wrists," Robin Blair asked. "Isn't that right?"

"Yes, the same priest."

"Does he still have the stigmata?"

"I haven't seen Father Bartholomew today," Ferrar replied, "but from what those coming out of the church say, he still has the bandages on his wrists."

"Well, there's probably going to be a lot more people tomorrow, after this report," Robin Blair said, wrapping up with Ferrar.

Castle's cell phone rang and he could see on the caller ID that it was Archbishop Duncan.

"Are you watching the local news?" Duncan asked, with concern obvious in his voice.

"Yes, I just saw the news report with that Spanish reporter outside St. Joseph's," Castle said.

"This could turn into a circus," Duncan said, obviously alarmed. "Are you sure releasing Father Bartholomew from the hospital was a good idea?"

"The priest is obviously well if he can hear all those confessions," Castle answered. "Unless you want me to commit Father Bartholomew to a psychiatric facility, we don't have much choice."

"Just the same, this situation is beginning to get out of hand."

Castle understood the archbishop's concerns. Yes, putting the priest in a psychiatric facility would limit the access of the press. But, in his gut, Castle wanted more data. He wanted to see what would happen when Father Bartholomew returned to St. Joseph's. Seriously disturbed psychiatric patients had a way of acting out their illnesses that made treating them easier. With Father Bartholomew back in the parish, would the stigmata heal or flame up again?

Since he took Father Bartholomew as a patient, Castle had studied enough about Padre Pio on the Internet to realize that Padre Pio had manifested stigmata for what amounted to around four decades. At fifty-four years old, Castle did not have four decades left for active psychiatric practice. Besides, a million dollars was a lot of money, but even a million dollars did not pay for decades of analysis with a priest who was determined to act out for the rest of his life the passion and death of Jesus Christ. Bartholomew was yet a young man. Castle wanted to know what was going on with him right now, not after the years of psychoanalysis it might take to cure him, if he could be cured at all.

"Committing Father Bartholomew will cause a lot of attention, too, especially after the reports on the stigmata begin circulating," he said. "Besides, I'm scheduled to see Father Bartholomew in my office on Monday. Let's give it until then."

Reluctantly, the archbishop agreed. "We'll leave it in God's hands, then," he resolved.

"At least for now," Castle said. "But I share your concern. With the media publicity Father Bartholomew is already getting, this is not going to be a case confined to New York City for long."

"Next thing we know, people are going to be camping outside the church all night, just to get in to see Father Bartholomew," Duncan said. "From there, word of mouth will take over and we will have people all over the country—probably all over the world—following what happens at St. Joseph's. How many people do you think there are with cancer in this city that would like an instant cure? If there's one, there's thousands and pretty soon they will all be demanding to see Father Bartholomew in the confessional."

"Wait until Fernando Ferrar catches on to the Shroud," Castle noted. "When he figures out how much Bartholomew looks like the Shroud, it will be the perfect story to go viral on the Internet. All it would take is for Ferrar to do another YouTube video about Father Bartholomew, Jesus, and the Shroud of Turin to add to the videos on the Internet showing Father Bartholomew getting the stigmata while saying Mass."

"No need to wait," the archbishop said with a tone of resignation. "The videos showing how much Father Bartholomew and the man in the Shroud of Turin look alike are already running on the Internet. Just go to YouTube and search Father Bartholomew's name. You will find one running that's particularly well done. By my count, a half million people have already viewed it."

"This case just gets bigger and bigger," Castle said, amused.

CHAPTER TEN

Outside St. Joseph's the street scene was mayhem. People were running from the church screaming. "Get help quick" summed up the panic as people dialed 911 on their cell phones. Inside, the faithful who had lined up to have their confessions heard by Father Bartholomew stood up or kneeled in bewilderment, worried that the collapsed priest lying on the church floor had died. Dozens of people were recording the scene on cell phone videos, determined to be the first to broadcast Father Bartholomew's collapse to their friends or to the world via the Internet. Outside, hundreds who had lined up around the block, waiting for their confessions to be heard, started pushed their way inside, determined to get a look for themselves before the miracle priest died.

"You've got to get over here right now," Morelli insisted to Dr. Castle on his cell phone. Morelli's voice sounded panicked.

"Slow down," Dr. Castle said, trying to get Father Morelli to calm down enough to explain what's going on. "Where are you and what's happening?"

"I'm at St. Joseph's. Bartholomew is unconscious. He was hearing confessions again tonight and he had some kind of seizure. Evidently, he staggered out of the confessional and collapsed on the church floor. There were a lot of people in the church waiting to go to confession and there's a large crowd outside that was waiting for their turn."

"Where's Bartholomew now?"

"We just carried him off the main altar. We're in the sacristy."

"Okay, stay with him. I'll be right there."

There was no time for Castle to call his driver and limo. Hailing a cab would be a lot quicker. With any luck, if he left immediately, he would be at the church before the ambulance arrived.

Running out of the apartment, he grabbed his medical bag. He had called downstairs to the doorman and by the time the elevator landed him on the ground floor, the taxi was waiting for him.

Driving the few blocks to St. Joseph's, Castle called the emergency room at Beth Israel and ordered them to be ready to receive a priest who was likely to be in a coma after suffering a seizure. He wouldn't know if the priest had suffered a stroke or heart attack until he got to the church in what he estimated would take less than five minutes.

Pushing through the crowd outside the church, Castle made his way to the sacristy. Father Bartholomew was lying on the floor, unconscious.

"Can you tell me how Father Bartholomew collapsed?" Castle asked, opening his bag to get his stethoscope.

"I didn't see how it happened," Morelli answered. "The nuns called me after Father Bartholomew had already collapsed. Evidently Bartholomew was hearing confessions and he had some kind of seizure. He came out of the confessional holding his heart and he fell unconsciously to the floor right outside the confessional. The nuns carried him to the altar. When I arrived, the nuns helped me move Father Bartholomew here, into the sacristy, where we could get him away from the people in the church."

Just then the paramedics arrived and took over.

"His pulse is weak," Castle said, "and I'm having trouble getting a read on his blood pressure. He's likely going into shock."

Quickly the paramedics lifted Bartholomew to the stretcher.

"I'm riding with you," Castle said, showing the paramedics his identification. "He's my patient."

The paramedics agreed, but they moved to block Morelli from getting into the back of the ambulance.

"This priest works for the Vatican," Castle intervened. "He needs to ride in the ambulance with us."

The paramedics looked like they were going to object, but in the rush they decided it was easier just to agree. Giving Morelli a hand, they lifted him into the ambulance and closed the doors.

"Head directly to Beth Israel," Castle directed. "I'm on staff there and I've already called ahead."

Once they were safely in the ambulance and the door was closed, the driver did his best to rush down Lexington Avenue with the siren blaring and the lights flashing. Within a block, a police cruiser joined them and led the way. Fortunately, it was almost 8 P.M. on a Sunday evening and the midtown traffic was relatively light. The ambulance and its police escort made quick progress toward Union Square.

Inside the ambulance, the paramedics and Dr. Castle were doing their best to stabilize the priest. Castle took a hypodermic from his medical bag and injected Father Bartholomew with a stiff dose of tranquilizer.

But instead of the tranquilizer causing Father Bartholomew to rest quietly, the priest began twisting violently. Castle wondered what could possibly be going on in the priest's mind to cause this apparent seizure. Was this an allergic reaction to the tranquilizer, or was it something else?

The paramedic riding in the back with them tightened the straps on the stretcher to hold the priest down. There was nothing in Bartholomew's medical history to suggest he was an epileptic, but Castle almost instinctively checked to make sure the priest was not swallowing his tongue. Still, Castle was concerned to see Bartholomew's eyelids begin fluttering. Then, suddenly his eyes opened and he began looking here and there, his eyes darting with the type of rapid eye movement associated with sleep disorders. *What is going on?* Castle wondered. *Is Father Bartholomew hallucinating?* Next, the priest screamed out a string of incomprehensible words and his face contorted in fear.

"Is he having an epileptic seizure?" one of the paramedics asked Dr. Castle.

"I don't think so," Castle answered. "I know the symptoms look like that, but there's nothing in his case history to suggest he is an epileptic."

"What's going on, then?" the paramedic asked urgently.

"It's hard to explain," Castle answered. "I'm his psychiatrist as well as his physician. I know it looks like an epileptic seizure, but I don't think it is. How far are we from the hospital?"

"Five minutes tops!" the driver shot back. "I'm doing the best I can!"

BARTHOLOMEW'S MIND WAS tripping in time once again.

In a jolt, he was back in ancient Jerusalem, this time being roughly led by a group of Roman centurions into a courtyard. His hands were bound with a rope the centurions used to force him forward against his will. After a few steps, he gave up struggling, realizing it was to no avail. He was headed to wherever the centurions were leading him. Once inside a small inner courtyard, the soldiers used the rope to fix his bound hands to a round iron ring that had been driven at about waist height into a small marble pillar ominously positioned at the courtyard's center.

A dozen or more soldiers poured into the courtroom, fighting with each other for position to get the best view from which to enjoy the intense beating they knew was about to take place.

Bartholomew could feel his robe being torn violently from his body. In an instant he was stripped naked, shamed to be standing there, completely exposed and totally vulnerable in this company of rough men.

"So this is the King of the Jews," the soldiers taunted, bending in mock bows before him as if he were on a throne, taking turns to approach him and spit on his naked body, aiming squarely for his face and genitals.

Struggling to recover from the insult, Bartholomew filled with fear as he saw two centurions with bulging arm muscles take up wooden-handled whips. Each flagrum consisted of three leather straps with lethal-looking, dumbbell-shaped lead weights attached to the ends.

Bartholomew froze in terror as the two centurions positioned themselves on each side, ready to get at his back, positioned out to them from the pillar. The centurion on the right was slightly taller than the centurion on the left, but both were impressively strong and had legs that looked like tree trunks.

The soldier on his right extended his left arm and flagrum above his head to get his full weight and force behind the blow he was about to flay across Bartholomew's back. Bartholomew buckled upon the impact. He cringed as the metal dumbbell ripped into his skin, then tore away tissue as the centurion forcefully pulled the flagrum away. In tandem, the second centurion lifted his whip with his right arm and repeated the scourging from Bartholomew's left side.

IN THE AMBULANCE, Castle and Morelli could not comprehend what was happening. Even though he was strapped tightly to the stretcher, Bartholomew's body twitched violently every few seconds. He screamed in pain and his head thrashed from side to side. Castle concluded that Bartholomew was experiencing some inner agony that was yet another manifestation of his neurosis, but Morelli was simply mystified. He took out his prayerbook and stole in preparation to give Father Bartholomew extreme unction, the final rites given by a Catholic priest at the death of one of the faithful.

Right then, Castle became alarmed to see that Bartholomew's shirt was filling with blood. He quickly loosened the stretcher straps around Bartholomew's shoulders so he could unbutton his black priestly shirt and examine him.

Exposing Bartholomew's chest, Castle could not believe what he was seeing. Accompanying every violent movement of Bartholomew's body, new wounds were appearing as if from nowhere. Castle's mind raced. It almost looked like Bartholomew was being wounded from the inside, especially since no one in the ambulance was striking him and there was no outside explanation for why new wounds were showing up right then before Castle's eyes.

Bartholomew looked as if he were trying to escape by violently twisting this way and that on the stretcher. It occurred to Castle that Bartholomew was desperately trying to turn his body completely around, to flip over from back to front, or even to position himself on one side or the other. Every time Bartholomew managed to twist around enough to expose a new section of his body, fresh wounds began appearing there, inflicted from some mysterious and unseen source.

Castle had never seen anything like this happening ever before, but his mind flashed to Bartholomew's description of how he had suffered the stigmata. While Castle discounted the possibility it was real, his immediate intuitive reaction was that Bartholomew was suffering a severe scourging, and the thought of ancient Roman whippings came to his mind. Castle's mind flashed on the scourging Jesus had received at the pillar as part of his torture leading up to his crucifixion and he began to worry that Bartholomew's neurosis was pushing him even deeper into personally experiencing the passion and death of Christ. Could it be possible that here in the back of the ambulance, Castle and Morelli were watching the scourge wounds appear on Bartholomew's body, adding the injuries of Christ's scourging at the pillar to the stigmata in Bartholomew's wrists?

To stop Bartholomew from thrashing about, Castle quietly injected a second dose of the tranquilizer, again to apparently no effect. Bartholomew's body continued twitching in spasms of pain, as if he were being beaten.

WITH HIS MIND back in the ancient courtyard, Bartholomew felt like a trapped animal. There was no escape from the repeated blows that drove him to his knees. The instant he fell, the centurions taunted him to get up. "What kind of man are you?" they jeered. "Can't even take a little beating?"

Since he was unable to get back to his feet, the centurions with the whips stopped long enough to kick him, then grabbed him by his arms and lifted him back to his feet. Once Bartholomew was upright, the beating resumed.

Bartholomew struggled to twist around to expose his front to the whips, thinking the soldiers might not beat him on his chest and genitals, but he was wrong. While he saved his back for a moment from further injury, the centurions whipped his forelegs and chest, not sparing his stomach and abdomen. No matter which way Bartholomew twisted, front or back, he suffered the continued blows of the flagrum, the lead weights tearing his skin away. With his wrists bound to the short marble pillar, there was no escape from the torture. For what seemed like more than an hour, they beat him, the centurions with the whips and the soldiers in the courtyard seeming to get an almost sexual pleasure from his suffering and pain.

"Why can't you save yourself?" the soldiers taunted, mocking his agony. "Where's your army now, King of the Jews? Why have your legions abandoned you?"

They laughed as he fell to his knees or fell to the ground, his upper body hanging from the metal ring, his bound hands suspended back above his head by the rope that held his wrists to the ring. "You cry like a woman!" they jeered. "This is the way a child would die. Do you want your mother? Stand up and take your punishment like a man."

More than once in the throes of his passion, Bartholomew's mind froze with alarm, realizing how the goal of his torturers was to bring him as close to death as possible, but not so far as to actually kill him, just prolong his agony and intensify his pain. Bartholomew knew this was a beating from which he would never recover. Somehow, he comprehended that this scourging was just the first act in a prolonged drama of death that would have several acts. The soldiers would beat him to a point where the injuries would cover every inch of his body, but he was by no means the first victim these brutes had tormented and he would by no means be the last.

In his horror, Bartholomew realized that these Roman centurions dressed in their military garb, with their wine-red tunics and tight-fitting leather bindings, were not savage beasts. To the soldiers this cruel courtyard was their temple of pain and Bartholomew their victim, with his hands bound by leather to their short marble altar of cruelty.

What they wanted was to intensify and prolong his anguish so as to intensify and prolong their pleasure at watching him suffer.

Even in their most sadistic impulses, these Roman centurions weren't so foolish as to allow their victim to die, lest they themselves be beaten for ineptitude. Prolonging the scourging was essential to the torment.

Bartholomew's entire body throbbed, but every time his mind threatened to go blank, the soldiers doused him with water, reviving him for more punishment.

The centurions paused only when it was time to pass the whips to fresh hands. The soldiers competed for the privilege of beating their bound victim, pushing one another aside as they lined up to be the next man wielding the flagrum.

As they arrived at Beth Israel, Bartholomew's bloody body went limp.

The paramedics moved quickly, fearful that Bartholomew might die before they could get him inside the emergency room. The paramedics moved Castle and Morelli aside respectfully as they pulled the stretcher from the ambulance, lowered the gurney's wheels, and rolled the injured man forward as quickly as they could.

Once he was inside the hospital, the ER team took over and went to work immediately. Stripping Bartholomew of clothes, they were shocked to see his body was severely injured front and back by hundreds of small cuts.

Pushing his way into the emergency room station, Castle was equally shocked to realize Bartholomew's injuries crisscrossed virtually every square inch of his body, from his shoulders down to his ankles. Trying to stay in the background so he wouldn't be thrown out, Morelli pushed himself into the ER right behind the psychiatrist.

Looking closely at Bartholomew's back as the ER doctors turned him over, Castle could see that the back wounds were about twice as numerous as the wounds Castle had suffered on his front side. Trying to estimate the total number of wounds, Castle picked a small area below the shoulders and counted. He could see dumbbell-shaped wounds clustered in groups of three. Taking into account that the injuries were fewer on his front side, Castle extrapolated and made a quick estimate that Bartholomew had suffered possibly as many as one hundred groups of what amounted to some three hundred separate dumbbell-shaped wounds.

Each wound was nearly identical—less than a half inch in length, with two small circles of injury defining the ends of each wound. Looking closely he could see what looked like lash wounds connected to each dumbbell-shaped wound. His mind envisioned a whip of three thongs that had a dumbbell-shaped weight tied at the end of each thong. He recoiled when he imagined that Bartholomew could have been hit by as many as one hundred different scourge blows. He wondered how anybody could survive a beating that brutal. What he was seeing of Bartholomew's naked body in the ER explained the anguish he had observed in the ambulance.

Standing in the background behind Castle in the ER, Morelli was coming to the same conclusions. Looking at Bartholomew as the doctors and nurses worked frantically to identify and treat his wounds, the thought flashed through Morelli's mind that here was the live image of the scourged man of the Turin Shroud.

Moving quietly forward, Father Morelli finally had the chance to begin administering extreme unction. Praying in a whisper, Morelli blessed Bartholomew's forehead with the sign of the cross and began bestowing on him the Church's last rites.

For several minutes, the doctors and nurses did the best they could to contain the bleeding. Then Bartholomew suddenly relaxed. His breathing became more normal and his vital signs, measured on the monitors, were strong.

"We need to send him to the burn unit," one of the ER doctors advised Castle. "His wounds cover his body. There's too many to stitch and we have to stop the bleeding. These wounds have to be cleaned out carefully to prevent further injury. Then his entire body will need to be sterilized to prevent infection. These aren't burns, but the burn unit has the kind of advanced treatment facilities and wound dressings he needs. He's suffered massive fluid loss in addition to loss of blood. He could go into shock at any time."

Castle agreed. Bartholomew would need intensive care for several days. He had the priest admitted to the burn unit and ordered monitoring of his circulatory system and heart. Castle was concerned Father Bartholomew's obvious trauma would cause hemodynamic instability, with the possibility that the priest's blood circulation might simply collapse. He also ordered twenty-four-hour monitoring for cardiac arrhythmia. For when Bartholomew could be transferred out of the burn unit to intensive care, Castle requested a private room, or a room in which the second bed would not be occupied. Castle wanted to maintain privacy for the priest and he was worried that a second patient or that patient's family would begin asking too many questions.

This time, the psychiatrist planned to keep the priest hospitalized for whatever time it took to figure out what was going on. If these injuries were psychosomatic, then Bartholomew's subconscious might continue inflicting serious injury on his body. Could this mental illness be stopped before Bartholomew's subconscious inflicted a fatal injury on the priest? Castle was not sure. The wounds he was seeing were so similar to the wounds of Christ's passion and death—the scourging at the pillar in addition to the stigmata on the wrists—that the prognosis could not be good.

Christ died on the cross. Would Bartholomew die imitating Christ's crucifixion? Castle tried to remember what he could of the wounds of Christ's passion and death that Bartholomew had not yet suffered—the crown of thorns, the nail through his feet, the spear in his side. Were these next? Castle didn't consider Bartholomew *consciously* suicidal, but subconsciously—that was a different matter.

Stopping by the burn unit, Castle consulted with the physicians and nurses on duty, making sure they understood his instructions.

Satisfied that he had done everything he could, Castle decided he would return to see the priest early in the morning.

As he stepped out of the hospital at First Avenue and Sixteenth Street onto Stuyvesant Square, he was surprised to see a crowd of some 250 people quietly holding lit candles. They had gathered in a silent vigil that Castle presumed was for Father Bartholomew.

He wondered how these people knew Father Bartholomew was here, but he did not have to wonder about that for long.

Catching sight of the doctor leaving the hospital's front entrance, Channel 5 reporter Fernando Ferrar stepped forward from the crowd with his film crew in tow. Seeing Ferrar rush at him with a microphone, followed by a mobile camera crew complete with bright lights, Castle had the answer to his question. Ferrar either had been monitoring police calls, or somebody at the television station had been tipped off.

The media circus was in full swing, even at this late hour on a Sunday night in New York City.

"Dr. Castle!" Ferrar shouted. "Can we ask you a few questions?"

Castle stopped long enough for Ferrar to shove the microphone in front of him. The lights from the TV crew illuminated the street around Castle in front of the hospital.

"Not right now," the doctor objected. "I'm not ready for a press conference."

"You are Father Bartholomew's doctor, right?" Ferrar pressed on. "Can you tell us what happened? We are hearing from ER that he had scourge marks all over his body. Is this a miracle? Father Bartholomew already has the stigmata in his wrists, so now has he been scourged at the pillar? Is Father Bartholomew becoming Jesus Christ?"

"Father Bartholomew has been admitted to the hospital," Castle affirmed. "That's all I have to say right now."

"Who is Father Bartholomew? Is he the Second Coming of Jesus Christ?"

"I'm a doctor," Castle protested, "not a priest."

"But you're also a psychiatrist," Ferrar said, playing to the television audience. "Is Father Bartholomew crazy?"

"I've said all I am going to say," Castle said, clearly irritated at being confronted on the street like this by a rude and overly aggressive reporter.

"How badly is Father Bartholomew injured?" Ferrar pressed on, undeterred by Castle's brusqueness. "Will he live?"

"That's it for now," Castle said, his voice bristling with the outrage he felt at this news assault. "Father Bartholomew is my patient and he has been admitted to intensive care. We will hold a press conference tomorrow, or the next day, but right now, this interview is over."

Castle excused himself from Ferrar and pushed his way roughly through the crowd of people quietly holding their candles and praying.

He grabbed the first cab he could find and headed back to his Fifth Avenue apartment. The circus was gaining momentum.

CHAPTER ELEVEN

Wednesday morning
Beth Israel Hospital
Day 14

B_y Tuesday night, Father Bartholomew had recovered sufficiently to be moved from the burn unit to a private room in the intensive care unit.

On Wednesday morning, Dr. Castle showed up at the hospital early, at 8 A.M., anxious to see how Father Bartholomew was doing.

As his limo approached Union Square, Castle could see that the crowd assembled outside the hospital had not gone away. Several hundred people appeared to be still keeping silent vigil. Determined to avoid another television hijacking, Castle had his driver take him to the private staff entrance underground.

Going directly to Bartholomew's room in the ICU, Castle was surprised to find Father Morelli standing at Bartholomew's bed, and a woman sitting on the bed, holding Bartholomew's hand.

Castle was sure he had given instructions that Bartholomew

was to have no overnight visitors. Visiting hours at the hospital did not begin until 10 A.M.

The priest from the Vatican might have talked himself into the room to be present with his fellow priest from New York City, but who was this woman and why was she here?

"She's family," the nurse said, reading Castle's mind as the doctor entered the room. "She says she is Father Bartholomew's sister."

What sister? Castle wondered. In their therapy session, Bartholomew said he was an only child.

Wearing his white physician's coat, Castle first said good morning to Father Morelli. The psychiatrist guessed from the priest's beard stubble and his rumpled clothes that Morelli had spent the night at Father Bartholomew's side, sleeping in the visitor's chair. There was a second bed in the room, but the sheets looked like nobody had slept there last night.

"I thought I said 'no visitors,'" Castle said pointedly, reproaching Morelli.

"I'm not a visitor, I'm his priest," Morelli answered sharply in return. "Sunday night, I couldn't leave Father Bartholomew alone. I prayed all through Sunday night that he would live. Monday and Tuesday, I came to the hospital during the night to check on Father Bartholomew, just to be sure."

"I told you on Monday that I thought Father Bartholomew was out of danger," Castle said.

"You did," Morelli agreed. "But I couldn't see how it would hurt anything if I spent the nights sleeping in the chair. What if you were wrong and Father Bartholomew had died? I'd never be able to explain to the pope why I wasn't right here at his side every minute."

Why argue? Castle thought. Castle knew he was on solid ground when he insisted that Morelli had no place in the analysis room in his office, but this was the hospital. Castle was the physician in charge but Morelli also had a point. In a way, Morelli was "the priest in charge," representing not just the Archdiocese of New York, but also the Vatican. Actually, Castle felt Morelli might be helpful here, especially if Father Bartholomew woke up.

Next, Castle decided he might as well introduce himself to the young woman and find out about her. But before he could say a word, she stood up from the bed and extended her hand to greet him.

"You must be Dr. Castle," she said calmly. "I'm Anne Cassidy, Father Bartholomew's half sister."

When she stood, Castle could see she was a beautiful and fully mature woman. Before Castle could say a word, their eyes met. Her soft blond hair flowed elegantly down to her shoulders and her deep brown eyes looked alive and vibrant.

He too immediately struck her as handsome, with his neatly trimmed graying hair and beard making him look very distinguished and professional, even more so in his full-length white medical coat.

Both instantly felt out of time and place. To Father Morelli, their meeting appeared a casual affair, nothing out of the ordinary. But for Dr. Castle and the woman he was meeting for the first time, the moment had an otherworldly quality about it.

Castle looked deeply into her brown eyes and somehow connected almost with her soul. He felt he was having the same impact on her. Her eyes locked firmly on his and her gaze seemed to penetrate to the depths of his soul as well. Each of them connected with the other at a level far deeper than words.

Castle felt like he was standing there for an eternity contemplating this bewitching woman, feeling for maybe the first time in his life not fully in command of the situation.

"I didn't know Father Bartholomew had a sister," Dr. Castle said, shaking her hand as if nothing out of the ordinary had just happened.

"He doesn't know he has a sister," Anne said honestly. "We have the same mother, but different fathers. We are half brother and half sister."

"How is it that Father Bartholomew does not know you're his sister?" Castle asked.

"My father was estranged from our mother after I was born," she answered. "Paul is about two years younger than me. This will be the first time we have ever met."

Castle filed this information away, to explore it in much greater depth as soon as he had the chance, with both Bartholomew and Anne.

"What drew you to the hospital now?" he asked.

"I live in Montreal. As soon as I read on the Internet about my brother getting the stigmata, I watched the videos. When the Internet reports said he had been hospitalized, I decided I had to be here. I got in my car and drove to New York. I got to the hospital sometime after midnight last night and I felt I had to see my brother right away. I begged them downstairs until somebody finally told me my brother's room number."

Listening to her soft voice explain how she managed to get herself to her brother's room, in direct violation of his instructions, Castle could not make himself feel angry. Instead, he felt instantly attracted to Anne. He realized she was much younger than him, probably in her early forties, about the same age as her brother. But he suspected she had strength of character that belied her young age and petite frame. Her knee-length blue dress draped her well-developed figure comfortably, almost sensually. Her long blond hair looked silky and soft. She had an expressive smile and delicate features. But more than anything, Castle was captivated by the intelligence and life he saw flashing in her chocolate brown eyes.

Castle instantly forgot having been irritated with her for showing up in the hospital room unannounced and against his "no visitors" order. Still, he felt he had to make the point that Anne and Morelli should not feel free to come and go as they liked. The hospital staff was certain to complain, especially if Morelli or Anne got in their way.

"Visiting hours at Beth Israel end long before midnight," Castle said as firmly as he could. He made a mental note to investigate what breaches of security had occurred that allowed Father Morelli and Anne Cassidy to spend the night in Father Bartholomew's room. "I won't allow either of you to be here again after visiting hours without my explicit permission. Do you understand?" he asked them both.

Both Father Morelli and Anne acknowledged that they understood and would comply with his instructions.

"Is my brother in a coma, Doctor?" Anne asked. "He hasn't woken up all night."

Castle looked at the chart and he could see that Bartholomew had stabilized overnight. As Castle had instructed, Bartholomew was continuing to get morphine intravenously.

"He went through an incredible amount of trauma on Sunday," Castle explained. "His wounds covered every square inch of his entire body, from his neck to his ankles. From the emergency room I had him sent directly to the burn unit, where they could treat his wounds and get him stabilized. With all the tranquilizers and painkillers we have given him, he may sleep most of the day today, maybe through the night. But technically, I'm not ready to say yet that he is in a coma."

Castle pored carefully over Bartholomew's chart and studied

the monitors in the room measuring the priest's circulation and heartbeat. Looking at the priest, he was surprised at how much color had returned to Bartholomew's face. When Castle had finally left the ER on Sunday night, Bartholomew had looked as white as a ghost. He thought Bartholomew would have been kept in the burn unit for several days.

Next, the psychiatrist lifted the covers back and examined the bandages on Bartholomew's body. Bartholomew looked like a mummy, wrapped in gauze. Using surgical scissors, Castle carefully cut the gauze at Bartholomew's chest so he could peel away the dressings and examine a small sample of the wounds.

Morelli and Anne waited silently for his verdict.

"From what I can see, Father Bartholomew is recovering faster than I ever imagined possible," Castle said, with obvious relief in his voice. "I don't claim to understand it, but the bleeding has stopped. His wounds appear to have closed and clotted, much more than I would have expected from the trauma I saw last night. Wounds this severe could easily have killed him. My biggest concern was that he would go into shock, but after the injuries stopped happening, he calmed down and his vital signs improved almost immediately."

"You know what these wounds are, don't you?" Morelli asked knowingly.

Castle suspected he knew what the priest was going to tell him, but he decided to let the priest go ahead and make the point.

"No, Father Morelli, I don't. Why don't you explain it to me?"

"These are the wounds Christ suffered when he was scourged at the pillar," Morelli said without any evident emotion. "Father Bartholomew is continuing to experience Christ's passion and death. I'm confident that if we take a close look at the wounds and examine them against the scourge wounds on the Shroud of Turin, we are going to find out they are identical."

That was pretty much what Castle expected Father Morelli would say. The same thought had occurred to Castle on Sunday.

"Well, I suspect you will have the opportunity to prove that point," Castle said quietly. "I have asked Dr. Lin to take CT scans and run an MRI on Father Bartholomew this afternoon. I doubt if I will have any results today, but Archbishop Duncan called me at six-thirty this morning. He wants results, too, and I believe he wants to introduce us to an expert on the Shroud of Turin recommended by the Vatican. I suggest we all get together tomorrow morning at ten in my office."

"What about me?" Anne asked. "Can I attend as well?"

"Yes, you're part of the family," Castle conceded. "Father Morelli can give you the address. But tonight I insist you find a hotel room and get some sleep. Security around Father Bartholomew will be tighter from now on, I assure you. As I said before, nobody will be permitted to stay overnight with him tonight. Understood?"

"Yes," Father Morelli and Anne both said.

"Good," Castle said firmly.

Then, turning to Father Morelli, Castle gave further instructions. "Tonight I suggest you return to the rectory at St. Patrick's Cathedral and get some sleep. The archbishop would probably appreciate a report from you in person, given all that has happened since Sunday."

"You're right," Father Morelli said. "I'll make sure Anne gets a hotel room and we will coordinate to be at your office tomorrow morning."

CHAPTER TWELVE

When he entered the conference room, Castle found the group had assembled. At the end of the room by the windows looking out on Central Park, Archbishop Duncan was talking pleasantly with a priest he had not met before. Castle guessed this was probably Father Middagh, whom the pope had mentioned on the telephone.

The archbishop was elegantly dressed in a black wool cassock trimmed in crimson silk. The cassock was bound at his waist by a purple sash that matched his purple skullcap. Around his neck was an elegant pectoral cross, suspended by a cord of entwined threads of green silk and gold. On the ring finger of his right hand, he wore a large gold ring that bore an image of Jesus. That image looked remarkably like the face of the man in the Shroud.

Standing there by the Central Park windows, the archbishop was a commanding presence. Duncan was in his mid-sixties, about ten years older than Castle, but clean-shaven. Looking at

Duncan's trim physique, Castle felt jealous. Castle had to force himself to exercise to stay fit, especially in his all-too-sedentary profession of psychiatry. The archbishop, Castle surmised, was probably thin by nature, to the point of appearing gaunt, and taller than Castle, at nearly six feet two.

Anne was seated at the table alone, waiting for the meeting to begin. She was wearing a nicely tailored beige suit that complemented her deep brown eyes perfectly and showed off the curves of her well-formed figure. Her blond hair was pulled back in a bun, giving her the more mature look Castle would expect of a professional woman in her early forties. Standing as the others came around to meet her, she introduced herself as Anne Cassidy, Father Bartholomew's half sister from Toronto.

"She's here today as a member of the family," Castle explained privately to Archbishop Duncan, taking him aside from the group.

"I didn't know Father Bartholomew had a half sister," Duncan said, surprised.

"I didn't know either," Castle said, somewhat embarrassed at Anne's sudden and unexpected intrusion into the case. "And from what Anne Cassidy told me yesterday at the hospital, I expect Father Bartholomew will be equally surprised to find out he has a half sister. From what I understand, the two of them have never met before, not until now. I plan to find out more about Anne Cassidy and I will report back to you later."

"Thank you," Duncan said. "The thing I appreciate most about a good mystery is solving it."

"I know exactly what you are saying," Castle said. "I feel the same way. Right now, Anne is here with my permission."

"Thank you for explaining that," Duncan said. "I understand."

As the meeting was about to begin, Archbishop Duncan sat

at the head of the conference table, with his back to the window. Castle took the other end of the table.

To Castle's right was Father J. J. Middagh, an expert on the Shroud of Turin. Sitting to the archbishop's left, Father Middagh was the living embodiment of the happy friar. Middagh wore a looser, more obviously worn cassock than the archbishop, one that covered but did not completely hide his ample paunch. Nearly bald, Middagh had a round red face and small wire-framed scholarly glasses gave him the appearance of being a well-fed bookworm who needed only a stein of lager beer and a thick tome to sustain him until dinner. In front of him was his laptop computer and a stack of books Middagh had brought along to buttress his presentation. As the meeting was getting ready to start, Middagh fiddled with a portable projector he had attached to his laptop for a presentation on a pulldown screen discreetly built into bookshelves that lined the far wall of the conference room.

Across the table from Middagh and to the right of the archbishop were Father Morelli and Anne. Morelli appeared to be wearing the same black suit and Roman collar that he wore the first time he meet Castle in the treatment room next door to explain his mission from the Vatican. He had his briefcase on the table and a stack of papers out for ready reference.

Archbishop Duncan started the discussion. "Pope John-Paul Peter I asked Father Middagh to join us here today because he is one of the top scholars on the Shroud of Turin. I have known Father Middagh for years and because he is a modest man, I will announce for him that his book on the Shroud will be published next week. Isn't that right, Father Middagh?"

"Yes, I have been working on what's going to turn out to be a two-volume treatise for more than a decade," Middagh confirmed. "My working title, *Behold the Face of Jesus*, says it all.

I am convinced the Shroud of Turin is the authentic burial cloth of Jesus Christ. I have brought with me some digital images that I used in the book."

"Father Middagh is a Benedictine priest and he works from a monastery located in White Plains, New York," Duncan explained. "By training, Father Middagh is a Ph.D. chemist who has taught chemistry at the university level. With that introduction, Dr. Castle, could you give us a brief update on Father Bartholomew's condition?"

"Yes," Castle said as he opened his medical file. "Father Bartholomew rested comfortably last night. He still has not recovered consciousness, yet I expect he will do so soon. From the CT scan and MRI tests that I had run yesterday, Father Bartholomew's wounds appear to be recovering remarkably fast, just as we saw with the stigmata on his wrists. We will know more in a few hours."

"Thank you," Archbishop Duncan said seriously. "Our prayers are with you, Dr. Castle, and with Father Bartholomew." Smoothly, Duncan shifted his attention to the subject of the meeting. "Dr. Castle, the pope has asked Father Middagh to join us as a resource to you on the Shroud. I suspect you can ask Father Middagh any question about the Shroud that you like. Where would you like to begin?"

"I want to start with the radioactive carbon-14 dating of the Shroud," Castle said immediately. He wanted to know if there was any proof the Shroud was a medieval fake. That would help him sort out whether there was any possibility Father Bartholomew was manifesting the authentic Jesus Christ, or just some medieval artist's idea of what Jesus looked like. "If I am correct, three separate carbon-dating tests have shown the Shroud was made somewhere around 1260 to 1390 A.D. If those results are correct, that would make the Shroud a medieval fake—maybe one of the best forgeries ever done in the history of art forgeries, but a medieval fake just the same."

"You are right about the carbon-14 tests," Middagh said. "But there was an important study published posthumously in 2005 by Raymond Rogers, who was a chemist and thermal analyst at Los Alamos. That study gives us reason to doubt the reliability of the carbon-14 tests. Ray Rogers was the director of chemical research for the Shroud of Turin Research Project in 1978. He was a personal friend of mine for many years. A year before he died, he submitted a paper to a peer-reviewed scientific journal; it was published after he died. Rogers basically argued that the cloth samples taken from the Shroud to be used in the radiocarbon testing were not representative of the main part of the Shroud, on which the image resides. Rogers argued that the 1988 samples came from a part of the Shroud that had been expertly rewoven sometime in the Middle Ages to repair damage to the Shroud."

"Was Rogers's analysis scientifically convincing?" Castle asked.

"Not everyone in the Shroud research community was persuaded, especially since Rogers dropped his opposition to the Shroud just before he died of cancer," Middagh answered honestly. "I had quite a few conversations with Rogers before he died and I am convinced he underwent a change of heart that was more than some sort of a religious conversion after he knew he was sick. Those who were on the Shroud of Turin Research Project in 1978 remember Rogers as one of the original skeptics. Then, when the original carbon-14 tests were conducted, Ray was very outspoken that the tests proved the Shroud dated from the thirteenth or fourteenth centuries. At the time of the carbon-dating tests, Roger openly announced he was confident the Shroud had been fabricated somewhere around 1260 to 1390 A.D."

"What changed his mind?" Castle asked.

"As I said, Rogers became convinced that the sample was not representative. In the past few years there has been a considerable scientific debate about how the cloth sample was taken from the Shroud for the carbon-dating tests. Pope John Paul II's decision to cut a piece of the Shroud for radiocarbon testing was very controversial. If the Shroud is the burial cloth of Christ, then cutting away a piece of the Shroud to destroy it in the burning process required by the carbon-14 test is almost a sacrilege. It's like destroying the only known artifact that may have had contact with the Savior. So the Church demanded the sample be cut from a corner of the Shroud that was already badly damaged."

"I understand," Castle said.

"Fellow Shroud researcher Barrie Schwortz recorded a video of Rogers just before he died, when Rogers knew he was close to losing his battle with cancer," Middagh said. "Schwortz is important because he was the official photographer on the 1978 Shroud of Turin Research Project. In the video, Rogers described how he became convinced the corner samples used for the radiocarbon tests came from a part of the Shroud that had been expertly repaired by the French Poor Clair nuns in to repair the damage from several fires the Shroud was in after it showed up in France in 1357. In one particularly threatening fire in 1532, the Shroud was nearly destroyed."

Middagh projected an image onto the screen that showed full-body views of the Shroud.

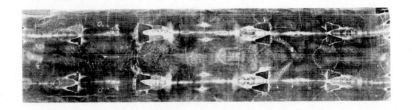

"You can see here the triangular patches that line each side of the body image along the length of the Shroud. The Shroud is a linen cloth that measures a little over fourteen feet in length. As you can see here, the body of the crucified man was laid with his back on the cloth. Then burial cloth was lifted over his head to cover his front side. That's why the image appears to have the two heads touching in the middle. The image appears that way when the cloth is once again stretched out full length."

"I understand," Castle said, letting Middagh know he was following the description.

"In a full-length view of the Shroud, there are sixteen triangular patches in total, eight on each side of the body," Middagh continued. "It's well documented that the medieval French Catholic nuns sewed those patches on this pattern of burn holes that runs the length of the Shroud. They did so to preserve the Shroud from disintegrating. The two rows of triangular patch repairs running up the length of the Shroud were too big for the type of 'invisible weaving' that professional weavers in the Middle Ages had perfected. Invisible reweaving repairs only worked on smaller damaged areas. Rogers came to the conclusion that the corner of the Shroud from which the radiocarbon samples were taken in 1988 had been altered in 'invisible weaving' repairs done in the Middle Ages. The repairs in this one corner were done so well that the reweaving was not evident to the naked eye, as were the eight triangular patches."

"If I hear what you're telling me," Castle said, wanting to make sure he got it right, "you believe that Rogers had a change of heart based on these scientific concerns?"

"Yes, I do," Middagh said. "If you are asking me if Rogers changed his mind because he knew he was going to die and he didn't want to face his Creator having denied the Shroud, just in case the Shroud was authentic, that's not what I believe happened. Rogers began changing his mind when two nonscientists, Joseph Marino and Sue Benford, got textile experts to examine microscopic evidence that cotton had been woven into the linen fibers of that corner where the carbon-dating samples were taken, in a series of repairs made to the Shroud. After the repairs were made, the repair areas were dyed so the cotton would match the linen to fool the eye into not seeing the reweaving repair. Rogers concluded that someone using materials that were not used in making the original Shroud did the reweaving with great skill. Looking back at the 1978 photos of the Shroud, Rogers realized the area chosen for the carbon-14 samples was different from the rest of the Shroud in that the sample area did not fluoresce the same, for instance, under the ultraviolet tests."

"So how did Rogers prove the 1988 carbon-14 sample was different from the main body of the Shroud?" Castle asked. "What was the methodology?"

Middagh answered slowly, trying to make sure he explained what Rogers had done so everyone in the room would understand. "In the paper Rogers published posthumously, he argued the 1978 STURP tests showed that the chemistry of the linen fibers taken from the main part of the Shroud differed from the 1988 radiocarbon samples in that the 1978 samples showed no sign of cotton having been interwoven with the original linen. In other words, the main body of the Shroud is completely made up of the original linen, with no cotton included in the weaving at all. Since linen is dye-resistant and cotton is not, the dye saturating the cotton was apparent to the eye under microscopic analysis, once interwoven cotton and linen fibers were compared. That there was dyed cotton in the 1988 sample proved to Rogers that the corner used to cut out the radiocarbon samples included the medieval reweaving. In other words, in the repairs made through the 1500s, sixteenth-century cotton was interwoven into first-century linen. That was the hypothesis that raised the possibility that the result of the carbon dating was wrong. The medieval cotton fibers interwoven into the sample could well have accounted for the carbon-14 test result that dated the Shroud somewhere around 1260 to 1390 A.D."

"Weren't there any samples for carbon-14 testing taken by STURP in 1978?" Castle asked.

"In 1978, the Church did not allow the STURP scientists to take samples for radiocarbon testing," Middagh answered. "But Rogers applied a different test to determine the likely age of the linen in the main body of the Shroud. From the tests made on the Shroud's linen, Rogers evaluated the rate of loss of vanillin in the linen fibers. Vanillin disappears in the thermal decomposition of lignin, a complex polymer that is in the cells of the flax plants used to make linen. The Dead Sea scroll linens, for instance, have lost all traces of vanillin. From this analysis, Rogers concluded that the linen in the main body of the Shroud also had lost vanillin. Hence the Shroud itself was much older than the carbon dating suggested, very possibly reaching back two thousand years to the time of Christ."

"Why did Rogers wait so long after the 1988 radiocarbon tests were announced to publish his results?" Castle pressed. "I can understand why some in the Shroud research community may be having trouble with Rogers. I have to ask you again: How do you know Rogers didn't just have a convenient change of opinion just before he died, as if he didn't want to be on the wrong side of the bet just in case there was a God and the Shroud was authentic? Well-known atheists making similar conversions just before they die might not be as rare as you think."

"If you knew Rogers, that is an especially good question," Middagh said. "When Rogers was healthy, he was characteristically outspoken. Before his change of mind, Rogers had been famous for saying he did not believe in miracles that defied the laws of nature. So, when the carbon-14 results were first published, Rogers was happy to dismiss the Shroud as a hoax. Still, Rogers was a credible scientist and he published the results of his microchemical tests in a credible peer-reviewed journal, even if he published the results posthumously. In my mind, the questions Rogers raised still stand, at least until the Church allows other, more representative samples from the main body of the Shroud to be taken and carbon-14 tested."

Morelli decided to jump in here, to support what Middagh was saying. "When Rogers published his results posthumously, it made a huge impact on the entire scientific community studying the Shroud, including me. When an outspoken expert like Rogers, who played a lead role in the 1978 STURP chemical analysis of the Shroud, publicly changed his mind on the accuracy of the radiocarbon dating, I began to doubt whether the carbon-14 results were representative of the Shroud as a whole. If medieval reweaving tainted the sample and the carbon-dating tests were biased as a consequence, the possibility was open once again that the Shroud might date from the time of Christ. Before he died, Rogers wrote on the Internet unequivocally that, in his opinion, the sample chosen for dating was totally invalid for determining the true age of the Shroud."

Though he listened carefully to the arguments Middagh and Morelli were making, Castle was still not 100 percent convinced. He made a mental note that Rogers's change of heart would have been more convincing if he had done his studies immediately after the 1988 carbon tests were announced, not after he knew he had cancer and just before he died.

Considering the carbon-dating discussion over for now, Castle looked through the notes he had taken in his telephone discussion with Gabrielli. "What about this medieval letter Bishop Pierre d'Arcis wrote to the pope in 1389, claiming the Shroud was a painting and that he knew who the artist was?"

"Scholars have argued the letter was motivated by jealousy and money more than an honest desire to state the truth about the authenticity of the Shroud," Middagh explained. "At the time the letter was written, Pierre d'Arcis was the bishop of Troyes and the Shroud was being exhibited in the nearby town of Lirey. Pierre d'Arcis did not like the pilgrims with their bags of gold going to a neighboring town and bypassing him. I'm pretty sure the letter might never have been written if the Shroud had been shown in Troyes."

Castle, no stranger to charging fees, appreciated the motive.

"Besides, we know the image on the Shroud was not painted," Middagh said. "The Shroud of Turin Research Project in 1978 tested on linen every painter's pigment known to have been used before 1532. Extensive tests were conducted on the samples to see how the pigments would have suffered the massive fire of that year. The medieval paints were chemically modified in fire and would have been washed away in the water that was used to extinguish the fire. Medieval paints were water-soluble and the 1978 STURP tests showed that no part of the image currently on the Shroud is soluble in water."

Castle was beginning to conclude that for every argument the skeptics produced about the Shroud, the believers managed to concoct a response. He wondered if he would ever get to the bottom of the debate with definitive scientific proof, one way or the other. It amused Castle, but in a way the case for the authenticity of the Shroud was a lot like the question about God's existence. Logic and science were not going to prove the Shroud was authentic, but he wondered if logic and science might end up disproving the authenticity of the Shroud. That's what so fascinated Castle about the work Gabrielli was proposing to do.

"So, you are convinced the Shroud was not painted?" Castle asked Middagh.

"Yes, I am," Middagh answered. "The image does not penetrate into the linen fibers the way you would expect paint to penetrate the cloth. At best, the image is one fiber deep, almost as if the image lies on top of the linen fibers. No fibers are cemented together, as you would expect paint to do, and the image does not cross fibers. The image areas are very brittle, with the image on the surface like what you would expect from material that had oxidized by dehydration. All the colored fibers are evenly colored such that an exposed fiber is either colored or not colored. There is no density of coloration on the fibers. What shading is apparent comes from the number of colored fibers we observe microscopically in any given unit area of the Shroud, not from a deeper or denser coloration of the fibers. The colored fibers are very uniformly colored. None of these observations are what we would expect if an artist had painted the image on the linen. The body image rests only on the very top of the fibers. The way the image is placed on the Shroud is consistent throughout—on the full-body dorsal image that resulted from the body laid on the Shroud and the distinct full-frontal body image that resulted when the Shroud was folded lengthwise over the body's head. Even though the body rested on the Shroud, the dorsal body image is also very lightly placed on the top of the fibers."

"I'm not an expert on medieval painting," Castle said, "but I've studied a lot of medieval paintings in Italian museums. The painter of the Renaissance who most studied anatomy was Leonardo da Vinci. I've spent hours examining his *Adoration of the Magi* at the Uffizi in Florence. There's never been a question

Leonardo was a genius and he used a sfumato style of painting in which he lightly created his images. Why isn't Leonardo a candidate for having painted the Shroud?"

"He is a candidate," Middagh admitted. "One problem is that Leonardo wasn't born until 1452 and the Church can date the Shroud earlier than that, certainly to the fourteenth century. The documented provenance of the Shroud that we know is the linen cloth in Turin goes back to the 1350s, when a descendant of Geoffrey de Charney, the Knight Templar who was burned at the stake with Jacques de Molay, the famous last Grand Master of the Knights Templar, had the Shroud first displayed to the public at a local church in Lirey, France. In other words, we can trace the history of the Shroud of Turin to a date before Leonardo was born."

Even that did not deter Castle. "There is one other possibility," he said. "Maybe the Savoy royal family who owned the Shroud in Lirey and brought it from France to Turin in Italy asked Leonardo to reproduce the Shroud to replace an earlier shroud that was an obvious forgery. Knowing Leonardo's expertise with human anatomy and the subtlety of his painting techniques, the Savoy family might have figured Leonardo's replacement forgery would be more convincing than their original. Why can't we assume Leonardo obtained a piece of linen made in the time frame of 1260 to 1390 A.D. that he thought would work? What if it turned out that Leonardo's shroud was so superior that the Dukes of Savoy destroyed the Shroud of Lirey and replaced it with Leonardo's duplicate? That would have allowed him to have been the artist in a theory consistent with the carbon-14-dating result."

"I understand your point," Middagh said, "but there are several problems, not the least of which is that we have no documentation historically that Leonardo ever worked in Turin or that he ever received a commission from the Savoy royal family."

"But it's an odd coincidence that the famous Leonardo self-portrait showing him as an old man with flowing hair down to his shoulders and a long beard ends up even today in Turin, one of the prize possessions of the Savoy family royal library in Turin," Castle added.

"I too once suspected Leonardo as the painter of the Shroud," Father Morelli interjected. "We also know Leonardo experimented with the camera obscura."

"How would a camera obscura be involved?" Castle asked.

"The camera obscura was a primitive light box that involved an early lens," Morelli explained. "The light box was constructed to capture through the lens an image from life that showed up upside down, with the top of the image showing up on the bottom, projected onto the back wall of the light box. The image could also be projected onto a cloth or canvas for painting. Leonardo also experimented with a wide variety of light-sensitive materials, including many wood resins and various tinctures made from plants and leaves."

Middagh jumped in. "But the theory is not that Leonardo painted the Shroud. I can't stress enough that the Shroud of Turin Research Project concluded in their 1981 final report that no pigments, paints, dyes, or stains were found on the Shroud's fibers. Over a five-day period in 1978, the Shroud of Turin Research Project did a definitive scientific analysis of the Shroud, using X-ray fluorescence analysis, ultraviolet fluorescence photography, and infrared photography, as well as microphotography and microchemical analysis. Their findings that there was no paint of any kind on the Shroud is still the definitive analysis."

"So why did you consider Leonardo a candidate?" Castle asked Morelli.

"The dates of the first known exhibitions of the Shroud in Lirey do rule out Leonardo," Morelli said. "But the most interesting theory is that Leonardo created the first photographic image when he produced the Shroud. The idea is that Leonardo may have coated the linen with a light-sensitive chemical mixture and projected the image onto the linen using a camera obscura. Books have been written arguing that the face of the man in the Shroud resembles images we have of Leonardo—most importantly the Leonardo self-portrait that is kept at the Biblioteca Reale in Turin. There have been a few books claiming that Leonardo used himself as the face in creating the Shroud as a photographic image. In other words, the authors argued that what we have in the Shroud is not the image of Jesus Christ, but a photographic image of Leonardo da Vinci."

"You reject that theory now?" Castle asked.

"I do," Morelli said. "There is no evidence in any of Leonardo's existing codex manuscripts that indicate he experimented with photography. He writes extensively about using a camera obscura, but as far as I can figure out, Leonardo used the camera obscura to assist him in his drawing and painting. None of Leonardo's existing notebooks discuss any experimentation with plants or chemicals to produce light-sensitive formulas."

"Aren't some of Leonardo's codex notebooks missing?" Castle asked.

"Yes," Morelli said. "But there is no corroborating evidence from anything written in Leonardo's lifetime that he came up with anything resembling photography. No image survives from the fifteenth century that even remotely resembles photography. The modern attempts to produce a Shroud-like image by photographic methods that would have possibly been known in the thirteenth to fifteenth centuries look crude, nothing like the Shroud. But still, the most important problem is that the dates don't work. No matter how you look at it, Leonardo was born after we can document that the Shroud had been exhibited at Lirey in France, and photography wasn't invented until about two hundred years ago."

"There's one more important piece of evidence," Middagh added.

"What's that?"

"There's human blood hemoglobin and blood serum on the Shroud, and the blood serum is only evident in ultraviolet fluorescence," Middagh said. "There is no way any artist in medieval times could have used ultraviolet fluorescence to paint human blood serum on the Shroud so it could be discovered centuries later, when UV fluorescence was invented. Besides, how would an artist paint blood serum that is invisible to the eye on specific places on the Shroud? Medical doctors examining the Shroud confirm the blood found on the Shroud, including the blood serum, is exactly where they would expect to find blood traces if the wounds displayed on the body of the man in the Shroud came from a crucifixion."

Castle, a medical doctor with extensive surgical experience, wanted to know more about the blood detected on the Shroud. "How exactly does the blood appear on the Shroud? Does the blood appear only on the top fibrils, as does the image of the body? Or does the blood saturate the Shroud?"

"Most of the blood we observe on the Shroud comes from direct contact the linen had with the body," Middagh answered. "The most prominent bloodstains appear as solid stains, for instance the blood streaming from the wrist wounds or the blood on the forehead from what would have been the crown of thorns. These bloodstains penetrate the Shroud, and so on the frontal image, the bloodstains from the crown of thorns show up on the part of the cloth resting on the body and bleed through to the top of the cloth. The same is the case with the dorsal image. Pools of blood resulting from direct contact with the body do saturate the Shroud. Even more interesting, the Shroud of Turin Research Project found that the bloodstains on the Shroud are composed of hemoglobin with high concentrations of bilirubin, which would suggest blood flows from wounds that were clotting. In other words, the blood flows that penetrated the Shroud occurred while the crucified man was yet alive. That these blood wounds show up on the Shroud means the crucified man was placed in the Shroud almost immediately after death, without being washed or embalmed."

"But these are not the only type of bloodstain we see on the Shroud, right?" Morelli asked, prompting Middagh to elaborate.

"Right," Middagh answered, picking up the discussion. "As I mentioned, the blood on the Shroud also gives a positive test for serum albumin. Under ultraviolet fluorescence photography, the serum separation shows up as a lighter ring around a darker blood center, very typical of postmortem blood flows. The serum stains were not visible to the naked eye but were clearly seen in the ultraviolet fluorescence photography. So, the bloodstains tell a very complex story of the wounds suffered by the man in the Shroud in life, as well as the blood that drained from the body after death."

"So far, I think I follow what you are saying," Castle said.

"Just to be sure, let me recap," Middagh responded, wanting to make sure the discussion was clear to everyone. "The evidence suggests that the crucified man was laid on the Shroud almost immediately after death. The blood flows suggest the man was placed in the Shroud without being washed clean or in any way embalmed or otherwise prepared for burial. We see the same evidence on the front and back images of the man in the Shroud. Remember, the Shroud wrapped over the man's head to cover his front side. This accounts for the head-to-head images of the man's front and backside we see on the Shroud's approximately fourteen-foot full length."

"Dr. Castle, as a physician, I'm sure you can appreciate what the presence of the hemoglobin and serum albumin on the Shroud mean," Father Morelli said.

"I believe I'm following what's been said so far," Castle answered, "but why don't you tell me what specifically you have in mind. I want to make sure I understand your point precisely."

"Just this," Morelli continued. "The blood evidence on the Shroud either means the image was imprinted on the linen of the Shroud by a body that had suffered the injuries we see, or by a forger who painted in blood and appreciated not only the anatomical nature of the wounds, but also the exact nature of the blood flow that would have resulted from crucifixion wounds while the victim was alive, as well as from the serum flow that would have continued even into death."

"I don't rule out an expert forger," Castle said directly. Morelli had a point. "Many people in the Middle Ages were as brilliant as today, even if they lacked our modern technology."

"The forger would have had to have been sufficiently brilliant to have painted onto the Shroud serum stains not visible to the naked eye, anticipating that in later centuries we would have and use the type of ultraviolet fluorescence technology we would need to check for serum in attempting to document the authenticity of the Shroud," Morelli added.

"Are you saying Leonardo wasn't that brilliant?" Castle countered.

"In Leonardo da Vinci's day, the study of anatomy was pretty primitive and the understanding of blood composition and circulation was not well advanced," Morelli responded.

Middagh interrupted this discussion to draw everyone's attention to a point in the discussion he wanted to make sure no one missed. "There's an important conclusion we can draw about the blood we find on the Shroud," Middagh said. "The bloodstains that penetrate through the Shroud and show up on the backside of the Shroud are very different from how the body image formed on the Shroud. We know the blood and serum inhibited the image formation on the Shroud. The Shroud of Turin Research Team in 1978 had instruments that could detect parts per billion of any substance on the Shroud, and the scientists concluded there is no body image under the blood and serum stains. What this means is that the blood flows from life and the blood serum draining from the body after death were both imprinted on the Shroud first, when the body was laid on the Shroud and it was pulled over the head to cover the front part of the body. The body image formed on the Shroud at a later time. In other words, frontal and dorsal body images appear to have been imprinted on the Shroud simultaneously, sometime after the body had rested in the Shroud and after all blood fluids had stopped draining from the body."

"What exactly is your point?" Castle asked.

"My point is simple," Middagh answered. "We know from studying the Shroud that there were two distinct steps in which the image was formed: first the blood was deposited by direct contact, then the body image was formed subsequently by a process we don't understand."

"What can you tell me about the wrist wounds?" Castle asked Middagh, wanting to know what the Shroud might tell him about Father Bartholomew's stigmata.

Middagh searched through his slides until he found the one he wanted, a close-up of the wrist wounds on the man in the Shroud. The image he displayed on the projection screen showed somewhat more of the man's body than did the close-up of the hands and wrists that Morelli had brought with him from the Vatican.

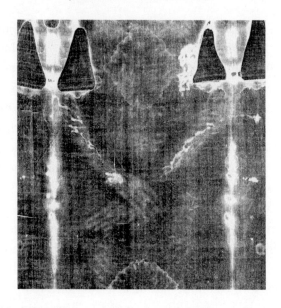

Middagh continued: "Most classical pictures of Jesus show him being crucified by being nailed through the palms of the hands. But as you can see here, the man in the Shroud appears to have been nailed through the wrists. It is an interesting detail, but none of the four gospels that discuss the crucifixion—Matthew, Mark, Luke, or John—say whether Christ was tied or nailed to the cross. Most of the ancient crucifixion nails recovered by archeologists in excavations throughout the wider regions of the Roman Empire give no indication what limb they had pierced. But we know the ancient Romans nailed people to the cross if they wanted the crucifixion to be particularly brutal or particularly short, and Church tradition supports that Christ was nailed to the cross."

Castle wanted to make sure he understood the negative image he was looking at. "Don't most negatives have a mirror effect in which, for instance, right is transformed to left in the negative?" he asked. "The negative shows the left arm crossed over the right arm. Is this really the other way around?"

"You're right, in that sorting out the right/left orientations of various images of the Shroud is confusing, even for experts," Middagh said. "But since the Shroud itself is a negative image, the mirror-effect reversal occurs in what we see in the Shroud with the naked eye. If you look at the Shroud, it appears the right hand is crossed over the left. I'm showing you a photographic negative, which once again reverses left to right and vice versa. In other words, the photographic negative has it right. In the corpse of the man in the Shroud, the left hand was crossed over the right. All the photographic negatives I am going to show you are correct for the left/right orientation of the man in the Shroud as he was buried."

"Thank you for explaining that," Castle said. "I'm beginning to get the point that the photographic negatives are perhaps the best way to see the crucified body of the man in the Shroud."

"I agree," Middagh said. "I'm showing you the negative photographs because the image is more clearly seen when the brownish-red image on the Shroud is transformed into the white and gray-tone shadings of the negative. Also, I'm showing you the negative photographs because the left/right orientations you see in the negative are true to the left/right orientation of the cruci-fied man himself. If you don't follow all this technical discussion precisely, it doesn't matter. Just remember that the images I'm showing you have been flipped appropriately so you are looking at the body the way it would have looked in death."

Studying the wrist and forearms image, Castle could see the wound in the wrist of the man in the Shroud correctly po-sitioned in the carpal area, the right place for a crucifixion, and the absence of the thumbs in the image confirmed once again Castle's presumption that driving a nail through the wrist in that location had probably damaged the median nerve, causing the thumb to bend back reflexively into the palm of each hand.

All this was consistent with his earlier discussion with Morelli and with Dr. Lin's analysis of Father Bartholomew's wrist wounds.

Looking closely at what appeared to be two streams of blood flow on the left forearm, Castle judged both streams of blood had come from the same puncture wound in the wrist. He estimated that the arms would have been extended at about a 65-degree angle with the horizontal to cause the blood to flow in the pattern he was observing on the forearms. The blood flows appeared to extend from the wrist to the elbow, which would have been consistent with the outstretching of the arm in crucifixion. Castle was beginning to have no doubt that in the Shroud he was looking at the image of a crucified man.

Whoever forged the Shroud in medieval times had to have a remarkable understanding of human anatomy and the mechanics of crucifixion to have produced an image that would stand up to current medical analysis confirmed by twenty-first-century technology.

"Again, we don't know exactly what the cross that Christ died upon looked like," Middagh said. "Typically the vertical beam of the cross stood permanently implanted at the place of execution. The victim often carried the crossbeam to the place of crucifixion, with the crossbeam carried on the shoulders, behind the nape of the neck, like a yoke. The Roman executioners pulled back the condemned man's arms to hook them over the crossbeam to hold and balance it. At the place of crucifixion, the victim was nailed to the crossbeam at the wrists, or the arms were bound and tied to the crossbeam. The Roman executioners then used forked poles and maybe a pulley to lift the crossbeam up to where it could be slotted into a notch at the top of the vertical beam to form the cross. Depending on how deep the notch was cut, the crossbeam might have been flush with the vertical beam, like the cross-stroke on the letter *T,* or maybe it fit into a deeper slot, forming the traditional four-point cross we see in most religious paintings from the Renaissance period until today."

Castle listened, with his mind translating what he was hearing into medical detail. With the massive trauma the arms of a crucified man suffered from bearing the weight of his body, especially as the horizontal beam of the cross was lifted to the vertical beam, there was no doubt nails had to be placed through the wrist. Otherwise, the crucified man could fall off the crossbeam as it was being elevated to the vertical beam of the cross. If the crucified man were to stay on the cross any length of time, the arms would end up supporting his weight, so the wrists had to be pinned to the crossbeam firmly enough so as to not come loose. Had the Shroud of Turin demonstrated anything different, it could be disqualified immediately as an artist's rendering. Whether Father Bartholomew appreciated the medical facts of crucifixion or whether he was merely manifesting what his subconscious recorded from the Shroud, Castle did not know. But Father Bartholomew's stigmata were also in his wrists, not the palms of his hands.

Looking closely at the projected image, Castle clearly recognized what appeared to be the scourge marks he saw manifested on Bartholomew yesterday. Looking at the photographs of the Shroud that Morelli had shown him from the Vatican, Castle had not focused on the scourge wounds, although those were obviously apparent in the body above and below the crossed arms, once you began looking for them. "Are those the scourge wounds that appear to cover the body?" Castle asked Middagh.

"Yes," Middagh said. "Let me show you a close-up image of the scourge wounds suffered by the man in the Shroud."

Middagh projected onto the screen a dorsal image showing the scourge wounds on the shoulders and back of the body.

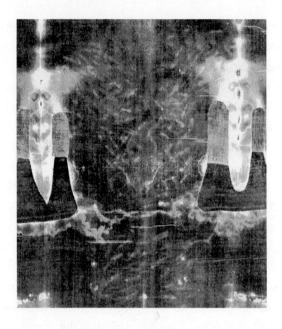

"As you can see, the man in the Shroud shows signs of an extensive beating from a whip. The scourge wounds are especially heavy on the shoulders and the backs, extending down the buttocks and the back of the legs. I have other images here that show the same pattern of scourge marks on the man's front side, although there are not as many scourge wounds on the chest or front of the legs as there are on the backside."

Seeing these wounds now, Castle could see the obvious resemblance to the wounds he saw on Bartholomew Sunday.

"We have to get detailed photos of Father Bartholomew's wounds," Father Morelli said insistently. "From what I saw of Father Bartholomew in the ER, I believe the wounds he suffered all over his body will match precisely what we are seeing as the scourge wounds on the Shroud."

Silently, Castle agreed.

"If this is the historical Jesus Christ we are looking at in the

Shroud, then the wounds on the Shroud document exactly where Jesus was beaten," Morelli said. "I believe we are going to find one-for-one that Father Bartholomew has exactly the same wounds that we are seeing on this slide right here, not more and not fewer, but precisely these."

"I've already ordered Dr. Lin at Beth Israel Hospital to take very detailed examinations of Father Bartholomew's body wounds, not just photographic, but also CT scans, as well as a full-body MRI," Castle commented, "as soon as Father Bartholomew is strong enough to undergo that."

"We look forward to seeing the results of those tests," Archbishop Duncan said.

"My guess, Archbishop Duncan, is that Father Morelli's supposition is correct," Castle added. "I too suspect Father Bartholomew suffered these exact wounds Sunday night. Where we differ is most likely in the interpretation. Even if the wounds Father Bartholomew suffered are identical in every detail to the scourge wounds we appear to see on the man in the Shroud, that still does not prove Father Bartholomew is manifesting miraculously the wounds Christ suffered in his passion and death. Father Bartholomew told me he has studied the Shroud for a long time. His years of study undoubtedly impressed on his subconscious all the details of the Shroud we are looking at today."

Archbishop Duncan was skeptical. "Do you really believe the subconscious is that powerful?"

"Yes, Archbishop Duncan, I do," Castle said without hesitation. "Your subconscious is what keeps your body going. You depend on your subconscious to keep your heart beating and your blood circulating. Your subconscious regulates your breathing. You have to consciously override your subconscious to hold your breath. I could go on. What do you think keeps you alive during the night? It isn't your conscious mind."

Anne was fixated on a more fundamental part of the discussion. "Does all this mean my brother was scourged exactly like Jesus was scourged at the pillar?" she asked, her voice giving away the horror she felt at the thought.

"Maybe yes and maybe no," Castle answered. "Not to be flip, but I don't want us jumping to conclusions. First off, we don't know that your brother's wounds are going to match what we are seeing here exactly, not at least until I compare the hospital photos of his wounds to the wounds we are seeing on the Shroud. But most important, I don't want anybody jumping to the conclusion that Bartholomew is suffering a repeat of Christ's passion, not even if the wounds are identical. I'm a psychiatrist and I'm interested in what's going on in Father Bartholomew's mind. For me, his body manifests his mental reality, possibly his religious beliefs. That's as far as I'm prepared to go right now."

"We all understand," Archbishop Duncan said, making sure everyone in the room knew he was not disagreeing with Dr. Castle's analysis by insisting on any different interpretation, at least not right now. "I understand your point about the subconscious. We don't want to jump to any conclusions here."

While they were talking, Middagh found and displayed another image from the Shroud, this time a detailed close-up of a group of scourge wounds on the upper back of the man in the Shroud. The close-up clearly showed the dumbbell nature of the wounds.

"The ancient Romans typically scourged a man before they crucified him, both to further punish him as a criminal and to weaken him so he would put up less resistance when they ultimately fixed him to the cross," Middagh said. "The Romans could also control how long a man would survive the crucifixion by how severely they beat a condemned man. The more vicious the scourging, the shorter the time a crucified man would live on the

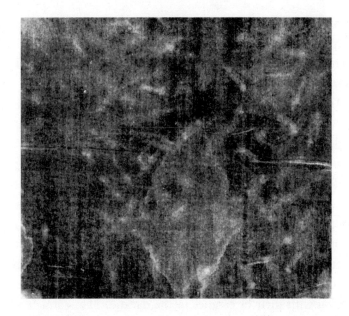

cross. Judging from the beating the man in the Shroud received, the Roman executioners wanted him to die pretty fast. Jesus went up to Jerusalem at the time of his death to celebrate Passover. Traditionally, the Last Supper is interpreted as a Passover meal. From the beating the man of the Shroud received, the Romans may have wanted Jesus to die fast, so he could be buried before sundown on the Sabbath."

Castle listened to the historical explanation but his mind was focused on the wounds themselves. The dumbbell nature of the wounds from the Shroud seen in close-up looked exactly like the wounds he observed on Bartholomew.

Middagh picked up on this exact point. "As you can see here in the close-up of the scourge wounds on the upper back, each wound shows the dumbbell-shaped weights the Romans fixed into the ends of the leather straps of their whips. Typically, the Romans used a handheld whip, or flagrum, a short handle with two or three leather thongs attached. Sometimes, instead of a dumb-bell piece of metal, the Romans just fixed two small metal balls on the ends of the leather thongs, a configuration that caused the wounds to look like dumbbell wounds just the same."

Anne could not believe what she was seeing. "How could Father Bartholomew be beaten like that and survive?" she asked Castle in disbelief.

"Right now, we are not sure how your brother was injured," Castle answered, irritated that hospitals were notorious rumor mills. All Anne had to do was ask a few questions and the nurses and orderlies would probably have filled her in on all the gossip about her brother. Immediately, Castle's mind flashed on the television reporter who accosted him leaving the hospital last night and on the crowd of silent believers who held vigil outside the hospital with their lit candles in the darkness. How much additional information did Fernando Ferrar have by now to broadcast on television?

Reluctantly, Castle realized this was going to be an impossible story to contain, even if he gave no press conferences. He suspected Anne was already concluding her brother was replicating the passion of Christ. He was certain that in no time at all the story that Father Bartholomew had been mysteriously scourged by unseen assailants would be circulating throughout New York City, possibly around the world, now with the added detail that the scourge wounds he manifested were exactly like the scourge wounds on the Shroud of Turin, wound for wound, blow for blow.

Just then Castle's cell phone rang. It was the hospital. Bartholomew was coming out of sedation. The nurse on duty was calling him as instructed, so he could be there to examine the priest as soon as he was once again conscious.

"I'm sorry," Castle told the group in his conference room. "But we're going to have to resume this at another time. The hospital just called and Father Bartholomew is coming around. I've got to get there immediately."

"I want to come with you," Anne said urgently.

Morelli chimed in: "I'd like to go as well."

"No," Castle said politely but firmly. "Neither one of you has any medical training as far as I know. I'm sure there will be an appropriate time for you to visit with him, but now I need to examine my patient alone."

"I'd like some time to speak with you privately," Anne said. "Can we arrange a time to get together?"

Thinking quickly, Castle realized he could use the drive time questioning Anne, to find out exactly how she fit into Father Bartholomew's life and why nobody seemed to know anything about her, until now. Asking to meet with him privately, Anne must have seen the same need to explain her background in more detail, Castle guessed.

"Okay, you can ride with me in the car to the hospital," Castle said. "That will give us a few minutes to get started."

"Thank you," Anne said appreciatively. "When we get to the hospital, I promise I will stay out of your way."

"Father Morelli, you join Anne in the waiting room of the ICU at Beth Israel, if you want, this afternoon," Castle instructed. "If everything goes well, you and Anne should be able to visit with Father Bartholomew for a few minutes later today, after I examine him."

"I'll do that," Morelli said appreciatively.

Next, Castle turned to apologize to Archbishop Duncan for having to leave the meeting so abruptly. "You will excuse me, your Eminence, but I have to leave immediately," he explained. Castle wanted to be sure he was properly respectful, especially with Fathers Morelli and Middagh, two representatives of the Vatican, in the room. "I'm sure you will understand, but I want to be the first to talk with Father Bartholomew when he regains consciousness."

"Certainly," Archbishop Duncan said graciously, as Castle gathered up his papers to leave. "We are available to you on a twenty-four-hour basis. The pope has made it clear that right now nothing is more important to the Catholic Church than Father Bartholomew and the Shroud of Turin."

CHAPTER THIRTEEN

Thursday noon
Return to Beth Israel Hospital
Day 15

Castle sat with Anne in the back of the limo headed downtown. He estimated the ride would take about twenty minutes, depending on traffic, and he instructed the driver to get to the hospital as fast as possible.

Riding with Anne, Castle felt conflicted. He had to admit he was physically attracted to Anne, yet he was uncomfortable not knowing who exactly she was and how she fit into the puzzle.

"You'll have to excuse me," he began, "but I'm still not sure how your family history fits together. You said your father separated from your mother shortly after you were born."

"That's right," Anne said. She folded her hands quietly in her lap, resolved to tell Dr. Castle the story. "My mother and Jonathan Bartholomew, the man who was Paul's father, had been high school sweethearts. That was over forty years ago, when the Vietnam War was reaching its height under President Nixon. Jonathan got drafted in the 1970 lottery and was sent off to Vietnam. A few months later, my mother heard he had been killed in combat. She mourned his loss. After that, she met my father. They got married and I was born."

"So why did Paul tell me he had no siblings?" Castle asked.

"A few months after I was born, Paul's father-to-be unexpectedly came walking out of the Vietnam bush. Everybody was shocked. Jonathan Bartholomew was treated as a hero. It turns out he had been captured by the Viet Cong and he escaped. But when he came back to the United States, my mother was already married to my father and she was pregnant with me."

"Okay," Castle said patiently, used to hearing complicated life stories from his patients. "What happened then?"

"My mother was always in love with Jonathan. When he came home, she began seeing him, even more in love with him than ever. She tried to hide the relationship from my father, Matthew Cassidy, but it didn't work. When my father found out, he gave my mother a choice."

"Is that when they got divorced?"

"Not immediately," Anne said. "My mother said she would try to stay in the marriage. But when I was about one year old, my mother announced she wanted a divorce. My father took it very hard, but granted her the divorce, on the condition that she would agree to give him sole custody over me. My mother agreed. Once the court decree was final, my father moved to Canada with me as an infant. My father never saw my mother again. After that, my mother married Jonathan Bartholomew and Paul was born about a year later."

"Did you ever reconcile with your mother?"

"No, I didn't. My father told me my mother had died giving birth to me. When I found out the truth, I learned I had a brother I never knew about. But I didn't attempt to contact Paul, out of respect for my father."

"How did you find out the truth?"

"My father died a year ago, of cancer. When I was going through his papers to settle his estate, I found the divorce papers. That's when I discovered who my mother really was. I did some research and found out the true story, including that Paul was my brother."

"What happened to Paul's father?" Castle asked.

"I'm not sure," she answered, "but from the research I did, it seems Paul's father was killed tragically in a work-related accident, about three months before Paul was born. As best I can find out, Paul never knew his father, just like he never knew anything about me."

Anne's information about Paul's father fit what Bartholomew had told Castle, that he never knew his father because his father had been killed before he was born. Castle felt sure that when Bartholomew had insisted he was an only child, the priest's mother had never told him anything about having a different husband and a daughter born prior to her marriage with his father. Father Bartholomew was certainly in for a surprise.

"What was your mother's name?" Castle asked.

"Anne, just like me," she answered. "As I explained, my father was Matthew Cassidy and Paul's father was Jonathan Bartholomew."

"Did you try to see your mother after you found out about her?"

"No," Anne said quietly. "It was too late. She had died a few years earlier."

"And you say you never met your brother until now?"

"No, we've never even spoken."

Still, Castle wanted to make sure he understood how the pieces fit together. "But when I saw you in the hospital, you said you came from Montreal to be with your brother. What I guess

I didn't fully appreciate was that you had never seen him before. What you are telling me now is that Paul still does not know you exist."

"That's right," Anne said. "It's all happened so fast since my father died. I wasn't sure what I wanted to do about meeting my brother. But then, when I read on the Internet about Paul suffering the stigmata, I realized I had to come here and be with him."

"So, in the last year or so, you knew you had a brother, but you never made any effort to contact him. I want to make sure I have that right."

"That's right," she said. "Like I said, I'm still not sure Paul knows anything about me, just like I knew nothing about him until after my father died. I'm not sure how much our mother, Anne, told Paul about her true family history before she died."

Castle listened carefully to her story, determined to watch how Bartholomew greeted his sister once they were introduced at the hospital.

"What do you do in Montreal?" Castle asked.

"I'm an accountant, a numbers person. I work for a Canadian export firm. We export wood products to the United States."

"And you never married?"

"No, I guess I never found the right person."

There were parts of the story that made sense to Castle. He could understand why Anne never married. He himself had not found another woman he felt was capable of replacing Elizabeth in his life. Finding the right person was hard, especially as he got older. He enjoyed his relationships with women, but typically they were casual—a dinner date, or a theater date. Women friends were easy, but living with a woman seemed to involve a lot of compromises in a lifestyle he was pretty happy to not change at all, especially the older he got.

Still, he had to admit, he wasn't sure he accepted as true every-thing about her story as she told it. "Just out of curiosity," he said, "I would like to see those divorce papers. It might help me bet-ter understand Paul's relationship with his mother." Castle knew seeing the divorce papers would provide confirmation for Anne's story.

"The only problem," Anne said, "is that I left all my papers in Canada. About all I have with me is my Canadian passport." She reached in her purse and retrieved it. "You're free to take a look at this, if you want."

Castle looked through the passport. She was identified as Anne Cassidy, and the date of birth worked. Her residence was listed as a street address in Montreal. The passport photo was clearly Anne. It was reassuring to Castle that the passport information confirmed her story.

Still, as a professional psychiatrist, he suspected there were many more levels to the story that Anne wasn't telling him, at least not right away. Almost certainly there were psychological implica-tions to her birth and the separation of her parents that Anne had not fully appreciated herself, especially since she had learned the truth so recently. How had she felt when she learned her mother abandoned her and that her father had lied to her all these years? Unless Castle placed Anne in analysis, he was not sure this ques-tion would ever be fully answered. Still, Castle felt confident that when Anne met her brother, she was certain to confront aspects of herself and her brother's birth story that were impacting deep levels of her subconscious right now, even if Anne could not yet perceive the impact consciously.

Castle also appreciated there were serious implications of this birth story for Bartholomew. If Bartholomew did not know about his mother's first marriage, how would he react when he learned his mother had hidden the truth from him that his father was not her first husband? Would he resent not being told he had a half sister living in Canada? A half sister he had never known existed? The questions raced through Castle's mind as he listened to Anne tell her life story in the limo.

The situation was complicated for Castle. Being truthful, he had to admit he continued to feel attracted to Anne, just as he had been the first moment he saw her. The thought passed through his mind that even though she was not in her twenties, Anne could probably have attracted a suitable man to marry her anytime she wanted, including now. Sitting with her in the backseat, he couldn't help admiring how her nicely sculpted legs looked in her sheer nylon stockings, especially as her dress rode up above her knees.

"Did you find a hotel room easily last night?" he asked her.

"I found a cheap room near the hospital," Anne said. "The hotel is okay and it's close to the hospital."

Despite the physical attraction he felt, Castle would never cross the line to act on those impulses with a patient or a member of a patient's family. Castle reminded himself that his concerns with Anne had to remain professional. Now that she had surfaced, she was certain to fit into his analysis of Father Bartholomew. Castle's instinct was to make sure Anne stayed more directly in his sight. Her story had too many psychological implications to be ignored. "It sounds like this may be your first time in New York?" Castle guessed.

"It is," Anne affirmed.

"Let me take care of the hotel room for you," Castle said. "You're in New York now and this is my city." Without waiting for her to respond, he reached for his cell phone in the pocket of his sport jacket and began dialing a number.

Listening, Anne realized he was calling the manager's office at the Waldorf Towers to reserve a one-bedroom corner suite on one of the upper floors for her, subtly making sure the suite was one of the larger and more elegant ones in the hotel.

From Castle's conversation with the manager, Anne could tell he was no stranger either to the Waldorf Towers or to the staff that ran the hotel. Castle asked for specific room details and appeared to know what the suite would look like simply by its room number.

"I don't know whether I can afford that level of luxury," Anne objected.

Castle smiled softly, pleased at her concern for expenses. "I'm not asking you to pay," he explained. "The Catholic Church is compensating me handsomely for taking your brother on as a patient and your accommodations at the Waldorf will be part of my expenses. I want to make sure you have a comfortable place to stay."

"Under those conditions, I accept," Anne said, feeling genuine appreciation for his concern over her.

As the limo approached the hospital, Castle could see that the crowd outside had swelled considerably. Hundreds more people were standing outside now and lit candles could be seen everywhere. A crowd had gathered in the open park across from the hospital main entrance. It was not standing silently, like before. This time there seemed to be a commotion going on. Observing closely, Castle was surprised to see people pointing up to the hospital rooms above.

Fernando Ferrar and his mobile video truck were on the scene, with Ferrar standing in front of the hospital giving what looked like a live remote broadcast from the scene. Ferrar's attention also seemed focused on one of the hospital rooms above.

Castle ordered the driver to take the limo to the private staff entrance underground.

As they entered the hospital, Castle made sure Anne was

comfortable in the ICU waiting room. Going down the hall to Father Bartholomew's room, Castle could see there was also a lot of commotion on the hospital floor.

"I've been dialing your cell phone," the chief nurse on duty said with relief as she saw Dr. Castle coming down the hall. "I'm glad you're finally here."

"We got here as quickly as we could," Castle responded. "What's the problem?"

"It's Father Bartholomew," she answered. "He's taken off all his bandages and he's standing at the windows without his hospital gown on. The nurses are trying to get him back into bed."

Entering the room, Castle could see Father Bartholomew standing at the window fully naked. His arms were outstretched as if he were being crucified and his head hung down on his chest as if he were still in his coma. Two nurses were trying to put a robe on him and get him back to bed, but Father Bartholomew wasn't cooperating. Castle was relieved to note the window came up to his waist, so that all Fernando Ferrar's television crew would get was a view of Father Bartholomew's chest and arms. But that was enough. No doubt Ferrar got what he needed for a national scoop.

On that point, Castle was precisely correct. Various hospital workers had tipped off Ferrar privately. He had been told that Father Bartholomew suffered the scourge wounds in addition to the stigmata on his wrists. Now he had visual proof for the world to see.

Dr. Castle took charge as he moved quickly to the priest at the window. He took a robe from one of the nurses and he began inserting Bartholomew's outstretched right arms into it. The nurse got the idea and she took over with the robe from there, determined to put the robe on Father Bartholomew whether he cooperated or not.

Speaking softly, Dr. Castle instructed Father Bartholomew to move away from the window, which he did. Step by step, Castle coached Bartholomew back to bed. He took the priest's blood pressure and he checked his pulse. Both were only slightly elevated. Looking at Bartholomew's chart, he could tell the priest had slept until about an hour earlier, when Castle got the call in his office that the priest had regained consciousness.

Seeing the priest naked, Castle was astonished to realize how remarkably Bartholomew's scourge wounds had healed. Gone were the open bleeding wounds, now covered in scabs and scars. He wanted to see Dr. Lin as soon as possible to see if the results Castle observed reflected internal healing of Father Bartholomew's wounds as well.

Once he was convinced Father Bartholomew was resting quietly and the nurses were back in control, Castle returned to the waiting room to tell Anne what had happened.

"I gave him a sedative and he's asleep again, resting quietly in bed," Castle explained to her. "The upset is over, for the time being, but I'm afraid you're going to have to wait here for a while longer. I have to meet one of the other doctors in the hospital to check up on the tests I had run on Father Bartholomew. After that, I will return here to examine Father Bartholomew."

"When will I be able to see him?" Anne asked.

"I'll check him again when I return and I will let you know then," Castle answered. "Meanwhile, please just rest comfortably here until I get back. Father Morelli will probably join you here shortly."

CHAPTER FOURTEEN

Thursday, early afternoon
Dr. Lin's office, Beth Israel Hospital
Day 15

Looking at the results of the previous day's tests in Dr. Lin's office, Castle was astonished to see what she had found.

She recounted the facts. "Father Bartholomew came to the ER with you on Sunday night. He had suffered what looked like wounds from a severe whip beating all over his body, front and back. The wounds were so severe that you had him admitted to the burn unit for treatment. This is Thursday afternoon, not quite four days later, and his wounds, as you can see, are nearly healed."

Castle took a close look at the CT scans and the MRIs. He could see that Dr. Lin was right.

"I don't understand it," Dr. Lin said. "I have never seen any case where wounds as severe as this patient suffered have healed so quickly."

"I don't have any medical explanation for it, either," Castle said. "Wounds as severe as what we observed in the burn unit should have taken weeks to heal."

Looking closely, Dr. Castle could see in Dr. Lin's tests the dumbbell shapes that marked the end of what appeared to be every lash of the whip. The CT scans and MRIs confirmed what he observed when he first checked Father Bartholomew's wounds in the hospital on Wednesday morning.

"I am going to ask a priest, Father Middagh, to come over here and meet with us," Castle said to Dr. Lin. "He is an expert on the Shroud of Turin."

"So you think Father Bartholomew's wounds are going to look like the wounds of the man in the Shroud?" Dr. Lin asked.

"There appears to be a resemblance," Castle said. "But remember, I'm a psychiatrist. I've established that Castle has studied the Shroud and his subconscious may be strong enough to have manifested those wounds by itself."

"Do you think Father Bartholomew is mentally ill?" she asked, following up.

"I haven't come to that conclusion yet. I'm just beginning the analysis."

"Just have Father Middagh call me directly," she said. "I'm sure I can make the time to see him today."

"What about the wrist wounds?" Castle asked. "Have they continued to heal?"

"That's another mystery," Dr. Lin said, turning to the CT scans and MRIs of Father Bartholomew's wrists. "In the first set of tests I ran, before these whipping wounds appeared, I noted that the wrist wounds had begun to heal from within."

"I remember that you could not confirm the wounds pierced completely through the wrists," Castle said.

"That's right," Lin said. "Now, in these tests I ran last night, the healing within the wrists is almost complete. The wrist wounds are only superficial wounds, on the top and back. I don't even see evidence of scar tissue within the wrists. It's almost as if the tissue has completely regenerated without any evidence of injury."

CHAPTER FIFTEEN

Thursday, late afternoon
Beth Israel Hospital
Day 15

I'm going to let you in to visit with Father Bartholomew," Dr. Castle told Father Morelli and Anne in the ICU waiting room. "But just for a few minutes. He is exhausted and he needs the rest."

From the moment Anne entered the room, Bartholomew sat up in bed, startled.

"Mother?" he asked in disbelief.

"No," Anne said, startled. "I'm your half sister."

"But I don't have a sister," Bartholomew said. "You look identical to my mother twenty years ago, when she was forty years old."

"My name is Anne," she said.

Bartholomew was startled as well. "Anne was my mother's name."

"I know," Anne said. "She was my mother, too, and I was named after her."

Observing closely, Castle concluded Bartholomew's reaction

confirmed the truth of Anne's story. Remarkable though it was, Bartholomew appeared to have had no idea that he had a half sister, let alone one who so closely resembled their mother, even in name.

Just then, Castle's cell phone rang. It was Dr. Lin. "Father Middagh has just joined me," she said. "Can you meet with us in my office?"

"Yes," Castle answered. "I'm still in the hospital. Do you mind if I bring Father Morelli with me? The pope sent him here from the Vatican to help us with Father Bartholomew's case."

"No problem. Bring him along."

Giving Anne some time alone to visit with her brother, Dr. Castle and Father Morelli headed off to Dr. Lin's office. Castle was looking forward to comparing Father Middagh's images of the man in the Shroud with the CT scans and MRIs that Dr. Lin had taken of Father Bartholomew.

When Castle and Morelli arrived, Middagh was already hard at work analyzing the two sets of images. "It's remarkable," Father Middagh told Castle and Morelli as they settled into Dr. Lin's conference room. "I'm not skilled at reading CT scans and MRIs, but with the assistance of Dr. Lin here, I believe Father Bartholomew's scourge wounds match almost precisely the scourge wounds we observe in the man in the Shroud, blow for blow. Where Christ was beaten, Father Bartholomew was beaten. I don't see any blows that were missed, even on the back, or the legs and the feet. Even the dumbbell wounds are identical. It's hard to believe we are looking at two separate men who lived two thousand years apart."

"Do you agree, Dr. Lin?" Castle asked.

"This is really the first time I've looked at the Shroud of Turin," she said. "So I'm no expert. But reading the CT scans and MRIs, I do see the points of resemblance Father Middagh is pointing to."

"What about the wrist wounds?" Dr. Castle asked Middagh.

"They appear identical again," Middagh said. "As far as I can tell, the wounds in Father Bartholomew's wrists are placed exactly where we see the wrist wounds in the Shroud."

"Do you agree?" Castle asked Dr. Lin.

"Again, my first impression is that Father Middagh is right," she answered. "Except for the healing I see in Father Bartholomew's tests, his CT scans and MRIs are similar to the injuries in Father Middagh's computer images of the man in the Shroud."

Dr. Castle took in their conclusions without comment. In his mind, Castle was calculating that Bartholomew's rapid recovery could be a sign that the wounds were psychologically induced in the first place. If Bartholomew's subconscious was causing him to manifest the wounds of the man in the Shroud, his subconscious might equally bring him back to normal once the drama of the wounds being inflicted was over.

"What do you make of it, Dr. Castle?" Father Morelli finally asked him.

"It's pretty much what I expected," Castle answered. "What I need to do now is interview Father Bartholomew some more privately. When he suffered the stigmata, he said he experienced in his mind that he had returned to Golgotha and that he took the place of Christ being nailed to the cross. I want to see if he had the same experience with these more recent wounds."

"So, you suspect Father Bartholomew returned to Jerusalem to take the place of Christ being scourged at the pillar?" Morelli asked.

"Yes, I do. At least in his own mind, I believe Father Bartholomew went back in time and became Christ being scourged."

Morelli listened intently. "Went back in time? Does that mean you are becoming a believer?" he asked Castle.

Castle corrected himself. "I meant that Father Bartholomew *felt* he went back in time."

Morelli pressed further. "So you think he was hallucinating?"

"In a sense, yes," Castle answered. "Much of what goes on in the mind does not happen that way in what we call 'reality.' I know how compelling this evidence looks to you and I know how much Father Bartholomew looks like the man in the Shroud, but that's simply because he has long hair and a beard."

"And now we have the wounds that are very similar," Morelli added.

"I understand," Castle said, without granting any conclusions.

"Do you think Fernando Ferrar is going to broadcast his film of Father Bartholomew standing at the window?" Morelli asked.

"I have no doubt about it," Castle answered without hesitation.

"What are you going to do about it?" Morelli wondered, sounding panicked.

"For starters, I'm going to call the archbishop," the psychiatrist answered, taking out his cell phone. "Other than that, I'm not sure there is anything I can do."

CHAPTER SIXTEEN

Thursday, 5:00 P.M.
Archbishop Duncan's office, St. Patrick's Cathedral rectory
Day 15

Fernando Ferrar's broadcast from outside Beth Israel had been aired on national television all afternoon. His reports showed Father Bartholomew at the window, naked from the waist up, holding his arms out as if he were crucified. Ferrar focused on the scourge wounds on Father Bartholomew's chest and the stigmata in his wrists. "Has Christ returned?" Ferrar asked the audience. The news segment showed video clips of the ambulance rushing Father Bartholomew to the Beth Israel emergency room on Sunday and of Dr. Castle leaving the hospital that evening. "Is Father Bartholomew a madman?" Ferrar asked. "Why won't the archbishop talk?"

The next images shown were of the Shroud of Turin. Ferrar narrated: "Several knowledgeable experts have come forward to document that the wounds being displayed by Father Bartholomew resemble the Shroud of Turin." The report next showed the main library on the Columbia University campus on New

York's Upper West Side. "Today I was able to interview Dr. Richard Whitehouse, a professor of medieval studies at Columbia University who has devoted decades to studying the Shroud of Turin."

The report showed Ferrar interviewing Dr. Whitehouse in the professor's office. "Tell me, Dr. Whitehouse, what first drew your attention to Father Bartholomew and the Shroud of Turin?"

"There's a long history of religious believers going back centuries exhibiting stigmata, most commonly the nail wounds Christ suffered on his wrists when he was crucified," Whitehouse said. "But when I saw your video of the wounds on Father Bartholomew's chest when he was in the hospital window today, I was surprised. Most people who experience the stigmata do not also experience wounds that look like the scourging that the gospels say Jesus Christ took at the pillar."

"So you compared this to the Shroud of Turin?" Ferrar asked.

"Yes, I did," Whitehouse acknowledged. "Your video images weren't clear enough to say for certain, but the pattern of wounds on Father Bartholomew's chest and arms looks similar to the wounds we see in the Shroud of Turin."

As Whitehouse said this, viewers saw side-by-side images: negative photographs of the torso of the man in the Shroud, and Father Bartholomew with his arms outstretched and chest naked in the window of his Beth Israel hospital room.

"It's also remarkable, don't you think, how much Father Bartholomew with his long hair and beard looks like Jesus?" Ferrar asked the professor.

Whitehouse proceeded carefully. "Again, I can't say the man in the Shroud is Jesus. That is still the subject of a lot of debate. But I can say that the face of the man in the Shroud and Father Bartholomew with his long hair and beard do resemble each other."

As Whitehouse answered, the camera showed close-ups of

Father Bartholomew's face as seen through the hospital window and the face of the man in the Shroud.

"There you have it." Ferrar concluded his report. "Has Jesus Christ come back to life in the person of Father Bartholomew? Is the Second Coming upon us? So far, we have had no official comment from the Vatican."

EARLY THURSDAY EVENING in Rome, a television rebroadcast of Ferrar's news report from outside the hospital had a big impact at the Vatican. "I think you need to hold a press conference as soon as possible and Father Morelli should attend to represent the Vatican," Pope John-Paul Peter I told Archbishop Duncan over the phone. "It's better if the press knows the Vatican is involved."

"What do you want us to say?" Duncan asked.

"I doubt if there is much you can say," the pope answered. "Let Castle do most of the talking. He will be limited by the doctor-patient relationship, so there is little he can disclose, but I think he will be successful in damping down the enthusiasm of the press to sensationalize Father Bartholomew, if that's possible to do."

The press conference was set for 5 P.M. ET on Thursday in Archbishop Duncan's office at St. Patrick's Cathedral in New York City.

The press conference was packed. Multiple video crews broadcast back to their home studios through remote satellite uplinks via trucks parked on the side streets along the cathedral.

A table was set up in the front of the room for the press conference. Archbishop Duncan sat in the middle, flanked by Dr. Castle on his right and Father Morelli on his left.

The archbishop introduced the psychiatrist, allowing Dr. Castle to make a short introductory statement.

"Father Bartholomew was admitted to Beth Israel last Sunday

under my care," Castle told the press. "There has been much speculation that Father Bartholomew's wounds are the wounds suffered by Jesus Christ two thousand years ago. There also has been some speculation that Father Bartholomew's wounds closely resemble the wounds displayed by the man in the Shroud of Turin. At this point, I can confirm neither."

"Is this what the Vatican thinks?" A reporter had interrupted, determined to ask the first question of Father Morelli.

"The Vatican is working with Archbishop Duncan and Dr. Castle," Morelli affirmed. "The Vatican has come to no conclusions."

"It sounds like the Catholic Church is stonewalling," Fernando Ferrar told Archbishop Duncan aggressively. "Why has the Vatican not responded to the questions from the news media about whether Father Bartholomew is manifesting the wounds that scholars like Dr. Whitehouse at Columbia see in the Shroud of Turin? Why have you waited until now to make a statement to the public?"

"If we were stonewalling, we wouldn't be giving this press conference," Duncan said firmly. "The Church is first and foremost concerned about Father Bartholomew's health. I can assure you that the Church is taking seriously all questions about Father Bartholomew, including questions that concern the Shroud of Turin. We will update you as soon as we have something more definitive to say. Right now, we would only ask the people who are coming to St. Patrick's Cathedral or Beth Israel Hospital to stay home. My office is working with the mayor and the New York Police Department to control crowds and make sure the streets of the city remain passable. Father Bartholomew appreciates your prayers, but he asks you to stay home and pray, for the safety of everybody involved."

"Does the archdiocese believe Father Bartholomew is Jesus Christ?" Ferrar asked in a follow-up question.

"The archdiocese and the Vatican have reached no conclusions about what is happening to Father Bartholomew. We are working with Dr. Castle and we will notify the public once we have anything more definitive to say."

Ferrar persisted. "Dr. Castle is a psychiatrist. Does that mean the Catholic Church thinks Father Bartholomew is crazy?"

"Again, we have no comment," Archbishop Duncan said resolutely.

Fernando Ferrar was rapidly becoming an international press celebrity, as his television news reports about Father Bartholomew were rebroadcast around the world—in Italy by RAI, by Univision and Telemundo to the Spanish world in North America, and by countless other networks in dozens of different languages.

Rather than put the controversy regarding Father Bartholomew to rest, the press conference only fueled speculation and interest in the case.

That evening, the crowd in vigil outside Beth Israel grew to well over a thousand people.

Within twenty-four hours of Father Bartholomew's appearance in the window of his hospital room, over ten million viewers had viewed Ferrar's broadcasts on YouTube.

The next morning, the New York tabloids hit the newsstands with top headlines that read SECOND COMING—IS JESUS IN NEW YORK CITY? and BURIAL SHROUD OF CHRIST COMES TO LIFE IN NEW YORK PRIEST? The front pages of both newspapers carried photographs of Father Bartholomew at the hospital window and the Shroud of Turin.

CHAPTER SEVENTEEN

Thursday night
Dr. Stephen Castle's apartment, New York City
12:00 A.M. ET in New York City, 6:00 A.M. Friday morning in Rome
Days 15–16

Gabrielli telephoned Castle from Bologna. "I think I am very close to reproducing the Shroud using only materials and methods that were known in the thirteenth century. If I succeed, this will be the crowning achievement of my career."

"How did you do it?" Castle asked.

"I have been experimenting with red ochre, a form of iron oxide that was a common paint at the time the Shroud was forged, and with vermilion, a red pigment that medieval painters typically formed from powdered mineral cinnabar, or red mercury sulfide. I also found a way to make linen photosensitive with a colloid mixture of various plants and mercury salts that alchemists used in the Middle Ages."

"I'm following you so far," Castle said.

"By covering a student with a combination of the red ochre and vermilion, I have managed to get the image to take hold by a combination of rubbing the linen against the student's body and exposing the linen, with the student underneath it, to the type of light sources a camera obscura lens concentrates from sunlight."

"Okay," Castle said. "Then what?"

"I bake the linen in an oven and wash the result in water. The end result looks a lot like the Secondo Pia negative, with the image visible in the white highlights of what otherwise looks like a negative."

"Are you sure this is the way the Shroud of Turin was produced?" Castle asked.

"A lot of what I'm doing was first suggested by Walter McCrone, the scientist on the 1978 Shroud of Turin Research Project who claimed the Shroud showed signs of iron oxide that proved it was painted. Others have suggested that a mixture of egg white and bichromate produces a photosensitive mixture that works when painted on the linen."

Castle filed away that information, pleased to know Father Middagh was not the only person who could cite the 1978 Shroud of Turin Research Project to suit the needs of his argument.

"Besides, it doesn't make any difference if the Shroud was created by the methods I am using," Gabrielli said. "All I need to prove is that I can produce today something that looks very much like the Shroud of Turin by using only materials that were known to exist when the carbon-14 tests show the Shroud was created, around 1260 to 1390 A.D."

The comment caused Castle to challenge Gabrielli on the carbon-14 tests. "I've been show evidence by the Vatican that the samples for the carbon-14 tests were taken from a corner of the Shroud that had been rewoven with cotton after the 1352 fire that damaged the Shroud."

Gabrielli shot back derisively. "The Church has gone to great lengths to discredit the carbon-14 tests. First the Shroud defenders attacked the carbon-14 process itself, claiming it could be inaccurate. But three different labs, all very credible, came up with about the same result. The problem is that carbon-14 dating is a very accurate scientific process. Then the believers claimed the samples were contaminated with biological debris from the Middle Ages. Now the argument is that the carbon-14 dating samples were from a rewoven part of the Shroud. Once we show that argument to be false, the Shroud defenders will come up with another one. The truth is that the carbon-14 tests were done correctly and the Catholic Church just can't stand it."

"How about the blood on the Shroud?" Castle asked. "Will your Shroud contain blood?"

"That's easy, especially since the Shroud of Turin Research Project proved a lot of blood on the Shroud came from direct contact. I could easily saturate parts of the linen with blood to look just like the Shroud. All I would have to do is get some blood samples. If you want, I can even get some samples from fresh corpses, to make sure I include the serum albumin on the Shroud, evidence the Shroud believers say proves Christ's dead body rested in the Shroud."

"Are you confident your Shroud will get world attention?"

"Most of my work does," Gabrielli said boastfully. "I have an international audience that follows my work debunking miracles, just as you are followed worldwide for the books you write attacking religion. When my duplicate shroud is ready, I plan to hold a press conference here at the university. I'm sure it will draw a crowd, especially with your Father Bartholomew drawing global attention on television and on the Internet. Here in Italy, I saw the report on RAI last night. It even included a clip of you at the press conference with the archbishop."

Castle was not surprised. "How did I look?" he asked jokingly.

"Good," Gabrielli said, "but I think you've gained about ten

pounds since I saw you last. You need to come over here to Ita
and do some walking around Rome and Florence."

Castle laughed, appreciating that Gabrielli probably had ;
point. Castle thought a trip to Europe would be a welcome idea
right about now. "When are you going to show your shroud handiwork to the world?"

"That's what I called to ask," Gabrielli answered. "When would
you like me to show it?"

"How about next week? I'm planning a trip to Princeton tomorrow to meet one of Father Bartholomew's advisors from
when he was a physicist. Then comes the weekend. You'll get more
attention if you wait until the middle of next week. How about
next Thursday? We will get coverage on Friday that will carry us
through the weekend news cycle. That should give us the chance
to get maximum news coverage worldwide."

Gabrielli thought for a minute. "Sounds good to me," he
agreed. "Next Thursday it is. I will start preparing the press release
right away."

CHAPTER EIGHTEEN

Dr. Castle had his limo swing by the Waldorf Towers to pick up Anne Cassidy. It was a beautiful fall day and Castle looked forward to the trip to see Dr. Horton Silver at Princeton University. He thought the ride would give him time to find out more about Anne and he looked forward to whatever insight Silver could give him about Paul Bartholomew's career as a physicist.

Castle wore a camel-hair sport coat he particularly liked and a blue button-down oxford shirt with no tie. In the pocket of the sport coat he had neatly arranged his trademark four-point linen handkerchief. Anne looked fresh in a light blue linen dress suit, highlighted by an Italian designer scarf she tied around the open collar of her tweed dress jacket. Under the jacket she wore an attractive black silk shirt. Castle noted how well Anne's outfit set off her blond hair and deep brown eyes. Once Anne was comfortably

in the backseat of the car next to Castle, the driver set out for the Lincoln Tunnel and New Jersey.

"What did Paul have to say when you introduced yourself to him?" Castle finally asked as they headed down the New Jersey Turnpike.

"At first, he couldn't believe it," Anne said. "He thought I was his mother come back to life. He said I looked exactly like she did when she was my age."

"Was he right?" Castle asked.

"I don't know for sure," Anne said with some hesitation. "When I was growing up, I never really knew much of anything about my real mother. I would ask my father to tell me about my mother, but he always put me off, saying something like 'That was a long time ago.' My father was not the most talkative man, especially when it came to personal matters."

Castle probed. "Certainly you must have wanted to see photos of your mother. You must have had some idea about who she was."

"Like I said, my father told me that my mother had died giving birth to me. He had one or two photos of them together that I remember seeing, but over the years even those photos got lost, probably in one of our many moves."

"So you didn't always live in Montreal?" Castle asked.

"No," Anne said. "My father was a lawyer and he worked for the Canadian Pacific Railway. I grew up in western Canada, in Calgary, where the Canadian Pacific is headquartered. It wasn't until I was a teenager that my father got a promotion by switching to the Canadian National Railway. That's when we moved to Montreal, when I was in high school. The Canadian National is headquartered in Montreal."

"Your father never remarried?"

"No, I think he was always very much in love with my mother.

I can't remember him even dating when I was a child. He was always there at home for me, playing the role of both mom and dad as I was growing up."

Castle began to see strange reverse parallels in Anne's life and the life of her half brother. Anne was told her mother died giving birth and Paul was told his father died in a work-related accident three months before he was born. Anne and Paul had the same mother, though Anne knew almost nothing about her mother and Paul was equally in the dark about his father. Anne Cassidy claimed never to have known her mother and Paul Bartholomew claimed never to have known his father, though they both had the same mother in common. Neither Anne Bartholomew, their mother, nor Matthew Cassidy, Anne's father, ever remarried. Over the years, Castle had become used to sorting out complex family histories. Discovering Anne, he believed, added an important piece to this puzzle.

"I'm sure I'm not the only person ever to be separated at birth from a mother," Anne said.

Castle agreed. "Still, you are one of the lucky ones. Very few people separated at birth ever get a chance to reconcile with a lost brother, or to find out the truth about their parents. After your father died, you learned the truth about your mother and now you are back together with Paul."

"I know it's hard to believe," Anne finally said, "but I think Paul is right. I feel surprisingly close to my mother now that I have met Paul. When Paul first saw me, he almost passed out. Judging from Paul's reaction when he first saw me, I guess I do look a lot like my mother did when she was my age. I understand how hard it must have been for Paul to accept he had a half sister he had never heard about. Yet, after we had a chance to get acquainted, he embraced me and I felt like we had never been separated at all."

"Why do you think you mother never told Paul that he had a half sister?" Castle asked.

"Since I never spoke with my mother, I'm only speculating, but my guess is that she did not want Paul to know her first husband was still alive, or that she had divorced him in order to marry Jonathan Bartholomew when he returned from Vietnam."

"So, you think your mother might have been embarrassed about the divorce with your father?"

"I'm not sure," Anne answered. "From the way I put the story together, my mother would never have married my father if she still thought Jonathan Bartholomew was still alive in Vietnam and coming back to her."

Castle admired how willing Anne was to accept the truth. It took some courage to come to New York to be with her brother after all these years. She obviously did not want her brother to suffer alone, not when she knew he shared her flesh and blood.

"Are you deeply Catholic like your brother?" Castle asked.

"No," Anne said. "My father was a Lutheran and I was raised Protestant."

"How about now? Do you believe in God?"

"Yes, I do," she said, "though I have to admit I'm not much for attending church regularly. Still, I can't accept that everything happens by accident. I have to believe there is a reason I found my brother and deep down I believe that reason has to do with God."

Castle saw no point in arguing with Anne about religion. He increasingly suspected she might help him better understand her brother.

As the limo entered Princeton, Castle enjoyed seeing once again how an Ivy League town looked. The open greens of the campus reminded him of Cambridge and his days at Harvard University. Finding the Physics Department headquartered in the modernistic Jadwin Hall, completed in 1968, was a bit of a shock.

But despite the sweeping windows and central open spaces of Jadwin Hall, Professor Horton Silver's office was pretty much what Castle had expected—floor-to-ceiling books and papers with one lonely window in the back that struggled to blend the ambient sunlight with the glare of Dr. Silver's slick widescreen monitor. Once the chairman of the Physics Department, Dr. Silver was now an emeritus professor.

Dr. Silver looked every bit the eccentric Dr. Castle expected to find. Silver's hair was just that—silver, and largely unkempt. His thick glasses seemed to protrude a quarter inch from their wire frames. Silver was comfortably attired in a loose-fitting sweater that looked as though it had reached its prime twenty years ago, complementing his baggy jeans and well-worn sneakers. Castle and Anne sat in straight-backed wooden chairs in front of the professor's desk, while Silver sat in his armed swivel chair positioned at the desk's helm so he could easily watch the monitor while they talked, moving the mouse and clicking at will even as he was conversing with his two guests.

"As I mentioned to you on the telephone, this is Anne Cassidy, Father Bartholomew's half sister," Castle said, introducing Anne.

Silver stood up and shook Anne's hand cordially. "I didn't know Paul had a sister," Silver said.

"It's a complicated story," Anne said. "But we have different fathers and my mother divorced my father before Paul was born. Paul never knew he had a half sister and we have just now been reunited."

"That's good," Silver said, obviously not interested in probing the details.

"As I understand it, Paul Bartholomew was one of your undergraduate students," Castle said, getting to the main purpose of the conversation. "Paul evidently was one of your protégés. You encouraged him to become a physics graduate student and you supported his appointment to the faculty of the Institute for Advanced Study."

"Yes, that's right," Silver said. "Bartholomew was one of the most promising physicists ever to work at Princeton or at the Institute for Advanced Study and we've had more than our share of Nobel Prize winners over the decades. In my estimation, Paul was well along his way to adding his name to that list, before he decided to quit."

"Why did he quit?" Castle asked.

"His mother died. She was sick for quite a while, as I remember. She had amyotrophic lateral sclerosis."

"She was sick for some time," Castle said.

"That's how I remember it. At any rate, when she died, Bartholomew wasn't the same. He lost his interest in physics. I couldn't figure it out at the time, but I remember him telling me he had despaired of the possibility of finding God in an equation."

"Did you ever meet Paul's mother?" Anne asked, anxious to see if he could supply her with any memories of their mother.

"I met her a few times," Silver recalled. "But, you've got to understand, I was Paul's academic advisor and then I was chairman of the Physics Department when he was a graduate student. I try not to intervene too heavily in the personal lives of my students. I'm a physicist, not a psychologist, and I built my career on knowing my limitations."

"As I understand it, you tried to discourage Paul from leaving his career as a physicist. Is that right?" Castle asked.

"Yes, I did. I could see he was emotionally crushed when his mother died. Paul had only two things in his life: his love of physics and his love of his mother. He was devoted to both. I had given up thinking Paul would ever get married. As I recall he had a few girlfriends, but relationships were hard for Paul. Women were too emotionally demanding and Paul was afraid of marriage. I'm sure, Ms. Cassidy, you will agree with me that a man who can't make a commitment to a woman is not a very good prospect for marriage."

"Maybe that's why I've never been married," Anne said, with a knowing smile. "Men like my brother marry their jobs and his attachment to our mother would not be very promising to a woman looking to be the center of his life as his wife."

"It was his commitment to theoretical research that consumed Paul," Silver said, wanting to be precise. "That's why I recommended him to the institute. The institute is a separate organization, not part of Princeton University. We are very close and the faculty here at the Physics Department typically works closely with the physicists at the institute. But the faculty at the institute have no students and they are not required to teach any classes. The faculty are not even required to write any books or articles, unless they want to. You might say that getting an appointment at the Institute for Advanced Study is one of the best academic jobs in America. You get paid handsomely and you are free to pursue whatever studies you want. Paul's devotion to theoretical research in physics fit right in."

"What was Paul working on when his mother died?" Castle asked.

"Do either of you have any background in physics?" Silver asked.

"None whatsoever," Anne volunteered.

"I took undergraduate physics in college," Castle said.

"That's about what I expected," Silver said with a smile. "Paul was working in advanced particle physics, the cutting edge of physics today, and he was trying to postulate the unified field theory that Einstein failed to formulate at the end of his career."

"I'm not sure I know what that means," Castle said.

"I'm not surprised," Silver replied as he clicked his mouse, preparing to type in a short answer to an email. "I will try to keep this simple so you both get the basic idea."

Castle and Anne agreed that made sense.

"In the last century, quantum mechanics challenged our fundamental understanding of time and space, just as did Einstein with relativity theory. In other words, physicists like your brother came to understand we do not live in a world defined by the four dimensions of length, width, height, and time. We frequently use the example of a famous novel Edwin Abbott published in 1884, called *Flatland*. In Abbott's flatland, the characters in the novel lived in a two-dimensional world in which there was only length and width. The world was flat in that no object had any height. This opened up an interesting possibility. Creatures like us who live in the added dimension of height take on magical properties in flatland. If you hover above flatland, you can enter the two-dimensional world as if you appear from nowhere. Then, if you leap out of flatland, it looks like you have disappeared. Appearing here and then there gives the impression you have walked through walls in flatland, when all you have really done is to hover above it in the dimension of height, waiting to choose when you want to enter the next room. Vanishing from the world of flatland and rematerializing suddenly out of nowhere is incomprehensible to flatlanders, who have no concept of height, but is no problem whatsoever to you, provided you live in three dimensions. Do you follow me?"

"Yes, I think so," Castle said for himself and Anne.

"You've got to read the books written by Michio Kaku," Silver said. "He's a theoretical physicist at the City University of New York. He's written several books explaining advanced physics to laymen and he's brilliant at it. Kaku uses another example. When H. G. Wells wrote his novel *The Invisible Man* in 1897, he showed the limitations of our four dimensions. There is this stranger who is completely covered with white bandages around his face, a hat that covers his head, and dark glasses. The invisible man turns out to be a Mr. Griffen of University College, who has discovered a way to make himself disappear by changing the refractive and reflective properties of human skin. Instead of using his discovery to better the human condition, Griffen uses his ability to disappear to commit a score of petty crimes. The point is that by learning to tap into invisibility as a fifth spatial dimension beyond length, width, and height, the invisible man is able to manifest the type of powers we typically attribute to ghosts or phantoms."

"So, what is the point?" Castle asked bluntly. "I'm sure I would benefit from taking one of your graduate courses, but I'm afraid I would turn out to be a disappointing candidate for a physics Ph.D."

Silver got the message. "My point is that physicists like your brother and me have come to believe that we may live in a universe that has as many as ten dimensions, not just four."

"What are the other six?" Anne asked. "Is this what my brother was searching for?"

"Yes," Silver acknowledged. "It is. Specifically, your brother was working with complex equations that explain observations particle physicists make when observing subatomic particles in complex and ridiculously expensive machines like the Large Hadron Collider at CERN on the French-Swiss border near Geneva. Physicists like Paul Bartholomew were investigating what we call 'M-Theory,' sometimes called 'the Theory of Everything,' an advanced version of what we physicists call 'string theory.' We can postulate that instead of a four-dimensional world, maybe we live in ten-dimensional space. A bumblebee flying in ten-dimensional space could conceivably go everywhere at once, without seeming to be anywhere."

"I don't get it," Anne said.

"Neither do I," Castle added.

"Don't worry," Silver said. "Nobody really gets it."

"What are the additional dimensions?" Castle asked. "Do you have names for them, or can you describe how they work?"

"Not really," Silver said. "That's the type of question Paul was working at answering when he was here in Princeton at the institute. Physicists fifty years ago would have said all this is nonsense, but the top physicists today worldwide are considering phenomena like time warps, or what astronomers call 'worm-holes,' physical constructs where you can enter in the universe here and come out in a parallel universe where everything is the same except maybe that you didn't die."

"It sounds like science fiction," Castle said critically. "So you are telling me that modern physics consider all these H. G. Wells phenomena to be possible?"

"Modern physics does not rule out time travel, if that's what you are asking," Silver answered. "Nor does it rule out that a lot of what we experience in our four dimensions might look very different if we could see the same phenomena in the ten dimensions or more that might truly define our universe."

For Castle, what he was hearing from Dr. Silver connected immediately with what Father Bartholomew had told him in their therapy session. Bartholomew had cautioned Castle not to rule out that his after-life experience may have happened exactly as he experienced it. What Castle realized listening to Silver was that Bartholomew was trying to tell him something that modern particle physics was seriously contemplating: for instance, that an afterlife may exist as a parallel world in which we remain alive. Bartholomew objected when Castle insisted his slippages in time back to Golgotha two thousand years ago on the day Christ died had been strictly a trick of Bartholomew's subconscious. What if Bartholomew, instead of being psychologically disturbed, had just slipped in time and space so he could experience one or more of the dimensions beyond? Dr. Silver said many modern physicists accepted them as real.

Castle had struggled to understand how someone as brilliant as Paul Bartholomew could fail to see that his physical manifestation of the hair and beard of the man in the Shroud of Turin, or the stigmata he experienced, were obvious manifestations of a psychological disorder. Maybe what Bartholomew was trying to tell him was that the interventions into his life, including the scourge marks he experienced, were really happening, not in our four dimensions, but through an intervention from a dimension beyond our here and now.

Dr. Silver had just explained that the invisible man appeared and disappeared at will, just as the third-dimensional hyperbeing appeared and disappeared in flatland. To Castle, the idea was bizarre, but if we truly lived in a world not bounded by our four dimensions, maybe Rod Serling was right after all. Was it possible the *Twilight Zone* was more reality than we ever thought it was? Is it possible we live in the *Twilight Zone* and don't realize it?

"Do you know that Father Bartholomew claims to have suffered an after-life experience in which God asked him to return to earth?" Castle asked Dr. Silver.

"I've been reading about it in the newspaper and watching the news reports on television," Silver answered. "I'm not an expert on the Shroud of Turin or the stigmata Paul claims to be manifesting."

"What sense do you make of what's happening to Father Bartholomew?" Castle asked, anxious to get the physicist's perspective. "Do you think what he is going through right now has anything to do with his career as a physicist?"

"I'm not sure," Silver answered. "All I know is that Paul Bartholomew is not only a priest, he is also a brilliant physicist. What he is going through with the stigmata and the Shroud may just be his most recent scientific experiment. I wouldn't put it past Paul to use himself as his own human guinea pig in the most recent phase of his search for God. Truthfully, that's what I think."

"So you don't think my brother is crazy?" Anne asked.

"We are probably all a little bit crazy," Silver answered with a grin. "But if your brother is crazy he reached that stage through the other side."

"What do you mean?" Castle asked. "What other side?"

"Paul was always so brilliant that he was beyond most human beings, even at the Institute for Advanced Study," Silver explained. "That's why I think he had few friends and never married. It was always hard to understand Paul. He was a loner by nature, except when it came to his mother."

"I understand," Anne said quietly.

"Maybe I can explain it to you with one more example," Silver said, seeing that Castle and Anne were doing their best to understand what he was talking about. "I'm not sure this will help, but what if we live in a complex reality where a person could be both dead and alive at the same time?"

"How is that possible?" Castle asked.

"Simple," Silver answered. "The person is dead and alive at the same time because the universe has split apart into a parallel world. In one world the person is dead, but in the other world the person is very much alive. People in each world insist that their world is the only real world and that all other worlds are imaginary or made-up. Universes might split up into millions of branches. In one branch you live to be ninety years old and never marry. In another branch you die tragically young, fighting bravely in combat. In one branch you have ten children; in another branch your only child dies at childbirth and you never have another one, or at least that's what you are led to believe."

"What's the point?" Anne asked.

"The point," Silver said, "is that you would have no way of knowing which reality was real. Maybe they are all real, simultaneously. Maybe you live in all of them at the same time. How would you ever tell the difference?"

Castle and Anne thanked Dr. Silver for being so generous with his time. The professor dismissed it, saying he hoped his comments helped. Silver's experience was that most laypeople left his office much more confused than when they arrived. He had long ago given up on being able to explain modern advanced physics to anyone but the most advanced graduate students.

On the ride back to New York, Anne and Castle were quiet for a long while.

"Dr. Castle, what do you think that was all about?" Anne finally asked.

"I'm not sure what I think," Castle answered, "but I'm sure your brother would have understood every word."

"It reminds me of something he said to me when we were alone in the hospital," Anne said.

"What's that?"

"At the time, I wasn't sure what Paul meant," she began slowly, wanting to be sure she explained this carefully, "but he said we were all stuck in time."

"Stuck in time?"

"Yes, that's what he said. And when I asked him what he meant, Paul said we live our lives like the future is ahead of us, unknown, and that the past is behind us, completely determined."

"Did Paul see it differently?"

"Yes," Anne said. "Paul said the truth is our destiny is determined for us when we are born. Our future draws us forward, much like a seed contains the mature tree. Paul said it's our past that's a fiction. We invent stories about who we were and where we came from to explain things that happen to us in life. Our memories are faulty and the stories we tell about ourselves change, often depending upon what is happening to us now. Maybe that's why he gave up physics."

"What do you mean?" Castle asked.

"Maybe Paul came to the conclusion that it was his destiny to find God, but that in physics he wasn't getting there. Then our mother died. Paul said at that moment he realized he wanted to be reunited with his mother. Maybe he decided God, not physics, was his doorway to the dimensions he needed to travel to get back together with his mother. That's why he decided to become a priest."

"Why exactly is that?" Castle asked.

"Maybe because Paul concluded he did have a vocation all along. That's what he told me. That he had been resisting God, thinking he could find God through an equation. When Mom died, he gave up and decided that accepting God in his heart was the only way to find God here on earth."

Castle reminded himself that Bartholomew had told him much the same thing, that finding God involved an experience, not an intellectual exercise.

"One thing about what Dr. Silver said bothers me," Anne said, with a concerned look on her face.

"What's that?" Castle asked.

"If Dr. Silver is right, how would we ever be sure anything happening here is the way we think it is happening?"

"I've dealt with that question for decades in psychiatry," Castle said. "Today was the first time I realized that physicists are asking the exact same question."

"Does anyone have an answer?" Anne wanted to know.

"I doubt it," Castle said with resignation. "I go about my job every day confident I see the world the way it truly is. But truthfully, I don't know."

"Wasn't that Dr. Silver's point?" Anne speculated.

"What's that?" Castle asked.

"When it comes to somebody as brilliant as my brother, maybe nobody can ever be sure what is real. That's what I think Dr. Silver was trying to tell us today."

CHAPTER NINETEEN

Castle began the weekend thinking about Anne. Sitting at his desk and sorting through his correspondence, he came across an invitation to attend a black-tie charity dinner that night at one of his favorite French restaurants. Castle had put the invitation aside, thinking he would figure out who to ask to be his date, but when Father Bartholomew's case took center stage, Castle forgot about social obligations, at least for the moment.

On impulse, he called Anne at the Waldorf.

"I know, it's spur of the moment," he said, "but why don't we go to this together tonight. It will be a great meal and the speeches will be mercifully short. If we get bored, we can skip out early."

"But I didn't bring any evening clothes with me," Anne said worriedly. "Otherwise I'd be flattered to be your date tonight. Living in Montreal, I love French cuisine."

"Evening clothes is a problem we can solve," Castle said, anticipating he might get to spend the day with Anne. "You're just a few blocks from Saks and I can easily swing by with my limo. I don't very often get the chance to buy a fashionable evening gown for a beautiful woman."

"Flattery will get you everywhere," Anne said, happy Castle couldn't see her blushing. "Give me a half hour and I'll be downstairs at the Towers entrance."

"You've got a deal," Castle said with enthusiasm, as he headed off to make sure he looked his best to impress the young woman who was rapidly capturing his eye.

At Saks, Castle found himself actually enjoying shopping, especially with Anne willing to flirt as she changed dresses, trying to make up her mind.

"Don't worry about the cost," Castle told her. "You're my guest tonight."

Anne selected what Castle thought was a particularly stunning full-length black strapless evening gown that came with a matching cashmere shawl designed to keep her shoulders warm. The Saks sales staff had no trouble finding the perfect Italian-made black shoes and just-right color of sheer Italian nylons to go with the outfit. As Anne twirled this way and that with the cashmere shawl wrapped tightly around her shoulders, Castle marveled at how perfectly her choice highlighted her blond hair and deep brown eyes.

On the way back to the Waldorf, Castle said, "I will come up to the suite to pick you up at seven tonight."

"I'll be ready," she said with anticipation, thinking this day was already one of the best dates she had ever had.

With Anne safely back in the Waldorf, Castle took the limo to Beth Israel. He wanted to pay Father Bartholomew a professional visit.

At the hospital, Castle found Father Bartholomew resting alone and comfortably in what had become his private ICU room.

Castle read Bartholomew's chart and quickly examined his wounds. From all signs, Bartholomew was recovering rapidly, much as Castle had expected, despite the severity of wounds that should have killed even a healthy and strong young man, which Dr. Castle knew this priest truly was.

"The way you are healing," Castle told Bartholomew, "I can't justify using costly hospital space to keep you here."

"As far as I am concerned, you can check me out right now," Father Bartholomew said, hoping Castle might listen. "I'm anxious to get back to my parish."

"When I do agree to release you," Castle continued, "it will be to the care of Archbishop Duncan and Father Morelli. I'm going to insist you stay with them at St. Patrick's rectory, before I even consider releasing you to go back to work at St. Joseph's. I'm not sure you've looked outside recently, but there are still a few hundred people standing out there holding candles and praying for you."

"The archbishop's residence is good for me," Bartholomew said. "I will do as you say."

Before he left, there was one thing Castle had to ask Bartholomew. It had been bothering him since yesterday and the conversation he and Anne had with Dr. Silver.

"Paul, I have to ask you something," Castle said, sitting in the chair next to the bed.

"What's that?"

"Your sister and I went to Princeton yesterday and we visited with Dr. Silver."

"That must have been interesting," Bartholomew said. He had no idea Castle and Anne had made the trip.

"Dr. Silver did his best to explain to us your work in physics, about how advanced particle physics says we live in a world of more than four dimensions."

"Right," Bartholomew said. "So what's your question?

"Just this," Castle said directly. "When you say you tripped in time and went back to Golgotha, what did you mean?"

"I meant just that," Bartholomew said. "My experience is that I am back on Golgotha on the day Jesus died. Even more, I am experiencing myself as being Jesus. It's like I am being scourged at the pillar and nailed to the cross."

"But how could you or anybody else have any objective proof that you weren't just going back to Golgotha in your mind?" Castle said. "Even your stigmata don't prove to me that you were really at Golgotha. The same with the scourge injuries you suffered. You could have produced both sets of injuries through psychosomatic mechanisms."

"Right now, I can't prove it to you objectively," Paul said.

"That sounds like you think there will be a time when you can prove it?"

"Yes, I believe that time will come."

Castle probed. "What do you mean?"

"Just this," Bartholomew said. "I think there is a reason I am Jesus."

"Is that what Jesus has told you?"

"Yes," Bartholomew said. "I know you believe I am imagining all this, but if I am right, you will continue to be intrigued by the Shroud. When you finally realize that you cannot prove the Shroud is a forgery, you will then be ready for an experience that will change your life. None of this is happening by accident, Dr. Castle."

"What do you mean?"

"My destiny is not just to find my mother. It's like I told you in our first therapy session in your office: my destiny is to unlock for the world the codex of the Shroud of Turin."

"We will see, Paul," Castle said, not convinced Paul wasn't simply slipping further into his delusion. "We will see."

Leaving the hospital, Castle called Father Morelli on his cell phone. "I'm checking Father Bartholomew out of the hospital. Can you be here later this afternoon to pick him up? I want him to stay with you at St. Patrick's."

"I can be there in an hour," Morelli said.

"Good," Castle said, "and I will want to see you both in my office early on Monday morning for a therapy session."

"How early?"

"Make it eight o'clock. Father Bartholomew will be my first patient of the day."

When Morelli agreed, Castle left the hospital, confident Father Bartholomew would be in good hands until Monday.

CHAPTER TWENTY

Saturday evening
New York City
Day 17

As Castle put on his tuxedo for the evening with Anne, he called the Waldorf room service and ordered up a chilled bottle of his favorite champagne and some of the hotel's best caviar.

Arriving at Anne's suite at 7 P.M., he was delighted to find her looking beautiful in the black strapless evening gown, her hair done up perfectly. The hotel's beauty parlor was top-notch.

"The champagne and caviar are a nice surprise," Anne said, welcoming him into the living room of the suite.

"This way I thought we could miss the cocktail hour at the restaurant," Castle said with a smile. "I'd much rather spend the time talking with you."

He enjoyed the pleasure with which Anne sipped the champagne and tasted the caviar. "You're going to spoil me living like this," she said, unafraid to show much she was enjoying the moment.

"I hope so," Castle said, raising a glass in a toast. "Here's to many more evenings together."

The limo ride to the French restaurant was nice and short.

Once inside the restaurant, Dr. Castle introduced Anne to several of his friends before they were shown to a relatively private side table, a banquette facing into the room.

"I hope you don't mind," Castle said, "but while attending these charity events is sometimes a social necessity, I still prefer to dine as privately as possible."

"Fine with me," Anne said, relieved she was not going to be thrown into a long evening of conversation with people she didn't know.

"Meeting you has been the silver lining in my taking on your brother as a client," Castle told Anne as they proceeded through the first course accompanied by a delicious French white wine Castle had perfectly selected.

"It's been doubly important for me," Anne added. "I'm thrilled to be reunited with my brother."

"Is your brother the person you expected to find?" he asked.

"In a way, yes," Anne answered. "Reading about my brother on the Internet, I realized how devoted he was both to his career in physics and to our mother. Now meeting him, I believe he is a very driven person. I have to admit I don't understand all his concerns, but the conversation with Dr. Silver in Princeton yesterday helped."

"What do you mean?"

"It's hard to explain, but all my life I have had the sense that I too am somehow suspended in time. After my father died, it was like I reconnected with a hidden life I never knew I had, not until I found those divorce papers. Now, in meeting Paul at the hospital, it somehow doesn't feel like we were ever separated. When I first saw him lying there unconscious, I panicked, worried that he might slip away before we had a chance to connect. When we were alone, I held his hand and I felt we were the same flesh. I understood him without him having to say very much. I'm sure I would have loved Mom and I'm sorry I never had the chance to meet her."

Castle listened carefully, moved at how much Anne cared for her brother.

"Do you really think all this is being caused by psychological problems my brother is going through?" Anne asked.

"That's what I'm trained to think," Castle said. "Still, the discussion with Father Middagh and Father Morelli about the Shroud has presented me with a lot of information I never considered before. I remain convinced the carbon-14 testing is likely to be correct and that means the Shroud has to be a forgery. The story about the carbon-14 sample being contaminated is a little bit too convenient for me. Still, I have to admit, the image of the man in the Shroud has begun to haunt me."

"It haunts me, too," Anne said, "especially when Paul has come to look so much like the man of the Shroud."

"Then I had no idea modern physics was so seriously considering other dimensions," Castle said. "The idea of parallel worlds and time travel had always seemed just science fiction to me."

"Do you think it's real?" Anne asked.

"I don't know, but your brother and Dr. Silver both seem to think other dimensions are a reality and they are the professional physicists. After all, your brother was appointed to the Institute for Advanced Study and Dr. Silver still considers him to have one of the most brilliant minds in physics that he has ever seen. That's quite a compliment coming from an emeritus professor who used to head the Physics Department at Princeton."

"My brother insists his life will unlock the meaning of the Shroud," Anne said. "That's what he told me when we were alone. He said that's why he looks so much like the man in the Shroud. He believes that his life and Christ's life are uniting as one, as if the two thousand years between them had never happened."

"That's more than he has told me," Castle said, making a mental note to add the information to his file.

"Paul also made me feel like my destiny and his were linked," she went on. "He said that I was meant to find those divorce papers and I was destined to come back and meet him."

Sipping the red wine and finishing the entrée, Anne could see the room was getting ready for the speechmaking to begin.

"I was thinking," she said coyly, "that maybe we could have dessert back at the hotel, unless of course you think you need to stay for the conclusion of the evening here."

"A great idea," Castle said with enthusiasm. "I've already made my donation to this charity for the year, so it seems to me that in my case the speeches we are about to hear are superfluous."

Back in the limo, Castle called the Waldorf Towers room service and arranged to have another bottle of champagne brought to Anne's suite, along with some chocolate soufflé.

When they arrived, Castle was pleased to see room service had been so efficient. The room was arranged for dessert for two by candlelight, just as Castle hoped it would be.

Finishing the dessert and champagne some forty minutes later, Castle decided it was time to excuse himself for the evening.

"You're a charming woman," Castle told her sincerely. "But you are also the sister of a patient. I want to thank you for a delightful evening. When this is all over, I hope I can ask you out to dinner again, maybe on less formal terms."

Anne was flattered by his comments. "I'd be honored to accept, Stephen," she said, happy to already be on somewhat less formal terms with a man she admired as much as she did Dr. Castle.

CHAPTER TWENTY-ONE

Castle slept late, enjoying a Sunday morning he hoped would lead to a day totally without patients.

But just as he was rolling over in bed, ready for another round of sleep, his cell phone rang.

"Dr. Castle, I hate to bother you again," Father Morelli said in a clearly worried tone, "but you have to get over here right away."

Not again, was Castle's first thought. "What is it this time," he said, not attempting to disguise his annoyance. He suspected this was going to develop into yet another Father Bartholomew crisis.

"Before I was awake, Father Bartholomew got dressed and left the rectory. He went over to St. Patrick's Cathedral and he has begun to say Mass. I'm there now, standing in the back vestibule."

"Doesn't sound like anything out of the ordinary," Castle said, trying to figure out what exactly was the problem. "I didn't want him out in public, but it doesn't sound like anything unusual is going on."

"It might not seem much to you," Morelli said, "but Father Bartholomew put on purple vestments to say Mass. It's not Advent or Lent. Today there is nothing special in the liturgy. Father Bartholomew ought to be wearing green vestments."

"So what?" Castle said, still feeling irritated at being disturbed, particularly this Sunday morning.

"Violet is the color that designates royalty and penance," Morelli told him. "It makes no sense to wear purple today unless Bartholomew is focused on Christ's passion again."

"How's that?" Castle asked.

"After he was scourged at the pillar, Christ was covered in a purple robe and mocked with the crown of thorns," Morelli said. "I am afraid of what might happen next."

"I'll be right there," Castle said, resolving it was best to go to St. Patrick's immediately, rather than regret it later.

As the taxi approached St. Patrick's Cathedral, Castle could see Fernando Ferrar's mobile broadcasting truck was parked on Fiftieth Street.

Rushing inside, Castle found Father Morelli in the vestibule at the back of the church, at the Fifth Avenue main entrance.

"There was nothing I could do," Morelli said pleadingly to Castle. "Ferrar charged past me saying I could call the police if I wanted to throw him out. He agreed not to put on the lights and begin taping unless something happens. So far nothing has."

"How far along are we with the Mass?" Castle asked.

"We are not yet at the Communion blessing," Morelli said, "but it's coming up right after the sign of peace is given."

Through a wireless microphone, Father Bartholomew's voice could be heard clearly throughout the church. "Lord Jesus Christ, you said to your apostles: I leave you peace, my peace I give you. Look not on our sins, but on the faith of your Church, and grant us the peace and unity of your kingdom where you live for ever and ever."

The hundred or so worshippers responded in unison, "Amen."

"The peace of the Lord be with you always," Father Bartholomew continued.

"And also with you," the worshippers answered.

"Let us offer each other a sign of peace," Father Bartholomew said, signaling for the worshippers to turn and give a kiss or handshake of peace to those with and around them.

Right then it happened. As Father Bartholomew reached to greet the altar boys, he grabbed his head and let out a scream. The pain took him to his knees. Castle reacted immediately, running up the central aisle to the altar.

As before, Bartholomew's mind tripped. Instantly he was back in the courtyard where his body had just been scourged unmercifully.

The centurions who had just beaten him were resting, breathing heavily, their naked upper bodies glistening with sweat. Methodically, they worked to free him from the pillar, making sure his hands still remained tied together at the wrists. Once free from the pillar, his body slumped hard to the pavement.

Two centurions picked him up roughly by the armpits and dragged his limp, nude body across the ground, his body leaving a trail of blood in his wake. When they got him to a corner of the courtyard, the centurions rudely twisted his body so it faced forward into the room, then lifted him onto a square stone that formed a hard, cold seat where two walls met. A centurion wearing a helmet with the red plume of command pushed Bartholomew's head hard back against the wall and grabbed his beard to yank open his mouth. Down his throat the centurion poured what tasted like a pungent mixture of old wine mixed with some sort of foul-tasting drug. He choked violently, struggling to get a breath.

The helmeted centurion laughed as he slapped Bartholomew hard across the cheek. "What's the matter?" he derided Bartholomew. "Doesn't the wine agree with you, Your Highness?"

The helmeted centurion backed away to allow two of his more brutish compatriots to grab Bartholomew by the shoulders, shoving him just far enough forward that they could throw a mantle of purple—the color of royalty—around his shoulders. "All hail, the King of the Jews!" they said as they tied the robe at his shoulders. Open in front, the robe did nothing to hide the embarrassment of his nudity.

Moving quickly, two more of the soldiers in the courtyard jammed onto his skull a cap they had formed from a thornbush growing in the courtyard. Taking rods, they beat the crown of thorns into his head, making sure it fit down on him like a hat.

Bartholomew screamed as the sharp thorns tore into his scalp, leaving gaping, bleeding wounds around his entire head. The centurions made sure their blows forced the long thorns deep into his scalp.

When they were finished pounding the skullcap of thorns onto his head, the centurions placed into his bound hands the wooden switch canes they had used to hammer the thorns. Bowing before him, the centurions honored Bartholomew as if he were sitting on a throne, holding a royal scepter as a symbol of his sovereign authority.

Finished with their rough work, the centurions resumed taking turns mocking him.

REACHING THE ALTAR, Castle lowered to scoop Father Bartholomew off the floor into his arms. Moving Bartholomew's ample hair aside with his fingers, Castle recognized immediately that the priest's scalp wounds extended from his forehead in a circle around his head, with punctures obvious everywhere across the top of the priest's scalp. Rushing behind Castle, Father Morelli dialed 911.

Screams went up from worshippers who stood seemingly frozen in the pews, unable to comprehend what was going on. Others grabbed cell phones and began recording. A few ran from the cathedral in panic. Some started crying, while others were unable to utter a sound.

Directing the action from the side of the altar, Fernando Ferrar had his film crew turn on their lights and begin taping. He quickly led the film crew directly to the altar, almost on top of Dr. Castle.

Just then, Father Bartholomew's arms shot out left and right in a straight line from his shoulders.

In a series of sharp, jerking movements, Father Bartholomew's body began lifting from the floor, as if he were levitating.

With his arms outstretched like one nailed to the crossbeam of a crucifix, Father Bartholomew lifted off the ground. His shoes fell from his feet as he floated high above the altar to where he was clearly visible throughout the church.

BARTHOLOMEW'S MIND SNAPPED immediately back to Golgotha. The rough centurions with the stale breath who had nailed his wrists to the crossbeam were standing below him, waiting as a group of soldiers using a pulley mechanism lifted the crossbeam up from the ground in several strong yanks, to a height where it could be slotted down into the vertical pole of the crucifix that was permanently implanted at this fearsome site of execution.

The pain was indescribable as Bartholomew's wrists bore the full weight of his body swinging free in the air as the crossbeam made its slow journey upward.

With a jolt, the crossbeam fell into the slot, giving the immediate signal for the two centurions with the mallets to go back to work. One centurion roughly forced the sole of his right foot flush against the upright beam. The other centurion moved simultaneously to bend his left leg so his left foot rested on top of his right foot. One centurion held the feet in that position as the other began driving yet another long nail through his feet. The nail entered his left foot through the long metatarsal bones forward of the heel, which lead down to the toes. With studied blows, the nail continued through the left foot onto the right foot below. The centurion angled the nail to be sure it also passed through the metatarsal region of the right foot, angled back toward the heel. Once it was through the right foot, the centurion drove the nail home into the wood of the upright beam.

Their work finished, the sweating team of soldier executioners looked with satisfaction on the crucified man, hanging with his weight supported entirely by the nails through his wrists and feet.

Bartholomew's mind went cold in shock as he realized he had been pinned to the cross to die. The damage done to his nail-pierced and scourge-beaten body was so severe that he could not last long. Still, the pain was anguishing. Even breathing was excruciating. He realized he would have to lift himself up using the nail in his feet as a pivot, just to relieve the pressure on his lungs long enough to exhale—otherwise, he would suffocate.

For Bartholomew, now nailed to the cross, the thought was terrifying beyond comprehension that the Roman executioners had calculated the torment of crucifixion so precisely that each new breath would require a cruel repeat of this macabre dance in which his arms and feet would have to work together in their passion, raising him up and lowering him down. To stay alive even one instant longer, to avoid suffocating from the weight

pressing down on his diaphragm, he was now forced co
ously to scrape his bones and flesh in synch against the na
this final hour of life, the practiced Roman crucifiers had
fully enlisted Bartholomew's body to complete their work
execution.

WATCHING THE NAIL wounds appear on Father Barthol
omew's feet, with the priest suspended in air above the altar of
New York's great midtown Catholic cathedral, several still in the
cathedral let out even more terrified screams. They echoed around
the church's vaulted ceiling, adding to the horror of the event.

Then, as suddenly as he had levitated, Bartholomew's body
came crashing to the cathedral's floor.

Examining Father Bartholomew quickly, Dr. Castle could see
that the stigmata on the priest's wrists had opened once again,
as gaping, bleeding wounds. Reaching under the priest's purple
vestments, the doctor felt blood soaking the tunic, meaning the
scourge marks on his body were likely also raw and bleeding.

Running into St. Patrick's, the New York Police Department
assisted Father Morelli in shutting down Fernando Ferrar's film
crew and escorting them outside.

The ambulance medics rushed in and took over. Within a
minute Father Bartholomew was in the ambulance, headed back
to the hospital.

"His pulse is weak," Castle told the medics. "His blood pressure is probably low and falling. He's in the first stages of going
into shock. But don't be alarmed; he's been through this before."

"I don't understand," one of the paramedics said loudly as he
jumped into the back of the ambulance.

"It's what I expected," Castle said, trying to calm things down.
"I'll explain it on the way downtown."

Squeezed into a corner in the back of the ambulance, Father Morelli quietly took out his stole and his prayerbook, ready to administer extreme unction once again to Father Bartholomew.

Dr. Castle ordered the driver to get to Beth Israel Hospital as fast as possible.

Ahead of them a police escort led the way once again with lights and sirens blaring.

CHAPTER TWENTY-TWO

Fernando Ferrar and his mobile television crew raced their van back to television news headquarters, a few blocks away from St. Patrick's Cathedral.

Already the editors were working to package his video into a breaking news segment, aiming to be the first with live coverage of Father Bartholomew and what was being called the "Miracle at the Cathedral."

Anchor Dave Dunaway broke into the Sunday afternoon coverage with a "news extra."

"I have with me here on the set today our correspondent Fernando Ferrar, who has just returned from St. Patrick's Cathedral here in New York City, where something extraordinary has just happened. New Yorkers are buzzing about what is being called the 'Miracle at the Cathedral.' Fernando was there. Tell us, Fernando, what happened?"

"It was quite extraordinary." Ferrar began with obvious

excitement at having just recorded the scoop of a lifetime. "Father Paul Bartholomew, the Catholic priest we have been covering— the one who has manifested on his wrists the stigmata, the nail wounds of Christ crucified on the cross—was saying Mass."

As Ferrar related what had happened, the national TV audience saw the video his crew had captured inside the cathedral.

"Just as the Mass was getting to Communion, the high point of the Mass, Father Bartholomew grabbed his head and fell to the ground. Our film crew was inside the church and we rushed forward to get a close-up."

"Looking at this for the first time, it's quite remarkable," Dunaway said. "It looks like blood is coming through his fingers as he grabs his head there. He looks like he's in severe pain."

"That's right, Dave," Ferrar said. "You're not going to believe this, but what it looked like to me was that Father Bartholomew was suffering the wounds Christ received with the crown of thorns."

"How is that possible?" Dunaway asked in amazement.

"Wait," Ferrar continued. "That's not half of it. Just watch the film clip. Within a minute or two, Father Bartholomew's body looked like it was being jerked upward in several distinct motions."

"I can't believe it," Dunaway said. "It looks like the priest is levitating."

"He was," Ferrar said anxiously. "At least, that's how it looked to me. But there's more. As you can see, his arms were outstretched, just like he was the one being nailed to the cross. And then—take a look at this close-up—the nail wounds on his wrists began bleeding again."

"It's amazing. I can't believe it," Dunaway said again, unable to control his sense of befuddlement at what he was seeing with his own eyes. "Is this some kind of magic trick?"

"Not that I could tell," Ferrar said seriously, "and I was standing right there, not ten feet away from Father Bartholomew when he levitated above the altar today at St. Patrick's Cathedral. It happened just like you are seeing, only a few blocks from here, right in the heart of midtown Manhattan, right on Fifth Avenue."

"It looks like Father Bartholomew was unconscious," Dunaway observed. "Was he still alive?"

"As far as I can tell, he was alive."

"How long did he stay like that, completely suspended in air, just like he was crucified?" Dunaway asked.

"It was only a few minutes," Ferrar answered quickly, anticipating what was coming next. "But look at this close-up. Hanging there, the priest's legs looked like somebody was positioning them to be nailed to a cross."

"That's right," Dunaway said. "It looks like the left foot is being placed on top of the right foot and then—what's this? It looks like the feet are being nailed. I can see the bleeding wound on the left foot on top. I can't see any nail, but I can see the wound developing. Could that possibly be what is happening?"

"Follow the close-up," Ferrar said excitedly. "It's exactly what is happening."

"I just can't believe it," Dunaway said in astonishment. "Are those the nail wounds on his feet?"

"Yes, that's exactly what is happening," Ferrar said. "You can see the feet beginning to bleed. When the camera pans back, you can see all the wounds—the forehead bleeding with the crown of thorns, the wrists bleeding from the nails. Underneath those purple vestments, the robes the priest is wearing for Mass, I'm told the scourge wounds opened up again on his body and began to bleed."

"But the cross is invisible and there is no crown of thorns," Dunaway pointed out. "There aren't any nails being driven through his wrists or his feet. I don't understand how what I'm seeing could possibly be happening."

"That's why it's being considered a miracle," Ferrar said. "There were about one hundred people in the church at the time attending Mass and they all stood there spellbound, not knowing what was happening. One woman said it looked like Father Bartholomew was experiencing in his own body the passion and death of Jesus Christ."

Just then the video showed Anne running forward and screaming, as she saw her brother suffering Christ's passion and death. On the video, her blood-curdling scream seemed to reverberate throughout the cathedral.

"Who's that?" Dunaway asked.

"I'm told that is Anne Cassidy, the priest's half sister," Ferrar answered.

"How long did Father Bartholomew stay levitating above the altar?" Dunaway asked. "It's incredible—this happened in midtown Manhattan just a few minutes ago."

"It seemed like an eternity that Father Bartholomew levitated there above the main altar in St. Patrick's Cathedral," Ferrar answered. "But it was less than five minutes from start to stop. You're seeing it on the video just as it happened. I don't think we edited anything out."

"How did it end?" Dunaway asked.

"As soon as his sister screamed, Father Bartholomew collapsed to the ground and it was over," Ferrar said. "It's on the next part of the video. Let's watch—you can see it happening."

"Remarkable," Dunaway said as he watched the remaining video. Anne screamed and fainted; the police and ambulance personnel rushed into the cathedral.

"I never would have believed it, except for your video," Dunaway said. "It's the most remarkable news video I've ever seen in my life."

"I know," Ferrar said. "I stood there entranced, watching as it happened. We have the best video crew in the business. They just kept videotaping and going for those close-ups while I stood there in disbelief."

"Is that the end of the video?" Dunaway asked. The program returned to the studio to show Dunaway and Ferrar sitting side by side at a desk on the set.

"Yes, that's it," Ferrar said. "As you saw right at the end of the video, the New York police rushed over to surround our video crew. We were told to stop filming and we were promptly escorted outside the cathedral onto Fifth Avenue."

"Where is Father Bartholomew now?"

"I believe he was taken by the ambulance to Beth Israel Hospital in lower Manhattan," Ferrar answered. "The man who came to Father Bartholomew's aid late in the video is his physician, Dr. Stephen Castle."

"Stephen Castle, the psychiatrist?" Dunaway asked.

"Yes. The other priest who rushed to the altar was Father Marco Morelli, a Jesuit the pope sent from Rome to work with Father Bartholomew."

"So, you're saying the Vatican is involved with Father Bartholomew's case?"

"Yes," Ferrar said. "I'm told Pope John-Paul Peter I has taken a personal interest in Father Bartholomew and I believe I can confirm that Dr. Castle has been hired by the Vatican to take Father Bartholomew on as a patient."

"The Vatican must think Father Bartholomew is crazy. Why else would a psychiatrist be hired to treat him?"

"I don't know if the Vatican thinks Father Bartholomew is

crazy, or if the Vatican is just being careful," Ferrar said. "Based on reports I filed over the past few days, Archbishop Duncan is also very deeply involved in this case. The Catholic Church is taking the case of Father Bartholomew very seriously."

"I can see that," Dunaway said, appearing suddenly distracted. "I'm being told by the control room that we also have a news clip of a press conference Archbishop Duncan and Dr. Castle held last week. I think we are going to play a clip from that now."

That evening the network televised an hourlong special report, *The Miracle at the Cathedral*, hosted by Fernando Ferrar.

Nielsen reports the next day showed the broadcast was one of the most-watched Sunday evening news shows ever, with over ten million people tuning in.

Geraldo Rivera, move over! Ferrar thought as he left headquarters that evening around midnight. He was confident his career was made now.

CHAPTER TWENTY-THREE

When he entered the conference room, Dr. Castle found the group had assembled. Archbishop Duncan was not there, but Father Morelli and Father Middagh were, as well as Anne. She still looked tense, obviously concerned about her brother.

After Ferrar's TV reports, Father Bartholomew's story was the buzz on the Internet. Videos taken from TV coverage of the levitation in the cathedral had received more than fifteen million views online in less than twenty-four hours.

"Father Bartholomew is resting comfortably at Beth Israel Hospital," Castle told the group as he began the meeting. "If the experience with Father Bartholomew's previous wounds is any guide, I expect his wounds will heal quickly and that Father Bartholomew will recover rapidly, much more so than would normally be the case with such severe wounds."

Anne was relieved to hear this, but still, she was not convinced.

"Can Father Morelli and I return with you to the hospital this afternoon to see my brother?"

"I'm not sure," Castle said. "At the end of this meeting, I expect to get a report on his condition and I'll make a decision then."

"Okay," Anne said compliantly.

Castle shifted gears unexpectedly. "At this meeting, I'm interested in learning more about the wounds we see on the man in the Shroud of Turin. As you all know, the world press is widely reporting that Father Bartholomew is now suffering the same wounds Jesus Christ suffered in his crucifixion, now including the crown of thorns and the stigmata in his feet. Pictures of the Shroud of Turin and Father Bartholomew are being juxtaposed on the Internet, on television, and in the print media internationally. Father Morelli explained to us last time that the Shroud of Turin provides a remarkably detailed view of the crucifixion of Jesus as described in the gospels of the New Testament, as well as the practice itself as described in contemporary Roman accounts. What I want to know in this meeting is this: Is there any basis on which we can discredit the comparisons the international news media are making between Father Bartholomew and Jesus? Given what we can learn about Roman crucifixion practices from studying the Shroud of Turin and what we know of the crucifixion of Jesus Christ from the New Testament, is there any basis for saying that what is happening to Father Bartholomew is *not* what happened to Jesus Christ?"

Father Middagh was prepared for this. "Let's start with the nail wounds on the feet."

"Okay," Castle said. "I'm listening."

Middagh projected an image from his computer onto the screen at the end of the conference room. "This is a view of the feet and calf area of the legs from the posterior image of the man in the Shroud. Remember, you are looking at a negative image in which left and right appear exactly as they would appear in the body of the crucified man in the Shroud. The image of the left foot shows only the heel area. The images of the feet are on the dorsal side of the body and were formed by blood contacting the Shroud, as we discussed before."

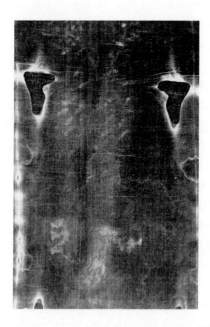

"In simple terms, what does all this mean?" Castle asked.

"It means the Roman executioners placed the sole of the right foot flat against the upright beam of the cross. Then they bent the left knee and twisted the body so the instep on the bottom of the left foot rested on top of the right foot. One nail appears to have been used to drive through both feet. The wound looks like it is in the metatarsal area of both feet, which would have been just forward of the small cuneiform bones just above the heel. The Roman executioners could have a different calculation with the feet than in nailing the wrists."

Studying the slide, Castle followed the explanation clearly.

"As we discussed before," Father Middagh went on, "the nails had to go through the small bones in the wrist, not the palms of the hands, because the hands nailed to the cross had to carry most of the weight of the body. The feet were different. The feet nailed to the cross did not have to carry body weight, but a crucified man would need to push down on the feet in order to lift himself up so he could breathe. In a way, the metatarsal region of the foot is more like the palm of the hand. If a man were crucified upside down, the feet would have to be nailed through the small cuneiform bones above the metatarsals. But the Romans needed to leave that region of the foot intact so the crucified man could push down with his legs to lift his body up. Basically, the nail in the feet just rode back up toward the heels as the crucified man lifted up to breathe."

"The pain had to be excruciating," Castle said.

"It was," Middagh said. "In fact, the word 'excruciating' derives from the Latin *ex crucis,* which denotes 'from being crucified.' The point of crucifixion was to make the death painful beyond description. Most people who were crucified died of suffocation. The weight of the body hanging down on the arms tended to fix the muscles needed for breathing in an inhalation state. To exhale, the crucified man had to pivot his weight down against the nail in his feet to allow the diaphragm to force the air out of his lungs. The nail in the feet rubbing on the bones in the feet would cause searing pain. In the process of breathing, the man's elbows would flex, causing the wrists to rotate around the iron nails, resulting in burning pain along the damaged median nerves leading to the thumbs. Eventually, the muscles tired and cramped, and the crucified man died of cardiopulmonary asphyxia."

Castle quickly grasped the anatomy of crucifixion. "What does the frontal view of the man in the Shroud show about the feet?"

"The feet in the frontal view are less distinct in the Shroud," Middagh said, "so you won't see much from the slide. From the ventral view, the bloodstain on the left foot is clear. The left foot was the foot placed on top, so we can see where the nail pierced the metatarsal area, about two-thirds of the way up the foot toward the heel from the toes. In the dorsal view of the man in the Shroud, we saw more clearly the sole of the right foot that rested flat against the cross. Hidden in the Shroud images of the feet are the parts of each foot that were inside after the left foot was crossed on top of the right. In other words, we don't have a very good image of the bottom of the left foot or the top of the right foot. But we can clearly see from the ventral view that the left knee is bent and the body rotated from the hip to accommodate the left leg resting partially on top of the right leg. Crucified this way, the lower part of the body would have been twisted somewhat away from the left, with the knees protruding most likely to the right. The crucified man's back would have rubbed against the wood of the upright beam of the cross each time the man lifted his body up or down in the process of breathing. In doing so, the scourge wounds on the back would have been reopened and rubbed raw."

In his mind, Castle quickly reviewed the many painted images of crucified Christ that he had seen in museums around the world. What Middagh was describing differed from the painted images in several important aspects. "So you don't think, then, that the feet of the man in the Shroud were nailed to any footrest that he could have used to support his weight?"

"The Shroud shows no evidence of a *suppedaneum*, or footrest," Middagh answered. "You've got to remember the precise way Roman executioners fixed a man to the cross depended upon how long the Romans wanted the man to live. The arms and legs could be tied to the cross, which would prolong the time the man had to suffer. A footrest or even a little seat or *sedile* was fashioned as a block of wood and nailed to the upright crossbeam so the man could rest his buttocks. Again, these niceties prolonged the death. A fully adult man crucified this way could last two or three days, possibly longer, providing he had not been scourged to within an inch of his life and that he had been tied to the cross instead of nailed. With a *suppedaneum* and a *sedile,* breathing was easier and the problem became dehydration and thirst, with the crucified man more likely to die from a combination of thirst and exposure, rather than asphyxia."

"The problem in Christ's crucifixion was that the Roman executioners were up against the Sabbath," Morelli interjected. "To comply with Jewish law, Christ had to be dead and buried by sundown. In Jerusalem, two thousand years ago, much more so than today, everything in the Jewish community was expected to come to a total standstill once the sun went down on Friday."

"That's right," Middagh said. "From the evidence of the Shroud, there was no footrest or seat on the cross. The man's body was allowed to hang free, supported only by the nails in the wrists and the nail in the feet. The other variable was that the man in the Shroud shows evidence of a brutal scourging, back and front, from his shoulders to his heels. Crucifixion itself was meant to be a relatively bloodless process. The Roman executioners were expert in placing the nails so as to avoid piercing an artery. If they made a mistake and pierced an artery, the man could die in a matter of minutes. Making that mistake, a Roman centurion would have faced severe punishment for incompetence. But by scourging a man just short of the point where the scourging itself killed him, the time the man lived on the cross would have been shortened. This is what looks like was done to the man in the Shroud."

"If all else failed," Morelli added, "and the crucified man was living too long, the Romans typically took what amounted to a sledgehammer and broke the man's legs below the knees. With the legs broken, the only way the man could breathe was by raising and lowering his body by using his arms and pivoting against the nails in his wrist. As you can imagine, breathing like this would barely work at all and the pain of even trying to do so would have been unbearable. Once the legs were broken, death tended to come a few minutes later. Typically, those crucified died from a combination of pulmonary asphyxia and cardiac arrest."

Middagh added a point of clarification. "In the case of the man in the Shroud, the legs show no sign of being broken. Instead, the right side shows evidence of having been pierced by a Roman spear. This follows the accounts of the crucifixion in the New Testament and in Christian tradition that the legs of the two criminals crucified with Christ were broken, but Christ was spared this indignity. Thinking that Christ was already dead when sundown was approaching, a Roman centurion named Longinus took his spear and pierced through Christ's side to his heart. This would have left no doubt Christ was dead."

So far, what Middagh was describing confirmed what Castle had observed at Beth Israel of Father Bartholomew's wounds. The feet wounds looked like punctures from the top of the feet, as indicated by the skin forced down into the wound on top of each foot. The trauma evidence was that the left foot had been on top of the right, with a straight line evidencing the wound from the left foot through to exit Father Bartholomew's right foot. The skin on the sole of each foot was pushed out, as Castle would have expected to see from an exit wound caused by a nail or a spike.

"The ancient Romans had crucifixion down to a cruel science," Morelli added. "Sadists were particularly adapted to the work and Roman executioners who weren't good at what they did usually didn't last very long. Roman executioners were particularly good at taunting and tormenting the condemned as they were scourged, beaten, and crucified. With Christ's case, there was ample opportunity for humiliation, as evidenced by the crown of thorns."

"What does the Shroud tell us about the crown of thorns?" Castle asked Middagh.

"The blood flows on the forehead of the man in the Shroud appear to be from puncture marks that would be consistent with a crown of thorns. Particularly noticeable is the long blood flow above the left eye that seems to form the number 3. The puncture wounds and bloodstreams are also visible in a circle around the head in the dorsal image. Moreover, if you look closely, you will see matting on the hair on the top of the head, both in the frontal and posterior views of the man in the Shroud. This would suggest the crown of thorns was actually a cap of thorns that was beaten or hit into the scalp to cause fairly profuse bleeding. As you know, wounds to the scalp tend to bleed heavily."

Studying the Shroud, Castle could clearly see the same types of scalp wounds that Father Bartholomew suffered yesterday. His scalp wounds were from punctures and the punctures were on the top of his head, not just in a circle around his head at the level of his forehead.

"In the frontal view, you can clearly see the blood flows from the scalp wounds soaked down into the hair," Middagh went on. "Again, these blood flows occurred while the man in the Shroud was living and they were transferred directly onto the Shroud as bloodstains. The blood from the crown of thorns is distinct from the image of the man and was transferred onto the Shroud before the image appeared. Again, we know this because there is no body image formed under the blood flows on the head. The blood flows from the crown of thorns are more evidence the man was placed in the Shroud directly from the cross and shortly after he died."

"Looking at all this, one thing doesn't fit together," Anne said, obviously perplexed.

Castle expected that she was going to be upset at the suffering her brother was going through. Obviously, this was a concern Anne repeatedly expressed. But this morning something else was on her mind.

"If I am getting this right, first my brother experienced the stigmata on his wrists and then he suffered the scourge injuries. Is that correct?" she asked.

"That's right," Castle said.

"Now we see my brother experiencing the crown of thorns, then he levitates and gets the stigmata in his feet, right?"

"Yes," Castle said once again. "That's right. What's your point?"

"My point is that it's out of order," Anne said. "The way Christ suffered his passion and death was that first he was scourged at the pillar, then the crown of thorns was placed on his head. He didn't suffer nail wounds until later, when he was crucified. If my brother is manifesting Christ's passion and death, the order of his injuries is all wrong."

Castle could see that Anne had hit on an important point. "What do you think it means?" he asked her.

"I'm not entirely sure," Anne answered. "But I think it must have something to do with what Dr. Silver told us at Princeton."

"What do you mean?" Castle pressed again.

"I think it has to do with time," she explained. "My brother told me he felt his mission was to decipher the message of the Shroud for the world. Maybe he's showing us that time does not necessarily happen like we experience it. Maybe the events of Christ's passion and death are all still happening somehow, as if those moments never ended. If that were so, my brother is able to go back and key into this moment or that moment of Christ's torture and death, but he doesn't necessarily have to do so in the sequence the events were seen to have followed some two thousand years ago."

"It's an interesting idea," Castle said.

"I mean, think about it," Anne said. "In a way, Christ's death preceded his scourging and crowning with thorns."

Castle struggled to follow this point. "I was following you up to now, but you just lost me."

Anne began to explain. "It's about how the tree defines the seed. Father Middagh has just explained that the way the ancient Romans crucified people depended on how the executioners wanted the crucified man to die. We just heard that the Romans scourged Christ to within an inch of his life because the Sabbath was approaching and Christ had to die quickly on the cross, in order to comply with the rules of the Jews that Christ's body had to be buried by sundown Friday. So, in that regard, the death of Christ was a reality that even two thousand years ago preceded his scourging at the pillar and determined exactly how he was crucified—whether or not he would have a seat to rest on and a footrest, for instance."

"There's another point here," Morelli said, picking up on the theme. "In a way, the Shroud of Turin is a book. Examining the wounds of the man in the Shroud gives us clues as to exactly how he was punished and killed. We read motivations into the crown of thorns, namely that Christ was mocked as the supposed King of the Jews, a concept the Roman centurions thought laughable. Otherwise there would have been no point in the mock crown designed to torment Christ."

"My brother continues to use the word *codex* to describe the Shroud," Anne said. "He said the Shroud was a codex, a secret message that he intended to decipher. My brother also said he never quit being a physicist and that this was the crowning experiment of his life. What my brother researched was time. Like Dr. Silver told us, my brother, when he was at the Institute for Advanced Study, was working out advanced particle physics equations in order to prove we live in a universe that may involve ten or more dimensions, not just the four dimensions we think we live in. The point is that time is not as we experience it every day, not a logical progression from birth to death, from infancy to old age—not a straight line at all."

Just then, Castle's cell phone went off, interrupting the meeting.

Castle took the call. Archbishop Duncan was on the other end of the line.

"The pope would like to talk with you," Duncan said simply.

This did not entirely take Castle by surprise, not after the worldwide attention Fernando Ferrar's video broadcast had received. "Okay, when?"

"At one P.M. today," Duncan said. "If you are available, my office will arrange a three-way conference call with the Vatican, to include you and me with the pope."

"That will work," Castle said. "I want you to call me on my private landline in my office."

"Will do," Duncan agreed.

"Unfortunately, this meeting is over," Castle announced to the group in the conference room. "That was Archbishop Duncan and we've got an important conference call with the pope at one P.M. today."

"Should we wait to go to the hospital with you?" Anne asked.

"No," Castle said. "You go ahead. The hospital emailed me,

and the report on your brother this morning is that he is out of the burn unit and resting quietly in intensive care."

"Do you see any reason for me to go to the hospital?" Middagh asked.

"No," Castle answered. "I think it's better not to confront Father Bartholomew with a crowd. Your presentation today has been very helpful. Thank you, again."

CHAPTER TWENTY-FOUR

Monday afternoon
Dr. Stephen Castle's office, New York City
1:00 P.M. ET, 7:00 P.M. in Italy
Day 19

The conference call came through to Dr. Castle's office on time, as expected.

"Can Father Bartholomew travel?" the pope asked Castle immediately.

"I'm not sure," Castle answered. "I'm going to the hospital this afternoon to check on him. If his last injuries are any indication, he should recover rapidly. I can confirm it this evening, but I expect Father Bartholomew is going to be much stronger in a day or two. What do you have in mind?"

"I want to bring Father Bartholomew to the Vatican," the pope answered. "We need to manage this situation from Rome. Father Bartholomew's story is drawing tens of millions of believers and skeptics around the world and it's more than Archbishop Duncan can or should have to handle on his own."

"Thank you, Holy Father," Duncan said, relieved that he might soon transfer primary responsibility for Father Bartholomew to the Vatican. "I think I need to stay here in New York, if only to deal with the press. That's a responsibility that should fall to me."

"Agreed," the pope said. "You've got millions of people in New York and the United States who are now closely following Father Bartholomew."

"We're getting swamped with press requests," Duncan noted.

"Even in Italy, Father Bartholomew has become a sensation," the pope said. "Italians love the stigmata. When I was a boy growing up in the 1950s, Padre Pio was all the rage in Italy. He was on all the televisions. Every newspaper or magazine you picked up had a story about Padre Pio. I never was in favor of him being canonized, but then I guess a lot of Italians would say I'm prejudiced. I'm from northern Italy and Padre Pio was from southern Italy."

Castle understood. "Are you implying you've concluded Father Bartholomew is a fraud?"

"I'm not implying anything," the pope responded. "I just want Father Bartholomew in Rome where we can deal with him directly. This is the age of twenty-four-hour cable television news and the Internet. Father Bartholomew is an international celebrity. Have you seen how many people are watching the videos about Father Bartholomew on the Internet? In Italy alone the numbers are in the millions."

"Am I off the case, then?" Castle asked.

"No," the pope answered quickly. "If you can, I want you to clear your schedule and come to Rome with Father Bartholomew. I'm arranging for a chartered jet to arrive there tomorrow morning. The jet will have hospital facilities and I will send along a Vatican medical staff—provided you determine Father Bartholomew can leave tomorrow evening and be here in Rome on Wednesday morning."

Castle thought quickly. "Okay," he agreed. "I'm going to be at Beth Israel Hospital a little later today and I will begin figuring out when we can travel. How long do you think we will be in Italy?"

"I have no idea," the pope answered. "Until this thing is over. That's all I can say at this point."

Castle considered carefully what that might mean in terms of his commitments to his patients. "It will be complicated," he said quietly, "but I'll do it."

"One more thing," the pope added.

"What's that?"

"I want you to bring with you Father Morelli and Father Middagh. It's time for Father Morelli to return to the Vatican. We are going to need Father Middagh's expertise on the Shroud."

"What about Anne Cassidy?" Castle asked. "She's Father Bartholomew's half sister. Should we bring her, too?"

"By all means," the pope said. "She's family. But there's one more person I want you to bring, and this one might surprise you."

"Who's that?" Castle asked.

"That television reporter," the pope said. "I want you to invite Fernando Ferrar and his mobile television crew. I'm going to send you a large airplane and you will have room."

"But won't that just make it a circus?" Castle wondered out loud.

"It's going to be a circus no matter what we do," the pope answered. "His boss will send Fernando Ferrar to Rome to report for the television network, regardless of what we do. If we try to keep him out of the tent, we're only going to raise his suspicions. Let's prove to him the Vatican has nothing to hide here. There's no better way to do that than for the Vatican to extend him an invitation to come to Rome at our expense."

"Any restrictions on what Ferrar can film or report on?" Duncan asked.

"None, as far as I'm concerned," the pope answered. "That is, unless Ferrar or his camera crew get in the way of Father Bartholomew's medical treatment. I'll let you, Dr. Castle, make that judgment call. You are still Father Bartholomew's attending physician. There should be no concern about Father Bartholomew getting excellent medical care in the flight across the Atlantic. Father Bartholomew may be leaving the hospital, but the chartered airplane I'm sending you will be the next best thing."

Thinking through the trip, Castle realized that his associate, Professor Marco Gabrielli, was planning to unveil his modern Shroud duplicate at a press conference in Bologna on Thursday.

He explained this to the pope and archbishop.

"Should I plan to attend Gabrielli's press conference?" Castle asked the pope.

"Absolutely," the pope said. "You should attend and you should bring everybody with you, including Fathers Morelli and Middagh. Let them see firsthand what Gabrielli is capable of producing."

"What about Fernando Ferrar and his camera crew?" Castle wondered.

"Absolutely," the pope said again. "Take Fernando Ferrar and his video crew as well. On Thursday morning, the Vatican will charter another airplane to take you from Rome to Bologna. Coordinate with Professor Gabrielli so the press conference doesn't start until after you get there. If your friend Gabrielli proves the Shroud is a fake, so be it. Let Ferrar broadcast the story live to the world from the press conference."

"I admire your courage, Holy Father," Dr. Castle said.

"Courage has nothing to do with it," the pope said firmly. "I'm not about to let the credibility of the Catholic Church rest on whether or not a relic is authentic. Nor am I going to bet on a priest who may turn out to be mentally disturbed. My job is to run the Catholic Church, absent the Shroud of Turin and absent Father Bartholomew."

As soon as the conference call with the Vatican was over, Castle telephoned Gabrielli in Bologna to tell him he would be arriving in Italy on Wednesday morning and would be attending the press conference in Bologna on Thursday in person.

"That's great news," Gabrielli said with enthusiasm. He was also very pleased to know Castle was bringing along Fernando Ferrar and his television crew.

"This is going to be a huge international event." Gabrielli was bubbling with excitement. "Wait until you see my Shroud. I think it's the crowning achievement of my career."

"Have you seen the videos of Father Bartholomew levitating in St. Patrick's Cathedral?" Castle asked.

"Of course I've seen them," Gabrielli answered. "I think every man, woman, and child in Europe has seen them. Too bad Bartholomew isn't Italian. He might be our next saint, but first he would have to be prime minister."

Castle laughed at the thought. "What did you think of the levitation?"

"Oldest trick in the book," Gabrielli answered with conviction.

"What do you mean?"

"Every stage magician in the world has a levitation trick," Gabrielli explained. "I'm sure you have seen them. The beautiful young woman assistant walks onstage with almost no clothes on. The magician appears to hypnotize her. He lays her down horizontally and appears to put her to sleep. Then he moves his hands about magically and appears to be causing her to rise into the air, still sound asleep. To top off the trick, the magician runs a hoop all around the levitating woman to show there are no ropes or wires that are lifting her up. When he brings the woman back to earth and wakes her up, she appears to have had no recollection of anything that just happened."

"So, you are saying Father Bartholomew's miracle was nothing more than a magic trick?"

"That's exactly what I am saying," Gabrielli said in a tone of certainty.

"So explain to me," Castle said. "How's it done?"

"Easy. First you have to understand that nobody in the history of the world has ever levitated, not Hindu mystics and not Jesus Christ, though I will admit that his ascension into Heaven has to have been one of the world's greatest illusions. I only wish I had been there to see it."

Castle listened with quiet amusement to Gabrielli's assessment of Father Bartholomew's miracle. "So how is the levitation trick done?"

"Usually with hydraulics," Gabrielli said. "The magician stands behind the levitating woman just right, so as to hide a hydraulic lift bar behind him that connects to a steel bed on which the sleeping woman rests. Sometimes the woman wears a thin body veil that helps hide the steel bar bed and the hydraulic mechanism."

"How does the magician get away with passing a steel hoop all around the levitating woman to indicate there're no wires involved?"

"The hydraulic lift bar can be built with a U-shape that connects the bar to the steel bed. The magician can move the hoop around the U-shape to create the illusion he has passed the hoop completely around the woman. Actually, he just moves the hoop to the end of the U-shape and then reverses direction. It looks like he has gone all around her, but actually he hasn't. Remember, most magic tricks involve misdirection."

"Do you think this is what Father Bartholomew did?" Castle asked. "Did he fake his levitation by using tricks an accomplished magician would easily recognize?"

"I don't know. But after Father Bartholomew collapsed, I doubt if you, or anyone else, did much to search around that altar to see if there were any magician's mechanisms around. I also doubt you checked around to find out if Father Bartholomew had any accomplices who were in on the illusion."

"What do you mean?"

"Well, you said Fernando Ferrar and the film crew were inside the cathedral when Father Bartholomew levitated, right?"

"Yes, they were," Castle said, intrigued by where Morelli was going with this. "Ferrar and his film crew were already in the cathedral when I got there."

"Well, video cameras and news crews are not routinely admitted inside Catholic churches, and I doubt Fernando Ferrar had Archbishop Duncan's permission," Gabrielli said. "Who tipped Ferrar off to be at the church that morning?"

"I don't know."

"Ferrar has a vested career interest in being the only reporter to film Father Bartholomew's supposed miracle, right?"

"Yes, that's true."

"And Father Bartholomew had a vested interest in making sure his miracle was filmed."

"I guess you could look at it that way."

"Well then, I wouldn't rule out Ferrar as being an accomplice," Gabrielli said, satisfied that he had made his point. "Maybe Ferrar both filmed the event and operated the hydraulics that made Father Bartholomew's levitation possible. When Father Bartholomew sister screamed and fainted, that was perfect for the misdirection needed to end the illusion. All attention went to her.

Nobody paid any attention to the priest, until he then collapsed on the cathedral floor. I couldn't have designed the illusion better myself."

Castle had to admit he had not thought about these possibilities before. "I guess that's why you are the world's expert on debunking miracles," he commented. "I guess I just don't think like a magician."

"I've made a career debunking the paranormal," Gabrielli said proudly. "I don't believe in levitating priests and I also don't believe in Christ being resurrected or ascending into Heaven. It's not our subject today, but I'm convinced Christ's resurrection and his ascension are two of the better illusions ever produced by any professional magician anywhere, if they happened at all. As far as I'm concerned, Christ as a magician makes Houdini look like a schoolboy. Right now, what I want to debunk is the Shroud of Turin and I think I'm well along the way to doing so."

"And you are pretty confident the Shroud you have produced will make your point that the Shroud could have been a fake."

"In my opinion, the Shroud *has* to be a fake," Gabrielli said strongly, "and I believe I'm well on my way to proving how a brilliant medieval forger could have made a fortune pulling it off."

CHAPTER TWENTY-FIVE

At Beth Israel, Dr. Castle met with Dr. Constance Lin in her office to go over Father Bartholomew's most recent CT scans and MRIs.

"It's pretty much the same story," Dr. Lin said. "All the old wounds opened up again—the stigmata in the wrists and the scourge wounds all over the body. Then we have the new wounds, the stigmata in the feet and the head puncture wounds that would be from the crown of thorns."

"Do the stigmata on the feet pierce completely through the feet?" Castle asked.

"Again, it could be that the wounds penetrated the feet when they were first made," Lin answered. "But I took these CT scans and MRIs only a few hours ago, and the stigmata wounds on the feet are healing nicely and the stigmata in the hands appear almost completely healed."

"How about the puncture wounds on the head?"

JEROME R. CORSI, Ph.D.

"Same scenario. The puncture wounds are healing, maybe a little slower than the scourge wounds. But the bleeding in all the wounds has stopped. Father Bartholomew is recovering once again in record time and I have no explanation for you on how or why it's happening."

Castle understood. "This is pretty much what I expected to see."

"At least, it's about the same as we saw before," Lin said. "Father Bartholomew will probably suffer no permanent disabilities from these wounds, though wounds of this severity would have killed most people when they were first inflicted."

"I know," Castle said. "Believers worldwide consider Father Bartholomew's case to be a miracle."

"What do you think?"

"About the same as I always thought," Castle said without emotion. "Father Bartholomew's subconscious is particularly strong."

Visiting the priest, Castle found him awake, in the company of Anne and Father Morelli.

"I suppose you've heard we're going to the Vatican?" Castle asked Father Bartholomew.

"Archbishop Duncan called me a few minutes ago and let me know," the priest said.

"We will leave tomorrow evening and we'll fly all night. We'll arrive Wednesday morning."

"Am I going to be okay to make the trip?" the priest asked.

Castle reassured him. "The Vatican is sending a charter airplane with hospital-like medical facilities aboard. You'll be fine."

During the limo ride back to his Fifth Avenue apartment, Castle called his favorite hotel in Rome, the Hassler in the Piazza della Trinitá at the top of the Spanish Steps, and reserved two suites, one for himself and the other for Anne. He still wanted to keep Anne close at hand, both so he could keep an eye on her and so he could immediately get any additional insights she might have about her brother.

Father Bartholomew was to stay under Vatican care in Agostino Gemelli University Polyclinic. The hospital, known in Rome as the official hospital of the popes, kept a suite of rooms permanently reserved for the pope or top Vatican patients. Father Middagh would be put up in the Vatican's visiting priests' quarters and Father Morelli would return home to the private apartment he maintained year-round in Rome.

CHAPTER TWENTY-SIX

Tuesday evening
Flight from JFK Airport, New York,
to Leonardo da Vinci–Fiumicino Airport in Rome
Day 20

Dr. Castle and Anne took the psychiatrist's limo to the airport, following behind the ambulance that carried Father Bartholomew.

Castle was impressed by the police escort, which shortened the trip from Beth Israel in midtown Manhattan to JFK to around thirty-five minutes, despite late afternoon traffic.

Arriving at the international terminal for private passengers, Castle could see that the private jet sent by the pope was the customized Boeing 767 that Alitalia kept reserved for heads of state, including the pope. The customized interior included ample first-class seats, a conference room for meetings, several private sleeping quarters for VIPs, and an infirmary in the rear. Among the crew were a medical crew from the Vatican, including two nurses and a physician.

Once Fathers Morelli and Middagh were on board, together

with Fernando Ferrar and his three-man video crew, the pilot was ready to take off. Leaving JFK at around 6 P.M. Tuesday, their estimated time of arrival was early morning Wednesday in Rome. They would gain six hours in the time zone changes involved in going to Italy, making the night a short one, despite a cross-Atlantic air trip of some 4,260 miles.

On the flight over, Dr. Castle did his best to make himself scarce. The Alitalia crew served a multicourse dinner, complete with excellent Italian wines.

Still, Fernando Ferrar managed to get him alone as they were finishing the meal with an assortment of fine cheeses and after-dinner drinks.

"I understand you cannot talk to me about Father Bartholomew because that would violate doctor-patient confidential privileges," Ferrar began. "But could you answer me one question?"

"What's that?" Castle asked, hoping one question had to be harmless. Besides, he could always decline to answer.

"You have all the money in the world, so you don't need to take Father Bartholomew's case for the money. What is it, then? Why are you interested?"

"Don't necessarily assume money isn't important," Castle said, correcting him.

"Okay," Ferrar said. "I concede the point."

"But to answer your question, I guess what drives me is the people. I've worked with Archbishop Duncan and Pope John-Paul Peter I before, when he was a cardinal. They asked me to take on this case and I guess I couldn't refuse."

"Why not? I doubt you take every case you're asked to take."

"You're right," Castle conceded. "But let me ask you. Why did you take up this story? You're obviously ambitious, but is that the extent of why?"

"Maybe," Ferrar answered. "Is there anything wrong with being ambitious?"

"No, not necessarily. But there's lots of stories out there. Why this one?"

"In my case, I'm intrigued," Ferrar said. "I was raised Catholic in Puerto Rico. The Shroud is fascinating to me and you have to admit, Father Bartholomew is a good story."

"Yes, he is," Castle said. "But what if it turns out all this is a fraud, or that Father Bartholomew is just mentally ill? Will you report that?"

Ferrar thought for a minute. "It would be a lot less interesting story," he finally said. "I guess I would report it, but who would care? People want to believe in God. They want to believe in miracles."

"I know," Castle said, moving in for the kill. "I would even go so far as to say people need to believe. But that is not my question. My question is about you. Do you want to believe? Is that why you're doing the story? Is it because you want the Shroud to be the burial cloth of Christ and you want Father Bartholomew to be a miracle man?"

Again, Ferrar thought before he answered. "I see where you're headed. You're a smart guy and I don't want to fall into your trap. Let me answer you this way: To tell you the truth, I'm not really sure about the Shroud, or about Bartholomew. But what I know is this—I'm covering the story because there is a good chance it's all true. Otherwise, I wouldn't waste my time."

"And from my point of view, it's just the opposite," Castle countered. "I took on Father Bartholomew as a patient because there's a good chance it's all false. Otherwise, I wouldn't waste my time."

CHAPTER TWENTY-SEVEN

Thursday morning
Bologna, Italy
Day 22

The eight passengers—Dr. Castle and Anne Cassidy, Fathers Morelli and Middagh, Fernando Ferrar and his three-man crew—fit comfortably in the eight-seat, two-engine Citation XLS the Vatican had chartered for the forty-seven-minute flight from Rome to Bologna.

Two limos picked up the passengers at the airport and transported them to the University of Bologna, where chemistry professor Marco Gabrielli was preparing for the press conference of his life.

When Castle and Anne walked into the auditorium-style conference room with its tiers of raised seats, Gabrielli was backstage, carefully going over his notes one last time. Castle counted some fifty correspondents who were present, including Reuters from Great Britain, the Associated Press from the United States, and Agence France-Presse. Italian journalists sat in the front row behind name cards reserved for *Corriere della Sera* in Milan, *La*

Repubblica from Rome, and *La Stampa* from Turin, among others. Video cameras from RAI in Italy and TV5 in France were prominent among the European television crews set up in the back row of the stylish facility. Quietly, the American video crew set up their camera among the others in the back of the room, as Fernando Ferrar positioned himself alone, in the center of the auditorium. Fathers Morelli and Middagh sat in the row behind Dr. Castle and Anne Cassidy, off to the side of the auditorium.

Each auditorium seat came equipped with earphones. A dial built into the desk allowed the occupant to select one of four languages: Italian, French, English, and German. Behind a glass panel off to the side of the room, opposite where Dr. Castle and the others sat, were four translators ready to do a simultaneous broadcast to the conference participants.

At precisely 11:30 A.M. local time, Dr. Gabrielli stepped to the podium, flanked by two assistants in lab coats. Behind each assistant was an easel with the display boards covered by a white cloth. He looked dapper in his finely tailored beige cashmere sport coat and black turtleneck sweater. For once, his freshly cut and nicely combed black hair was a good match for his closely trimmed Van Dyke beard. From the way he was dressed and groomed, Castle judged Gabrielli was at the top of his game. The impression was reinforced the minute Gabrielli stepped to the podium. As he surveyed the audience, Gabrielli's trademark wry smile and his darting green eyes gave the impression that he was indeed the cat who had caught the mouse.

"Good morning," Gabrielli began confidently. "Welcome to the University of Bologna. I am Dr. Marco Gabrielli, senior professor of chemistry here. My complete academic resumé will be provided to you in the press packets we will hand out at the end of the session. We will take questions at the end of my short presentation."

Looking out at the audience, Gabrielli was pleased to see Dr. Castle in attendance. Almost imperceptibly, Gabrielli nodded recognition to his friend and associate in the audience.

"My expertise at the University of Bologna has in recent years been extended to exposing frauds in a wide range of paranormal phenomena, including supposed miracles involving a variety of statues of Jesus Christ, the Virgin Mary, and various saints that have been claimed to be crying tears of blood, to an exposition of the chemistry by which religious mystics have been able to self-produce the illusion of the stigmata, the nail wounds of Christ's crucifixion appearing typically on their wrists."

Having given more than one press conference in his career, Gabrielli planned to cut to the chase.

"Today I am here to announce that I have successfully reproduced the Shroud of Turin using only materials and methods known to be available to medieval forgers who were working in the period between 1260 and 1390 A.D., the dates the carbon-14 tests done on the Shroud have established for its date of creation."

At Gabrielli's instruction, his first assistant removed the cloth from the first easel, exposing a life-size photograph of the frontal image of the crucified man depicted in the Shroud of Turin. "This, as you see, is the original Shroud of Turin. This image is a life-size photographic negative that shows the crucified man's features in white highlights."

At his instruction, the second assistant removed the cloth from the second easel, showing for the first time Gabrielli's life-size reproduction of the Shroud on a modern strip of linen made, under Gabrielli's direction, to match the Shroud of Turin's exact weave pattern and size. When the image was exposed, even the jaded members of the press seemed to let out an audible gasp. The first impression of everyone in the room was that Gabrielli had done it. His reproduction was startling in how much it looked exactly like the original, down to the beard and mustache of the crucified man, the scourge marks visible on the body, and the nail wounds seen in the man's wrists and feet.

"I'd like you to meet my model," Gabrielli said, motioning to the back door of the auditorium.

Out stepped a handsome, bearded man in his early thirties, wearing a long, flowing white robe designed to enhance the effect.

"This is one of my senior graduate students," the professor said. "Roberto d'Agostini."

Everyone in the room was instantly impressed by how much d'Agostini looked like an icon of Jesus Christ that had stepped right out of the Shroud itself. Even Castle was impressed. D'Agostini had the same square face and beard with a forked opening in the middle, the same long hair that drooped to his shoulders and trailed into a ponytail that stretched down his back to his waist. He had the same long, elegant fingers as the man in the Shroud of Turin. Even their ages seemed similar. D'Agostini appeared to be in his early thirties and Christ, according to tradition, was thirty-three years old when he was crucified.

But truthfully Castle wasn't sure whether d'Agostini or Father Bartholomew had done a better job in making themselves look like the man in a Shroud, so he guessed it was a toss-up. If d'Agostini looked somewhat younger than the man in the Shroud of Turin, Father Bartholomew in his early forties looked somewhat older. That was the only significant difference Castle could discern.

"While I can assure you that Signore d'Agostini's beard and mustache are authentic, there was no reason for him to appear nude today," Gabrielli said. "The wounds you see in my shroud were painted on his body, based on a detailed analysis of the wounds we see in the Shroud of Turin. We transferred the body image to the linen cloth of the Shroud duplicate by a series of carefully designed rubbing methods and exposure to ambient light."

D'Agostini gathered up his robe and took a chair to the side of Dr. Gabrielli. Sitting quietly, he looked every bit as composed and serene as did the man in the Shroud.

"While the press packet will give you a more complete description of my methodology, let me simply say that I used red ochre and vermilion paints, common coloring materials available to medieval artists. I followed, among others, the scientific conclusions of Dr. Walter McCrone, the American chemist and leading expert in microscopy who was a member of the team of scientists allowed by the Vatican to examine the Shroud over a five-day period as part of the 1978 Shroud of Turin Research Project. To produce the image on my Shroud, we treated the Shroud with a light-sensitive coating made from a proprietary mixture of egg albumin and various plant extracts. The primary paint I used was an iron oxide formula commonly known as red ochre, which I supplemented for detailed painting with a mercuric sulfide mixture known in the Middle Ages as vermilion. I produced the final result by exposing the finished product to various heat treatments in a specially designed industrial ceramic furnace. I would remind believers that the Shroud of Turin does not show substantial traces of iron oxide or mercuric sulfide today because the paint pigments on the original Shroud faded away over the centuries."

The video cameras at the back zoomed in for close-ups of both shrouds, as the reporters at their desks furiously made notes.

"In conclusion," Gabrielli said, "please realize that this is only my first effort. My goal today was simply to demonstrate to you that materials and techniques commonly available to medieval artists were more than sufficient for a skilled and brilliant forger to have produced the Shroud of Turin in his studio. I think you will agree that the shroud duplicate that you see before you has fundamentally the same characteristics you see in the original Shroud of Turin. My goal is to dispel the myth that the Shroud of Turin displays unexplainable features that could not be produced by human hands. I believe you will agree with me that the shroud duplicate I have produced in the last few weeks goes a long way to proving that the Shroud of Turin is no more authentic than religious statues claimed to bleed real blood."

When Gabrielli finished, a flurry of reporters raised their hands to be the first to ask a question.

In politically astute deference to his countrymen, Gabrielli chose an Italian press reporter from the first row to ask the first question. Gabrielli asked the reporter to identify himself before he asked his question.

"I'm Silvio Brunetta from *La Repubblica* in Rome," he said as he stood up. "How do you expect the Vatican to react to your shroud?"

Gabrielli chuckled. "Truthfully, I don't expect any reaction," he said. "The Vatican has always been cautious not to confirm the Shroud of Turin as the actual burial cloth of Christ. The group that I do expect to go berserk are the scientific members of the Shroud of Turin community around the world who have a vested interest in defending their decades of research trying to prove the Shroud is real, despite the carbon-14 evidence to the contrary."

A second questioner introduced himself. "I'm Vittorio Graviano with *Corriere della Sera* in Milan. I see on your shroud that you even duplicated the burn holes and water damage we see on the original Shroud. Can you tell us how you added these effects?"

"Certainly," Gabrielli answered. "As I said, I wanted my shroud to look as much as possible like the original Shroud. So, after we placed the image of Signore d'Agostini on the cloth, we scorched the cloth and soaked it with water, to duplicate as much as possible the patterns of damage you see on the original. To finalize the results, I added blood and blood serum to the image, in the exact areas we see bloodstains on the original. To be authentic, I used human blood."

From there, Gabrielli was peppered with questions for half an hour. No, he answered, he was not an atheist. "I'm a Roman Catholic," he asserted. "Just not a very devout one."

He stated that he did not hate the Vatican and that he did not want to hurt Christianity. "My goal is not political," he argued. "I'm a professional chemist who teaches here at one of Italy and Europe's oldest and most prestigious universities. I expose fraud. My goal is to prevent gullible people worldwide from being deceived even today by a forger who had a plan to get rich in the thirteenth or fourteenth century."

Gabrielli stated that his goal was not to get rich by his efforts.

Asked whether he produced the shroud because of the recent fame of Father Paul Bartholomew in the United States, Gabrielli admitted that the attention generated by the American priest was his inspiration. "Yes," he said. "And I understand that Father Bartholomew has been brought to Rome by the Vatican and I am looking forward to meeting him. Maybe after that I can give you a report on how I believe Father Bartholomew is producing the illusion of his stigmata."

That Father Bartholomew had been brought from the United States to Italy by the Vatican was news to all in the room, except of course for Dr. Castle and the contingent that had traveled with them from New York.

Fernando Ferrar spoke up.

"I'm Fernando Ferrar, a television reporter from New York," he said, introducing himself. "I can confirm that Father Bartholomew is in Rome. My news crew and I traveled with him on the Vatican-chartered airplane that left JFK Airport for Rome this Tuesday evening."

Heads in the audience turned, as various reporters decided they would interview Ferrar as well as Gabrielli before they rushed out to file their stories.

"My question, Professor Gabrielli, is this." Ferrar continued: "Just because you can duplicate the Shroud of Turin does not mean the original isn't authentic."

"What do you mean?" Gabrielli asked, puzzled at the supposed question.

"Maybe somebody could duplicate Leonardo da Vinci's *Mona Lisa*, but that doesn't prove Leonardo didn't paint the original."

"What's your point?" Gabrielli shot back.

"My point is simple." Ferrar pressed on. "It's a lot easier to duplicate something than to create it in the first place. I don't see that you produced the 'positive' from which your negative image with the white highlighting was taken. How did a medieval painter think to create a negative that would not have been recognized as such until Secondo Pia first photographed the Shroud for the 1898 exposition?"

"This is just my first effort," Gabrielli said defensively. "I will be refining my techniques in the future and producing more examples to show how the Shroud of Turin could have been forged. Remember, I can't prove the Shroud was forged. I can only prove the Shroud *could* have been forged."

"Isn't that a lot like trying to prove that the Declaration of Independence could have been printed on a modern copying machine?" Ferrar asked, hoping he might get an answer. "Maybe you could get from a copy machine a document that would be indistinguishable from the original, but what would it prove? Just because you can copy a document doesn't mean the original isn't authentic."

"If you recall, I stressed that I used only medieval materials and techniques," Gabrielli said, smiling in a condescending way. "Copy machines were obviously not around in the thirteenth or fourteenth centuries."

Then, looking to Dr. Castle and seeing him nod with satisfaction, he decided it was time to bring the press conference to an end. "Thank you for coming," Gabrielli announced. "That concludes the formal part of our news conference for today. Press packages will be handed out in the back of the room as you exit."

But before Gabrielli could leave, reporters circled him and blocked his escape in their determination to ask him one more question before he got away.

The still photographers roamed about, taking close-up shots of Gabrielli surrounded by the gaggle of reporters, of d'Agostini, who was more than willing to pose alongside Gabrielli's shroud, and of Gabrielli's shroud itself. The video crews moved through the crowd with their handheld cameras, getting the fill-in footage they would need to give the press conference some background context. Almost immediately, one of the reporters with a cell phone camera scooped the television reporters by posting a video of the press conference on the Internet.

Within the hour, video of Gabrielli's news conference was being seen by millions worldwide, both on the Internet and on television.

The headlines from a largely nonbelieving and predictably cynical world press were much as expected: ITALIAN SCIENTIST REPRODUCES SHROUD OF TURIN and SCIENTIST PROVES SHROUD

OF TURIN IS A MEDIEVAL FORGERY seemed to capture the general tenor of the stories going forth that afternoon from the conference room in Bologna.

On the airplane ride back to Rome, Castle was amused at how right Gabrielli was. He had two Shroud supporters with him in the persons of Fathers Morelli and Middagh. Despite Archbishop Duncan's initial effort to sell Father Morelli to him as a devil's advocate Jesuit, Morelli admitted he had crossed over long ago, convinced the scientific evidence weighed in favor of the Shroud's authenticity, despite the carbon-14 dating.

Middagh and Morelli did nothing to hide their displeasure at having to listen to an hour or more of talk from Gabrielli, who they thought lacked expertise in Shroud research.

"The Shroud of Turin Research Project discredited Walter Mc-Crone," Middagh said.

"Gabrielli all but admitted today that the traces of iron oxide on the Shroud are minimal," Morelli added in an irritated tone. "Besides, the straw yellow color of the body image on the Shroud doesn't match the color of any forms of ferric iron oxides that are known to exist."

"Science by press release," was how Middagh summed up Gabrielli's performance before the international media. "He's a publicity hound, nothing more and nothing less. If he were a true scientist, Gabrielli would have presented his findings to a peer-reviewed academic journal. Otherwise, it's just show business."

Listening to Fathers Middagh and Morelli grouse, Castle was convinced he was in the first stages of hearing the Vatican's unofficial rebuttal, even though Castle was certain Pope John-Paul Peter I would never take any official position on the Shroud.

"How many times do we have to prove that the Shroud was not painted," Morelli wondered. "Red ochre is an earth pigment that would have washed off when water was thrown on the Shroud in the 1532 fire. McCrone was an old fool who was the only member of the Shroud of Turin Research Project to think the Shroud was painted. That was his opinion going into the research project and that was the prejudice he held until he died."

"Besides, there's the issue of the blood on the Shroud blocking the formation of the image," Middagh said. "How many times do we have to explain that there were two distinct steps in which the image was formed: first the blood was deposited by direct contact, then the body image was formed by a process nobody so far has explained satisfactorily. I'm sure all Gabrielli did was throw blood here and there on top of an image he already created. Look closely and I'm sure you will find a body image under the globs of blood Gabrielli painted on his shroud. If that's what Gabrielli did, he missed an important point and his duplicate shroud will end up doing nothing to discredit the authenticity of the Shroud of Turin."

When they landed in Rome, Morelli got a call from the Vatican.

"The Vatican says we should all rest up tonight," Morelli told Castle.

"Why?" Castle wondered.

"The pope has chartered the plane for us once again tomorrow morning," Morelli explained. "They have scheduled us a trip to Geneva. Seems there is a scientist at CERN the pope wants us to meet."

"Are we invited?" Ferrar asked, not wanting to be excluded.

"Yes," Morelli said, "and the pope suggests you will want to bring along your video crew. The Vatican has requested for you to videotape the interview."

"Sounds good to me," Ferrar said.

"One more thing," Morelli said to Castle. "The pope wants Professor Gabrielli to go along. Do you think you can arrange that? The pope will schedule an airplane to take Gabrielli directly to Geneva and return him home at the conclusion of the day."

"I don't know," Castle said, not entirely surprised at Pope John-Paul Peter I's decision to include his chemist friend on the field trip to CERN. "I will telephone him and find out."

CHAPTER TWENTY-EIGHT

Friday
CERN, Geneva, Switzerland
Day 23

The name CERN derived from the acronym in French for Conseil Européen pour la Recherche Nucléaire, or European Council for Nuclear Research. CERN was formed in 1952 as a provisional body charged with building a world-class fundamental physics research organization in Europe. The guts of CERN were underground, consisting primarily of the Large Hadron Collider, a twenty-seven-kilometer-circumference circular tunnel built below the surface of the earth in the area between the Geneva airport and the Jura Mountains. CERN physicists use the Large Hadron Collider to smash protons together in an attempt to understand the "big bang," which many modern physicists and astronomers believe was the origin of the universe.

Within minutes of Dr. Castle's arrival from Rome, a limo delivered Professor Gabrielli from Bologna. Once the group was together, they were escorted down a central elevator to the office of Dr. Ruth Bucholtz, an internationally renowned particle physicist.

In the past year, Dr. Bucholtz had the personal pleasure of presenting the results of her decade-long research on the Shroud of Turin to Pope John-Paul Peter I in a personal two-hour audience in the Vatican. In a conference room adjoining her office, Dr. Bucholtz set up the equipment she would need to demonstrate her conclusions about the Shroud.

Dr. Bucholtz greeted them with her thick German accent. Castle judged her to be in her early sixties. He had to admit she looked attractive in the gray pinstriped pantsuit she wore for the occasion, instead of her more customary white lab coat. Her shoulder-length silver hair blended nicely with her distinctive gray eyes. By training, Dr. Bucholtz was a Ph.D.-level physicist who studied at the Technische Universität München, or Technical University in Munich, one of Germany's most highly acclaimed research universities in chemistry, engineering, physics, and mathematics. After graduation, she joined the physics faculty at the University of Heidelberg, where she remained until 1990, when she accepted a full-time senior research position at CERN.

Dr. Castle took the opportunity to introduce the others to Dr. Bucholtz as they took their seats in the conference room to watch her presentation.

"Do you mind if we video your presentation, Dr. Bucholtz?" Fernando Ferrar asked.

"No," she answered. "I have no objection whatsoever. The Holy Father when he spoke to me yesterday from the Vatican expressly asked my permission.

"Thank you for coming here today," she began, addressing Castle and others. "After Professor Gabrielli's most interesting presentation yesterday in Bologna, the Vatican called and asked me if I would be willing to share with you the results of the research I have been doing on the Shroud of Turin for the past ten years. It may surprise you that a physicist like myself with a specialty in advanced particle physics should take an interest in the Shroud of Turin, but I estimate that after you view my presentation you will understand what drew my interest."

Castle was not surprised. Father Bartholomew was also a particle physicist. Castle assumed Bartholomew and Bucholtz shared a lot of scientific perspectives and conclusions.

With this, an assistant in the back of the room lowered the lights. Bucholtz had projected from the computer a photograph of the Shroud of Turin displayed in the specially built vacuum-sealed display case in the Chapel of the Shroud in the Cathedral of St. John the Baptist in Turin. "As you know, the Shroud is a relatively ordinary piece of linen, but what I want to explain to you here today is why I have concluded that the Shroud contains a quantum message that we can only begin to decipher with the advance equipment we have here at a world-class particle physics research laboratory such as CERN. You will have to trust me for now when I claim that the Shroud is a blueprint to a completely new understanding of our universe, an understanding for which we will have to invent a completely new science of physics."

This got everyone's immediate attention, particularly Castle's. What did Dr. Bucholtz mean by a "quantum message"? What type of advanced equipment had Dr. Bucholtz used to decode the message she claimed to have read in the Shroud? What new "blueprint" could this ancient relic possibly contain? Castle was not sure. Neither was any of the other guests in the room.

"I want to start by showing you some images that were developed by Dr. John Jackson and Dr. Eric Jumper in 1976. Dr. Jackson, then an air force officer, was working as a physicist at the U.S. Air Force Academy while Dr. Jumper was an air force captain working as an assistant professor of aerodynamics with Dr. Jackson. At that time, they were utilizing a NASA-developed VP-8 Image Analyzer that was designed in the 1960s to create relief maps of the moon from astronomical photographs. Their goal was to produce topographic images that would be useful to NASA and to the U.S. astronauts preparing for moon landings. Dr. Jackson, as I am sure most of you know, went on to be a primary organizer and scientific leader of the thirty or so scientists he assembled to make up the 1978 Shroud of Turin Research Project. At present, Dr. Jackson heads the Turin Shroud Center of Colorado, with his wife, Rebecca, in Colorado Springs."

Next, Dr. Bucholtz displayed on the screen a copy of the 1931 photograph Giuseppe Enrie had taken of the Shroud of Turin.

"When Jackson and Jumper placed this famous 1931 photograph of the Shroud of Turin into the VP-8 Image Analyzer, they were startled to see a three-dimensional image. What jumped out was the face of the man in the Shroud of Turin in the accurate 3-D detail they would have expected to find from the 3-D topographic images the machine was design to create for moon craters. By comparison, when Jackson and Jumper analyzed a normal photograph taken of a person, the result was not a three-dimensional image, but a rather distorted jumble of light and dark shapes. The two-dimensional photograph lacked the necessary information coded within the image to produce a 3-D picture of the person, unlike the image of the Shroud."

Everyone in the room understood the point when Bucholtz projected onto the screen the three-dimensional green-tone image of the face of the man in the Shroud as produced by the VP-8 Image Analyzer. Instead of seeing the face as a flat, two-dimensional image, the man in the Shroud appeared almost alive. The nose, cheeks, hair, beard, and mustache all stood out, while the eyes receded as one would expect.

"The difference is that the lights and darks of normal photographic film result solely from the amount of light reflected by the subject onto the film. In sharp contrast, the image in the Shroud contains precise data that record density in direct relationship to the distance the subject was from the film. In other words, the closer the cloth was to the body, for instance at the tip of the nose or in the cheekbone, the darker the image that was formed on the Shroud. The more distant the body part—for instance, the eye sockets or the neck—the fainter was the image recorded on the Shroud. As you will see in this next slide, we get the same three-dimensionality when we examine the full-length body of the man in the Shroud in the VP-8 Image Analyzer."

Again everyone in the room was impressed by the lifelike nature of the green-tone image Bucholtz projected on the screen: the man in the Shroud shown in a frontal view from the top of his head to the fingertips of his crossed hands to his feet.

Next, Bucholtz projected onto the screen an image of the shroud that Professor Gabrielli had unveiled the previous day in Bologna.

"Professor Gabrielli, I'm sure you will recognize this as the shroud you produced to prove that medieval materials and methods could have been used to produce a forgery?" she asked.

"Yes," he said. "That certainly looks like the shroud I created. Where did you get the picture?"

"The Vatican had it delivered to me yesterday," she said. "But then for the past twenty-four hours your shroud has been all over the Internet and television, so getting a copy would not have been difficult. I just wanted to use the photograph you yourself produced."

"Did you examine it in the VP-8 Image Analyzer?" Gabrielli asked, anxious to know the results.

"Yes, I did," Bucholtz said, as she projected the results on the screen. "There are only one or two functioning VP-8 Image Analyzers yet around. Fortunately, CERN has one of them. As you can see, the results are disappointing, much like when we project a normal photograph through the analyzer. The green-tone result shows a forest of uneven lines with no dimensionality whatsoever. So I would have to say that in this respect, you failed to prove your point."

Rather than become defensive, Gabrielli decided to concede the obvious. "I'm afraid that up until now, I didn't really appreciate the three-dimensionality of the Shroud of Turin. Obviously, in my next attempt, I will have to take that into consideration."

Next Dr. Bucholtz turned to a large apparatus she had set up in the corner of the conference room. Castle could see that the machine was built around a series of lasers.

"I have designed this machine to project holographic images into three-dimensional space," she explained. "Without giving you a physics lesson, you should know that holograms are a major advancement in our ability to represent three-dimensional objects. Holograms are formed by scattering intense beams of light onto an object, typically by lasers, so that the interference pattern generated by multiple lasers hitting the object allows us to produce a three-dimensional image of the object."

Bucholtz grabbed an ordinary credit card she had placed on the table in front of her for this demonstration. "You have all seen holograms, typically on the security elements built into credit cards that show you flying birds or some other three-dimensional object when you hold the credit card at varying angles to the light. When you rotate the card, it looks like you are seeing the three-dimensional image from different angles, even though the credit card itself remains two-dimensional, completely flat, other than the raised letters and numbers imprinted into the card's face."

At that point, Bucholtz turned on her laser machine and an image of the man of Turin appeared as if floating in space in front of them, as a three-dimensional hologram. Without saying a word, Bucholtz manipulated the hologram so it rotated 360 degrees, permitting Castle and his guests to see the full frontal and dorsal images of the man in the Shroud. Then Bucholtz adjusted some more gears, and the image appeared to jump right into the room, rotating in front of them as if a holographic Jesus Christ had suddenly come alive in their presence.

Fernando Ferrar had never seen anything like this, unless it was at a theme park back in the United States. He went back to his camera crew to make sure they were capturing the hologram, as best they could, on video. Looking through the lens himself, he was thrilled. The camera captured the hologram floating in space in front of them. It looked almost like Bucholtz had made the man in the Shroud come alive.

"As you can see," she said, "I have gone one step further from the earlier demonstration on the VP-8 Image Analyzer that established the information on the Shroud was three-dimensional. What I have proved by this demonstration is that the information on the Shroud is holographic, such that you see the results right here before your very eyes. In other words, holographic information is encoded within the image of the Shroud. Until very recently, our technology did not allow us to read this information and interpret it—"

Father Middagh interrupted. "One question, please. The image of the man in the Shroud is lined by the burn marks and the triangle repairs the nuns sowed onto the cloth several hundred years ago. The burn areas destroyed parts of the image, such that we have lost the shoulders of the man in the Shroud and the forearms. Why is it that we see those parts of the body reconstructed in the hologram?"

"An excellent question," Bucholtz said. "Without giving you the technical explanation, just accept that one of the more interesting characteristics of a hologram is that each part of the holographic image contains information about the whole image. My team here at CERN and I have learned how to take a partial holographic image, such as the Shroud, and reconstruct the whole from the parts that survived."

"Very impressive," Middagh said.

"Professor Gabrielli, you will have to be sure your next two-dimensional shroud contains enough information properly coded so that I can lift a three-dimensional holographic image off it." Dr. Bucholtz made her suggestion gently, careful to mask her skepticism. She seriously doubted Gabrielli would ever be able to produce that result, especially if he was serious about limiting himself to materials and methods available to thirteenth- and fourteenth-century artists.

"So noted," said Gabrielli, showing no sign of having taken any offense at the suggestion. Gabrielli indeed believed he could do it and his mind was already calculating several possible methodologies he might use in the effort to re-create what he was now seeing for the first time.

"My next challenge was to explain how the image might have been placed on the Shroud," Bucholtz went on. "I began by noticing an important characteristic of the Shroud image. While the bloodstains on the Shroud may have resulted from direct contact with the body, the body image we see on the Shroud could not possibly have been produced by direct body contact."

"What do you mean?" Castle wanted to know, not sure he was following her explanation.

"If a cloth lies on top of a person and an image is directly transferred by contact from the body to the cloth, that image would be distorted when the cloth was lifted from the body and stretched taut," she explained. "Let me show you a series of images that illustrate my point."

Returning to her laptop computer, Bucholtz projected onto the screen several photographs of models used to produce shroudlike images by direct contact. One of the models, in particular, had been painted head to toe. When the cloth was lifted off his body, the image looked extended and distorted, fatter than the model and out of proportion to his body.

"I came to the conclusion that the image on the Shroud could have been produced only if the body somehow floated in air," she said. "The Shroud rapped around the man's head had to have floated above and below the body, such that both the upper and the lower part of the Shroud were pulled completely taut in a horizontal position to the body, so as to prevent any distortion of the image when it was transferred to the cloth."

Returning to her hologram machine, Bucholtz next generated a three-dimensional hologram of the body of the man in the Shroud floating in midair. His arms could clearly be seen resting on his abdomen and his left leg was bent forward above the right leg; also, both legs showed the bending at the knee that would have resulted from the trauma of the crucified man raising and lowering his body to breathe.

After making a few more adjustments, Bucholtz caused the Shroud itself to appear in three dimensions, wrapped around the man, but suspended above and below the body in parallel lines. Everyone in the room could see the body of the man in the Shroud projected in space before them, as if they were watching a 3-D movie, but without the red-and-blue glasses. The long linen cloth was wrapped around the head of the dead man lying on an unseen plane in space, such that the Shroud stretched taut at a distance of several inches above and below the body, reaching down to the feet on both the upper and lower sections.

Bucholtz rotated the image into the room, so the audience could see from multiple different angles the hologram of the man suspended in the air with the cloth hovering above and below him as if in parallel planes.

"If you think about it," she said, "the dorsal image could not have been formed so perfectly as it is if the man were lying on a rock bed in a tomb. His back would have been pressed down into the cloth and distortion of the image would have been inevitable. The same is true with the frontal image. Gravity would have pulled the cloth down on the man resting on his back dead in the tomb. Wrinkles and folds would have been inevitable. The amazing thing about the image on the Shroud of Turin is that there are absolutely no distortions. The muscles of the back and buttocks are not pushed in or distended from the man lying on his back. This type of image reflects no effect of gravity whatsoever."

Looking at the hologram floating in midair as Dr. Bucholtz talked, Gabrielli was becoming more and more convinced he was witnessing just another version of a magic show, with the only difference being that this one was produced by a highly paid physicist with an expensive piece of advanced imaging machinery. Most magicians aren't so lucky to have the resources of CERN at their disposal.

"The image we see on the Shroud could only have been produced if the image projected up and down simultaneously, from some imaginary plane that ran through the middle of the body of the man himself," she continued. "You have to see here how the linen burial cloth is stretched out above and below the body as if they were two parts of one artist's canvases framed and positioned above and below the body ready for painting. Now I will draw a plane through the center of the man lying on his back. From this plane, the image is simultaneously projected upward and downward, with no spillover of the image from front to back, and with no evident distortion caused by gravity."

"Of course, an artist would not have worried about the physical transfer process," Gabrielli said in objection. "An artist would have worked on a stretched canvas and painted intentionally without the distortions of a cloth lying on the body at all. It would have been completely natural to have painted a front and a back image separately, each without distortion."

"Yes, you have a point," Bucholtz conceded, "but I disagree with you that the image was painted at all. The Shroud image was imprinted on fibers of cloth that are one-tenth the diameter of hairs on your head. The image was created by what at a microscopic level would look like random coloration, much like how newsprint looks like dots when magnified. You would have needed an atomic laser machine that could place the image on the Shroud as we see it. Unfortunately, high-resolution atomic microscopes like we have available here at CERN were not available to artists working in the thirteenth and fourteenth centuries. The very top of the linen fibrils of the cellulose fibers of the Shroud demonstrates colorization from an extremely rapid dehydration and oxidation process. It is almost as if the Shroud fibers aged in an instantaneous process similar to effects we observe with radiation. The reddish brown sepia or yellow-straw image on the Shroud appears almost as if formed in the process of the Shroud being scorched."

"So how then do you explain how the image was formed?" Gabrielli asked, rapidly losing patience with an explanation he still considered to be nothing more than the ramblings of a theoretical physicist speculating about a religious relic outside her area of expertise.

"I believe the suspended body of Christ in the tomb entered what we call in general relativity an event horizon," she answered.

"Excuse me if I don't know what an event horizon is," Gabrielli replied. "I'm just a simple chemist, not an advanced particle physicist like you."

"An event horizon is a boundary in space-time where the normal laws of physics no longer apply," she said. "We observe event horizons, for instance, in the area surrounding black holes in space, where light that is emitted from within the black hole is never able to escape to an observer standing outside the black hole."

"So you are telling us, then, that Christ suspended like your hologram shows, between the sheets of the Shroud, and entered one of these so-called event horizons where his body radiated into some other dimension. Is that it?" Gabrielli asked, intending to be sarcastic.

"Yes, that is exactly what I am trying to say," Bucholtz answered, not realizing that Gabrielli was trying to be facetious.

"So, in other words, the Shroud of Turin, in your opinion, is a kind of time machine. Is that it?" he asked.

"In a way, I guess you could say that," she said. "My conclusion is that Christ's body entered an event horizon in which his physical body transitioned into another space-time dimension. My hypothesis is that at the moment of transition, the body transitioned into another space-time dimension with an instantaneous burst of radiant energy. The burst of radiant energy at the instant of transition was what seared the linen cloth and formed the image. In other words, what we see today as a brownish red image imprinted on the linen Shroud was created almost as an energy scorch, as Christ's body transitioned almost as pure energy through an unseen event horizon. Importantly, my theory validates Einstein's famous equation that energy is a function of mass and the speed of light. In transitioning dimensions, the mass of Christ's body transformed into a burst of energy that moved through our dimensions of space and time with the speed of light."

Castle was not sure he comprehended the physics behind what Dr. Bucholtz was saying, but he connected instantly with the discussion at Princeton with Dr. Silver. Dr. Horton Silver and

Dr. Ruth Bucholtz were saying the same thing. Deciphering the code built into the Shroud demanded comprehension of a particle physics world defined by multiple dimensions coexisting with our known dimensions of length, height, width, and time. This was what Father Bartholomew had told both of them. The point was that understanding how the Shroud was formed was not possible until advanced particle physics had pushed the envelope beyond Einstein's theory of general relativity.

"This is why the Shroud is a negative that shows a mirrorlike reversal of the way right and left appear to the naked eye," Bucholtz said. "When Christ's body transformed into radiant energy, a negative was burned into the linen of the Shroud, such that the transformation of Christ's body was a function of mass converting into energy, producing a flash of light that left the brownish red burn marks on the cloth."

"Excuse me, Dr. Bucholtz," Fernando Ferrar said from the back of the room. "I want to make sure what you're telling us. You're talking about the resurrection of Jesus Christ, aren't you? With this burst of radiant energy that burned the image onto the Shroud, aren't you saying the Shroud image was formed by the energy generated when Christ resurrected from the dead? I want to report this, but I want to be sure I get it right."

"I guess I am," she said. "What I am describing is how Christ's body transfigured, much like we see the New Testament gospel describing Christ after the resurrection. Christ appears to the apostles after the resurrection almost magically, as if he chooses to leave and reenter our normal four dimensions through an unseen fifth, special dimension. The importance of quantum physics is that it allows us to see our world bounded by length, width, height, and time, but it allows us to envision a multidimensional universe that is not bounded by our ordinary understanding of time and space. What the Shroud evidences is that human beings can transform the mass of their bodies into energy so as to make the transition into another dimension with the speed of light."

"That's all well and good," Ferrar said, not sure he really understood a word of what Dr. Bucholtz was saying, "but what does this have to do with the resurrection of Jesus Christ?"

She did her best to explain. "The image of the man in the Shroud, in my judgment as a professional physicist, could only have been created by a phenomenon in which the man in the Shroud passed through into an extraordinary dimension, where, if he had been perceived as dead, he was suddenly seen as alive. In other words, it is completely conceivable to me that the man in the Shroud emerged with a transfigured body that would appear to us in our dimensions, if we could perceive it at all, as being not a physical body, but rather a body that was composed of part spirit and part physical material."

"Okay." Ferrar persisted. "Then what you are describing is the resurrection of Jesus Christ?"

"I am a physicist, Mr. Ferrar," Dr. Bucholtz said, acknowledging her limits. "You are asking a religious question that I am not qualified to answer. But you can interpret what I am saying as consistent with the description of Christ's resurrection in the New Testament, if you want to."

Ferrar appeared pleased with that answer.

Listening carefully, Marco Gabrielli decided to interrupt, determined to take the discussion down to a much more practical level.

"Excuse me, Dr. Bucholtz," Gabrielli began, "but if I understand you directly, a key point you are making is that the image of the man in the Shroud of Turin is three-dimensional. Is that correct?"

"Yes," she said. "And more importantly, that the three-dimensional image has the characteristics of a hologram. In other words, we can lift a hologram of the man in the Shroud from the information contained in the brownish red image."

"So, to produce a Shroud by means of artistic forgery, all a painter would have to do is to paint an image that was three-dimensional in nature with holographic characteristics embedded in the two-dimensional information. If I understand you, that is what the Shroud of Turin does. Is that right?"

"Yes," she said, a bit tentatively. "I guess that's right."

He pressed on. "So the trick is to convert the three-dimensional holographic information into the two dimensions of a flat drawing, right?"

"Where are you headed, Professor Gabrielli?" Bucholtz asked, wanting him to get to the point.

"Where I'm headed is that a brilliant forger who could think three-dimensionally might have been able to accomplish the two-dimensional image artistically, without the use of any advanced technology or hologram machine," he said.

"What do you mean?"

"What I mean is this." He started carefully. "The Shroud of Turin is two-dimensional. Studying how the image appears on the Shroud of Turin should be the key to learning how to draw three-dimensionally on a two-dimensional surface. It's kind of like how a camera obscura teaches you to draw with perspective. Once you understand how the principles of perspective work, you don't need a camera obscura anymore. You learn how to draw a three-dimensional image on a two-dimensional surface with the skill a painter develops by understanding perspective."

"I see your point, Professor Gabrielli," Bucholtz said. "But the Shroud was created before the principles of holograms were understood, so a medieval artist such as you are postulating must have been a remarkable genius."

Gabrielli conceded that. "I agree. But we may differ in that I do not tend to discount the genius of prior ages, as you may be inclined to do."

Castle could see where Gabrielli was headed.

Rather than being impressed that Bucholtz was in the process of deciphering what Father Bartholomew liked to call the "Shroud codex," Gabrielli merely understood Bucholtz as establishing a higher bar he would have to hurdle to make his forgery convincing. He would have to learn how to produce two-dimensional images with three-dimensional qualities.

CHAPTER TWENTY-NINE

D_{r.} Castle was ushered into the pope's office, anticipating his first face-to-face meeting with Pope John-Paul Peter I, the man he had first met when he was Cardinal Marco Vicente.

Also scheduled to be in attendance were two Vatican physicians who had examined Father Bartholomew at Agostino Gemelli University Polyclinic since his arrival from New York on Wednesday morning. After their discussion, Father Morelli had arranged to bring Father Morelli from the hospital to visit with the pope and Dr. Castle in person.

The pope's office was as ornate as Castle had imagined, with expensive paintings on the wall, and an elegant, hand-crafted, gold-embossed wood desk with a red leather desk pad expertly embedded into the writing surface. Looking around, Castle saw gold everywhere: in the side chairs at the pope's desk—one of which he now occupied—in the woodwork, even in the wallpaper. Thick antique Middle Eastern rugs, hand-woven into intricate patterns, covered the floor.

Ushered into the room next were Dr. Guilio Draghi, the attending physician at Agostino Gemelli University Polyclinic, and Dr. Giorgio Moretti, a top psychiatrist from Rome whom the Vatican had asked to meet with Father Bartholomew to confirm Dr. Castle's analysis. The priest ushering the doctors into the room made the necessary introductions.

When the three physicians were settled in their gilded chairs in front of the pope's desk, the doors to the Holy Father's living quarters opened and Pope John-Paul Peter I walked into the room.

Castle was struck by how small the pope was, no more than five feet, eight inches tall, he judged. Somehow, speaking to Marco Vicente by telephone, Castle had remembered him to be a much taller man. Still, wearing the white cassock and white skullcap of the pope, highlighted by the golden chain and cross that hung down across his chest, Vicente carried himself with the obvious dignity of his office. Bowing down to kiss the papal ring on his finger, Castle was impressed by the pope's neatly trimmed white hair and the obvious warmth exuded by his soft, olive-colored eyes.

"Gentlemen." The pope began the meeting as he settled into the seat behind his desk. "I would like to ask you to share with me your medical opinions about Father Bartholomew. We are very pleased to have with us today Dr. Stephen Castle, a top psychiatrist from New York City. Dr. Castle and I have a history of working together that stretches back to when Archbishop Duncan was first appointed to head the Archdiocese of New York. I am going to ask you all to speak with me frankly, as I much prefer to have the truth about Father Bartholomew, regardless of how harsh your opinions may be."

Dr. Draghi began. "Holy Father, we have examined the CT scan and MRI tests that Dr. Castle had sent from Beth Israel Hospital and we have repeated the tests here in Rome. Our results are identical. Father Bartholomew displays the wounds of Christ's passion and crucifixion exactly as we see in the Shroud. Father Bartholomew exhibits the stigmata in his wrists and feet. His body shows the scourge marks we see in the Shroud, with an exact match blow for blow. His head from the brow around to the back and on top of the head throughout show the same puncture wounds we see on the Shroud resulting from a cap of thorns, not simply a circular crown of thorns banded around his head at the level of the forehead."

"I understand," the pope said.

Draghi continued. "Moreover, our tests show the same result as we saw at Beth Israel. The wounds Father Bartholomew suffered could have been fatal to an average man of his age and physical condition. Yet the wounds have healed remarkably fast and completely, so much so that I cannot now determine after only a few days since the last incident if the nail punctures in his wrists and feet ever went all the way through. There is substantial healing evident from within on all the wounds we see on Father Bartholomew's body. I have no medical explanation for how or why."

"What does the psychiatric evaluation show?" the pope asked Dr. Moretti.

"You must understand that my results are preliminary, Holy Father," Dr. Moretti began, carefully hedging his conclusions. "But I tend to agree with Dr. Castle that Father Bartholomew is suffering from a form of multiple personality disorder. Father Bartholomew is under the illusion that he suffered an after-life experience in which he was given a choice by God to return to life. He believes he can see Jesus and speak with Jesus. He believes that Jesus instructs him in the confessional to give to confessants the precise spiritual advice they need in order to be healed miraculously by the intervention of Jesus. Father Bartholomew further believes his mission from God was to return to life so he could prove the Shroud of Turin is the actual burial cloth of Jesus Christ."

Listening, Dr. Castle was relieved to hear the Italian psychiatrist chosen by the Vatican agreeing with his diagnosis.

"So, Dr. Moretti, if I understand you correctly: Father Bartholomew, in your opinion, is psychologically disturbed, is that right?" the pope asked.

"Yes, Your Holiness, it is."

"And you, Dr. Castle, agree with that analysis?" The pope pressed on.

"As Dr. Moretti noted, my analysis is also preliminary," Castle said carefully. "Neither Dr. Moretti nor I have had much time to work with Father Bartholomew in a therapeutic setting. But, yes, I do concur that Father Bartholomew is suffering from a severe multiple personality disorder in which he has come to identify his ego with Jesus Christ. As you know, Father Bartholomew has managed subconsciously to alter his physical appearance to represent the icon of Christ depicted in the Shroud. I believe all his wounds are psychosomatic in nature."

"So then, Drs. Moretti and Castle, am I correct in assuming that neither of you is prepared to assert that Father Bartholomew's stigmata and other injuries have convinced you that the Shroud is authentic?" the pope asked directly.

"That's right, Your Holiness," Moretti said. "My conclusion is that Father Bartholomew is suffering from a psychological disorder that proves nothing about the Shroud."

"I agree wholeheartedly," Castle said. "Even when he was a physicist at the Institute for Advanced Study in Princeton, Father Bartholomew was always a loner. He never married. As far as I can tell, the only person Father Bartholomew was ever close to was his mother. When his mother passed away from amyotrophic lateral sclerosis, a progressive nerve disease, Paul Bartholomew went into a crisis that was the beginning of his current psychological disorder."

"Dr. Castle, do you think Father Bartholomew can be cured?" the pope asked.

"I don't know, Your Holiness," Castle answered. "As I told you and Archbishop Duncan when I agreed to take this case, Father Bartholomew's case might take years of psychoanalysis and even then I can't promise results."

"Do you agree, Dr. Moretti?" the pope asked, wanting to make sure both psychiatrists had a chance to express their professional opinions clearly.

"Yes, Your Holiness, I do."

The pope sat back in his chair and folded his hands in his lap. "It would be easy for me to dismiss Father Bartholomew, except that now there are millions of Catholics out there who believe in Father Bartholomew. What's more, with Father Bartholomew manifesting the man we see in the Shroud, millions are now convinced that the Shroud too is authentic. I cannot just dismiss Father Bartholomew without being accused of engaging in a cover-up. People today do not believe official commissions, whether they are about the assassination of President Kennedy in Dallas or whether Adolf Hitler died at the end of World War II instead of escaping to Argentina. Now we have Professor Gabrielli trying to prove the Shroud was a medieval forgery. Up until now, Gabrielli has been a minor celebrity, known primarily in this country, where he has been trying for years to prove that Padre Pio, whom we canonized, is as fake as a statue of Jesus that cries blood. But instead of that, Father Bartholomew has managed to give Gabrielli an international stage. What do you gentlemen suggest I do?"

The three physicians sat silently, thinking.

"Does the Vatican have to do anything?" Dr. Moretti asked.

"It's a good question," the pope said, "but after trying for the past few days to convince Professor Gabrielli that duplicating the Shroud will be no easy business, I think I've failed. Do you agree with this, Dr. Castle?"

"As I disclosed to you from the beginning, Your Holiness, you know I have been working in association with Professor Gabrielli," Castle answered. "I'm sure you are all aware of the books I have written and that I profess no affinity for relics like the Shroud that tend to inspire belief in God even if the relics are false. So there is no need for me to hide my beliefs from this group."

"Rest assured," the pope said, "your book *The God Illusion* was translated into Italian and did quite well in the bookstores."

"Thank you, Your Holiness," Castle said. He knew the pope was right. "I can tell you for a fact that our meeting at CERN did nothing but convince Professor Gabrielli that he needs to refine his methods in his next try. I have no doubt that the next shroud that my friend Gabrielli fabricates will resemble the Shroud of Turin even more convincingly."

"This is why I tried to tell Pope Paul VI that permitting scientists to examine the Shroud of Turin was a bad idea," the pope said with obvious frustration. "I got nowhere with Pope Paul VI. He even had to go out and tell the world that the Shroud was a 'wonderful document of Christ's passion and death, written in blood,' or something like that. For my part, I think the Shroud of Turin and Father Bartholomew are both sideshows to a genuine belief in God. Deep down I agree with Dr. Castle, at least in part. The last thing I want to do is to turn the Catholic Church back into a medieval relic factory."

The pope leaned forward in his chair and began tapping the

top of his desk rhythmically with the fingers of his right hand. Silently, he prayed for patience, and guidance from above.

After a moment or two, the pope picked up his phone and instructed that Fathers Morelli and Bartholomew be brought into the room.

Almost instantly, Father Morelli was pushing into the room a wheelchair containing Father Bartholomew. The priest from New York looked almost exactly the way he had looked the day Dr. Castle first met him. Sitting comfortably in the wheelchair, Father Bartholomew was dressed once again in a flowing white robe that together with his long hair and beard gave the impression that he was Jesus Christ reincarnate.

Father Morelli wheeled Father Bartholomew to center stage, positioning the wheelchair between the Italian doctors on the priest's right and Dr. Castle on the left. Going to the back of the room, Father Morelli brought forward a side chair that he moved so he could sit slightly behind and to the right of Father Bartholomew. By the positioning of the chairs, Castle got the impression the deck was stacked, the Vatican on one side and him on the other.

"Your Holiness, excuse me if I cannot get up to kiss your ring," Father Bartholomew said humbly.

"That won't be necessary," the pope said, unable to completely disguise the irritation he felt at seeing Father Bartholomew in person for the first time. In truth, the pope felt considerable sympathy for the priest. He knew Father Bartholomew was suffering and that his wounds had to be extremely painful. Nor was he convinced that Bartholomew was insane. Conceivably, Father Bartholomew was confronting the Church and the world with a new reality that everyone would have to pay attention to, whether they liked it or not. Still, Father Bartholomew was causing the Church a worldwide commotion and the pope worried that Father Bartholomew's crisis would be bad for the Church. "I assume you know everyone in the room."

Looking around, Father Bartholomew acknowledged that he did. "It's been my good fortune to have had the professional assistance of each of these distinguished doctors," Bartholomew said deferentially.

"Father Bartholomew, please excuse me if I get directly to the point," the pope said, displaying less patience than he had planned to show in this meeting. "I agree with these gentlemen that you are suffering a psychological illness from which you may never recover."

"I understand that, Holy Father," Father Bartholomew said deferentially.

"Quite frankly, I don't know what to do with you," the pope said, expressing openly how perplexed he felt. "Even if you came back from the dead with a photograph of Jesus Christ taken in Heaven, I doubt I could ever declare as a matter of Catholic dogma that the Shroud of Turin is anything more than an artifact worthy of veneration. Do you understand that?"

"Yes, Your Holiness, I do."

"The minute I would declare the Shroud of Turin to be the authentic burial cloth of Christ, it would be just our luck to have some scholar unearth a lost Leonardo da Vinci notebook in which he recorded the methods he used to create the Shroud."

Saying nothing, Father Morelli appreciated the dilemma. While years of study had led a once-skeptical Morelli to conclude the Shroud was authentic, he did not think it was possible to establish beyond any possible doubt that the Shroud was Christ's burial cloth. In the final analysis, Morelli agreed with the pope. One would probably always need a leap of faith to see the Shroud as authentic, just as one always needed that leap to believe in the existence of God.

"As all you gentlemen know, my papacy has been predicted to be the last," Pope John-Paul Peter I said with a steady resolve in his eyes. "Who knows? Maybe the prediction is right. But I will not gamble my future or the future of the Catholic Church on the Shroud of Turin. The moment I would make that proclamation, I would simply empower those like Professor Gabrielli, who is resolved to demonstrate how easily the Shroud could be some clever medieval artist's idea of a joke."

Everyone in the room sat silently, digesting the importance of what the pope was saying.

"Furthermore, I don't fully appreciate how you have raised the stakes," the pope said pointedly to Father Bartholomew. "Do you understand that?"

"I'm not sure I do," Bartholomew answered, showing his confusion at the pope's statement.

"It's pretty easy if you think about it for a moment," the pope said, fighting to keep his irritation from being obvious in his voice. "If we end up exposing you as a fraud or a nutcase, I've still got a problem. There are millions of people out there who believe in you and they're ready to turn on me if I don't. Do you understand me now?"

"Yes, Your Holiness, I guess I do," Bartholomew said tentatively. "There is just one thing, however, if you will permit me."

"What's that?" the pope answered.

"The Shroud of Turin is the authentic burial cloth of Jesus Christ and I have returned to life to prove that," Bartholomew insisted. "I'm not a fraud and I'm not crazy."

"I wish you would stop sounding like you're the one who's been crucified and resurrected, not Jesus Christ," the pope said, fighting back frustration. "Maybe we should start seeing if we can update Michelangelo by painting your face in the Sistine Chapel's scene of the Last Judgment, so you can be sitting there next to Jesus Christ on Judgment Day. Look at you! Don't you think it's arrogant to make yourself out to be the Second Coming of Jesus Christ?"

"Actually, Your Holiness, you don't need to paint my picture in the Sistine Chapel," Bartholomew said, doing his best to answer the pope with humility. "But Jesus Christ and I were both resurrected and I think I can prove it to you, if you'll just give me a chance."

"How's that?" the pope asked.

"I've never seen the Shroud in person, and I would like to do so," Bartholomew said.

"I'm sure that can be arranged," the pope said calmly. "But why would I do so?"

"I believe that if I can see the Shroud of Turin in person, I can prove to you it is the authentic burial cloth of Jesus Christ. I also believe I can prove to you that Jesus encoded in the Shroud an important message for all time that it is my responsibility to decode. If I fail on either of those points to persuade you, then I will admit to the world that you are right and I am psychologically disturbed. If I fail, I will readily agree to undergo the years of psychoanalysis the doctors here think I need to be healed of my delusions."

The pope resumed tapping his desk with the fingers of his right hand. "The problem with your proposal is that it is one-sided."

"How's that?" Bartholomew asked.

"You control the outcome and it's up to you to say whether you will undergo psychoanalysis. How do I know you won't just see the Shroud and say that it proves you were right?"

"Excuse me, Your Holiness, but I don't think you fully understood my proposal."

"So, what did I miss?"

"What I said was that I wanted to see the Shroud of Turin in person and that if I failed to convince you the Shroud is authentic, then I will submit to psychoanalysis. It will be entirely up to you. If we see the Shroud of Turin together, in person, and you come away unconvinced, then that's it. I will make a public statement that I have been misleading people and I will withdraw from public view into medical treatment."

The pope stood up from his desk and leaned forward, with both his arms extended in front of him so the palms of his hands rested on the top of the desk. He looked Bartholomew squarely in the eye. "You're a physicist, Bartholomew, and I have been told you are a genius," the pope said with resolve. "But I warn you not to tempt God. As smart as you think you are, God is smarter."

"I know that," Bartholomew said, "and I don't plan to tempt God or to disappoint you in what I propose to do."

"And there's one point on which I will concede you're a lot like Jesus Christ."

"What's that, Your Holiness?"

"You are a troublemaker who is causing the Roman Catholic Church great consternation, just as Jesus Christ caused consternation for the ancient Romans trying to govern Israel."

"And maybe like Jesus Christ, I will change the world," Bartholomew said, defending himself. "My mission here is not to cause trouble but to affirm Jesus Christ in his passion, death, and resurrection."

The pope turned to Father Morelli. "Any reason you think we shouldn't accept Father Bartholomew's proposal, Father Morelli?" the pope asked. From the beginning of this affair with Father Bartholomew, the pope had relied upon Morelli's advice. Besides, the pope knew there was no one who had spent more time with Father Bartholomew since this all began than Morelli had. The pope relied upon Morelli's judgment and trusted his loyalty to the Vatican. Morelli would never recommend anything that might hurt the papacy.

"I don't see why not," Morelli said simply. "I'm sure we can arrange to bring Father Bartholomew to Turin to see the Shroud, and I don't see what we have to lose. Either something happens that convinces you the Shroud is real and that Father Bartholomew does have a mission from God, or Father Bartholomew has offered you a way to put an end to all this drama."

The pope sat down and looked carefully at everybody in the room, one at a time. Praying silently for wisdom and guidance, he had made his decision.

"Okay, Father Bartholomew. I'm going to grant your request," the pope said, resolved to go forward. "Father Morelli will make the necessary arrangements."

Hearing that his request had been granted, Father Bartholomew solemnly made the sign of the cross, slowly touching his forehead first, then his stomach, and finally his left shoulder and his right shoulder. Grateful that he was given permission to see the Shroud of Turin in person, Bartholomew felt confident he was going to achieve the mission for which he had returned.

"Now, gentlemen," the pope said with finality, "if you will please excuse me, I have some work to do."

CHAPTER THIRTY

The Turin Cathedral requested until Friday of that week to prepare the Shroud for private viewing. The pope decided to use the time as an opportunity for Dr. Castle and the others to have a meeting at the Vatican Library with Dottoressa Francesca Coretti, a Vatican Library senior staff researcher who had been studying the history of the Shroud for decades. Her particular area of academic specialty involved researching religious icons and Church traditions since the time of Christ in the first century. Her goal was to find icons of Christ that looked like the face of the man in the Shroud of Turin and Church traditions involving a burial cloth of Christ that might document the existence of the Shroud of Turin from before the 1260–1390 A.D. dates established by the carbon-14 testing for the creation of the Shroud.

Pope John-Paul Peter I was confident Dr. Bucholtz's presentation had made an impact on Dr. Castle, but there was yet another dimension to the Shroud the pope wanted Castle to understand.

The Shroud had held the attention of believers for centuries. Millions around the world revered it as the authentic burial cloth of Jesus Christ. While Castle, as an atheist, tended to discount the importance of religious experience, the pope knew that as a psychiatrist Castle could not dismiss the deep emotional impact the Shroud had made in hundreds of millions of lives through the past centuries. Still, there was a mystery of lost knowledge about the Shroud, and the pope wanted to see if he could make that a subject for Dr. Stephen Castle's contemplation.

At the pope's suggestion, Father Morelli had invited Professor Gabrielli and Fernando Ferrar, along with his video crew, to attend the interview with Francesca Coretti, as well as to attend the private viewing of the Shroud in Turin arranged for Friday.

"If you're concerned with millions putting pressure on the Church over the Shroud, why do you invite our biggest critic and the New York television news to attend?" Father Morelli had asked the pope, objecting to opening these two private audiences to the public by inviting the world press and a critic of the Shroud with a growing international reputation.

"The truth is that Fernando Ferrar and Professor Gabrielli counterbalance one another," Pope John-Paul Peter I answered.

Morelli did not immediately get the point. "How's that, Holy Father?"

"Gabrielli will do his best to prove that whatever happens is just more evidence the Shroud of Turin is a fraud," the pope said, "and Ferrar will be doing just the opposite. Ferrar's interest is in promoting Father Bartholomew's alleged miracle as authentic. Besides, if I exclude either one of them, the other accuses me of bias. If I exclude them both, the world accuses me of conspiracy. Let them both attend and we'll leave the results up to God."

Morelli saw the wisdom of the pope's argument and he made the necessary arrangements without further discussion.

Welcoming the group to one of the Vatican Library's many conference rooms, Francesca Coretti looked very much the part. Castle judged her to be about fifteen years younger than him, in her late forties. She was attractively thin and strikingly dressed, with her knee-length gray dress complementing her elegant shoulder-length black hair and her jet-black eyes. The straight lines of her nose and chin were nicely set off with the round large lenses of her scholarly looking gold-frame eyeglasses. Coretti had received her doctorate in medieval art history from the University of Milan. She was one of the most highly regarded staff professionals at the Vatican Library, trusted by the pope for her painstaking investigations and honest judgments.

In keeping with the décor of the Vatican Library, the conference room Dottoressa Coretti selected provided a colorful background with a ceiling decorated with magnificently hand-painted frescoes that illuminated scenes of papal history.

Surveying the room, Ferrar's camera crew picked up a corner from which they thought they could cover the meeting. To capture the flow of the meeting, one of the crew broke out the mobile camera, deciding to roam the room during the meeting to get different perspectives on the discussion and close-ups as needed. Ferrar had in mind using this footage as part of a TV documentary he planned to put together when he got back to New York.

As the group settled into the conference room, Coretti singled out Father Middagh, shaking his hand and greeting him warmly. "We are all looking forward to the publication of your magnum opus on the Shroud. When is the publication date?" she asked enthusiastically.

"We are planning to publish *Behold the Face of Jesus* as a two-volume work," Middagh answered. "The first volume will be issued in January, with the second volume to follow a year later."

Turning her attention to the group, Coretti began by making

a dramatic statement: "We can trace the history of the Shroud of Turin back to the time of Christ. The mystery that a living likeness of Jesus Christ survived the crucifixion began even before Christ died."

This statement got Castle's attention. "How's that?" he wondered out loud, not having heard this before.

"The legend is that a woman named Veronica wiped the face of Christ with her veil as Jesus carried the cross to Golgotha," she said, "and that Christ in gratitude supernaturally left an imprint of his face on the veil. Veronica is a name derived from the Latin word *veritas,* for 'truth,' and *icon* for 'image.' So the very name Veronica signifies 'true image' in Latin. The Sixth Station of the Cross, still celebrated today in Catholic churches throughout the world, is dedicated to Veronica wiping the face of Jesus on the way to Golgotha. The Via Dolorosa is the path traditionally marked out through the Old City of Jerusalem as the route Christ took on the way to his crucifixion. The Sixth Station of the Via Dolorosa is located on the site reputed to have been Veronica's home at the time of Christ's crucifixion. The story is that Veronica came out of her house, saw Jesus suffering, and took pity on him by wiping his face with her veil."

"Is there any reason to believe the story of Veronica is true?" Castle asked. "That the name derives from the Latin for 'true image' makes it sound like the story is apocryphal, that the character of Veronica was made up around the idea that a likeness of Jesus survived after his death."

"Clearly, whether or not Veronica existed is debatable, despite the Stations of the Cross and the Via Dolorosa," Coretti said. "Yet the story suggests the early Christians believed a true image of Christ existed. I believe what was known as the Veil of Veronica was actually what we see today as the Shroud of Turin. We have good historical authority to prove the Shroud of Turin was actually folded and framed so that only the face was visible for veneration. Just seeing the face of Christ, not the whole body image, would have been consistent with the Shroud of Turin being responsible for the Veil of Veronica we find related in early Christian writings and venerated in the Stations of the Cross."

Coretti passed around the table several books illustrating the Veil of Veronica and documenting the Sixth Station of the Cross on the Via Dolorosa. The mobile camera moved in to get video of the group looking through the books. Ferrar made a note to stay behind after the meeting to get Coretti's permission to take detailed shots of the various illustrations she was sharing with the group.

"We can pick up the story of the Shroud in the first century after the death of Christ," Coretti said. "There is a legend involving the Image of Edessa, named after the ancient Turkish city of Edessa, which is modern-day Urfa. In the early fourth century, Eusebius, an early historian of Christianity, said he translated an ancient letter in which King Abgar of Edessa wrote to Jesus, asking Jesus to heal miraculously an illness he had that was thought to be incurable. After Jesus died, an evangelist named Thaddaeus is said to have brought the Shroud to King Abgar in response to his request. The image brought to Abgar was said to have miraculously and instantly cured him of the leprosy that had paralyzed his legs. Tradition links the story of King Abgar with a face of Christ known as the Mandylion in the Greek Orthodox Church. We have many images of the Mandylion that closely resemble the man in the Shroud. The idea is that the Mandylion, which typically shows only the face of Jesus, was the Shroud of Turin folded and placed in a display frame so only the face could be seen."

"Why would anyone believe this story?" Gabrielli asked.

"We have found frescoes of the Cloth of Edessa in Turkish

churches dating back to around 1100 that look a lot like the face of the man in the Shroud. The man in the Shroud, the Cloth of Edessa, and the various images we have of the Mandylion in Greek Orthodox churches look a lot alike. Portraits of Christ on the gold coins of Byzantine emperor Justinian II, from around 692 A.D. in Constantinople, closely resemble the Cloth of Odessa and Mandylion images and look almost identical to the face of the man in the Shroud."

Coretti passed around books containing photo illustrations of these various faces of Christ. Gabrielli looked unconvinced. All it proved to him was that at some point, maybe around 500 A.D., the image of Christ that artists accepted became an icon. After that, all images artists painted or otherwise represented of Christ had to look like the icon to be accepted; otherwise people would not recognize the image, or would be be confused.

"We can prove with almost absolutely certainty that painters in Constantinople prior to 1200 must have seen the Shroud of Turin," she said.

Castle thought this point was more interesting. He wondered how Coretti was going to prove her assertion.

"The Pray Manuscript, an ancient codex written between 1192 and 1195, is preserved in the Budapest National Library," Coretti said. "The Pray Manuscript contains illustrations that portray the burial of Christ, showing Christ removed from the cross being placed on a burial shroud. The figure of Christ in the Pray Manuscript displays facial and body features consistent with the Shroud of Turin, including the crossed shape of the arms in front of the body and the suggestion that the burial cloth of Christ used the unique herringbone twill we see in the weave of the Shroud of Turin. Interestingly, the Pray Manuscript depicts no thumbs in the hands of the dead Christ, another feature that appears to have been copied from the Shroud of Turin. The nails driven through Christ's wrists would have damaged the median nerves, causing the thumbs to retract into the palms. A medieval artist is unlikely to have invented this important anatomical detail. The Pray Manuscript traces back to Constantinople."

"Most importantly," Middagh added, just to make sure nobody missed the key point, "the various images we have of the Cloth of Edessa, the Mandylion, the gold coins of Justinian II, and the Pray Manuscript all predate the carbon-14 dating that places the creation of the Shroud of Turin at around 1260 to 1390 A.D."

Coretti nodded in agreement. "We also have the memoirs of French Crusader Robert de Clari, who documents that he personally witnessed a ritual in Constantinople where a cloth depicting the crucified Christ was raised by a mechanism the Byzantines designed to make it appear as if the Shroud was rising from a casket. Various Byzantine sculptures and paintings from the twelfth and thirteenth centuries show a Christ looking almost identical to the man in the Shroud—same beard, same crossed arms, same missing thumbs—rising from a casket. As bizarre as it may sound today, the Byzantine church in Constantinople before 1200 A.D. appears to have used the Shroud of Turin in some sort of a ritual ceremony reenacting Christ's resurrection. Again, the early Church believed the Shroud contained not just the true image of Christ but a lost mystery about the ancient secrets at the heart of the resurrection itself."

Then, sorting through the piles of books on the table, she found one in particular. "This is the book I published ten years ago on the Shroud of Turin and the Knights Templar," she said. "It was titled *The Secret History of the Knights Templar.*"

Gabrielli laughed, particularly pleased to learn of this. Any ancient artifact he could tie in with the Crusades and the Knights

Templar immediately increased its value dramatically. Gabrielli was well-known for saying, "Every good medieval conspiracy theory needs a connection to the Knights Templar and the Crusaders in Jerusalem."

"The Knights Templar were accused of worshipping a bearded head they brought back from Jerusalem as a relic from the Crusades," Coretti said. "The accusation was that the bearded head was Baphomet, a grotesque representation of the devil, typically seen as a goat-man, that the Knights Templar used in their worship of Satan. I disagree. I think the bearded head the Knights Templar venerated was the framed Shroud of Turin looking like it did when it was displayed as the Cloth of Edessa or the Mandylion in Byzantine Constantinople. A panel of wood found during World War II at a Knights Templar site in Templecombe, England, had been above a plastered ceiling. The panel contained a painting with a distinctly Shroud-like face. Carbon-14 tests placed the wood panel in the Templar period, around 1280 A.D. So there is good evidence the Knights Templar possessed the Shroud and that they venerated it, much as the early Byzantine Church in Constantinople venerated it."

"There is another strong connection between the Knights Templar and the Shroud of Turin." Middagh joined in, supporting Coretti's argument. "We know that the Shroud of Turin was brought to Lirey, France, in the 1350s, by a descendant of Geoffrey de Charney, the Knight Templar who was burned at the stake in 1314 with Jacques de Molay, the famous last Grand Master of the Knights Templar. French and Venetian knights of the Fourth Crusade besieged Constantinople, along with the Knights Templar. Then, on April 13, 1204, they entered the city and looted it. Geoffrey de Charney was married to one of the leaders of the Fourth Crusade. So it is entirely possible that the Knights Templar were responsible for getting the Shroud of Turin from Constantinople to France. From Lirey, France, we know the Shroud traveled to Turin, where it has remained ever since."

Gabrielli made detailed notes about Geoffrey de Charney and the Knights Templar, deciding not to challenge any of this history.

"Then there is the pollen analysis," Coretti said. "If the Shroud had been forged in France during the fourteenth century by Leonardo da Vinci, for instance, we would not expect to find microscopic traces of pollen embedded in the cloth as residue from plants we know are found only in locations such as Jerusalem or Turkey. Yet this is just exactly what we do find. Dr. Middagh, would you like to explain the research?"

"Certainly," Middagh said, pleased to have another chance to contribute his expertise to the discussion. "In 1978, Swiss criminologist Max Frei worked with the Shroud of Turin Research Project to obtain samples of dust from the Shroud by applying dabbed strips of sticky tape onto the cloth's surface. Dr. Frei correctly assumed the dust samples would contain microscopic spores of pollen that would provide clues to where the Shroud had been over time. Under microscopic analysis, pollen spores have a hard outer enzyme shell that remains resistant to change for thousands of years. If the Shroud contained only French or Italian pollen spores, the results of the analysis would support the hypothesis that the Shroud had been forged in Europe in the years 1260 to 1390 A.D."

"But this is not what we found," Coretti quickly added.

"Right," Middagh said. "Before his death in 1983, Frei had identified fifty-eight varieties of plant on the Shroud, permitting him to conclude the Shroud was once in the Middle East. Frei found pollen samples he identified as from plants found in Jerusalem; other pollens were characteristic of the areas around Edessa and Constantinople; there were also pollen spores common to Europe. Frei concluded the pollen had been deposited on the Shroud from its various public expositions over the centuries. At one time or another, the Shroud must have been exposed to the air not only in Jerusalem, but also in southern Turkey, including the surroundings of Constantinople, which is now Istanbul. Frei's analysis established definitively that the Shroud did not originate in France or Italy."

"One last point," Dottoressa Coretti said. "In 1978, when they were working with the NASA VP-8 three-dimensional Image Analyzer that I believe you heard about at CERN, Dr. John Jackson and his longtime associate Dr. Eric Jumper discovered what looked like coins resting over the eyes of the man in the Shroud of Turin. Then in 1980, Father Francis Filas of Loyola University in Chicago, a Jesuit like our Father Morelli here, and Michael Marx, an expert in classical coins, identified the object over the right eye as a Julia lepton coin with a distinctive design of a sheaf of barley. Pontius Pilate minted the Julia lepton, equivalent to a low-value Roman mite, between 29 and 32 A.D. to honor Emperor Tiberius Caesar's wife, Julia. The word *lepton* designates 'small' or 'thin.' The lepton with the distinctive barley sheaf design was minted only once, in 29 A.D. Putting coins on the eyes of the dead has a long history in the Middle East. In various religious traditions the coins are seen as providing the money to pay for the trip to Heaven, not just keeping the eyelids closed in death—"

Middagh interrupted. "Please allow me to elaborate why various Shroud researchers consider the coins to be an important discovery.

"Of course." Coretti acquiesced, certain she would appreciate his explanation.

"The coins on the Shroud had a misspelling," Middagh explained, preparing to point out why the detail was important. "The coins were Roman and the emperor's name would have been spelled in Greek on the coins as TIBERIOU KAISAROS. The problem was that the recognizable writing on the coins on the Shroud was UCAI, formed by the end of TIBERIOU coming together with the beginning of KAISAROS. That would seem to indicate a misspelling, where the C should have been a K. It was a problem, that is, until several similar coins were found with the misspelling. In a way the misspelling confirmed that the researchers were looking at real coins that had been placed over the eyes of Jesus in death. Had an artist painted in the coins or had the researchers been seeing what they wanted to find, the likelihood is the spelling identified in the Shroud would have been correct."

Father Morelli jumped in. "If you will permit me, I want to add an important point here, before we leave the issue of the coins, even if it means raising some questions about what Dr. Middagh has just explained."

"By all means, go ahead," Middagh said graciously.

"In recent years, Dr. Jackson has come to doubt whether the coin information is verifiable. He has raised the question whether minor marks or imperfections seen in the weaving of the fabric might be misinterpreted as having significance—such as seeing coins, or traces of letters and writing of various kinds on the Shroud. Moreover, Dr. Jackson's wife, Rebecca, a Jew by birth, has objected, pointing out that Jews in the first century would have considered it a religious violation to place anything so crassly related to civil government as a coin on the body of a Jew being buried in accordance with Jewish law."

"Whether or not there really were ancient coins on the eyes of the dead man in the Shroud seems irrelevant to me," Gabrielli said.

"Why is that?" Father Morelli asked.

"Simple." Gabrielli began explaining. "Putting ancient coins on the eyes of a dead Jew could easily have been the work of a brilliant forger. In a curious way, I almost think the Roman coins, if they are over the eyes, prove the Shroud is a fake. Maybe the forger didn't know Jews in the first century did not put coins on the eyes of dead people being buried. Probably the forger was calculating that someday, someone in the future would discover the coins and be tricked into arguing the Shroud had to be real because no forger would have ever had the forethought to put them there. But if the coins are there and they violate Jewish burial traditions in the first century, then the Shroud has to be a fake."

Castle thought Gabrielli had a good point.

"In my next attempt to duplicate the Shroud"—Gabrielli said, wanting to make sure his bottom-line point was clear—"I could easily replicate the coins over the eyes, or just about anything else the scientists end up finding microscopically on the Shroud."

Castle figured that in the final analysis Dr. Jackson was right about the coins. "I'm not sure Gabrielli is right here that the coins prove the Shroud had to be forged," he said. "But if I follow the discussion, the coins are capable of being seen only through a high-powered microscope and I agree it would be easy to see subjectively what you wanted to see. The weave of the linen appears very coarse. I think that with a microscopic image you could imagine seeing anything you wanted to see."

Castle once again reached the conclusion that all the research regarding the Shroud, regardless of how scientifically conducted or academically verified it was, was still subject to debate and argumentation, especially by a scientist as clever as Gabrielli.

CHAPTER THIRTY-ONE

Friday
Turin Cathedral, Turin, Italy
Day 30

For days, the staff of the Turin Cathedral worked in a side chapel specially designed for displaying the Shroud in private viewings. With the greatest of care, the Shroud was removed from the case in the cathedral where the Shroud is preserved in an atmosphere of inert gas scientifically designed to preserve the Shroud from deterioration. Visitors to a private showing are permitted to see the Shroud directly in front of them, stretched on a frame built to display it, without the bulletproof glass covering that is used to protect the Shroud at public exhibitions.

On Thursday, the day before the private showing arranged for Father Bartholomew, the Turin Cathedral museum staff ushered Fernando Ferrar and his video crew into the side chapel. Cardinal Giovanni Bionconi had given Ferrar permission to bring in high-definition cameras to film the Shroud in advance of the private showing planned for the next day.

On Friday morning at 10 A.M., the hour appointed for the

private viewing to begin, the cathedral staff first ushered into the private chapel Dr. Castle and Anne Cassidy, followed by Father Middagh and Professor Gabrielli.

Castle was amazed at how overwhelmed he felt viewing the Shroud in person for the first time. He had expected that seeing so many photographs of the Shroud since taking on Father Bartholomew as a patient would have jaded him to the experience. But standing in front of the actual Shroud for the first time, Castle was impressed.

To begin with, the size of the cloth made the object in real life appear much bigger than the photographs had suggested. Somewhat larger than fourteen feet long and three feet wide, the Shroud seen in real life was an impressive relic. It stretched vertically along the full length of the display frame that filled the back wall of the specially designed side chapel, with its blacked-out windows.

Castle's next impression was that the image seen in real life was much more subtle than he had imagined. For what seemed like several minutes, Castle had to adjust his eyes and strain to make out the subtle reddish brown lines of the figure's full-length frontal and dorsal images. Then, as he studied the Shroud inch by inch, the image became gradually more distinct.

When he was finally able to clearly make out all the lines in the body, including the scourge marks front and back, Castle was hit with the emotional impact of the image. Here in front of him was the full-body image of a man who had been tortured and crucified two thousand years ago. Yet the face looked serene, as if finally at peace in death. The arms crossed modestly in front of what was obviously a nude body reinforced the impression of serenity, at least until Castle allowed himself to appreciate the brutality of the nail wounds on the wrists and the evidence of blood flows along the arms. Was it possible he was looking at a true image of the crucified Christ? Even though he was a committed atheist, the thought still crossed Castle's mind as he looked on the Shroud for the first time in person.

Marveling at the Shroud in front of him, Castle concluded that if the object were a fake, this was very possibly the most magnificent and most subtle painting ever done. He had seen many Leonardo paintings, including the *Mona Lisa* and the *John the Baptist* in the Louvre and the *Last Supper* in Milan. Yet no Leonardo painting held a candle to the Shroud. The Shroud, if Leonardo truly had painted it, was Leonardo's crowning achievement.

Leonardo's sfumato style required a subtle touch, such that brushstrokes were not evident at all. Leonardo's drawings in his notebook sketches were intricate in their detail and fidelity to nature. But the delicacy with which this brutal image of a crucified man had been left on cloth was breathtaking. Perhaps no artist who ever lived had done more to bring anatomy to life than Leonardo, but the detail of the body of the man in the Shroud defied comprehension. Somehow Castle had the feeling the man in the Shroud was yet alive, only sleeping, or that had just died an instant earlier and the naked body enclosed in the burial cloth would still be warm to the touch.

Anne was equally moved. For her the yellow-straw colors of the linen itself and the subtle brownish red lines of the body created a feeling of warmness she had never before felt looking at art. She felt an immediate attachment to the life of the man in the Shroud as she began to read his struggles and hardships in the dark shadows that defined the closed eyes and in the blood soaking his brow and hair from the crown of thorns. Yet there was a quiet dignity in the soft but firm line that formed his mouth and the elegant nose that gave his face a look of majesty, despite the obviously cruel death he suffered. Looking on the Shroud for the first time in person, Anne felt certain that Jesus had defied his

crucifiers by living even to this day in the preservation of this serene image stretched before her.

Father Middagh crossed himself and said a quiet prayer. He
had first seen the Shroud in person during the 1998 exhibition,
but the impact it made on him today was double the initial impression. After decades of study, spending every waking hour por-
ing over the available evidence in his attempt to prove the Shroud
of Turin was the authentic burial cloth of Jesus Christ, Middagh
felt his life was now fulfilled. He thanked God he was given the
chance to see the Shroud one more time in person before the
publication of his two-volume treatise. Studying the Shroud at
this moment, Middagh felt he had been blessed to proclaim correctly, in the most appropriate title he could have chosen for his
life's work, *Behold the Face of Jesus.*

After a few minutes, Cardinal Bionconi accompanied Pope
John-Paul Peter I into the room. They were joined by a delega-
tion of clerical dignitaries from both the Vatican and the Archdiocese of Turin. Entering the room, each of these top clerics of
the Catholic Church hierarchy paused in their conversation as
soon as they came into the presence of the Shroud. Castle contemplated that this private viewing of the Shroud had a special
feeling of reverence about it. Having toured the Sistine Chapel
many times, Castle was always struck at how the Michelangelo
frescos on the ceiling and walls had inspired conversation along
with awe. Here, in this private chapel, it was different. The Shroud
inspired an awe that was heightened by silence as onlookers
stood before the centuries-old cloth stretched out full-length for
viewing.

The last to enter the room was Father Bartholomew, in a
wheelchair gently pushed forward by Father Morelli.

Ferrar's eyes followed Father Bartholomew into the room,
waiting to see what would happen. Looking to his camera crew

chief, he got a nod of confirmation that they were capturing every detail.

Father Morelli wheeled Father Bartholomew to the front and center of the group. He was speechless like everyone else in the room, soaking in every detail of the Shroud.

Seeing the Shroud in person, even Father Bartholomew was struck by how precisely his body had come to resemble the man in the Shroud. The hair and beard, the square and serene look of the face, the wounds in the wrists and feet, the scourge marks that crisscrossed the body—every mark had been duplicated on his body, with precision. Father Bartholomew realized his long white robe hid from the others in the room the evidence of the injuries that marked the body of Christ as seen in the Shroud. But what he did not fully appreciate was how the robe itself intensified the immediate impression of those in the private chapel with him that in truth Father Bartholomew had become Jesus.

"Father Bartholomew, here is the Shroud of Turin," Pope John-Paul Peter I proclaimed loud enough for all to hear. "Now what is the demonstration you asked us here to witness? You can be assured you have our full attention."

Rather than answer directly, Father Bartholomew motioned to Father Morelli to lock the wheels of his wheelchair and place up the footrests, so he could stand to his full height in front of the Shroud. Taking his time to lift himself so as not to fall, Father Bartholomew rose from his chair and turned to face the group. "This is the moment God promised if I agreed to return to life," he said quietly and respectfully to the pope. "I am honored that you and the others are here to share the moment with me."

Then, with his back to the Shroud, Father Bartholomew lifted his arms perpendicularly to his sides, as if he were being crucified on the cross. At the same time, he kicked from his feet his shoes. He stood up from the wheelchair and bent his left knee so he could twist his body just right to lift his left foot on top of his right.

AT THAT INSTANT, Bartholomew's mind tripped and he was back at Golgotha, struggling to take his last breaths on the cross. The pain in his feet and wrists from the nails had caused him to hallucinate. He had screamed out loud, but in vain, to the prophet Elijah, whom he had imagined seeing right there at the foot of the cross, standing in front of him, waiting patiently to deliver his spirit to God, their Father.

As his last instants grew near, the skies around Jerusalem darkened suddenly, as if a great and unexpected storm had arisen. The light of late afternoon receded instantly into the twilight of early evening. Storm winds swirled the dust around them as an unearthly cool hung in the air at this lonely hill where he was about to die. Twisting on the cross to exhale what might be his last breath, Bartholomew felt a final burst of cold energy shoot up and down his spine. In the corner of his eye, he saw a lone centurion approach his cross with a spear.

IN THE PRIVATE chapel at the Turin Cathedral, everyone in the room felt paralyzed as they stood watching Father Bartholomew's body twist before them into the final death throes of crucifixion. His body, unsupported by any footrest on the cross, sagged, with his knees jutting even more sharply and outward to the right as his body weight shifted down.

Then in shock, Dr. Castle and the others realized the stigmata wounds had opened again and had begun bleeding profusely on both Father Bartholomew's wrists and feet. The long white robe hid what Dr. Castle was sure were the reopened scourge wounds. His suspicion was confirmed as the bleeding from an unseen crown of thorns began to flow heavily into the hair on the crown of Bartholomew head, with streams of blood pouring down his forehead into his eyes and soaking the long hair Bartholomew wore down to his shoulders.

Then the wound opened on his right side. Seeing this, Castle's mind immediately made the connection. Father Bartholomew had just suffered the final wound of Christ's passion and death. The centurion on Golgotha had just pierced his right side with his spear, puncturing his heart to make sure the crucified man was truly dead. A mixture of blood and clear fluid poured from Father Bartholomew's right side, producing a large, bloody stain—precisely where the spear mark was also evident in the man on the Shroud stretched behind the priest. Bartholomew suffered in his own body the final death throes of Christ, crucified two thousand years before.

BACK ON THE hill of his death outside Jerusalem, Bartholomew felt nothing form the spear, but he heard, as if his soul were receding rapidly out of his body, another centurion proclaim, "Truly this man was the Son of God." The earth shook from a sudden earthquake and the sky turned to pitch black as lightning and thunder framed the horizon. The last person Bartholomew saw before his spirit completely departed his wrecked and twisted body was his mother, standing in tears at the foot of the cross. At that instant the veil of the temple was rent in two, from the top to the bottom.

IN THE TURIN chapel, Bartholomew's hung body began levitating once again. Castle strained his eyes, but somehow a burst of radiant light that he did not understand began extruding from Bartholomew's wracked body.

Spellbound and unable to comprehend what they were experiencing, everyone in the room was equally frozen in a combination of wonder and fear. Castle's mind raced back to Dr. Bucholtz's comment that the image had been transferred to the Shroud in a blinding flash of almost pure light, shining brilliantly. Could that be happening again?

Frantically, Ferrar's camera crew made sure they were capturing what was happening, both with the high-definition camera they had brought to document the Shroud and with their mobile equipment. Ferrar's heart beat rapidly. Whatever was happening, he was willing to bet the next few moments would make him famous worldwide.

Levitating now at the level of the Shroud, with his back to the Shroud, Father Bartholomew's body suddenly went horizontal, at a distance of about three feet above the floor. Instantly as he reached horizontal, a plane of pulsing blue light crossed through his body from head to toe, rotating him so he faced outward into the room, still completely levitated, with his back facing the Shroud.

Silently, Father Bartholomew's robe disappeared in a burst of radiance, leaving him completely naked. Bartholomew's left hand folded across his right hand, with the fingers modestly covering his pelvic area. All the wounds were now clearly visible on Bartholomew's tortured body. With Bartholomew levitated against the Shroud like that, the one-for-one identity of the two bodies was unmistakable. Slowly Bartholomew's body rotated around the blue light plane that appeared to hold him in midair. The wounds on his backside were equally apparent to everyone in the room, as were their identity to the dorsal wounds of the man in the Shroud.

Castle's mind raced to anticipate what was going to happen next. Bucholtz had said an event horizon opened up in the tomb where Jesus had been laid to rest. She said the Shroud of Turin had rested above and below a levitating Jesus in the tomb, such that the burst of brilliant light that marked his passing into the next dimension would leave no distortions in the image, negating the idea that the image had transferred from contact with the body. Castle realized Bartholomew's body was positioned for the transition.

The radiant light from the blue event horizon line began penetrating every square inch of Bartholomew's body; his body was transfiguring into a light-created being. Rapidly disappearing from sight were his flesh and blood. Almost imperceptibly, a rumbling noise arose as if from a distant horizon. Just then thunder could be heard in the hills outside Turin, and even though the windows in the private chapel had been covered to prevent light from entering, flashes of lightning seemed to penetrate the coverings and burst around the room.

Looking around, Castle could see that everyone in the room, including himself, was being covered with electricity that looked like the luminous plasma of St. Elmo's fire. It surrounded them and danced in a continuous coronal discharge from a source unseen.

Just then, Bartholomew's eyes opened and he called out to Anne what sounded like "Mother, please join me. We are returning home."

Puzzled at what Bartholomew meant, Castle looked to his side, where Anne had been quietly positioned since they entered the room. He was astounded to see her moving forward toward her brother, as if she were in a trance.

Looking at her closely, Castle could see that she too was levitating and that she was walking with her feet about one foot above the floor.

Castle strained his eyes to comprehend what he was seeing, but

Anne seemed to have exchanged her twenty-first-century clothes for the veil and robes common to Jewish women two thousand years ago.

Bartholomew stretched out his hand to receive Anne. The moment the two touched, a burst of illumination filled the room. Castle and everyone else in the room felt the pulse pass through their bodies as if an electric shock had hit them. Forcibly, he and the others were thrown to the ground. The rumble of thunder and the flashing of lightning filled the private chapel as if all Heaven had burst loose and its energy was pouring forth in waves pulsing through every cell of their bodies. For what seemed an eternity, the vibrations made every tissue of bone and muscle in Castle's body quiver as if he were going to burst apart.

Then, as quickly as the event began, it was over.

Gone was the brilliant illumination.

Gone also were Father Bartholomew and Anne Cassidy.

Those on the floor, including the pope and the cardinal, moved slowly, their bodies aching throughout from the surges that had penetrated them. Castle was beginning to understand they had been hit by translucent, pure impulses of irradiant energy.

"What happened?" was the inevitable question, with the only answer being the pathetically inadequate "I don't know."

Father Morelli was the first to recover sufficiently to notice the only tangible evidence of the transcendent phenomenon they had just experienced.

"Look," Morelli said, struggling to stand. "The Shroud—the image has gotten brighter."

Castle's immediate reaction was that the inexplicable splendor of pure light had rattled Morelli's brain. But then he looked for himself. Sure enough, Morelli was right. The reddish brown lines that had previously defined the image of the man on the Shroud faintly to the naked eye had darkened decidedly, showing much more definition in the figure. The wounds now stood out in great detail, and the anatomical features were also more visible.

But that was not all that had changed.

"And the eyes have opened," Father Middagh said with astonishment as he weaved back and forth, suggesting his ability to remain upright on his feet was very uncertain at best.

Castle thought Middagh had lost his mind, until he looked. Once again, Castle was astounded. Before, the eyes of the man in the Shroud had been closed. Now the eyes of the man in the Shroud were wide open, looking straight ahead. The once solemn and serene face now looked as if the Christ figure within were about to begin speaking.

Ferrar forced himself to his feet and rushed over to his camera crew. Reviewing the video, Ferrar saw they had recorded everything, including the illumination. "Keep taping." Ferrar encouraged the camera crew, doing his best to make sure the cameras were still running. Ferrar did not want to lose a second of anything that happened.

Positioning himself in front of the cameras, Ferrar began what would be his afternoon newscast a few hours from now, relayed by satellite from Rome to New York and from there broadcast to every corner of the globe.

"You won't believe what just happened," Ferrar said into the camera with a look of disbelief on his face.

Castle was sure that was correct. If it had not been recorded, no one would have believed it.

From what Castle was provisionally putting together, he was beginning to conclude that Father Bartholomew had won his challenge with the pope. What had just happened before them in this small, private chapel in the Cathedral of Turin was unprecedented, uncaptured in human history.

As best Castle could figure, Father Bartholomew had just

transitioned into a dimension beyond and he had taken Anne with him. As Dr. Bucholtz had warned him, the Shroud of Turin was a codex into ancient mysteries he and others would have no choice but to decode. Even more than a codex, the Shroud was a portal, an entry point into the dimension beyond.

Looking within himself in those first moments after the event, Castle had to admit that he was now willing, for the first time in his life, to consider the possibility of God, or at least of the existence of dimensions he had never before contemplated as existing.

Maybe Father Bartholomew was right that creating an experience beyond what we consider the normal laws of nature, in full view of the world, was the mission God sent him back to earth to accomplish.

But if Castle thought, even for a second, that his religious conversion was going to be immediate, picking up Gabrielli off the floor was all he needed to plant his feet firmly once again on terra firma.

"That was the best magic trick that I ever saw in my life," Gabrielli said, brushing himself off and rearranging his clothes. "How do you think the pope did it?"

CHAPTER THIRTY-TWO

Friday night
Hassler Hotel, Rome, Italy
Day 30

That evening, Dr. Castle returned to Rome in a daze.

He decided to go to the rooftop restaurant at the Hassler and have dinner by himself, hoping he would find the quiet time to sort out what he had just experienced.

Twilight was coming and the lights of the Vatican highlighted Rome with a magic that tonight he saw through different eyes. Perhaps Father Bartholomew had been right after all. Castle had always understood that religion could not be achieved by reason alone. Bartholomew was right in asserting that Castle had never gone through an experience that required him to believe in God. For the first time in his life, Castle was wondering if he had just gone through that type of experience.

As he sipped his wine and tried to decide if he had the appetite for dinner, the maître d' approached him with a package.

"The signora you had dinner with here earlier this week left this package at the front desk for you today as she left the hotel," he explained. "She said you would probably be dining here alone tonight and she felt certain you would want to have this."

Befuddled, Castle tipped the maître d' generously and accepted the package, having no possible idea what it might contain.

A purple ribbon bound the contents in wrapping paper Castle recognized from one of the shops he and Anne had visited in the past few days along the Via Condotti, just below the hotel on the Spanish Steps, at the Piazza di Spagna.

He opened the package with haste, finding within it a letter and a photo album. The letter was from Anne.

"By the time you read this, I will be gone," Anne wrote. "What you must know is that I am and always was Paul Bartholomew's mother. After his car accident, when we were reunited before God, I promised that if Paul would accept the mission to return to life, I would return as well, to accompany him. So, you see, I invented Paul's half sister in order to explain my presence back in his life. Seeing me in the hospital, Paul recognized me immediately. But when Paul and I spoke with one another privately in the hospital, I explained to him how it had to be. I could not come back as his mother. Everyone knew I had died of Lou Gehrig's disease."

Castle took a drink of his wine, struggling to grasp what Anne was telling him.

"When the authorities investigate Anne Cassidy in Canada, they will find that Anne Cassidy never existed. Obtaining documentation such as a passport these days is unfortunately easy to do."

Reading this, Castle motioned the waiter over to the table and asked for a double scotch, no ice. "Please bring it immediately," Castle told the waiter. "I need it now."

"*Subito,*" the waiter said compliantly in perfect, crisp Italian, as he rushed off to bring Dr. Castle his drink.

The waiter rushed back with the scotch, as ordered. Castle took a strong swig, then another.

He resumed reading.

"The photo album is Paul's photo album, from when he was a baby. You will see there is no father for Paul in any of the photographs. You will see that the woman you knew as Anne Cassidy is the same woman that appears in the photos as Paul's mother, Anne Bartholomew. There never was a Vietnam War hero named Jonathan Bartholomew who returned mysteriously from being missing in action. What I portrayed about being Paul's sister also required me to make up the story about Matthew Cassidy. There also never was a father who took me to Canada when he learned my mother had always loved the soldier who never existed. When you find Paul's birth certificate, you will find the father is listed as unknown. You can search for Paul's father if you want, but that is a secret I plan to share with you in the afterlife, when we are reunited in the presence of God."

Castle finished the scotch and ordered another. It was beginning to look to him like he might end up drinking his dinner that night.

"I know you do not believe in God," she wrote. "I am sure it will take you time, maybe even years, to sort out and understand the events of the last month. I only wish I could be there to assist you."

Thanks a lot, Castle thought, reading that. When he had accepted Paul Bartholomew as a patient, Castle truly had no idea what he was getting himself into.

"Paul's destiny was to decipher the Shroud codex for the world. Paul struggled to find God in an equation, until he gave up the idea and decided to be a priest. Professor Gabrielli will try to convince the world that my disappearing with Paul was an elaborate trick. Dr. Bucholtz will understand that we transitioned through what she calls an 'event horizon' to another dimension people have called 'Heaven' for millennia, dating back to the writing of the Bible. You will have to decide for yourself what you have seen with your own eyes, from the first moment you met Paul in your office."

For Castle, the idea was beginning to settle in. Anne was either delusional or the entire experience with Bartholomew would have to be explained in mystical terms Castle considered suspect by nature.

"Had things been different, we might have been lovers," she wrote. "If you believe what Dr. Bucholtz told us about parallel worlds, in another time in another dimension, we might yet be lovers. The care you took to include me and provide for my comfort was noticed and appreciated. The affection I saw you express for me, I felt for you in return."

Castle asked the waiter to return to his table. He asked the waiter to bring him one more scotch, but he had also decided to have dinner. "Let me see the menu," Castle asked politely.

Castle paged through the photo album. The mother with the baby Paul Bartholomew was unmistakably the woman he knew as Anne Cassidy.

"Know that I and Paul are eternally grateful for all you have done for us both," Anne wrote in conclusion. "You became part of our destiny the moment you accepted Paul as your patient."

She signed her name simply, in the same firm hand with which she had written the letter.

Castle knew he had a lot of thinking to do, but one thing was certain. He needed some distance to gain perspective. He took out his cell phone and called Gabrielli.

Castle began a little tentatively. "Marco, I've been doing some thinking since we got back from Turin."

"And what have you concluded?" Gabrielli asked, having no idea where his friend and associate was headed.

"Maybe you should write that book about the Shroud on your own," Castle suggested. "I'm not sure I'm ready to be your coauthor."

Gabrielli thought quickly. He was not about to let go of the opportunity of a lifetime to debunk the Catholic Church. "Well, I will miss your help," he said, "but I guess that just means more royalties for me."

Castle agreed, said good-bye, and wished his friend good luck.

The next call he made was to Norman Rothschild, the venerated psychiatrist who had brought Castle into the profession. It was afternoon in New York and Rothschild answered the phone when he recognized Castle's name showing up on his caller ID.

"How's Rome?" Rothschild asked.

"A little more interesting than I had anticipated," Castle answered.

"I can tell from the tone of your voice. I've been worried about you since you first briefed me on your new patient, Father Bartholomew. I've been following the television reports."

"I figured you would," Castle said.

"What's going on?" Rothschild asked. "I haven't heard anything since you left for the Vatican."

"I can't explain it to you now; it's too complicated. But I'm sure you will be catching up, once you turn on the television. Will you have time for dinner early next week, after I return to New York?"

"You know I will," Rothschild said affirmatively. He was looking forward to seeing Stephen in the city. "When are you flying home?"

"I will leave Rome on Sunday," Castle said. "I'll take tomorrow to rest. Can we have dinner Monday evening?"

"Of course we can," Rothschild said enthusiastically. "I will clear off my calendar whatever I need to clear. Call my office and my assistant will work out the details."

"Sounds good," Castle said appreciatively.

"Just tell me this," Rothschild said seriously, wanting to be sure before they ended the conversation. "Are you okay or do you need some assistance right now? I have colleagues I trust in Rome."

"I've been through a lot," Castle said, "but I think I'm okay for now."

Ending the call, Castle decided to turn his attention to dinner.

"What does the chef recommend?" he asked the waiter politely, ready to accept just about anything the waiter had in mind.

CHAPTER THIRTY-THREE

Sunday evening
New York City, 8:00 P.M.
Day 32

Anchor Dave Dunaway had Fernando Ferrar appear in person on his Sunday evening broadcast to promote the hourlong special on Father Bartholomew and the Shroud of Turin that Ferrar had produced for national broadcast the coming Wednesday. Since Friday, Ferrar's video of the events that transpired in the Chapel of the Shroud had been broadcast by the network and picked up on the Internet.

"What is the official status of Father Bartholomew and Anne Cassidy?" Dunaway asked.

"According to Italian law enforcement authorities, both are listed as 'missing persons,'" Ferrar reported. "I was there in the Chapel of the Shroud in Turin, Italy, when the burst of light flooded the room. The pope was standing within five feet of me at the time. What I experienced, I can't explain. But what I think happened is that Father Bartholomew and Anne Cassidy's bodies seemed to vaporize into what I can only describe as pure energy. It looked to me like they disappeared right through the Shroud."

While Ferrar was speaking, the audience saw the video of the moment—the light flash as Father Bartholomew stood there and reached out to Anne; as he grabbed her hand, she was absorbed into the light. It looked like both were vaporized, with the light leaving the room through the Shroud. When it was over, the pope and the others in the room were on their knees or knocked flat on the floor. When the commotion settled in the chapel, Bartholomew and Anne were gone.

"When I got back to my feet, I noticed that the eyes of the man on the Shroud had opened," Ferrar said. "I couldn't believe it, but before that the eyes were closed. I know that for certain. The day before the private showing with the pope and Father Bartholomew, the archdiocese allowed our video team to bring in high-definition cameras to record very detailed images of the Shroud for broadcast. We must have been in the Chapel of the Shroud doing the HD taping for somewhere around five hours last Thursday. I got a chance to study the Shroud very closely with my own eyes."

Again, as Ferrar talked, the broadcast showed images of the video team taping the Shroud, a close-up of the closed eyes in the image of the Shroud before the event, and the open eyes after the event.

"You interviewed Dr. Ruth Bucholtz, an internationally renowned particle physicist, didn't you?" Dunaway asked. "What does Dr. Bucholtz think happened last Friday in Turin, Italy?"

"That's right," Ferrar said. "We caught up by remote from Rome with Dr. Bucholtz in her office at CERN in Geneva, Switzerland. I believe we have a clip of that interview now."

A split screen showed Ferrar in the television studio in Rome and Dr. Bucholtz in her Geneva office, being interviewed by Ferrar remotely.

"What you filmed, I believe, is the first documentation of an 'event horizon' in which people passed from our normal four dimensions into one of the additional dimensions required by advanced particle physics to explain quantum phenomena observed since Einstein first formulated the general theory of relativity," Bucholtz said.

"Can you translate that for our audience?" Ferrar asked. "I'm afraid you lost me once you started talking about quantum physics and Einstein. I barely got through physics class in high school."

"Sure," Dr. Bucholtz said, smiling at Ferrar's self-putdown. "I think what your video shows really happened. It was not a trick. Father Bartholomew and Anne turned into pure energy. They transitioned from earth to some other dimension that we humans do not normally experience."

"I was raised Catholic," Ferrar said, "and what you are saying sounds a lot like the resurrection of Jesus Christ, especially when we are talking about the Shroud of Turin. Are you saying Father Bartholomew became Jesus and Anne Cassidy was like the Virgin Mary? According to what I was taught in Catholic catechism, Jesus died on the cross, was resurrected, and ascended into Heaven. His mother, the Virgin Mary, also died and was assumed into Heaven. Is this what you are talking about?"

"I'm not saying that Father Bartholomew became Jesus or that Anne Cassidy was the Virgin Mary," Dr. Bucholtz said to clarify things. "But I think they both went through an experience that the New Testament describes as the resurrection of Jesus and the ascent into Heaven of Jesus and his mother."

Cutting back to the studio in New York, Dunaway had a look

of amazement on his face. "I can't believe what I'm hearing," he said to the national audience. "You're telling me that Dr. Bucholtz is an internationally respected physicist who works at CERN in Geneva, Switzerland. Is that right?"

"Yes, it is," Ferrar affirmed.

"And she believes in resurrections and ascents into Heaven?" Dunaway asked. "Is that consistent with being a scientist?"

Ferrar laughed quietly in agreement. "It seems like the world of advanced particle physics and the world of religion may be a little closer than we typically assume."

"But Bucholtz wasn't your only interview, right?" Dunaway skillfully shifted the focus of the discussion. "You also interviewed a well-known skeptic."

"That's right," Ferrar said, picking up Dunaway's segue. "I also interviewed Dr. Marco Gabrielli, a professor of chemistry on the faculty of the University of Bologna. Gabrielli has made a career debunking religious and other paranormal phenomena. He's best at exposing frauds, like statues of Jesus that appear to cry tears of blood, when all that's involved is filling a porous cavity in the statue's head with a liquid solution that looks like blood. Here's what Professor Gabrielli told us."

Another split screen showed Ferrar in the television studio in Rome interviewing Gabrielli in his office in Bologna.

"It was classic misdirection," Gabrielli said on camera. "Every magician in the world since before the time of Houdini knows their illusions depend on creating a diversion that distracts the attention of the audience. That burst of light that blinded all of us in the Chapel of the Shroud was one of the best I've ever seen. We were all thrown into confusion, even me. Who knows what really happened? Sure, it looks like Father Bartholomew and Anne Cassidy vaporized into pure energy and disappeared through the Shroud, but can you prove to me there wasn't a trap door in that room that allowed them to escape without any supernatural effects whatsoever?"

"So you disagree with Dr. Bucholtz, then." Ferrar pressed the chemist. "You don't think we witnessed any 'event horizon' or 'passing into another dimension'? Nothing supernatural as far as you're concerned, is that right?"

"Right." Gabrielli said without any hesitation whatsoever. "Magicians have been making people disappear for generations. Usually they use a curtain, or they have a person go into some sort of a cabinet or box before the magician makes them disappear. But I have to admit that a blinding flash of light is every bit as good as any physical apparatus magicians have designed over the decades to pull off their disappearing tricks."

"Are you trying to duplicate the illusion right now?" Ferrar asked.

"Absolutely," Gabrielli said. "And I am pretty well along the way to figuring it out. My only questions now are who was paying Father Bartholomew and Anne Cassidy for pulling off this trick, and how much money did they walk away with? I also wouldn't mind tracking them down so I could prove to the world they are frauds. That should be pretty obvious after I find out where they went to spend their money."

"Well, that should settle it, don't you think?" Dunaway asked Ferrar as the camera returned to the New York studio.

"It might," Ferrar said, "except for one thing."

"What's that?" Dunaway asked, looking surprised.

"We've managed to find a picture of Anne Bartholomew, Father Bartholomew's mother," Ferrar said as the picture went up on the television screen. "When we set that photo side by side with the recent photos of Anne Cassidy, the woman who came on the scene as Father Paul Bartholomew's half sister, the two women look exactly alike."

The photo of Anne Cassidy came on the screen next to the old photo of Anne Bartholomew, the mother of Father Bartholomew, and the resemblance was obvious.

"So, to find out for sure if Anne Bartholomew and Anne Cassidy are the same person, we consulted an expert in face-recognition software," Ferrar said. "Michael Winters, in Concord, New Hampshire. Winters is founder and CEO of a company that works with casinos to find card counters and cheats even when they try to disguise their facial appearance."

"Very interesting," Dunaway said, now looking intrigued. "What did you find out?"

"Here's a clip from the special," Ferrar said. "I interviewed Winters in his home office by remote video this morning."

The split screen came up on camera again. Ferrar in the New York studio was talking with Winters at his computer in his New Hampshire office.

"So, if you are following me," Winters said in the clip Ferrar had chosen for the promo with Dunaway, "the one dimension of a person's face that is hard to change is the distance between their eyes, measured from pupil to pupil. People can get their noses or their chins modified relatively easily by plastic surgery, but not the distance between their eyes."

The camera focused on Winters's computer. On one half of his computer monitor, Winters showed a photo of Anne Barthol-omew from when her son was an infant; on the other half Winters showed a photo of Anne Cassidy from a few days earlier.

"As you can see," Winters said, "the distance between the eyes of the two women is identical."

Winters typed in a few keystrokes, and the two photos began to merge.

"As you can see when we overlap the two photos, in this case all the facial features in the two photos match almost perfectly."

"What's your conclusion?" Ferrar asked.

"My conclusion is that these two photos show the same woman," Winters said, looking up from his computer monitor. "I believe I can say that with a ninety-nine-percent confidence level. In my years of working with this software, I can think of only two or three other cases where the faces have matched up so perfectly."

"So there you have it," Ferrar said to Dunaway as the scene returned to the New York studio. "We're going to have to let you, the viewers, decide whether our recorded video documenting that Father Bartholomew and Anne Cassidy disappeared into the Shroud of Turin is a paranormal event that confirms Christ's resurrection and the authenticity of the Shroud, or whether Father Bartholomew and Anne Cassidy are nothing more than top-notch charlatans who could show up any day with their next magic act."

"I can't wait to see your special," Dunaway said. "When does it broadcast?"

"This Wednesday at eight P.M. Eastern Time," Ferrar answered.

"Well, I will be sure to be watching," Dunaway said, wrapping up the promo segment. "And I suspect I will be only one of the millions in your audience on the edge of their seats. What happened in front of our cameras in the Chapel of the Shroud in Turin, Italy, last Friday? A religious experience of the ages or an ingenious magic trick that was brilliantly pulled off? Watch this Wednesday at eight P.M. Eastern Time. *Father Bartholomew and the Shroud of Turin: Miracle or Magic?* We will present the evidence so you, the viewers, can decide for yourselves."

CHAPTER THIRTY-FOUR

Monday evening
New York City, 8:00 P.M.
Day 33

Norman Rothschild reserved a private room for dinner with Stephen Castle at his favorite midtown steak house.

Comfortably settled at their table, the two psychiatrists each ordered a single-malt scotch, as Rothschild selected a fine bottle of vintage French Bordeaux to accompany their steak dinners. Castle knew that the wine Rothschild selected would probably cost twice as much as the steak dinners put together.

At seventy-five years old, Rothschild looked younger and more fit than he did more than two decades ago, when he first met Castle. The reduced patient schedule that came with semiretirement permitted Rothschild a lifestyle that included more time for himself. A medium height man at five feet, ten inches, Rothschild followed a daily routine of briskly walking five blocks to get his favorite espresso and croissant each morning, and five blocks back to his midtown Park Avenue apartment. With a full head of silver hair to set off his ocean blue eyes, Rothschild always looked distinguished, whether he was attired in his jeans and walking shoes in search of his daily morning coffee or in his tweed sport coat and tailored pants, as he was tonight for dinner.

When Castle changed careers to go into psychiatry, Rothschild had helped prepare him for the profession by serving as his analyst. Ever since, Rothschild remained Castle's dedicated mentor, always ready to meet with Stephen to counsel him not only through difficult psychiatric cases, but also through the expected psychological challenges that confront all human beings in the course of life. Though he had sported a neatly trimmed beard when he was in his fifties, much like Castle's, Rothschild discarded the beard when he reached seventy, thinking he no longer needed the assistance of a distinguished beard to appear mature for his patients.

Prior to the meeting, Castle emailed Rothschild a summary memo he had written for the file detailing Father Bartholomew's case history. By giving Rothschild the opportunity to study the memo in advance of the dinner, Castle knew he would save a lot of time explaining the basic facts.

"I declined to be on Ferrar's television show," Castle explained as they enjoyed their drinks. "I pleaded doctor-client privilege, but in truth, it's just too soon for me to talk about any aspects of this case in public."

"I think that's wise," Rothschild said. "Did Ferrar give you any hint on the angle he was going to pursue?"

"Ferrar told me that Canadian law enforcement officials have told the network they can find no record of any Matthew Cassidy working for either the Canadian National or the Canadian Pacific railways. Ferrar also says the Canadian government has no record of ever having issued a passport to Anne Cassidy. I guess I was a fool just to look at Anne's passport and assume it proved anything."

"Don't beat yourself up too severely," Rothschild said. "You're only human and you're not a trained law enforcement authority. You're a psychiatrist, not a private investigator."

"I know," Castle said, "but I'm afraid I let down my guard, maybe because I liked the woman and wanted to accept her story."

"I suspected as much, just from how you wrote up the case file," the senior psychiatrist surmised. "You are usually pretty cool with women, but this time I detected you were on the verge of being romantically interested in her."

Castle knew better than to try to hide anything from Rothschild. There was not much about him that Rothschild didn't know, especially since he went into analysis with Rothschild right after Elizabeth had died. "I've never really loved any woman except Elizabeth," he said openly. "I have always thought that no other woman could ever live up to her standard, or maybe it was that I have always been afraid."

"Afraid of what?"

"Afraid that if I loved another woman, I might lose her, too, just like I lost Elizabeth."

Rothschild took a sip of his scotch, considering what Castle had just told him. "That's possible. But I think I sense an important change in you."

"What's that?" Castle asked.

"It sounds to me as if you're getting ready to make space for a woman again in your life; otherwise I doubt Anne or any other woman would have caught your attention."

Rothschild was probably right, now that he thought about it. "I have to admit I was physically attracted to Anne. She was approaching maturity with a beauty most younger women would envy."

"Who do you think Anne really was?" Rothschild asked as the appetizers were served.

"Of course, I've thought a lot about that," Castle admitted. "I spoke with Dr. Bucholtz at CERN by phone before I left Rome and she would like me to think Anne was a time traveler. Maybe Dr. Bucholtz is right."

"Do you have any idea who Paul Bartholomew's father was?"

"No, not really. Ferrar told me the network's reporters have tracked down Bartholomew's birth certificate and the father is listed as 'unknown,' just as Anne's letter said it would be. Maybe Anne was the reincarnation of the Christ's mother, Mary. Maybe Paul was conceived by virgin birth."

"You're being facetious, I take it?" Rothschild asked.

"Yes, in large part I'm being facetious. But I can't accept Marco Gabrielli's theory that Father Bartholomew and Anne amount to nothing more than a con-artist team. I saw Bartholomew's wounds with my own eyes; I watched as some of them were being inflicted. He suffered real pain, even if the injuries healed in record time. All that is consistent with my original diagnosis that Father Bartholomew was suffering from a multiple personality disorder and that his injuries were psychosomatically induced, but not a conclusion that he was a con man. Still, I have to admit that dealing with this case has forced me to face mysteries I can't explain by sheer reason alone."

Rothschild agreed. "How about Anne and Father Bartholomew?" he asked. "What have you concluded about them? Were they mother and son, or were they brother and half sister?"

Castle wanted to choose his words carefully. "Try as he will, I don't think Gabrielli is going to be able to prove Father Bartholomew and Anne Castle were charlatans." The Anne Cassidy I knew was the Anne Bartholomew I saw in the photographs of that album. They were one and the same person. Father Bartholomew may never have had a half sister, but he had a mother and I believe that mother was both Anne Bartholomew and the woman we knew as Anne Cassidy. I'm told Ferrar's television special this Wednesday has a face-recognition expert who's prepared to say on camera that Anne Bartholomew and Anne Cassidy were the same person."

Rothschild had suspected Castle would come to that conclusion. Even in death, Anne had somehow found a way not to abandon her only child. As impossible as that seemed, the possibility was what made the events his protégé Dr. Stephen Castle had just experienced so tantalizing.

The steaks were excellent. The Bordeaux was one of the best he had ever tasted. There was good reason this restaurant was one of Rothschild's favorites.

"What position has the pope taken on what happened last Friday?" Rothschild asked.

"Father Morelli assured me before I left Rome that the pope is planning to issue a statement this week to the effect that the Vatican has agreed to cooperate fully with Italian law enforcement authorities in the missing persons case involving Father Bartholomew and Anne Cassidy," Castle explained. "The Vatican is preparing to explain that the events surrounding Father Bartholomew are still under investigation. Immediately following that, Morelli told me, the Vatican will issue a second statement affirming that the Shroud of Turin is still regarded by the Catholic Church as a relic worthy of veneration. Morelli said the Vatican also plans to announce a new exposition of the Shroud this spring. Father Bartholomew's case has obviously renewed interest in the Shroud worldwide."

"What do you think the pope believes about the Shroud of Turin?" Rothschild asked.

"Honestly, I don't know," Castle said. "The pope has always played his cards very close to the vest with me. But I may have a clue in how the pope handled himself during the conference with the Italian physicians who examined Bartholomew for the Vatican. The pope made it clear that his job was to lead the Catholic Church and he wasn't about to bet his future or the future of the Catholic Church on any relic, regardless of how many millions of Catholics might believe it is authentic. I doubt the pope will change his mind on that."

This made sense to Rothschild. No mature CEO of any organization, whether the organization was the Catholic Church or one of the largest public corporations in the world, ever rolls the dice on something that is not 100 percent certain, unless they have no choice but to do so. "You respected Marco Vicente when he was a cardinal and I sense you continue to respect him now that he is pope," Rothschild said.

"Yes, I do." Castle spoke without hesitation. "I admire how he handled this case. He deferred to Morelli's judgment, much as a field general would defer to a top lieutenant. He agreed to allow Bartholomew to see the Shroud after Morelli argued it made sense to do so."

"Do you think Morelli was right?" Rothschild asked.

Castle thought for a moment before answering. He took a sip of the wine. "It's a tough judgment call, but I do think Morelli was right."

"How so?" Rothschild asked. "There's a huge controversy over whether what happened Friday was a miracle or a magic trick."

"I know," Castle said. "But I don't think the pope minds that controversy. It takes the issue off whether the Shroud is a medieval forgery and puts the world's attention squarely back on figuring out who Bartholomew really was and what he was all about."

"How about you?" Rothschild asked as he ordered a rare brandy to finish their meal. "Does any of this cause you to doubt your convictions as an atheist?"

"Do you want to know if I came out of this with any glimmer of a belief in God?" Castle asked with a smile.

"Yes, that's what I'm asking."

"I'm conflicted, maybe for the first time in my life, if you must know the truth," Castle said. "There was a lot to what Professor Silver at Princeton and Dr. Bucholtz at CERN said. Modern physics is clearly advancing into scientific areas that used to be reserved for religion."

Rothschild smiled slightly, expressing a trace of satisfaction. "I'd like to think that all those articles I've been sending you over the past few years on the big bang did not entirely escape your attention. The big bang has always sounded to me a lot like the moment of God creating the universe that the Bible describes in Genesis. But then, unlike you, I'm not a professed atheist. I'm Jewish and I'm comfortable with God, as long as nobody holds me to going to synagogue on a weekly basis."

Castle appreciated his point. "You're right, of course, in concluding that when physics begins contemplating God, I might have no choice other than to do the same. I'd like to believe there is a dimension where I might someday find Anne again. But I don't know if those are my emotions, not my head, thinking."

"Even for a psychiatrist as accomplished as you, telling that difference is sometimes impossible to do," Rothschild said. "But as to the issue of religion, I've fought with you since we first met. You've always told me we make up religions to compensate for the unknown—to explain where we came from, or what happens to us when we die. Or that we make up religions to control behavior, to say you will go to Hades if you don't do exactly what I say. I understand all that. But I'm wondering if you have caught a glimpse of what I always considered the real question."

"What's that?"

"The question is whether deep down there is an impulse built into us that compels us to create religions and to believe in God."

"What do you mean?"

"I can explain it to you in Freudian terms, if you want, but tonight I want to say it simpler than that."

"Okay, I'm open to that. Say it simply."

"You can dismiss the religions we create as defective, but you can't dismiss as a fact the continuing human need to create religions."

"You could well be right," Castle said. "I hate to admit it, but you could well be right."

"Do you think Father Bartholomew had a mission from God, like he claimed?"

"That's a harder question," Castle said. "Anne believed he did and I can't prove that he didn't. He conveniently escaped treatment before I completed my analysis."

Rothschild realized Castle had made a point he could not refute. "What are you going to do next?" Rothschild asked, moving on to the future.

"I'm going to take a couple of weeks off," Castle answered. "I need some time to recover from this experience. Besides, I did my job for the Vatican the best I could and I got paid generously for it."

"Are you going to go anywhere?"

"Yes, I'm going back to Italy," Castle said. "I can't get out of my mind something the pope said in our final conference, just before he agreed to allow Bartholomew to see the Shroud in person."

"What's that?"

"The pope said it worried him that there might just be a Leonardo da Vinci codex buried somewhere in the Vatican archives that explains exactly how Leonardo created the Shroud," Castle said. "In one our last conferences I think I met just the right person to conduct the search for me."

"Who's that?"

"Dottoressa Francesca Coretti, a Vatican Library senior staff researcher. She has a doctorate in medieval art from the University of Milan. She has been specializing in researching the Shroud for years. If the Vatican archives have some long-lost Shroud codex written by Leonardo da Vinci, I have a hunch Dottoressa Coretti might just be the right person to find it."

"She wouldn't happen to be attractive, would she?" Rothschild asked slyly.

"As a matter of fact, she is," Castle said with a knowing smile. "I judge her to be in her forties and attractively thin. She has this elegant black hair that matches her jet-black eyes perfectly."

"When are you leaving?" Rothschild asked.

"I'm booked for tomorrow, first-class to Rome, departing out of JFK late afternoon," Castle said, picking up the check.

"Makes sense to me," Rothschild replied, very happy to hear the news. "Take my cell phone number with you. I want to be the first to know when you find the codex you're looking for."

ACKNOWLEDGMENTS

My interest in the Shroud of Turin dates back four decades, when I first learned about the Shroud while attending St. Ignatius High School in Cleveland, Ohio.

In 1998, I traveled to Turin, Italy, where I had the opportunity to view the Shroud in person multiple times over several days. That Exposition that marked the hundredth anniversary of the 1898 exhibition of the Shroud, when Italian amateur photographer Secondo Pia took the first photographic images of the Shroud.

In researching this book, I was greatly assisted by John and Rebecca Jackson in Colorado Springs, Colorado. John, as mentioned in the novel, was a principal organizer of the 1978 Shroud of Turin Research Project.

Rebecca graciously provided many excellent comments in reading an early version of the manuscript. John and Rebecca run the Turin Shroud Center of Colorado and edit the extremely valuable ShroudofTurin.com website.

Barrie Schwortz provided the photographs used in the novel. Barrie was the official photographer of the 1978 Shroud of Turin Research Project. He edits another extremely valuable website, Shroud.com.

In writing this novel, I took the necessary liberties of fictionalizing events of the book and may well have represented the science about the Shroud or the photographic evidence in a manner John and Rebecca Jackson or Barrie Schwortz would dispute.

Neither should John and Rebecca Jackson or Barrie Schwortz be seen as endorsing the novel or the views expressed in the novel.

I am indebted to Bill Donohue, president of the Catholic League for Religious and Civil Rights, for his continued friendship and his support for my efforts to write a novel about the Shroud of Turin.

The novel benefited greatly from the insightful comments and suggestions of my close personal friend Dr. Stephen Friefeld, M.D., an accomplished surgeon in Springfield, New Jersey, as he closely read the manuscript throughout the drafting process.

Again, any limitations in telling the medical part of this story are entirely my own, given that my graduate academic training is as a political scientist, not as a medical doctor.

Several books were extremely helpful in conducting the research.

Frederick T. Zugibe's *The Crucifixion of Jesus* is an invaluable forensic inquiry into the ancient Roman practice of crucifixion, but also a key treatise on the medical examination of the Shroud of Turin.[i]

Equally important was the two-volume treatise by Raymond E. Brown titled *The Death of the Messiah,* an indispensable biblical analysis of the account of Jesus Christ's death as told by the New Testament gospels.[ii]

Among Ian Wilson's many important books on the Shroud of Turin, I found myself relying upon his 1998 book, *The Blood and the Shroud: New Evidence That the World's Most Sacred Relic Is Real.*[iii]

The 2000 book *The Turin Shroud: The Illustrated Evidence*[iv], resulting from Barrie Schwortz's collaboration with Ian Wilson, was also extremely useful.

For the theory that Leonardo da Vinci created the Shroud of Turin, I found most useful Lynn Picknett and Clive Prince's 1994 book, *Turin Shroud: In Whose Image? The Truth Behind the Centuries-Long Conspiracy of Silence.*[v]

Two books by Michio Kaku, the Henry Semat Professor of Theoretic Physics at the Graduate Center of the City University of New York, provided an excellent introduction to particle physics: his 1994 book, *Hyperspace: A Scientific Odyssey Through Parallel Universes, Time Warps, and the Tenth Dimension*[vi], and his more recent 2005 book, *Parallel Worlds: A Journey Through Creation, Higher Dimensions, and the Future of the Cosmos.*[vii]

Of the many video presentations available on the Shroud of Turin, the one I found the most useful was the 2007 DVD *The Fabric of Time.*[viii]

My wife, Monica, and my daughter, Alexis, graciously tolerated the countless hours I spent working alone, writing this book.

Finally, I want to thank my parish priest in New Jersey, Father Hernan Arias, in Morristown, New Jersey, who encouraged me to complete this book upon seeing the very first pages I had drafted.

[i] Frederick T. Zugibe, *The Crucifixion of Jesus: A Forensic Inquiry* (New York: M. Evans and Company, Inc., 2005).

[ii] Raymond E. Brown, *The Death of the Messiah: From Gethsemane to the Grave* (New York: Doubleday, Two Volumes, 1994).

[iii] Ian Wilson, *The Blood and the Shroud: New Evidence That the World's Most Sacred Relic Is Real* (New York: The Free Press, 1998).

[iv] Ian Wilson and Barrie Schwortz, *The Turin Shroud: The Illustrated Evidence* (London: Michael O'Mara Books Limited, 2000).

[v] Lynn Picknett and Clive Prince, *Turin Shroud: In Whose Image? The Truth*

Behind the Centuries-Long Conspiracy of Silence (New York: HarperCollins Publishers, 1994).

[vi] Michio Kaku, *Hyperspace: A Scientific Odyssey Through Parallel Universes, Time Warps, and the Tenth Dimension* (New York and Oxford: Oxford University Press, 1994).

[vii] Michio Kaku, *Parallel Worlds: A Journey Through Creation, Higher Dimensions, and the Future of the Cosmos* (New York: Doubleday, 2005).

[viii] Executive Producers Vance Syphers, Paul Schubert, and Joe Call; and Senior Producer David W. Balsiger, *The Fabric of Time: Are the Secrets of the Universe Hidden in an Ancient Cloth?* (Baker City, Oregon: Grizzly Adams Productions, 2007).